June Bug

June Bug

❀ ❀ ❀

CHRIS FABRY

Tyndale House Publishers, Inc.
Carol Stream, Illinois

Visit Chris Fabry's Web site at www.chrisfabry.com

TYNDALE and Tyndale's quill logo are registered trademarks of Tyndale House Publishers, Inc.

June Bug

Copyright © 2009 by Chris Fabry. All rights reserved.

Cover photograph of girl copyright © by Radius Images/Jupiterimages. All rights reserved.

Cover flourish elements copyright © by Shutterstock Images. All rights reserved.

Author photo copyright © by Herb Wetzel. All rights reserved.

Designed by Beth Sparkman

Edited by Lorie Popp

Scripture quotations are taken from *The Holy Bible*, King James Version.

ISBN-13: 978-1-61523-340-3

Printed in the United States of America

To Erin, Megan, Shannon,
Kristen, and Kaitlyn.
My June Bugs.

❀ ❀ ❀

PART ONE

Some people know every little thing about themselves, like how much they weighed when they were born and how long they were from head to toe and which hospital their mama gave birth to them in and stuff like that. I've heard that some people even have a black footprint on a pink sheet of paper they keep in a baby box. The only box I have is a small suitcase that snaps shut where I keep my underwear in so only I can see it.

My dad says there's a lot of things people don't need and that their houses get cluttered with it and they store it in basements that flood and get ruined, so it's better to live simple and do what you want rather than get tied down to a mortgage—whatever that is. I guess that's why we live in an RV. Some people say "live out of," but I don't see how you can live out of something when you're living inside it and that's what we do. Daddy sleeps on the bed by the big window in the back, and I sleep in the one over the driver's seat. You have to remember not to sit up real quick in the morning or you'll have a headache all day, but it's nice having your own room.

I believed everything my daddy told me until I walked into Walmart and saw my picture on a poster over by the place where the guy with the blue vest stands. He had clear tubes going into his nose, and a hiss of air came out every time he said, "Welcome to Walmart."

My eyes were glued to that picture. I didn't hear much of anything except the lady arguing with the woman at the first register

3

over a return of some blanket the lady swore she bought there. The Walmart lady's voice was getting all trembly. She said there was nothing she could do about it, which made the customer woman so mad she started cussing and calling the woman behind the counter names that probably made people blush.

The old saying is that the customer is always right, but I think it's more like the customer is as mean as a snake sometimes. I've seen them come through the line and stuff a bunch of things under their carts where the cashier won't see it and leave without paying. Big old juice boxes and those frozen peanut butter and jelly sandwiches. Those look good but Daddy says if you have to freeze your peanut butter and jelly sandwiches, then something has gone wrong with the world, and I think he's right. He says it's a sin to be mean to workers at Walmart because they let us use their parking lot. He also says that when they start putting vitamins and minerals in Diet Coke the Apocalypse is not far behind. I don't know what the Apocalypse is, but I wouldn't be surprised if he was right about that too.

You can't know the feeling of seeing your picture on a wall inside a store unless it has happened to you, and I have to believe I am in a small group of people on the planet. It was all I could do to just suck in a little air and keep my heart beating because I swear I could feel it slow down to almost nothing. Daddy says a hummingbird's heart beats something like a million times a minute. I was the opposite of a hummingbird, standing there with my eyes glued to that picture. Some people going outside had to walk around me to the Exit doors, but I couldn't move. I probably looked strange — just a girl staring at the Picture Them Home shots with an ache or emptiness down deep that I can't tell anybody about. It's like trying to tell people what it feels like to have your finger smashed in a grocery cart outside when it's cold. It doesn't do any good to tell things like that. Nobody would listen anyway because they're in a hurry to get back to their houses with all the stuff in them and the mortgage to pay, I guess.

The photo wasn't exactly me. It was "like" me, almost like

I was looking in a mirror. On the left was a real picture of me from when I was little. I'd never seen a picture like that because my dad says he doesn't have any of them. I've gone through his stuff, and unless he's got a really good hiding place, he's telling the truth. On the right side was the picture of what I would look like now, which was pretty close to the real me. The computer makes your face fuzzy around the nose and the eyes, but there was no mistake in my mind that I was looking at the same face I see every morning in the rearview.

The girl's name was Natalie Anne Edwards, and I rolled it around in my head as the people wheeled their carts past me to get to the Raisin Bran that was two for four dollars in the first aisle by the pharmacy. I'd seen it for less, so I couldn't see the big deal.

MISSING CHILD

Natalie Anne Edwards

DOB: *June 20, 2000*	Age Now: *9*
Missing Date: *June 16, 2002*	Sex: *Female*
Estimated Height: *4'3" (130 cm)*	Estimated Weight: *80 lbs (36 kg)*
Eyes: *Blue*	Hair: *Red*
Race: *White*	
Missing From: *Dogwood, WV*	
United States	

Natalie's photo is shown age progressed to 9 years. She is missing from Dogwood, West Virginia. She has a dark birthmark on her left cheek. She was taken on June 16, 2002, by an unknown abductor.

I felt my left cheek and the birthmark there. Daddy says it looks a little like some guy named Nixon who was president a long time ago, but I try not to look at it except when I'm in the bathroom or when I have my mirror out in bed and I'm using my flashlight. I've always wondered if the mark was the one thing my mother gave me or if there was anything she cared to give me at all. Daddy doesn't talk much about her unless I get to nagging him, and then he'll say something like, "She was a good woman," and leave it at that. I'll poke around a little more until he tells me to stop it. He says not to pick at things or they'll never get better, but some scabs call out to you every day.

I kept staring at the picture and my name, the door opening and closing behind me and a train whistle sounding in the distance, which I think is one of the loneliest sounds in the world, especially at night with the crickets chirping. My dad says he loves to go to sleep to the sound of a train whistle because it reminds him of his childhood.

The guy with the tubes in his nose came up behind me. "You all right, little girl?"

It kind of scared me—not as much as having to go over a bridge but pretty close. I don't know what it is about bridges. Maybe it's that I'm afraid the thing is going to collapse. I'm not really scared of the water because my dad taught me to swim early on. There's just something about bridges that makes me quiver inside, and that's why Daddy told me to always crawl up in my bed and sing "I'll Fly Away," which is probably my favorite song. He tries to warn me in advance of big rivers like the Mississippi when we're about to cross them or he'll get an earful of screams.

I nodded to the man with the tubes and left, but I couldn't help glancing back at myself. I walked into the bathroom and sat in the stall awhile and listened to the speakers and the tinny music. Then I thought, *The paper says my birthday is June 20, but Daddy says it's April 9. Maybe it's not really me.*

When I went back out and looked again, there was no doubt in my mind. That was me up there behind the glass. And I couldn't figure out a good way to ask Daddy why he had lied to me or why he called me June Bug instead of Natalie Anne. In the books I read and the movies I've seen on DVD—back when we had a player that worked—there's always somebody at the end who comes out and says, "I love you" and makes everything all right. I wonder if that'll ever happen to me. I guess there's a lot of people who want somebody to tell them, "I love you."

I wandered to electronics and the last aisle where they have stereos and headsets and stuff. I wasn't searching for anything in particular, just piddling around, trying to get that picture out of my head.

Three girls ran back to the same aisle and pawed through the flip-flops.

"This is going to be so much fun!" a girl with two gold rings on her fingers said. "I think Mom will let me sleep over at your house tonight."

"Can't," the one with long brown hair said. "I've got swim practice early in the morning."

"You can sleep over at my house," the third one said almost in a whine, like she was pleading for something she knew she wouldn't get. She wore glasses and weighed about as much as a postage stamp. "I don't have to do anything tomorrow."

Gold Rings ignored her and pulled out a pair of pink shoes with green and yellow circles. The price said $13.96. "These will be perfect—don't you think?"

"Mom said to find ones that are cheap and plain so we can decorate them," Brown Hair said.

"What about tomorrow night?" Gold Rings said. "We could rent a movie and sleep over at my house. You don't have swim practice Thursday, do you?"

They talked and giggled and moved on down the aisle, and I wondered what it would be like to have a friend ask you to sleep over. Or just to have a friend. Living on the road in a rolling bedroom has its advantages, but it also has its drawbacks, like never knowing where you're going to be from one day to the next. Except when your RV breaks down and you can't find the right part for it, which is why we've been at this same Walmart a long time.

"You still here, girl?" someone said behind me.

I turned to see the lady with the blue vest and a badge that said *Assistant Manager*. The three girls must have picked up their flip-flops and run because when I looked back around they were gone. The lady's hair was blonde, a little too blonde, but she had a pretty face that made me think she might have won some beauty contest in high school. Her khaki pants were a little tight, and she wore white shoes that didn't make any noise at all when she walked across the waxed floor, which was perfect when she wanted to sneak up on three girls messing with the flip-flops.

"Did your dad get that part he was looking for?" she said, bending down.

"No, ma'am, not yet." There was almost something kind in her eyes, like I could trust her with some deep, dark secret if I had one. Then I remembered I did have one, but I wasn't about to tell the first person I talked to about my picture.

"It must be hard being away from your family. Where's your mama?"

"I don't have one."

She turned her head a little. "You mean she passed?"

I shrugged. "I just don't have one."

"Everyone has a mama. It's a fact of life." She sat on a stool used when you try on the shoes and I saw myself in the mirror at the bottom. I couldn't help thinking about the picture at the front of the store and that the face belonged to someone named Natalie Anne.

"Are you two on a trip? Must be exciting traveling in that RV. I've always wanted to take off and leave my troubles behind."

When I didn't say anything, she looked at the floor and I could see the dark roots. She smelled pretty, like a field of flowers in spring. And her fingernails were long and the tips white.

She touched a finger to an eye and tried to get at something that seemed to be bothering her. "My manager is a good man, but he can get cranky about things. He mentioned your RV and said it would need to be moved soon."

"But Daddy said you'd let us park as long as we needed."

She nodded. "Now don't worry. This is all going to work out. Just tell your dad to come in and talk with me, okay? The corporate policy is to let people . . ."

I didn't know what a corporate policy was, and I was already torn up about finding out my new name, so I didn't pay much attention to the rest of what she had to say. Then she looked at me with big brown eyes that I thought would be nice to say good night to, and I noticed she didn't wear a wedding ring. I didn't used to notice things like that, but life can change you.

"Maybe you could come out and talk to him," I said.

She smiled and then looked away. "What did you have for supper tonight?"

"We didn't really have anything. He gave me a few dollars to get Subway, but I'm tired of those."

She touched my arm. "It'll be all right. Don't you worry. My name's Sheila. What's yours?"

"June Bug," I said. For the first time in my life I knew I was lying about my name.

❀ ❀ ❀

Johnson stared at the sun through the rear window. Pollen from the pine trees and dirt from a morning rain streaked it yellow and brown in a haphazard design. Three Mexicans climbed out of a Ford. Tools piled in the back of the truck and compost and some black tarp. One slapped another on the back and dust flew up. Another knocked the guy's hat off and they laughed.

The sun was at the trees on the top of the nearby mountain, then in them, and going down fast. An orange glow settled in and Johnson's stomach growled. He glanced across the parking lot at the neon liquor store sign next to the Checker Auto Parts, and his throat parched.

A newer RV, a Monaco Camelot, had parked at the end of the lot, and the owner pulled a shade at the front windshield for privacy. He wondered what driving one of those would be like. How much mileage it would get per gallon. The smooth ride on the road. Almost looked like a rolling hotel.

He sat up and looked out the front of the RV. The way they were parked gave him a good view of the store's entrance. An old guy with an oxygen tank pushed two carts inside. The man smiled and greeted a mom and her children.

Johnson hit the down arrow on his laptop. One green light on the wireless network from the coffee shop. He wished he had parked closer to the end of the lot, but he hadn't planned on getting stuck here.

A loud knock at the door, like he'd just run over someone's dog and it was under the back tire yelping. Johnson moved slowly, but he was agile in his bare feet. He caught a glimpse of the guy in the right mirror. Blue vest. Portly. Maybe thirty but not much older. Probably got the job through someone he knew. Johnson opened the door and nodded at the man.

"Just wondering how long you're thinking of staying," the man said. There was an edge to his voice, like he was nervous about something.

Johnson stepped down onto the asphalt that was still warm from the sun but not unbearable. "Like I said, I'm waiting on a part. If I could get out of here, believe me, I'd be long gone."

The man looked at the ground. "Well, you'll have to move on. It's been—"

"Three weeks."

"—three weeks and it could be three more before whatever part you're looking for comes, so I think it's best you move on."

"And how do you want me to move it? Push it to the interstate?"

"I can call a tow truck."

Johnson looked away. Boy Scouts at the Entrance sign were selling lightbulbs. Pink and orange clouds had turned blue, like something was roiling on the other side of the mountain. A black-and-white police car pulled into the parking lot and passed them. The man in the vest waved and the officer returned it.

"I'll give you one more night," the manager said. "If you're not out of here by morning, I'm calling the towing company."

Johnson wanted to say something more, but he just pursed his lips and nodded and watched the man waddle, pigeon-toed, back to the store.

The girl came out and passed the manager, smiling and swinging a blue bag. She had a new spiral notebook inside. She'd filled more of those things than he could count, and it didn't look like she was slowing down.

"Did you get your work done?" she said as she bounded in and tossed the bag on her bed.

Johnson opened the fridge and took out a warm can of Dr Pepper. "Enough."

"What did the manager guy want?"

"He said we'd won a shopping spree."

"He did not."

Johnson took a long pull from the can and belched. "He was just wondering how long we'd be here."

"I met a friend," the girl said, her face shining. "She's really nice. And pretty. And I don't think she's married. And she has the most beautiful eyes."

"June Bug, the last thing we need is somebody with her eyes on this treasure." He spread his arms out in the RV. "What woman could resist this castle?"

"She's not after your treasure. She just cares about us. She said the manager guy was getting upset that we've been here so long. Is that what he told you?"

"Nah, this is a big parking lot. We're gonna be fine. Did you get something to eat?"

June Bug shook her head and climbed up to her bed. "Almost finished with my last journal. I want to start a new one tonight."

"What do you put in those things? What kind of stuff do you write down?"

"I don't know. Just things that seem important. Places we've been. It's sort of like talking to a friend who won't tell your secrets."

"What kind of secrets?"

She slipped off her plastic shoes and let them fall to the floor, then opened the bag and took out a dark green notebook. "When you tell me what you're writing about on that computer, I'll tell you what's in my notebooks."

Johnson smiled and took another drink from the can, then tossed it in the trash.

At the storefront, the police car had stopped and the manager leaned over the open window.

2

On an impulse she could not explain, nor would she have wanted to, nor would she have had anyone to explain it to, Sheila Lempis bought an entire fried chicken dinner, complete with potato wedges and coleslaw, and headed out the door, keys jangling.

"Have a good night, Ed."

"You too, Sheila," the man wheezed.

She stowed her purse in her car, locked it, and took a deep breath. The RV was toward the middle of the lot, nearest the grocery entrance. She supposed she had seen vehicles in worse shape parked there overnight, but she couldn't remember when. Rust, a cracked windshield, balding tires. The vehicle was square, less aerodynamic than newer models, and with the price of gasoline she wondered how anyone could afford to drive such a thing. Inside had to be blistering in the summer heat and frigid during the winter. She imagined them chasing the sun in the winter and driving to cooler climates in the summer. The license plate had rusted off the front, but the back showed a faded outline of the state of West Virginia, and the words *Wild, Wonderful* were still visible.

Dark inside the RV and nothing moving. She clutched the blue bag and wondered who she could give the chicken to if they weren't there. Maybe Mr. Taylor, who lived behind her, alone after the death of his wife. All he had were those horses to keep him busy.

Sheila turned and walked toward her car but stopped when a fox trotted through the edge of the lot. The things were plentiful here all year round, but this one looked like it had just crawled out of a den after a long winter. Bony shoulders poked through its fur, matted and splotchy. It stopped and stared at her, sniffing at the wind, then disappeared as it loped around the building's corner.

The young girl's face passed through her mind as if in a dream, and Sheila couldn't walk away without trying. Those eyes, bright and intelligent, sparkling with life. Eyes that seemed to know too much and too little at the same time. Sheila had watched her wander through the store, pausing in jewelry, passing time leafing through books, in search of something. A locket. Something to read. Maybe a home.

Her father did not normally accompany her inside the store, and Sheila guessed from the food she bought that they had no working stove or refrigerator. Sheila had talked with no one about the two. When the manager noticed the "hunk of junk" in the parking lot, Sheila knew there would be trouble.

The father was not hard to look at. He was tall, with a square jaw and penetrating eyes. He had the stubble of a man stranded, though she had seen him carry a small black kit into the bathroom and exit clean shaven. His hair was a bit too long, even shaggy, but it was full and dark and just touched his eyes. He always paid with a dwindling wad of cash and didn't make small talk with the cashiers. He carried a certain strength about him that wasn't measured in muscles, though he surely had enough of those.

Sheila had spoken to him only once while he was waiting in the salon for his daughter's haircut. He had a current *Newsweek* in his lap, flipping through the pages.

"She's a real cutie," Sheila had said.

He looked up as if someone had caught him with a hand in the cash drawer. Surprised. Off guard. He glanced behind, catching sight of the girl in the mirror, and tipped his head back. "Oh yeah. She's something else."

"Are you finding everything okay?" she said, cringing at the words. "I've seen your RV in the lot for a few days."

He nodded. "Waiting on a part. The thing just gave out on us."

Sheila smiled, an uncomfortable silence creeping in. "We have a lot of people come through here on their way to California or the Northwest." She chuckled, though there was no reason to laugh, and her face burned. "Well, if you need anything, that's why we're here."

She retreated to customer service, her heart skipping a beat. It had been a long time since her heart had felt anything like skipping.

Sheila pushed a couple of errant carts into the stall to make a bit of noise and gritted her teeth. *Now or never. Just walk up to the door and knock. What's the worst that can happen?*

She knocked. Silence inside. A fat crow landed on the flickering light overhead and cawed. Maybe they didn't hear. It was a timid knock.

As she lifted her hand to rap again, she saw the RV dip to one side and squeak.

"It's her," the girl said inside. The side window was open. "It's the lady I told you about."

Sheila couldn't help but catch a faint reflection of herself in the dirty window. A pale likeness of the girl she used to be with more pounds and less hope. The curls had long ago straightened. The dream of finding someone she could share life with who wouldn't drink his way into the gutter had dissipated like morning fog. Her husband had lost his job and then his license. After a few treatment programs failed, she hung on long enough to pay the mortgage and their increasing bills while he watched the Broncos and the History Channel. He complained when she canceled the cable, but she had to do it. They lived exactly seven miles from the nearest liquor store at the time. When he wasn't watching TV, he was working on an old bicycle in the garage. When he'd finally gotten the thing fixed, he'd set off for his promised land.

But here she was at a stranger's door, trying again. Just showed the ache was still there.

The man appeared at the door in a white T-shirt and dirty jeans. Sheila looked down, trying to hide her embarrassment, catching sight of the plastic tarp on the ground underneath the engine where he had been working.

"I told the manager we'd be out of here as soon as possible," he said, his voice firm and a bit irritated.

She held up the bag. "I'm not here to kick you out. I brought you and your daughter some dinner."

He studied her for a moment, then opened the door and stepped down. "I appreciate it, but we're fine."

Sheila half whispered, "I know. I'm sure you can take care of yourself. I talked to her today and she . . . she's just so cute. I bought this on a lark. Thinking you might enjoy the hot meal."

He bit his lip and stared at her, his face pained, like he was trying to find the cure for cancer. Finally he reached out and took the bag, looking past the lock of hair that swept over his eyes. "You want to join us?"

"I really couldn't. I have to be going."

He gave a wry smile. "Now if we can accept this hospitality, the least you could do is eat with us—don't you think?"

Sheila heard something like clapping inside and a few thumps, like the girl was hopping. "All right. If you insist."

"Wait right here," he said. He closed the door. Inside the RV a flurry of activity. Someone cleaning furiously. Curtains pulled. Then he was back. "It's not the cleanest place in the world."

"It'll be fine. I even brought some paper plates and plastic forks."

❁ ❁ ❁

My dad had already had a nut roll, but he grabbed a piece of chicken and some potatoes and coleslaw and dug in. When I saw that, I knew it was going to be a good night. It had been forever since we'd had anybody inside the RV. Last time was probably down in Florida at one of the campgrounds where I made a friend, and her mom and her came over and helped us clean the place. It wasn't long after that that we packed up in the night and took off for South Carolina.

I think Daddy ate the chicken because he didn't want to talk.

Sheila picked at a little wing and grinned at me, saying if I didn't eat I would probably dry up and blow away. I suppose that happens to some people, but I have a pretty healthy appetite.

"How long have you worked here?" I said.

"This store's been open about four years. I started as a cashier and worked my way up. Before that I was working at a store out in Falcon, east of here."

"You ever been married?"

"June Bug, that's enough questions." Daddy wiped his hands on a napkin and poked at the grease in the corners of his mouth.

Sheila smiled. "I don't mind. Is June Bug your real name or just a nickname?"

I usually would have answered right away, but I took a quick bite from a leg and stared at my dad.

He shook his head. "It's both. June's her name, and I put the *Bug* on the end of it."

Sheila looked a lot more nervous in here than inside the store, and I can understand that because I feel a lot more comfortable in the RV than inside Walmart where people look at you like you don't belong.

"I was married to a sweet man who had a problem with the bottle," she said. "It finally got the best of him."

"What happened?" I said.

Daddy gave me *the look*.

"He'd been without a drink for a whole month when he fixed up a bike and took a ride to the liquor store. That night I was coming home and saw the police cars by the road. It looked like somebody in an SUV had hit a deer. When I got home and saw he wasn't there, I knew what had happened."

"I'm sorry," I said.

"It was going to happen one way or another," Sheila said. "I'm just glad he didn't take anybody out while driving drunk. He didn't treat me mean or anything. He didn't want to face life, I guess."

Daddy grabbed the salt from the counter and put some on his potato wedges. Then he squeezed the ketchup packets out like he always does, making a ketchup lake on his plate.

"Do you think you'll ever get married again?" I said.

I guess Daddy had resigned himself to my questions now because he just closed his eyes and chewed.

"I've thought about it," Sheila said. "But I don't want to make the same mistake. My father says I should come live with him and my mom on their ranch in Wyoming."

"They live on a real ranch?" I said. "With horses and cows and stuff?"

Sheila nodded. "Lots of horses and cows and more stuff than you can believe. Fifty years' worth of stuff in that house. I don't think I could breathe in there it's so packed."

"I'd love to live on a farm and have my own horse and a dog."

"You should drive up there when your part comes in," she said to Daddy. "They've got a lake where you can fish and mountains all around. Pretty much perfect if you don't get too close to the house. I know they wouldn't mind."

"If it's so perfect, why don't you go back?" Daddy said.

Sheila smiled. "Probably the same reason you like to travel in one of these. Just need space. And a life of my own. Feels a little like giving up to go back."

The dim fluorescent light from the parking lot was all we had to eat by since we didn't have electricity. The generator had gone out long before we arrived. I went to get my flashlight about halfway through the meal, but Dad told me to wait. He has this thing about carrying a little flashlight in his pocket everywhere he goes, and I keep mine under my pillow. He pulled out a half-used Yankee Candle and lit it. Daddy said I could never use a candle because once I lit one and put it on my bed and then went to sleep. He got pretty mad over that. The flickering candle made our faces glow around the table, and all of a sudden I got this warm feeling like we were living like regular people.

"What about you two?" Sheila said. "What brings you all the way to Colorado?"

"We've been on the road since I can remember," I said. "I think Daddy likes to spend as little time as possible in one place."

"That's not true," he scolded. "I wouldn't mind settling down someday to a ranch. Maybe have a couple cows."

"What do you do?" Sheila said.

"I'm a writer. I sell articles to magazines or whoever will buy them."

"He writes scripts too," I said.

"Yeah, but I don't sell many of those. I do some blogs for companies and such. And odd jobs here and there. Pays the bills most of the time."

Sheila's eyes twinkled. "That's exciting. You're probably famous."

Daddy shook his head.

"How do you get paid?" she said. "I mean, if you're traveling all the time, how do they send you the money?"

He hesitated. "I got a post office box or two."

"I'd love to see something you've written. You should send me a copy of an article." She wrote her e-mail address on a napkin.

"He doesn't use his real name on the articles. He uses a sumo-name."

"Pseudonym," he corrected.

"It's a fake name," I said.

Sheila laughed. "What I wouldn't give to be out on the road. Nothing to tie you down. Just pick up and go when you want. Beats working at Walmart."

"There are some drawbacks," Daddy said. "If you get sick, there's no family doctor. And no health care plan."

"But you don't have a mortgage or a car payment. I assume this is yours."

"Yeah, bought and paid for a long time ago."

"What's a mortgage?" I said.

"House payment," Daddy said.

We finished and there were a couple pieces of chicken left over. Sheila insisted we keep them, but my dad opened the refrigerator and showed her it was dark in there, so she picked up the plastic container.

I thanked her for dinner and told her she could come back

anytime. Daddy opened the door for her and walked into the parking lot. I blew out the candle and listened from the front window screen.

"That was real nice of you," he said. "Thanks for going to the extra trouble. She appreciated it."

"What about you?"

"I did too."

"I heard the manager tell one of our employees that he was calling the tow truck tomorrow if you were still here."

"You think he'd do that? just kick us out?"

"I think he'd kick his own mother off the property if she stayed too long. It's always the bottom line with him. Black-and-white, no grays." She looked up at him, and the flickering fluorescent light hit her face just right—a half silhouette and half halo. I thought this could be a scene from my life I might remember forever—the scene where I finally get a mother.

"I hope you don't mind me saying this . . . ," Sheila said.

Dad moved a few paces away, probably so I couldn't hear, but I got closer to the screen. "Let me guess," he said. "This is no life for a little girl. She needs a mother. Is that it?"

Sheila smiled. "She needs a school where she can make friends and go to Girl Scouts and learn how to cook."

You tell him, Sheila.

"She's learned a lot out here you could never learn in a classroom. I've taught her to read and write. She knows the country a lot better than most adults. She can tell you the capital of every state in the Union."

"She doesn't have a bicycle," Sheila said. And then she got quiet like she was sorry she had said it, but I wasn't.

I felt something warm on my cheek and brushed it away. It was like this lady I didn't even know knew me better than he did.

He nodded. "I know."

She turned to walk away and my heart almost broke. Then she stopped and looked back. "I put my street address and phone number on the napkin with my e-mail address. You could have the tow truck bring you there. I have some space by the garage where you could park. Just until the part comes."

"I'm going to walk over to the parts place in the morning. I'll bet it'll be in and we'll be on the road."

"Just in case you need it."

I watched her walk back into a dark spot in the parking lot. Before Daddy came inside, I jumped into bed and pulled the covers over me so he wouldn't see my eyes. He put a hand on my shoulder and whispered good night. I just lay there and didn't say anything, pretending I was asleep, this warm and hollow feeling down deep inside at the same time.

All I could think about was the name Natalie Anne. And if somewhere out there was a mother who was waiting for me.

A hard knock at the door woke me from a deep sleep. The sun glinted off the red rocks of the mountain across the interstate. Over there, a truck stop was coming to life with 18-wheelers pulling out in a line. Daddy's bed was empty at the other end of the RV, the covers all messed up, so I scrambled down and hit the linoleum.

It was the manager of the store, his hand cupped at the window, trying to see inside. I opened the door and noticed something leaning against the front of the RV. A pink bike with a white basket on the front and those streamer things on the handlebars. The thing took my breath away, and all I could do was stare at it and wonder where it came from and who had bought it or if it was some kind of mistake.

"Your daddy in there?" the manager said.

"No, sir."

The man sighed like I'd just told him the world was coming to an end on Thursday and he was going fishing on Friday. "Know when he'll be back?"

I shook my head.

"When he gets back, you tell him to come inside the store there and see me." He pointed to the Walmart like I'd never seen it before or like I was some little idiot kid who couldn't figure out two plus two. "You hear me?"

"Yes, sir. I'll tell him."

"If he doesn't get back before noon, I'm calling the tow truck. You have any way to get ahold of him?"

The man had just eaten a breakfast burrito or something because I could see white stuff between his front teeth and his breath smelled spicy. I wished I didn't have to talk with him and that Daddy was back.

"No, sir."

He swore, then mumbled something about leaving a kid out here alone as he pulled a pack of cigarettes from his pocket and lit one up. He looked down at the bike and scowled. At least that's the only way I can think of describing it. It wasn't a sneer; he kind of turned up his nose and said, "This your new bike?"

"I don't know."

He sighed again. "You tell him to come see me." Then he walked off fast, his shoes hitting the pavement hard. He pushed a couple of carts together and moved off toward the grocery entrance. I looked at my watch and it said 6:54.

There was a note taped to the bike's seat, and I climbed down to get it. On the envelope in big letters it said *JB*. Inside was a piece of paper with his scrawl in pencil. When he was teaching me to write, he used the big lined paper and made sure he always printed things nice and neat, but the rest of the time he let his hand go and it was hard to read.

> JB,
> I was thinking about what that lady said last night about you—I know you heard some of it. When I get back, let's find an empty spot on the lot and I'll teach you to ride. Your helmet is in a bag by my bed. Try it on but don't ride the bike

before I get back. I want to see your
face when you figure it out.
    If that manager comes by, tell him
I'm looking for the part. I'll be back
quick as I can.
    Daddy

I thought about running after the man and telling him where
Daddy was, but I figured I'd better leave well enough alone. I flew
into the RV and tried to get the helmet out of the box. It was a chore,
but I did it. After I'd pulled all the stickers off, I put it on and ran
for my mirror. The helmet was the most shiny and beautiful thing
I'd ever seen, but I couldn't figure out how to get the strap fastened
because it was too tight. On the counter was a little white bag with
a donut inside. I ate it while I went outside and walked around the
bike. It had white tires and white handlebars and white pedals, and
the rest of it was pink.

If this was the effect of having a mother, I was all for it.

❀ ❀ ❀

Sheila arrived a half hour early for work, her heart fluttering as she
exited the interstate and wound her way around the other grocery
and drugstores. She usually drove to the light and turned, but
she didn't want to get caught by it, so she pulled into The Home
Depot and drove to the end where she'd have a good view of the
parking lot.

The RV was still there.

She took the fresh loaf of banana-nut bread and knocked on the
door. No answer. She opened it and put the loaf on the counter. In
the light of day and with the shades open, she could see a bit more
of their lives. Everything the girl owned was on her bed. A pile of
notebooks mostly. Where did she keep her clothes?

The RV could have been worse, though Sheila wasn't sure how.

Maybe if there were raw meat on the floor and rats gnawing at it. The night before, the small living space had looked quaint in a way. Now it was just sad. It had to be difficult to live in a confined space without it becoming a trash heap, but these two clearly needed tips on clutter management. It looked like the girl slept in a sleeping bag on top of the mattress. A permanent campout.

A box of granola sat on the counter. An opened can of Pringles beside it. A half-eaten box of Oreos. A stack of old newspapers. Several blue plastic bags from the store. The couch, if you could call it that, was ripped and had crumbs strewn around, along with a torn cardboard box. His bed was unmade with only a throw draped over the mattress, no sheets. The computer sat on the floor by his bed. A half-empty cup of coffee from a nearby shop perched precariously on a shelf. Maybe the coffee shop was how he charged the computer and used the Internet.

Suddenly, something about his work didn't feel right. As soon as she'd gotten home the night before, she checked her e-mail to see if he had sent her a message, but there was nothing. Just a message from her sister about the negative effects of aspartame and how she needed to quit drinking diet soda. That and a few spam e-mails.

It was a glance at their lives, just a fleeting look at the way they lived, but she found herself judging them—him, really. Questions flooded. Where was the girl's mother? Was he on the run? If so, from who? Or what?

She'd had this feeling before, a stirring in the gut that something was amiss, something didn't fit. A sensation at the soul level, somewhere between marrow and bone and emotion that told her to be wary. At those times, she had dismissed the feeling as simple reserve, an unwillingness to commit to life, to move forward. And some of those moves had been disastrous.

This does not feel right.

Only one thing surprised her in the whole RV. By the head of the bed, on top of the built-in cabinets, next to several rolls of stacked toilet paper, was a weathered Bible. It sat open, as if it had been recently read. Her parents had kept a family Bible on a coffee table in the living room when she was a child. It was more of a good luck charm than anything, for the family certainly didn't read it, and they only hit church on the high holidays.

The sight made her want to run. She felt as if she were treading on some sacred burial ground and that brought a chill.

What if this guy is a serial killer and the girl was the daughter of one of his victims? The two don't look that much alike—no resemblance other than the eyes. Or he could be one of those perverts who kidnaps kids and moves from town to town until he gets tired of them and finds another.

She quickly retrieved the bread, stuffed it in her purse, and hurried out the door. Sweat trickled down her back, and she wiped at her forehead as she scurried across the parking lot in the hot morning sun.

The entrance hit her with a blast of cool air and a greeter said, "Good morning, Sheila." Delores was wiry and older, with a nice smile and hair that could be described only as patchy.

Sheila didn't want to face the crew and the questions that would undoubtedly be waiting, so she turned right, needing a refill of her blood pressure medication, a problem handed down from her mother. There was no one at the front counter, so she walked past the aisles of painkillers, diabetic supplies, and supplements until she found the pharmacist and two other workers staring at the black-and-white monitor for drive-up prescriptions.

"Isn't that cute?" a young assistant said. She had flowing black hair and a pretty face, and Sheila couldn't help but wonder if the dark-haired boy with the black trench coat and earring in his eyebrow who hung around at closing wouldn't be her undoing someday. An assistant manager has to know as much as she can about her employees and struggle with the information.

"She got it," the pharmacist said, laughing. "Look at her go! I wish I could record this."

Sheila moved to the end of the counter so she could see the monitor. In the empty lot behind the store stood a tall figure watching a smaller figure pedal a bicycle.

"Isn't that something," the assistant said, biting her lip. "I remember when my dad taught me to ride."

"It's like watching someone take Communion for the first time." Sheila turned and walked away.

❀ ❀ ❀

Johnson stood transfixed, watching the perfection of momentum, speed, and balance. Pink and white and a little girl smiling was the best thing he had seen all day. Maybe all year. He hadn't thought about a bike for June Bug, but now it seemed like the perfect fill to the void growing ever wider. The void of the present and the future.

He had loosened the straps for the helmet and positioned it on her head correctly, just as the box said. The back of the store seemed a good bet, less traffic and no slope. The only problem was that the aroma of fire-grilled food coming from the nearby Texas Roadhouse had his stomach growling.

It hadn't taken her five minutes to put it all together and begin to ride with abandon. Braking was still a foreign concept, but he guessed that was the way of children. Old people are more concerned with stopping than going. Kids just want to go, and he wasn't about to rain on her pedal parade. In time she'd get all the stopping she wanted and then some.

In a white T-shirt and jeans, he watched, his own childhood flooding back in a patchwork of memories like some quilt strung together from vulnerable moments. Riding by himself down the short gravel drive leading away from their house. Lost momentum, falling, skin on rocks. Blood. Laughter behind him. Some people viewed parents as those who stand on one side of a room and encourage you to walk, cajoling you to get up and try again. Johnson had experienced the opposite. It had taken years to shake the feeling of ridicule and scorn he expected just for getting up and putting one foot in front of the other. Since birth, his view of the world had always been of people—and even God—waiting for his fall and then piling on. Success was simply staying down and surviving.

It had only been recently that Johnson had begun the long climb out of the canyon of failure toward the glimmer of a thought that God may not be as full of scorn as he once thought. Things he heard some radio preacher say. Words on a page about an easy yoke and a light burden. He'd always looked at religion as a crutch for people who were too scared to do life by themselves. Now he wasn't so sure.

There were things he missed from his childhood—the lazy summer afternoons of lemonade and peanut butter and jelly sandwiches, friends, fireflies, tying strings to the legs of june bugs and following them like they were kites. But the truth was he longed to escape the past and the remembrance of things stored and locked away in the trunk of memory. Some nights he would lie on his bed listening to her soft breathing, cars passing, and he would try to get a picture of childhood in his mind, of some good thing he could hold, but the good thoughts were usually fleeting. Some men could put all that behind them and move on. For some reason he couldn't, and maybe that was part of the reason the girl was still with him.

June Bug navigated the Dumpsters and the empty 18-wheeler parked behind the store. To the north, a field with wild grass and flowers bloomed. To the west were mountains and above them dark clouds, as if something waited to descend.

A diesel engine chugged behind him, and he turned to see a tow truck at the light, pulling into the parking lot. He waved at June Bug but she had her face down, watching her feet like he'd told her not to do, the front wheel wobbling back and forth.

"Don't watch your feet, dummy," his father had yelled from the porch. *"Look up and keep your eyes on what you're headed for. You watch your feet and you'll wind up on the ground."*

"June Bug, we need to go," Johnson said, his voice echoing off the store wall.

She kept riding as if she didn't hear.

An employee in a blue vest stepped out a door and lit a cigarette.

The woman glanced toward the girl and blew a long trail of smoke in the air. "This her first bike?"

"Yeah."

"Like a duck to water, isn't it?" she said, smiling.

"Just about." He raised his voice again. "June Bug! Let's go."

She looked up and immediately put her feet out, scraping the pavement with her shoes until she stopped. "Why? I'm just getting started."

"We'll come back later. I need to go see about the RV."

"Okay, you go see about it and I'll stay here."

"I can't leave you here. Come on. You can ride more later."

Her shoulders slumped, and she pushed herself inch by inch until she came closer. "You promise?"

He nodded and waved at her to go ahead of him; then they moved past tire and lube and around the parking lot to lawn and garden. He caught up to her and grabbed the back of the seat before she rolled into traffic. Yellow lights flashed in the lot, and the big diesel was in front of the RV, backing up, its bed extended.

"What are they doing to our house?" June Bug said, getting off the bike.

"Guess we're being evicted."

"But I don't want to leave. I'm just starting to have fun."

"I know, but—"

"This always happens." She grabbed the straps under her chin with one hand and tried in vain to take them off. "The minute I start having fun, something goes wrong and we have to move."

He caught the bike as it fell. "I know it seems that way, but—"

"I hate it," she yelled. She had her helmet off now and slammed it to the ground with a loud crack. The doors to lawn and garden weren't working, and Johnson watched her run down the sidewalk to the other entrance and go inside.

He picked up the bike and carried it into the parking lot, stowing it on top of the RV.

The manager was there with the tow truck operator, a thin man with stubble and greasy hands. "Sorry about this, man," he said.

"Not your fault," Johnson said. He turned to the manager. "I went over for the part today, and they said it could be another couple of days."

The manager didn't make eye contact. "This is not an RV park. You're supposed to be here overnight."

The thin man put on his gloves and loosened the chain and fastened it to a hook on the front of the RV. "Where are we taking you?"

Johnson scratched his head. "I guess you could tow me to the lot where I'm having the part delivered."

He glanced at the manager and said, "I can't tow you to another parking lot. It's either to some address or the impound. And that's going to cost you to get it out."

Diesel smell wafted over them. The manager stood with his hands on his hips, as if he were powerless.

"Take him to this address," a woman said. It was Sheila and June Bug was with her. She handed the man a piece of paper. "There's a carport by the garage. I cleared it last night."

"Sheila —," the manager said.

"I'm just helping them out until they can get back on the road."

The manager looked at Johnson and shook his head. "He's going to be nothing but trouble. Him and that girl will bleed you dry."

3

Mae Edwards had been born in Dogwood, West Virginia, in a small shell of a house that still stood by the winding creek that worked its way from the north side underneath the interstate, by the train tracks, and down through the heart of the sleepy town. As water will do, it found its purpose by spilling into something bigger than itself—the Mud River. Dogwood, it is said, is a place where dreams die and good people live out their lives like the last three innings of a hopeless baseball game. Too many runs to make up but too much pride to quit. Mae knew about feeling behind. And she had felt that old, nagging desire to just quit several times, though she had never given in.

Only one thing kept her going.

She was at the table, clipping an article from the *Herald-Dispatch* and placing it in a pile on the plastic tablecloth dotted with coffee cup rings and stains from a thousand forgettable dinners.

Her husband, Leason, walked through the front door with another newspaper. He smelled wet, like an old dog that had just run through the dew-stained grass of the yard. "Here's you a fresh one," he said, plopping the newspaper on the table beside her.

"I thank you." She sipped her coffee.

She waded through the news like seining for minnows, her net the pair of scissors that seemed attached to her right hand. A man shot in Huntington. Police had released few details. A wreck of a church bus in Wayne County. Repairs on a bridge over the

Ohio were going to cost more than originally planned. Vandalism in Ritter Park.

He went to the refrigerator and opened it, grunting as he bent over to see shelves crammed with food and Tupperware containers. She was one to toss things, but he would not, and his choices were either a gastronomic paradise or a ticket to Cabell Huntington's emergency room, depending on which container he chose. Some jams and jellies in the door hadn't been opened since Kennedy was shot.

"I put one out over on the counter," Mae said, still staring at the headline, "Top Girl Scout Cookie Sellers to Be Honored."

Leason shut the door, then found the grapefruit, still cool to the touch, on a plastic cutting board. She'd put it out there for him to slice with the knife he'd sharpened the day before. Like always, he held half of the fruit to his nose, taking in the ripe citrus smell. The grapefruit spoons were in a dirty silverware drawer that went off the track when opened. She'd asked him a hundred times to fix it. He took the sports section from the new paper before he sat and tipped a generous dash of NoSalt to the grapefruit halves.

"See anything?" he said.

Mae sighed. "Not much. Not what I'm looking for."

Leason attacked the grapefruit, not noticing he was sending showers of juice across the table, all while checking the box score of the latest Cincinnati game. Another abysmal season, but Mae knew there was something to be said about loyalty to a team. Not like the players who jumped from one league to another simply because somebody gave them a million or two more. Leason had talked about the days when it wasn't the money that drove a team toward the pennant but just a passion for the game. He read the box score every day through the prism of that memory, then grabbed the life section and headed down the hall.

Mae shook her head. *I could set my watch to that man's bowel movements.*

She knew he would spend the next half hour in there doing the word jumble and reading the comics. Same time every day, rain or shine. She wasn't sure whether to be disgusted about it or to thank God for the regularity.

A half hour later the water chugged through the rusty pipes and the toilet gurgled into the septic tank, and the old man walked back through the kitchen, his belt askew and the varicose veins on his legs showing blue, and threw away his spent grapefruit.

Mae put her paper and scissors down and sat back, her coffee at arm's length, toying with the handle back and forth. "You think I should just give up, don't you?" she said, studying his face. "You think I'm crazy, still looking through the paper every day."

Leason leaned against the stove, wiping his hands on a paper towel from the dispenser he had mounted under the cabinets. "I never said that."

"I didn't say you said it. I said you *think* it."

He tossed the wadded-up towel toward the paper bag that served as their trash. Not even close. "If it helps you to keep looking for things that might give an answer, I don't care if you take a shovel and dig all the way to China. And you gotta do what you need to do. You don't need anybody telling you whether it's a good idea or not."

"You're supposed to support me in this."

"I just brought you the paper, didn't I?"

"I don't mean that. I mean support with your words and your thoughts."

"How in creation do you know a person's thoughts? Mae, you're not making sense. No sense at all."

Mae ran her hand across the tablecloth. Spreading the crumbs was all she was doing, but it still made her feel like she was doing something. The sound of his voice was both a comfort and a wound. She longed to hear what he was thinking, but every time she coaxed a few words out, it only reminded her of what she was missing. His words were a long, cool drink on a hot day, and over the years the drinks had become few and far between. "You think she's gone for good."

"I think the best time to find her was the night she disappeared.

After that the trail goes cold. And with all the sickos out there these days, it's hard to tell. It's just hard to tell."

"What you're saying is, after seven years, there's no use to what I'm doing."

He crossed his arms like an umpire listening to a coach's tirade. With as much heartfelt compassion as he could muster, he said, "I don't think we're ever going to know for sure what happened. I could be wrong. Something could turn up."

She closed her eyes tight and held them that way, as if doing so could bring the past into greater clarity. "There's something we're missing. There's something we're not seeing about this whole thing."

Leason spoke quickly. "What we're not seeing in this whole thing is that your daughter knows the truth—"

"Now don't you go bringing Dana in," she interrupted. "She's been tied up in knots about this ever since it happened."

"She sure has a funny way of being tied up."

He spoke about Dana like she wasn't his daughter. Always had. There was some disconnect between the two of them, and Mae had always felt in the middle.

"She shows it different; that's all," Mae said. "Look at you and me. I'm here clipping the newspaper almost seven years to the day, and you're ignoring it like you did from day one."

"I never ignored it. How dare you say that."

"You acted like it never even happened." Mae felt the tears coming and she turned away. This was the most they had talked about it since the anniversary two years earlier, and every time they did, it was like opening up some old wound that had barely scabbed over.

Leason stared at the empty birdcage by the refrigerator, his jaw set. He could say a lot more, she knew that, but he just stood there like a fifth head on Mount Rushmore, stone-faced and easing away from the fight. A few months after Natalie went missing—it was in the fall after the leaves started turning—Dana did the same thing, running off with some guy for a week or two and then returning and losing her job. Mae chalked it up to her grief, but she knew Leason didn't believe it. He thought Dana knew more than she was telling. He thought the sheriff was right in bringing her back and talking, the trail getting colder.

Leason swallowed something, perhaps his pride, and mustered the courage to break the silence. "How is it I could support you better?"

Mae let the question hang there in the air between them. She rested her forehead on the palm of her hand. "If I'd have known it was going to turn out like this, I never would have had children."

"You can't know how things are going to turn out. And you can't choose somebody's life for them. You don't have the power."

Mae folded, and she could tell Leason was watching. It happened like this around every anniversary. She'd go into her shell, and she wondered how Leason viewed these episodes. Theirs was not a great marriage, nothing for the ages, but it wasn't bad. And it was certainly worth saving.

She knew he still hurt because of the suspicion on him. He'd been a suspect in those early days when people were looking for anyone to blame, though Dana had said a white man with a leather jacket had stolen the car with Natalie in the back.

"I remember when I was a kid and we were moving up this way from the coalfields," Leason said. "We had this black dog that found us in the hollow down there. Just a mutt. We never even knew where he came from. Just showed up one day. Times were hard and Daddy said we didn't have enough to feed the rest of us and we couldn't keep him. But I felt for the little thing, so I used to find scraps from the table, crusts of bread and things, and put them out the back door when nobody was looking.

"That dog stayed with us. Made his home with us. Went out and scavenged the dump for food or caught a grouse and then came back and slept under our porch. He never got an invite from any of us except for me, but he was about as faithful as they come.

"After the war, Daddy decided to get out of the mines because of the machines and the dust and the black lung. He packed every-thing we had on a wagon and sent the rest of us over the mountain to come up this way. I don't know how he ever got that thing all the way here with those two plow horses he had, but I remember the day he showed up at my grandmama's house. Just sitting on that wagon, smiling from ear to ear, our stuff still tied on the back.

"I asked him where the dog was, and he acted like he didn't know what I was talking about. Then he said the dog fell in the river, and I knew he'd probably kicked it in or thrown something at it to get it to stop following him. And I cried like a baby about that dog and kept begging God to let me have him back. I'd tied this sea grass string around his neck as a sort of collar and cut a hole in a piece of leather and burned his name in there. We called him Percy. I don't know why. It seemed like a good name for a dog to a little kid.

"I dreamed about him one night, walking past hobo camps, coming through the woods, and escaping danger. Rainstorms and floods and all these adventures.

"About a year later—it was in the spring when everything was starting to bloom and the worms were coming up and the ground real soggy—my little sister started whooping out on the porch. Mama tried to get her to be quiet because she was sure the neigh-bors could hear. But what she was screaming was 'Percy, Percy, Percy!'

"Daddy was making breakfast in that big iron skillet, the eggs sizzling and popping, and he stayed there watching out the window while us kids ran out to see about all the fuss. Then I saw that old dog. From a distance it looked like Percy, but I wasn't sure. He came up real slow, like he wasn't really sure it was us. And then when he saw me, he took off running and I saw that sea grass string around his neck.

"I drove back down that way once just to take a look around, and I hit the trip meter while I was still in the driveway. When I pulled up next to where that old house had been, it was more than eighty-seven miles. That dog walked more than eighty-seven miles to come home to us. It took him a solid year and you could tell he was worse for the wear, but he made it. I don't know how in the world he found us, but he did."

Mae had been watching his hands as he told the story. She took a big swig of the tepid coffee. "Is there supposed to be some point mixed up with that?"

"I hope to say there is. When something you love gets lost, it will usually find its way back. It may take a while, but if it's out there, it'll return."

"She'd be almost nine now," she said. "Her birthday is coming up."

"The other point is, you have to let it go. You have to release even the chance that whatever you love is going to come back. That's where the power comes."

She turned to her husband. "That girl is alive. I know it just as sure as you and I are here talking. She's alive."

He nodded. "All right, then. I'll support you until you find her."

"I'm not giving up."

"I didn't think you would."

"Everybody in this town is going to eat their words about her being dead and buried. She's coming back here, and I'm going to raise her like she was my own."

Leason licked his lips and found an errant piece of grapefruit stuck there. "I'll be the first to drive you both to the mall."

Someone drove up the gravel driveway and Leason turned his head. "Wonder who that could be."

Mae stood and looked out the front hallway, past the Hummel figurines and family pictures and decorative plates and handblown glass swans and paperweights on a shelf in the entry. The two lights on top of the car were all she needed to see.

"Oh, dear. What's happened now?"

4

Sheila said her house wasn't that far away, but the tow truck driver didn't seem too happy about taking the RV back into the trees and up a couple of steep hills and around some winding roads. I was lost as soon as we pulled out of the parking lot. The driver fussed about how much gasoline cost and how he probably wouldn't break even this month, and I just listened, sitting in the middle seat with my dad on the right nodding and saying, "I know what you mean."

We finally made it to the address, but the man drove past the driveway and had to back up. Then he cussed when he saw it had tall pine trees on either side and was as winding as a snake to the house.

"If I hit one of these trees, you're going to have more trouble than replacing an engine part," he said.

My dad got out and walked the driveway, then guided the man until he got to a level place by the garage. "Sheila said to put it right here."

First thing I noticed was the barking coming from the garage. A big throaty bark like some kind of monster was in there. Lots of scratching at the door too.

While they got the RV unhooked, I went exploring. The house was red on the outside, the color of the wood used to build it. There was a wooden porch with some chairs set up real nice and a fireplace built right out in the yard. There wasn't a house I could see next to hers until I ran out a ways and looked through the trees. That's when I found the barbed-wire fence. Where there's a fence there's usually some animals, and when I saw a horse barn my heart went pitter-patter all over again.

I ran down the hill and stumbled onto an old basketball court where I could ride my bike, and there was a wire running from one huge tree all the way past the house that I later learned was called a zip line. You grabbed hold of a handle attached to a pulley and rode down.

I saw this beautiful horse standing by the barn, and it was all I could do not to climb right through the fence to go over and say hello. And when I saw that my dad and the tow truck guy were still trying to get the RV situated, that's what I did.

I have a long history with horses, and I like to draw them in my journals. One time there was this carnival where you could ride a pony around and around, and it was about as close to heaven as I ever hope to get down here. Just the feeling of riding on its back and holding the reins made my insides feel like they were about to burst. I closed my eyes and pretended I was out on the range, just me and my horse, with nothing but empty spaces, and I could choose any which way I wanted to go. It's kind of like the feeling of living in an RV, only you don't have to put gas in a horse.

When I made it close enough to reach out and touch the horse, my dad yelled. His voice spooked the animal and the thing reared up and I fell. Another horse came around the barn and ran near where I was—so near I could feel the ground shake. I turned over and pulled my legs up to make myself as small as I could. It wasn't something I did on purpose; it just happened.

Next thing I knew I was in the air over my dad's shoulder, and he set me down on the other side of the fence and crawled over it. There were six horses, not two, and for the first time I felt like we had hit the jackpot in life's lottery.

"You need to respect other people's property," my dad said, breathing hard. He pointed to a sign on the fence that I guess I should have seen. "You can't go wandering into somebody else's place. You could get in trouble or hurt or both."

"Yes, sir."

The tow guy had a sheet my dad had to sign and then pay him, which I'm not sure how he did. I sat by the fence and watched the horses run. I already had names for two of them—the one with the white spot above its nose was Giselle, and the black one that shook the ground when he walked was Goliath. My dad doesn't believe in naming animals or cars, which I think is just a lack of imagination, or maybe he wasn't allowed to do that kind of stuff as a kid.

"Can I ride my bike?" I said as we walked back to the house.

"Not on that road. Car comes around that corner and you're a goner."

"I just meant on that court over there."

"Okay, I'll get it down."

He had secured the bike on top of the RV with a bungee cord, so he climbed the ladder on the back. He's not much of a talker, but he sure is strong because he brought it down with only one hand. Then he carried it over to the court.

"How long we gonna stay?" I said as I got started.

"Hard to say. That part should be in any day."

"Do you like her?"

"Like who?"

"You know who." I laughed. "Sheila. I think she's pretty."

"You just like the horses." Dad walked back to the RV and then around to the porch, staring at something.

I let the bike fall and ran to him. "What are you looking at?"

"Nothing," he said. "Come on. Let's take a walk around the place."

Brown pine needles crunched under our feet. The grass was old scrub grass that grew in clumps, and in lots of places there was just the red dirt—not like the sandy clay you see in Alabama but a dusty red, like there are rocks everywhere just waiting to stick up from the ground. Dad says the wind and water make little rocks out of big rocks and then it makes dust blow around and I could see that on every window in the house. Dad says that's why every windshield in the state has a crack in it—because of the little rocks on the highway that kick up.

"Did Indians used to live out here?"

"They're not Indians, June Bug. They call them Native Americans." Dad nodded and pointed toward the horse farm. "There was a big massacre not far from here. Back during the Civil War."

"What happened?"

"It's too awful to talk about."

"What happened?"

I knew if I asked him enough times he'd finally tell me. That's what he did when we went to all those Civil War sites. He'd keep saying stuff like, "A lot of brave men died here, but I can't talk about it." That just got me more curious, and I'd ask more questions until he broke down and told me.

Dad sat back on a big rock and crossed his arms. "I think they were Arapaho and Sioux. No, Arapaho and Cheyenne. The government kept pushing them farther and farther west and giving them land here and there to hunt. But some in the group didn't like the treaties, thought it was their land, and hated all the people coming through their territory to the gold mines and pushing them out.

"The tribe camped near Sand Creek—we can go there on the way back east if you want. Anyway, these boys from the Army came through, and one of their leaders ordered them to attack. There were only women and children and old men there. The young men were hunting."

"They killed them?"

He nodded. "For a while they made it look like the soldiers were brave and stood up to those painted warriors, but it didn't stick because the truth came out. That'll always happen eventually."

I closed my eyes and tried to imagine such a horrible thing. I'm sure it was worse than what ran through my mind.

"What some people can do to others is just plain awful," he said. "Hard to understand what's going through their minds."

When Sheila got home from work that night she had a big smile on her face, and she acted like we were special guests coming from some foreign country. She had a couple bags full of stuff and one of those take-and-bake pizzas that I've been wanting to try. Pepperoni is my favorite and that's what this one was. I wondered if she knew or just guessed.

Dad asked if he could use her phone, and she told us to come on inside. I held my breath as I walked into the house because I was afraid that I wouldn't like the place, but there turned out to be no reason for being afraid. First of all when she opened the door to the garage this red dog raced through the kitchen with his tail wagging and his tongue hanging out almost like he was smiling. Around his eyes the fur was white like he was some old dog professor. He came right over to me, past my dad who was running interference (which I think is a football term), and licked me in the face. (The dog, not my dad.)

"Walter, stop it," Sheila said, pulling on his collar.

When Dad reached out to pet him, Walter growled.

Sheila wasn't too happy, and she scolded him. "These are our guests. Now you be nice to them or you'll be in the garage the rest of your life."

It was almost like Walter understood her, or at least he heard the tone of her voice, and the old thing dipped his head and loped outside to take a pee. You could see all the white splotches on the yard that were his favorite places. You might wonder what kind of person names her dog Walter, but I have to admit that the name fit just right. The only thing that would have been better was to have a girl dog beside him named Eloise or Mabel or something like that.

Sheila showed Dad the phone in the kitchen, and I just stared at the living room. She had one of those really thin TVs in the corner that you see at Walmart playing the latest movie over and over and a bookshelf that filled the whole back wall. The couch and love seat and other chair looked a little old, but the chair was so comfortable to sit in I wanted to stay there the rest of my life and read books and watch TV. There was a fireplace too. Not one of those that you flip a switch and the logs start burning, but a real one with real logs. I could imagine the snow piling up outside and the fireplace on and me on the couch reading a book with a blanket over my legs.

"You like to read, don't you?" Sheila said behind me.

"I've always wanted a bookcase for the RV, but there's no room. This one is amazing."

She showed me the section where she kept her classic stories, and there was a shelf up high for books on marriage and relationships and presidents and a couple on war. I could have stood there and looked at the spines of those books all night, but she offered to give me a tour of the house and I was anxious to see the rest of it.

Downstairs was another living room and a fireplace (the people who built this house sure did like their fireplaces and I can't blame them), but the room had boxes of stuff stacked up like somebody was moving in or moving out. Off to one side was a bedroom.

"This is my guest room," she said, flicking on a light.

There was a big bed and a dresser and a closet. It smelled musty in there, like nobody had been a guest in a long time.

"What's the stuff in the boxes?" I said.

She put a hand out and ran it over one. "My husband's things. I've been meaning to have Goodwill come and pick them up, but I just haven't had the heart."

"If it's clothes, maybe some of them would fit my dad." We shop at Goodwill stores all the time, and I figured it wouldn't make any never mind to her because she was getting rid of them anyway.

"Maybe I'll have him go through them. My husband was a little shorter than your dad and kind of skinny, but we'll see."

There was a bathroom with a shower down there, another bathroom on the main floor where the kitchen and living room were, and the third floor had three bedrooms and another bathroom. The whole place had hardwood floor that creaked when you walked on it, except for the downstairs, which had a thin carpet. The carpet looked worn and had lots of stains, and from the smell down there I half wondered if that was why Walter spent his time in the garage.

Sheila's bedroom was on the third floor. Her bathroom had a big bathtub with little jets in it. There were a bunch of different shampoos and body lotions on the counters, and I've never seen so much fingernail polish in my life.

The bedroom was neat—her bed was made like it was some hotel room, the corners all tucked in and everything. On the nightstand was a picture of Sheila and a young girl, smiling. I asked who it was and she said it was her niece and then she told me about her and that she was sick and not doing well.

"Do you have any kids?" I said.

She kind of smiled and frowned at the same time, as if I'd asked her something too personal, but she said no, she didn't have children but that she always wanted to.

"How come you live in this big house all by yourself?"

"I'm not by myself." She sat on the bed. "I have Walter."

"Yeah, but he stays in the garage."

My dad's voice came up through the heating vent. He was on the phone and sounded mad, like somebody had lied to him or something.

I smiled and sat down on the bed and looked at the cobwebs in the corner of the ceiling. There were definitely flaws in the house, but I would have stayed the rest of my life if it were up to me.

On the way over, we had passed a church made out of logs, and I imagined my dad dressed in a tuxedo, his hair cut, and Sheila coming down the aisle in a long white dress, her face with some blush on it so she didn't look so pale, me putting flower petals on the floor in front of her. I also imagined her side of the church pretty full and nobody on our side. And then I thought of the picture in Walmart and that my name wasn't Johnson and if that was true, my dad wasn't really my dad. Or maybe he was and he had taken me from my mother. I swear, it's hard to keep your mind from running sometimes.

"I was married once," Sheila said softly in a voice like a little girl. "But he passed away a few years ago."

"The bike accident," I said. "Was he wearing a helmet? Because my dad says you gotta always wear a helmet, even if it's just in a parking lot."

"Your dad's a smart man. No, he wasn't wearing a helmet."

Her closet was full of clothes in neat piles on shelves or hanging up and there were all sorts of colors. Probably one to match every one of those fingernail colors. I wondered what it would be like to have all this room for your stuff, and then I thought about what dad had said. "Do you have a mortgage?"

She shook her head. "A couple of years before my husband passed, he bought an insurance policy that paid the house off if he died."

That seemed like a lucky break to me, except that he died of course. "So you're not tied down to a mortgage?"

"No, that's one thing I don't have to worry about. There are still enough bills, though, and Walter nearly eats my whole paycheck each month."

From what my dad had said, living in a house was a bad thing. But as the miles rolled on, I'd look out at all those houses passing by and wonder, if it was such a great idea to live in an RV, why didn't everybody live in one? I'd see these big white houses in Kentucky with the white fences and wonder what it would feel like to go to bed inside something that never moved and didn't need parts. Then, because my mind tends to jump from one thing to another without a whole lot of warning, I wondered if my mother lived in a house and if she was waiting for me. Or maybe she'd gone out riding without a helmet like Sheila's husband.

Across the way a horse blew some air through its lips, and I stared out the window at them. This whole setup didn't seem bad at all.

"Who owns that farm over there?" I said.

"Mr. Taylor's there alone. His wife passed last winter."

All of a sudden I got an idea that we could trade Mr. Taylor the RV for his farm and he could go out on the road. You can meet a lot of people when you're traveling.

"You said something about liking horses last night," Sheila said.

"Oh yeah, they're just about my most favoritest thing in the world, except for little dogs."

She stood and looked out the window. "Well, maybe I can take you over there this weekend and he'd let you ride one."

"You really think so?"

"Maybe we'd need to soften him up a bit with some homemade apple pie or some nut bread, but I think we could arrange it."

She smiled and put a hand on my head, and it was the best feeling I'd had in a long time. I couldn't resist hugging her right then and there and burying my head in her side. Her perfume smelled so good I didn't want to let go.

Sheila turned and gasped. My dad stood in the doorway.

"I didn't hear you come up the stairs," she said. She didn't know that he has a way of creeping around without anybody noticing. I don't know how he does it or where he learned it, but it's an unfair advantage when we're playing hide-and-seek at a campground.

"The parts place said they lost the order. Just fell through the cracks, I guess. It's going to be another few days. They can FedEx it, but that'll cost at least—"

"Don't spend that extra money; that's silly," Sheila interrupted. "You can stay here for as long as you'd like. I've got plenty of room."

I could tell by the look on his face that the idea wasn't going to fly, so I quickly spoke. "You should see the house, Dad. She has so many books it would take me years to go through them all. Lots of the classics you like. Plus, she said that Mr. Taylor will let me—"

"Hold on, June Bug. We have our own place. We're not putting Sheila out any more than we already have."

"I don't mind," she said. "There are two bedrooms up here not being used. One downstairs. You can sleep there and she'll sleep on this level."

Dad shook his head. "I don't want to impose. You've done enough."

"Nonsense. It's no trouble. You're just parking your RV. And you might as well take advantage of this old house before it starts falling apart."

I was still hanging on to my dream of riding those horses, so when he said, "We'll stay in the RV. If I could hook up to your electricity, that would be great," I ran over to him and hugged him.

"She's making pepperoni pizza for us."

"Suit yourself," Sheila said. And then she walked downstairs real fast.

He looked at her bedroom like it was some lost jungle where there might be a city of gold. Then he spoke in a quiet voice and took my hand. "Don't get too attached to things around here, you understand? We might have to leave quick."

"I want to ride the horses. She said I could."

"Just don't get too attached."

Sheila gave me raspberry lemonade with my pizza and she offered Dad coffee or tea, but he just had the lemonade and she did too.

After supper, I went outside on the porch and sat next to Walter and rubbed his head while they stayed in the kitchen. I was watching some old bird fly from a pine tree to the fence and then over to the barn. It had black wings with white around, and it made a screeching noise. I think it's called a magpie, but I'm not sure.

"How does she do school?" Sheila said.

I moved close to the window so I could hear more.

"I homeschool her. Actually, I RV school her."

Sheila laughed. "Well, it looks like you've done a good job. She's as smart as Einstein and cuter than a button."

"To be honest, I don't have to do much. She tears through books like there's no tomorrow. I wish there was a way I could get her hooked up with a library, but moving around doesn't lend itself to that."

There was a pause. There are times when you want to turn up the volume on life and times when you want to turn it down and times when you just want to turn it off. This was a volume-up time for me. I guess Sheila was taking her time, thinking about what she was going to say because she didn't speak very loud when she did talk again.

"I don't want to overstep my bounds . . ."

"Didn't bother you in the parking lot last night."

Sheila laughed again. "A girl that age, moving toward this part of her childhood . . . It's important for her to learn girl things. Like how to cook and how to make a bed and learn some things about the house."

"She knows how to cook a few things."

"I'm not criticizing your parenting. It's just that there are some things a woman needs to teach a young girl. Things she should pick up from another woman. Has it been a long time since her mama was around?"

Another pause. "It's been a while."

I heard the refrigerator open and close and the clink of dishes.

"I expect that manager of yours thinks you're crazy letting us stay here," my dad said.

"He's not somebody I go to for advice on life, if you know what I mean."

Dad laughed.

"He cares, I guess. Thinks you might be bad news."

"And what do you think?"

"You're here, aren't you?"

"Yeah. He actually let us stay longer than I thought he would. Can't blame him for being cautious. This the first time you picked up a couple of strays?"

"It is. Except for Walter, of course. And he's a keeper."

I had bugged Dad about a dog for a long time, and he said it wasn't fair to bring an animal into a life like ours. Now, petting Walter and seeing him close his eyes in pleasure at my touch made me want to have a dog all the more.

"She can't go over to a friend's house to play," Sheila said. "I see her walking the aisles of the store, just staring at other girls. I'm not trying to be hard on you—you've done the best you can—but there are some things a father can't give. Some things only a mother can."

I listened close, thinking Dad was going to run out of there, but he didn't.

Then Sheila spoke again. "She's shown an interest in the horse farm next door. Is it okay if I talk with the owner about letting her ride?"

Walter put his head up.

"I don't think we're going to be here long enough to do much riding."

"It might take a few days for that part, though. And on the weekends I help Mr. Taylor clean his barn. If she helped, I suppose he'd let her ride as a fair trade. It teaches responsibility, that an animal comes with hard work—"

"I can see why you're in retail. You're good at sales."

Sheila chuckled. "I really think it would be good for her."

"Let me think about it."

Another pause. Then my dad said, "I was noticing a few loose shingles on the roof. You get a lot of wind out here, don't you?"

"Blows like a hurricane in the winter and spring."

"I'd like to repair those for you if you'd let me. I can't pay you for the hookup and for parking in your driveway . . ."

"There'll be none of that. I invited you here as a friend. I'm not hearing any talk about payment. That's like a slap in the face."

"All right, but let me work on the roof. And if that Mr. Taylor would let me help in the barn, I'd do that too."

"So she can ride?"

"Yeah, I guess it'll be okay. Just don't let her get too attached to those horses. She's probably already named them."

Walter put his head down, and his leg moved in a phantom scratch. I guess I hit the spot with him, and Dad's words made me feel the same way.

"You a handyman?"

"I can fix a thing or two."

"Writers do that sort of thing?"

"Writers do what they have to."

Walter's ears went up and he loped off through the yard. I wanted to follow him, but the conversation was too interesting. There was a long pause, and I figured Sheila was getting ready to back the question truck up and unload.

"What happened to her mama?" Sheila said. "Did she pass away? If it's something you don't want to talk about, I understand."

"It's complicated. Let's just say I was put in a position I didn't expect. You know, being a father and all wasn't what I had planned."

"But it's grown on you."

"Yeah, I guess it has."

"So her mother isn't dead."

"Not that I know of."

"You haven't spoken with her? Does she know where her daughter is?"

"Look, I appreciate what you're doing. I don't know where we'd be if you hadn't extended your kindness."

A chair moved back.

"I'm sorry. I didn't mean to pry."

"No, you have a right to know what you want to know."

"Sit down, please. I ask too many questions."

The chair creaked with his weight again. "Why don't we talk about you?"

"What do you want to know?"

"Something easy. Like why you're out here all alone."

"I like it here. It's peaceful. It's paid for. It's not far from work. It's the best of both worlds. Out in the country but close to civilization."

"It is nice, but that doesn't explain why you're alone. I know your husband died, but that was a while ago, right?"

"True. And I knew it was going to happen. It was a matter of time and whether he was going to give control to God or Budweiser. But it's hard to move on after something like that."

"You a religious person?"

"I try not to be religious. That sounds stuck-up. Like you just follow rules. I read somebody once who said religion is man's way to God. We make a list to follow that makes us good people in our own eyes, but we don't take into account what God wants."

"I read the Bible every now and then."

"Why?"

"Guess I'm looking for guidance. You know, like there might be something in there for me."

"Guidance for what?"

"Which way to go. What to do with her. That kind of stuff. I've never been a churchgoer. It's hard on the road to do that type of thing."

"Still, it seems like you want to give her something spiritual."

"I bought her a Bible storybook a while back. We'd read it at bedtime. David and Goliath. Daniel and the lions. She devoured it. She read the whole thing in one night."

"That's good. Shows she's hungry."

"Part of my dilemma. I can tell there're some things I can't give her. Things a little girl deserves. But I can't let her go either."

I'd never heard Dad talk about stuff like this. Was this what it was like to have a father and a mother? two people who cared about you?

"What are you running from?" Sheila said.

"Excuse me?" Dad said, almost choking on whatever it was he was drinking.

The two of them laughed until Sheila said, "It just seems like you'd want to settle down. If you're this anonymous guy driving around the country, you must be running from something."

"What's the difference in us out on the road and you here in this big old house by yourself?"

"Maybe everybody is running from something inside. It's just a little more obvious for you."

"You're probably right," Dad said. "Only it gets really hard to run anywhere when your engine part is sitting on a shelf in Michigan."

"Sleep here in the house," Sheila said all of a sudden. "No strings. The downstairs is all yours. You can close the door down there."

"I can't do that."

"Warm sheets. A soft bed. I'll keep Walter up here with me so he won't bother you."

"It's not that. I can't become more indebted to you than I already am. Makes me feel guilty sponging off you."

"Sponge away, John. I don't mind. You two are the only light that's been in this house for ages. You'd be doing me a favor."

"I appreciate it. I really do. But I can't."

"At least let her sleep in a real bed. The upstairs guest room has lots of frills and a canopy over it. It'll be like sleeping in a castle for her."

"What's not real about the bed she's got?"

"You know what I mean. Stay out in that motor home all you want, but don't deprive her. While you're here, I'll teach her a few things. Bake a cake or roll out some pizza dough. Take her to a movie and let her get sick on popcorn and candy. And buy her some nice clothes instead of those old tomboy ones she has."

"I never had a sister," Dad said, and there was an edge to his voice like he was hurt.

"There's no reason you would know any of this. That's my point. She's not going to get what she needs unless you let go a little. Let me help her. Let me help both of you."

5

Mae Edwards stood at the edge of the Dogwood reservoir in the shade, where the dew of the misty morning still left wet stains on her shoes. Clouds circled overhead, threatening rain. A swirl of lights illuminated trees and shrubs with an eerie glow as they waited for the sun to rise higher. The ascent of confused lightning bugs from the damp earth gave her little comfort, though that scene at evening had always brought with it a measure of familiarity and peace. As long as she could watch the fireflies rise, there was equilibrium with the world, a rightness to an earth gone mad in a hurry. People let old women die in hospital emergency rooms without moving a finger. Men kidnapped children and held them hostage in basements before killing them. There were sick people out there and some were close.

"I never thought this day would come," she muttered.

Leason shifted from one foot to the other like his back was giving out on him again, pacing along the freshly mown grass near a small sandy patch where the sheriff had told them to stay. There was already yellow tape on the battered dock where kids fished or watched fireworks on July Fourth. A handful of fishermen were in place on an inlet where the trees leaned out over the lake.

"There's nothing that says she's down there," Leason said.

"That's not what the sheriff thinks," Mae said.

Leason's jaw was set with an uncharacteristic hardness. "Sheriff doesn't know everything."

"He wouldn't have told us if he didn't think there was something to this."

A young man wearing a tie emerged from the woods, carrying a small notebook and a pen stuck in his shirt pocket. He had the look of innocence combined with an inner tenacity of an attack dog, and Mae guessed where he was from the minute she saw him. It took Leason a while longer to even notice his approach.

"Morning, folks," the man said just loud enough to be heard. There were burrs on the bottom of his pants, showing the length he had traveled to avoid the authorities. "You're Leason and Mae Edwards, right?"

"What's that got to do with you?" Leason said. He was usually genial, a man of few words, and allowed his wife to not only make their social calendar but also take the lead in each conversation. The tension of the scene was eating at him, though. His right eye twitched with what looked to Mae like the beginnings of pinkeye.

"You're from the *Herald-Disgrace*, aren't you?" she said.

The man smiled, familiar with the pejorative. "Yes, ma'am. Todd Bentley." He reached out a hand, but both of them stared at him until he took it back. "I was hoping I could ask a couple of questions."

"I read your story about the anniversary of Buffalo Creek," Mae said.

"Thank you."

"There's no thank-you to it. Looked to me like you were jockeying for some book deal. Some of those stories make you relive all the pain. Yours just made me feel sorry for the people you tracked down."

Bentley smiled. "I can assure you, ma'am, I'm not shooting for any book or movie deal. You don't get too many of those around these parts. Just trying to do my job as well as I can."

An emergency worker gave a yell and a diesel engine fired. Black smoke rose through the trees like some evil prayer and drifted toward the valley.

"How'd you hear about this?" Mae said.

Bentley moved closer. "I've got a friend at the sheriff's office. We've been waiting for a break in this case for a long time."

Mae could see the headline: "Seven-Year Mystery Solved." "This is going to sell you a bunch of papers tomorrow, isn't it?"

"With all the cutbacks, we need something. They've laid off half the newsroom since I've been working there. If you don't generate some stories of your own, you don't have a desk." Bentley took another step closer to Mae. "But really, Mrs. Edwards, there's a lot of people who have been interested in this story since day one. You've seen all the churches that have kept their vigils, their prayer chains. People have held out hope that this day would come and that we'd at least find out what happened to Natalie."

Mae recoiled when he spoke her name. As if he knew the girl himself. As if he were on a first-name basis. As if he cared. He had no idea. That girl was full of life with sparkling eyes. Mae still kept the DVD someone had made of the video clips of her birthday and her first pony ride and the trip to Camden Park with Natalie covered in cotton candy—she even had it in her hair. Mae had bathed the child herself that night and marveled at the sticky sweetness of life, and a few days later, at the senseless meaninglessness of the whole thing.

He was right about the prayer chains. Every church in the tristate had Natalie on its list, but as time went on, she dropped off each list one by one. Either God was powerless to do something about the situation or he just didn't care. And the people were just as powerless as he was.

"I want to be as accurate as I can so our readers get the truth," Bentley said. "That's my goal."

"The truth," Mae said, laughing through the pain. "You wouldn't know the truth if it snuck up on you and bit you on the butt."

A photographer snapped a few shots of emergency personnel at the edge of the lake. Then an officer waved his arms and made the guy move back behind the yellow tape. Obediently the man did, snapping more pictures.

Bentley nervously fiddled with his tie, smiling. "I'll give you that one. But if the truth held on long enough, we'd probably get a good picture of it."

Leason, still staring at the scene, shook his head. "Vultures is what you are. Preying on people's bad news. Just a bunch of vultures looking for carrion. Ought to be ashamed of making people's loss your stock and trade."

"Did the sheriff come and get you?" Bentley said.

"He sent one of his deputies. Said there was a scuba diving class early yesterday morning that spotted a car at the bottom. It didn't hit him until later that it fit the description, and they hustled out here this morning."

"He wanted you to be here?"

"Discouraged it, in fact," Mae said. "Didn't want us as part of a circus, but there are some things you just have to know."

Todd was scribbling as she talked, looking straight at her. "You've always maintained that your granddaughter was alive. Why have you thought that?"

There it was. The fishing had begun on this side of the lake. Looking for a money quote before they even pulled the car out of the water. Natalie was probably just a skeleton now. The fish and crawdads and whatever else lived down there had probably been at her. Water could make a body disintegrate over time. Mae had been at the Ohio when they pulled her uncle's body out after being in the water for only three days, and he was bloated and almost unrecognizable. Too much to drink and the water too swift and a man who never could swim. What would Natalie look like after seven years?

"I still believe she's alive," Mae said. "Some people call it blind hope. I know how much life that little girl had in her. But my resolve is being sorely tested; I can tell you that."

"Where's the mother? Where's Dana?"

Leason turned on the young man like a bull whose territory had been violated, but Mae held up a hand and he stopped, his face contorted.

"Just leave it," Mae said as if talking to an old dog that had dug through a double-ply trash bag for a chicken bone.

Leason hobbled down the uneven slope to the water and walked precariously along the bank to the staging area for the recovery.

"I'm not talking to you about her," Mae said. "None of your business. Or anybody else's."

"It just seems strange that the mother of the child wouldn't be here. Has the sheriff contacted her? Or maybe she's moved from the area?"

"You can't contact what you can't find," Mae said, her jaw set on the false teeth she'd had since she was in her twenties. "Can you imagine losing your only daughter like this? not knowing where she is? wondering every day if you're going to get a call that says they found a body? people believing the worst about you? I don't blame her for trying to move on with her life."

Bentley scribbled and nodded.

Mae waved a hand at him like she was done and took a few steps.

"Mrs. Edwards, is there anything you want to say to the community? the people who have stood with you?"

Mae turned and looked hard at Bentley. "I've already thanked those people myself. The ones who prayed and brought us meals and such, they know how much we appreciate their reaching out." She wasn't through. "But to the ones who called talk radio and whispered behind our backs like we did something wrong, well, as a Christian woman I don't have much to say that you could print."

"Mae!" Leason shouted from the bank. "They're pulling it up."

❀ ❀ ❀

Sheriff Hadley Preston had seen more than his share of gruesome things in his law enforcement career and in the military before that. The past few years most of his days had been spent answering calls about stolen property or domestic disputes and the occasional drug bust. He'd written his share of speeding tickets, knowing well the best wooded lots to park where unsuspecting motorists never saw him until he pulled behind them. That always gave him a sense of pleasure, seeing surprised faces in the rearview.

However, in the midst of regular days of patrols and the routine

desk work of a Mayberry existence, he'd stumbled onto the hor-
rific. Before his post in Dogwood County, he'd spent time in smaller
communities. He'd been the first on scene at the 7-Eleven in Red
House when a robbery gone bad had turned worse. The gunman
had fled after spraying the scene with bullets from a semiautomatic.
The eighteen-year-old girl behind the counter had died before she
hit the floor. Two kids toward the back of the store were lying in
a pool of their own blood and red Slurpees. An older teen was
hunkered down behind the hot dog warmer, shaking and unable to
speak. That day wasn't much fun.

Of course the strongest memory, the one that had defined his
waking moments—and many of his dreams—was the night of
November 14, 1970. Preston was seventeen and one of the young-
est volunteers with the Wayne County Civil Defense. That evening was cold and rainy, had been all day. The quintessential West
Virginia mid-November day. Not a night fit for anything but staying inside and watching TV. Wet leaves on the ground. Soggy earth
that smelled fertile and just waiting for winter to lock in and turn
everything hard.

His parents had gone to dinner at a friend's home in Barboursville.
He figured they would drink some Hudepohl and play Rook until
late. Preston had said he didn't want to go. In the intervening years,
he'd often considered what might have happened if he had taken
their invitation and wasn't one of the first people at the scene.

That night he'd left his cigarettes in the truck, and he ran outside without a coat to retrieve them from the dash. In the eerie mix
of dark and fog and rain and moisture that hung in the air, he heard
a plane's engine overhead.

Whoa, that thing is too low, he thought.

He got out of the truck, listening more than anything, looking
toward the airport, hoping what was about to happen wouldn't.
Then a horrible sound wafted over the ridge, unearthly, unforget-
table. The last moments of life for some people. The sound was
quickly followed by a ball of fire that cut through the haze and fog
and descending darkness.

Preston didn't wait for the phone call. He stuffed his cigarette pack in his shirt pocket and headed up Route 75 until he neared the road to the airport. There, along the ridge, he saw the scattered, burning debris. He parked the truck in a ditch and jumped out, heart pounding, an unlit Pall Mall hanging from his lips, and ran through the underbrush, then slogged through mud that pulled him in and rose to his ankles. Then halfway to his knees.

By the sound of the engine, this was not a small plane, and the wreckage confirmed it. The burning rubble was scattered for several football fields.

He made it to the upward slope of the hill, out of the marshy area, and stopped to listen. The air was still. A crow flew over, cawing. Tires on wet pavement. A VW Beetle with a flashing light on top pulled to the side of the road. Fire trucks in the distance, sirens blaring, getting closer.

For a moment, Preston concentrated on the *tick-tick* of rain on wet leaves. Fire licking the edges of burning engines and the hiss of cold rain on hot metal. In all of that he never heard a voice crying for help. Didn't hear one person calling out.

Then the sirens overtook the closer noise of the evening.

The pungent smell of jet fuel was all around, and he wondered if he weren't in some kind of rescuers' no-man's-land and if the hillside would be engulfed in flames like some napalm run in Vietnam. But there was something more driving him—the heart of a young man who believed he could find a survivor. On a plane that big, somebody had to have made it. It looked like it had clipped trees at the top of the ridge, and if that was true, perhaps the bottom of the plane had been taken out and seats could have been scattered . . .

Others were coming up the hill, shouting. Preston'd had the presence of mind to grab his long gray flashlight before getting out of the truck. It was on now, scanning the hillside like a beacon of hope. His foot hit a stone, and he cursed as it rolled through the wet leaves. He flashed the light in that direction and was stunned to see a face staring back at him. An older woman. A pearl earring in one ear. He had thought her head was a rock.

It was at that point that he knew this would not be a rescue. He fell to his knees in the wet grass, the light trained on the woman's face. Water droplets running down her cheek and down to her neck and to the ground.

"You see anybody?" someone said nearby. Then silence as the man saw his flashlight beam. "Lord, have mercy," the man said.

Preston didn't know how long he stayed there or how many other rocks he already had stepped on or over.

Finally an older man put a hand on his shoulder. "You with Civil Defense?"

He nodded and gave his name. "I heard the engine. It sounded too low. And then this awful noise. I got in my truck down there. My dad gave it to me last year for my birthday. . . ."

"Hadley, I want you to listen to me," the man said. "Are you listening?"

"Yes, sir."

"I want you to go home and change clothes. Get a coat on. A rain slicker. Put on a couple of sweaters. And if you have boots, put them on too and some fresh socks. It's going to be a long night."

It was. The longest of his life. He did as the man said and raced home.

When he returned to the hillside, there was talk about where the plane had come from and who it might be. A news reporter had found a wallet on the ground and had called the newsroom. Someone recognized the name on the driver's license. It was somebody from the Marshall football team. That's when the air got sucked out of the whole hillside. Word passed along one by one. This was the Herd's plane. Men moved like statues, stiff and aimless when they realized the truth.

"East Carolina," someone said. "They were playing East Carolina. Lost their last game."

People drove up, gawking, some parking and running through the brush to see what had happened. The team bus sat at the airport above, waiting. And the saddest part was when it left, empty, and snaked down the hill.

Not one of those people had a chance when the plane clipped the trees on the ridge and flipped. An airplane on approach was probably going a good 200 mph. When it hit the hillside, the violence of the crash had killed all seventy-five instantly.

Preston wondered what those last moments were like. If they had time to react. Throw their hands up. Say a prayer. Call out a name.

He spent the rest of that night taking orders from the Civil Defense leader on the ground. Their job was to pick up body parts and bag them. An arm here. A hand there. Legs. Torsos. He didn't find any bodies intact. None of them were lying in the wet leaves like they were just sleeping. They were torn apart and scattered like a farmer scatters fertilizer. Mixed up. Burned. He had never gotten the smell of seared flesh out of his mind, and he doubted he ever would.

He'd bend over and pick up a foot, then feel the gorge rising and turn away. Soon it was just dry heaves. Then he got used to it. That was the worst effect. You could get used to the carnage more quickly when it was all around.

He came to a wooded area, combing for any sign of human life, and he stepped on a smoldering tree stump. When he got to the other side, he realized it wasn't a stump. It was a man's body still buckled into that part of the seat. He went down again, this time in a catcher's crouch, trying to take in the terror of the scene.

"Here," somebody said, offering him a swig of Jack Daniel's. "Take it. You're going to need this before it's over."

The drink burned as it went down. He took another swig and handed the bottle back. His body took over. He simply did what he was told. Just get the job done.

In the days afterward, when the funerals came and the shock of that night set in, Preston decided he had to put it behind him. He would not think of it, not speak of it, and not let it affect him. His mother had asked what he saw, and he told her it wasn't that bad, that the people died in a split second. The worry on her face told the story.

With the diesel engine running, much like the sound of the

fire trucks on that night almost forty years earlier, Hadley Preston opened his eyes. The tension on the cable grew tighter and jiggled in the water like a bluegill nibbling at bait. The rise of the car was slow—painstakingly slow.

Leason Edwards had his hands on his hips, watching the drama unfold. Hadley walked over to him.

"Grim business," Leason said.

"It is at that."

"And the press is already swarming."

Preston hadn't noticed the reporter. He turned and saw Mae pointing a finger at him and shaking her head. "You want me to run him off?"

Leason shook his head. "He'd just come back and ask the same questions. Vultures is what they are. Looking for carrion."

"I wish you two hadn't come," Preston said.

"She wouldn't stay away. Couldn't keep her away with a good horse."

"I figured as much."

His deputy, Mike, waved a hand at the edge of the water. "It's comin' up, Sheriff."

Leason took a step toward the reservoir, but Preston put out a hand. "I think you ought to stay back. I'll call you over when it's time."

"All right," Leason said. He wiped his forehead with his palm. "Gonna be a hot one today, isn't it?"

"I believe it will be."

The trunk of the car was just underwater, like a snapping turtle coming to the surface. Preston had seen this car in his mind a thousand times, and like the fire on the hillside and the smell of jet fuel, it came back to him as he studied the mud-caked license plate he'd been searching for.

You live and you die, and that's about it, he thought. *Rain falls on the just and the unjust.*

His wife had always said he shouldn't dredge up the past. Let sleeping dogs lie. He wondered what she would say about this.

6

It took me a day or two to get used to sleeping in a bed where you don't have to worry about sitting up and banging your head against the ceiling, but once I did, it was a whole new world. And the sheets were nice and clean and didn't have all those pebbles and sand. Dad slept in the RV, and the three of us ate breakfast together like one of those families you see on TV or in the movies. Sheila made us eggs and bacon and had orange juice with the pulp floating in it and not like that orange juice you can tell hasn't seen an orange for a long time.

Before Sheila went to work that first morning when I'd slept in the bed, she looked at me kind of funny, like some brush fire had been sparked in her head, and she said, "Wait right here."

A few minutes later she came back with a couple of big bags that had other bags inside them, and when she finally got all the plastic layers off I couldn't believe it. There was this big doll with the prettiest face you've ever seen — it looked like a real, live person. And in the other bag were two more with different faces and clothes. I just stood there and looked at them, afraid to even touch them.

"Go ahead," Sheila said. "You can play with them."

I couldn't eat I was so excited, and I carried one of them around all day with me. Sheila said I could have a tea party if I wanted, but I wasn't much interested in that. I did have lunch outside, watching Dad work on the roof, nailing shingles and moving around up there like a cat. Before lunch he took his shirt off, and I could see the muscles and the big scars he wouldn't talk about no matter how much I asked him.

That evening after Sheila came home, we had supper together again. She made the best corn bread I'd ever tasted that almost melted in my mouth, and we ate corn on the cob and chili. Chili's not my favorite, but I didn't say that because I didn't want to be rude. She asked what I did all day, so I told her about running around the yard with Walter, riding the zip line, and staring at the horses. I'd built a little shady place by the fence with an old blanket I found in the garage, and I stayed there watching them swishing their tails and eating grass.

I went out on the porch after dinner and acted like I was in some other world, but I wanted to give Dad and Sheila a chance to talk. I was forming a plan to get them together because, as far as I could tell, this was about the best situation ever.

They started talking about the RV and that we'd be able to get on the road as soon as the part came. Sheila didn't say anything for a while, and there was a clink of dishes, like she had started cleaning up.

Dad said something about the roof and that he'd found a hole up there; then he stopped. "What's the matter?"

"You just don't see it, do you?" Sheila said. "When I gave June Bug those dolls, did you see what she did?"

"She played with one of them the whole day, didn't she?"

"Right. With just *one* of them. Most kids would see dolls like that and would right away want to have a tea party and sit them in chairs and have them talk to each other. She took one and went off in her own world."

"What's wrong with that? Maybe she just liked that one."

"She's a lonely little kid, John. She hasn't had interaction with any kids her age. It's like she's starving for it and doesn't even know she's hungry."

My dad wasn't quick with words, but when he spoke, I could tell there was some emotion. "I've done the best I could. She can read and write like nobody's business. We need to work on the social interaction thing, but—"

"I don't doubt you've done your best. I'm not saying you're a bad father. But June Bug needs a stable place. She needs friends. She needs to have a sleepover and cook s'mores at the campfire. She needs a mother to hold her at night and tell her stories. She needs to know where she came from and who her grandparents are. She needs a home. A sense of place. While we were making dinner, she told me that sometimes she stays up past midnight reading. She needs a set bedtime and somebody to enforce it."

A chair scraped against the floor. I could tell by the creaking wood that my dad had gotten up. "Now listen, I appreciate everything you're doing, but you also have to look at the positives. I admit she's no debutante. But she's been more places and seen more things in this country than most people combined. We've touched the Liberty Bell. We've been to the Alamo. Hiked the trail Lewis and Clark walked. Have you ever seen the sun come up on the Grand Canyon?"

"No, but that's not what I'm—"

"Just let me finish. I know I haven't done a good job in a lot of areas. I'm not going to be able to give her everything she deserves. But I can give her love, and if she only plays with one doll instead of fifteen, I'm not going to have a conniption. Maybe it's better to play with one instead of all of them. Ever thought of that?"

"I'm not saying it's wrong to play with one doll. But a girl goes through stages, and she needs a mother to help her through the changes. At least an older female who can teach her about things."

"I'll give you that. So what are you saying?"

"Why don't you let her stay here? I've been thinking about it, and I'd like to take her in. Both of you if you want. You could stay on the property and maybe find some work. There's a church I go to sometimes. I'd bet those people would love to come alongside you. Good schools. No commitment or anything from me. I just want to help."

"Camel's nose under the tent," my dad said.

"Excuse me?"

"Just an old saying. The camel gets his nose under the tent and pretty soon he's inside."

Sheila's voice got an edge to it, and it was all I could do to not go in there and try to break up the fight. "I don't appreciate that. You're saying I'm some calculating woman. I'm not. I just care about her and it's something I've been thinking about. I look at her and . . ." Her voice trailed off like somebody driving to a distant hill and then hanging there on top as they hit the crest.

I couldn't believe somebody would talk about me that way, and it made me want to run inside the house and hug her. Except it sort of made me mad that she thought I didn't have a good dad. I'd seen plenty of dads whack their kids just for hanging on to the grocery cart at the Kroger or Piggly Wiggly. He'd never so much as raised a hand toward me. Now, I won't say that he hasn't yelled at me when I get out of line, but I've never actually been afraid he'd hit me.

Sheila's words stirred up something. Maybe it was the fact that I'd never seen any pictures of my mother. Maybe it was those movies I've seen we rent for a dollar from the Redbox. Some are about families having problems and some mom wants to leave her husband because he works too much or kisses other women. I just wish I had those kinds of problems. I wish I had a mom who might run off with me. And now that I'd seen my face on the wall at Walmart, I thought there might be somebody out there waiting.

"I do appreciate it," Dad said. "You've been kind to both of us, and I know your heart is in the right place. I just don't think it'd be good to get tied down right now."

My heart did a flip-flop, and it felt like the air in my lungs got replaced by molasses.

"Why don't you talk with her?" Sheila said. "Give her a choice. Maybe you'd be surprised at what came out."

❀ ❀ ❀

Mae set her jaw as the car emerged from the water and just hung there, years of sludge and slime and algae running out like sand from an hourglass. A weaker woman would have looked away or buried her head in her husband's shoulder, but Mae was not weak. Never had been. And she wasn't about to start.

Sheriff Preston asked them to move back, said that what they were about to see might not be pleasant, but again, Mae wouldn't be moved. Leason tried to turn her around as the car rested on dry ground, but she pushed him away and edged closer.

A Channel 3 News truck pulled into the reservoir entrance, then past the barricades. The reporters would probably want the car back in the water so they could get their video. *And this is how it starts.* The national attention. The stories of a missing little girl found after all these years. It would be the top story on the Internet for about a day, and then everybody would forget and move on to something else. An Olympic runner who loses a medal. Or a pastor's wife who guns down her husband while he's in the pulpit. Or some sixth-grade teacher taking liberties. Mae didn't understand how a handful of people had the power to deem a story important or not. How could a select few gauge the interest of a nation?

The sheriff called his deputy, and they draped a tarpaulin over the side of the car. The camera guy from Channel 3 came running, shooting video as he went, finally getting close enough to have the deputy reach out and shove the camera away. The scene would be replayed over and over in the coming days on CNN and other news outlets.

"Is she in there?" Mae heard herself saying. She pushed through the gauntlet, and the deputy held out an arm like he was trying to hold back the tide with a toothpick.

"Mae," Leason yelled behind her. "No!"

She reached the car as the sheriff opened the back driver's-side door. The window was cracked and broken, and a good-size bass fell out and flipped and flapped on the ground. A guy in a wet suit grabbed it and took it back into the lake.

After seven years, the backseat didn't even look like a backseat. Black mud and minnows and crawdads mixed together in a scene trapped in time. On the seat, wrapped in mud and algae, lay a child's blanket and a stuffed animal of some sort, almost unrecognizable.

The sheriff leaned in and worked on something at the edge, moving his shoulders like it was some great struggle. Finally there was a dull click and he backed up, revealing a car seat with nothing in it but mud and sludge. The buckle was still fastened, but the straps—what was left of them—lay limp and lifeless. He put his head inside the car to examine the rest, then emerged and looked at Mae. "She's not in there."

Leason came up behind her, grabbing her shoulders to turn her away, but she shook him off. "I knew it. I told you all along she was taken. Just like Dana said. I told you!" She turned and a camera was on her and she nudged it. "Get out of my face."

"What happened to the girl?" Bentley, the reporter, said.

"She's not in here," the sheriff said, placing the black tarp back on the window. He instructed the divers to get in the water again.

The TV reporter shouted something, and Mae pushed her way through the gauntlet. She'd seen enough.

"Do you have any comment, Mrs. Edwards?" Bentley said, trailing the two of them.

"Nothing you could print," Leason said.

Mae stopped. "I've told you people all along that Natalie Anne is alive. She's been alive for seven years, and not a one of you has had the guts to believe me. Maybe now you will."

The dew had burned off, and the access road was dusty as Mae and Leason drove from the scene. The TV news camera took a shot of them leaving. Mae turned from the window as an officer lifted the yellow tape and Leason drove through.

"They should have believed Dana from day one," Leason said.

"Why should they? You didn't."

They rode home in silence, Mae's mind spinning with *who* and *what* questions. It was going to be a long day of people calling and asking more questions and coming by with food to ask questions. But now she had something concrete that she hadn't had for seven long years. Mae had reason for hope.

Sheriff Preston had the car loaded onto the back of a tow truck and hauled away, a grim picture frozen in time. The news truck left soon afterward, and all the onlookers headed home. A young girl who looked to be no more than ten laid a handful of daisies and wild-flowers at the edge of the water. Preston watched her walk away and shook his head.

The diver approached him with something, asking for a plastic bag. The sheriff went to the cruiser and poked through the backseat and the trunk, finally finding a white trash bag. He opened it and the scuba guy held out a long-handled knife.

"Looks like this could do some pretty serious damage," the scuba guy said. "I don't know if it has anything to do with it, but I uncovered it in the mud where the car was resting."

Preston studied the knife in the morning sunlight. That long in the water had left its blade rusted and the handle covered with growths, and there wasn't much chance of getting anything from it other than the serial number. Even that was dubious. But he'd seen this type of knife before.

"What do you think happened, Sheriff?" the diver said.

He let the knife fall in the bag, tied it tight, and tossed it in the open trunk. He got out another trash bag and placed the smelly car seat inside as well as the blanket and what was left of the stuffed animal and tied the top. "Something went royally wrong here, and it might have cost a little girl her life. To tell you the truth, I don't know. But I'm going to keep asking questions until I do."

Preston closed the trunk and drove away, deep in thought. He'd been there when the mother told her story the first time. Dana appeared to be in deep distress, as any mother who has just lost her child to a kidnapping would be. She had met a stranger at the Dew Drop Inn, she had said. Nobody in the bar remembered him. He had her drive into the country and pulled a knife on her. Then forced her to get out. She admitted it was a mistake bringing her daughter to a place like that and letting her sleep in the backseat while she was inside. That, to Preston, had lent credence to her story. She wasn't afraid of the unvarnished truth. She really did seem broken up about losing the baby.

The guy had tied her to a tree with some rope he had in his backpack and left her there, telling her if she tried to escape, he'd kill the little girl. She had burn marks on her wrists where she tried to get free, and later she had taken them to the tree where she'd been tied and showed them the missing bark on the other side. Everything about her story checked out, except the car and the girl had simply vanished.

Something kept gnawing at him about the car seat, however. Something about it wasn't right. He passed a car wash on a hill and doubled back and pulled up to the middle bay. There was an old boy washing a vintage Mustang in the first bay. Deck shoes with no socks, cutoffs, and a tank top. A semi driver was washing his cab in the third one. The mud flaps had Yosemite Sam holding two six-shooters.

Preston popped the trunk and pulled out the plastic bag with the car seat. He grabbed a few coins from his pocket and let them fall into the slot in the wall, clinking their way into the cash holder. The hose filled with water and gave a hiss through the nozzle, and a thin stream added to the puddle already growing on the concrete.

The pressure on the line felt like a snake trying to squirm free when he pressed the trigger, and just like that the car seat became visible. The material was corduroy, maybe a denim color, and it began to come apart with the force of the water. He had second thoughts about it as soon as he hit the back of the seat and it tipped over. He adjusted the nozzle so the stream widened to a spray and the mud and slime oozed from the material and the plastic.

The old boy with the Mustang was drying his car and sneaking peeks at him. Preston wondered what would happen if he ran the plates on the Mustang.

He let go of the trigger and the line tensed again. Tossing it aside, he knelt and held the front buckle in his hand. The seat was the old type that had a strap coming down over the child's head and torso. He knew enough about car seats to judge that this was probably a secondhand buy. These days half the people who bought fancy car seats had no idea how to secure them. He'd stopped cars and found he could tip kids forward as much as a foot with the slightest pressure.

The lock on the front of the car seat was still engaged. Above it was the strap, jagged and torn and hanging limp. Preston washed off the back and found the other end of the strap that had worked its way through the holes.

He sat on his haunches a few minutes, holding the pieces, working it out in his head. A strap like that wouldn't disintegrate in one place and stay intact everywhere else. There had to be a logical explanation for this, but for the life of him he couldn't figure it out.

"Hey, Sheriff." It was the Mustang owner wiping off his hands and arms with a chamois. "Somebody throw their kid in the Ohio?" He said it half laughing.

Preston just turned and stared.

The old boy shrugged and hopped in the car and fired it up. The engine still sounded tight, like some mechanical work of art that ought to be in a museum. The muffler needed work, but then guys like this probably wanted it loud so people would hear them coming.

Another car pulled into the first bay, a rusted minivan with several bumper stickers on the back door. One read, *My Karma Ran Over Your Dogma*.

Preston knelt there, hanging on to the buckle. Had it been cut? Whoever did it would have to be strong to get a knife through it.

A buzzer told him he had only thirty seconds left on the hose. He stood to return it but sprayed inside the plastic bag before the time was up. When the hose went limp, he dumped the blanket onto the concrete with a splat. The colors had faded but he could recognize the pattern. Noah's ark. He lifted the blanket and found a one-eyed bear with a ribbon still tied around its neck.

He put everything back in the trunk and closed it. The guy in the minivan was scrubbing the front grille, his ponytail swirling behind him. A tattoo on his shoulder of a hemp plant. To Preston all the scrubbing seemed an exercise in futility, a losing battle, sort of like his work, a picture of the culture right there in front of him. People rearranging deck chairs on the *Titanic* for a better view; only they didn't realize there was an iceberg dead ahead. The man never looked at him, but Preston could have sworn the guy flipped him the bird as he turned and got in the cruiser.

Preston's mind jumbled over the discovery. All those years wondering. In the days after the disappearance, he'd had a sense that the story he was hearing wasn't the truth. But in a tight-knit community that wanted answers and a quick arrest, he was cautious, tracking as many leads as he could until bringing Mae's daughter in for an all-nighter. The young woman never budged from her story, but something didn't add up then or now.

Every day for seven years he woke up with the nagging suspicion that there was a little girl's body decomposing in some shallow grave in the woods. He kept waiting for the phone call from some hunter, but the call hadn't come. Until last night.

He could almost piece it together—the timeline, the words of the young lady, the description of the perpetrator—but not quite. What happened that night? What was the truth?

There was no way around it. He had to talk to Mae and Leason's daughter again.

❀ ❀ ❀

On Saturday Sheila and I went over to Mr. Taylor's barn. The building looked ramshackle from the outside with weathered boards sticking out, and the whole thing leaned toward Pikes Peak. But it was a lot different inside. It didn't feel like it would fall down. Sitting on a hay bale and smelling all the smells of a barn was just about the best feeling on earth.

The horses came right over to us, and Giselle and Goliath ate some cornmeal out of my hand. Their hairy lips felt funny and I dropped half the food, but Sheila said she did the same thing her first time, and that made me feel better. Sheila wore these big rubber boots that came up to her knees — I guess because of what she was about to step in — and coverall jeans.

Mr. Taylor was a mean-looking old man with spidery eyes and skin that looked like the leather on his pointed boots. He was bent over at the shoulders and I thought he was going to pick something up, but then I realized that was just the way he stood all the time, like a tree that was weighted down with fruit. Only he didn't straighten once the fruit fell. Even though it was hot he wore a long-sleeved shirt and jeans. The horses walked toward him like he was their best friend.

"So we got us a helper, huh?" he said, glancing at me out of the corner of his eye and smiling. He had big white teeth just like the horses, and I wondered if those teeth were really his or if somebody had put them in for him.

Sheila introduced me as the daughter of a friend, and the old man didn't ask questions. "Well, it doesn't matter who you are in my book, as long as you're willing to work."

"That's me," I said.

He told me the troughs hadn't been cleaned in a long time, so I set to work chipping away and scrubbing at the wooden thing that looked like it was older than the barn itself. Sheila and Mr. Taylor went inside the stalls and moved the manure around so it wouldn't get too deep in there. That probably sounds disgusting, but to me it seemed like a lot of fun to get down in there. I wanted to help but Sheila said I should wait until I got some farm clothes and boots and I agreed with her because I just had one pair of shoes and they had tears in a couple of places.

A mouse hopped from underneath a bale of hay and bounced along. That thing could jump about a foot off the ground. I let out a scream and the old man laughed. He said it was a kind of jumping mouse that lived in the fields and that the Walmart almost didn't get built because of it. I thought it was funny that a little mouse could slow down a thing as big as Walmart.

Dad came running into the barn and the horses moved back from him and Giselle nearly stepped on my foot. Mr. Taylor coaxed her over to a stall, and Sheila made the introductions.

"You've got quite a little worker there on your hands," Mr. Taylor said.

"She's a keeper, isn't she?" Dad said. He turned to Sheila. "The part's in. Do you think I could run over to the place in your car? I'll bring it right back."

Sheila looked like someone had dropped an anvil on her head. "Oh, sure. No problem. Let me get the keys."

"I know where they are," Dad said. "I'll be back in a jiffy. How about a cookout tonight to celebrate? I'll pick up some stuff for the grill." He looked at Mr. Taylor. "Enough for the four of us."

"Oh no, I couldn't," the old man said.

"Sure you could," Sheila said. "It'll be nice to have some company."

"I'll go on strike if you don't come over," I said.

That made him laugh. "We'll see."

"See you soon," Dad said and he was off.

Mr. Taylor bent over and raked some dung out of the corner of the stall. "Your daddy know how to cook up a good burger?"

"He makes the best. He stuffs the inside with cheese and mushrooms and whatever you like. We haven't cooked out in a long time — ever since the grill we had broke."

"How long ago was that?" Sheila said.

"Maybe a year or two? All I know is I can smell that charcoal and my mouth starts watering."

By the time we finished at the barn and went to the house, Dad was back and had climbed underneath the RV, his legs sticking out, working on the part. There were white bags filled with buns and vegetables from a different grocery store.

Sheila had me take my shoes off outside and told me to come upstairs. "I've got a surprise for you."

I couldn't imagine what it was, and my heart jumped like one of those mice when I followed Sheila to her bathroom. She had a big bathtub that almost looked like a swimming pool.

"The only luxury I've allowed myself here is this Jacuzzi," she said, turning on the water and running her hand underneath. She took a plastic bottle from the shelf and poured in some thick liquid, and the bubbles starting foaming. Then she turned on the jets, and the whole bath rumbled and shook the floor. I thought the bubbles were going to lap over the top of the tub. When the water was high enough, she stopped it and said for me to get undressed and get in while she got me some clothes.

I closed the door and put my clothes in the corner and stepped in. The jets felt funny against my skin, but the water was warm and the bubbles smelled like the field of lilacs we had walked through when we'd stopped at a rest area in the Midwest. It smelled like summer to me, and now I was drenched in it.

Sheila came back in and hung a pretty cotton dress with red flowers all over it on the towel rack. I'd seen that exact dress while looking for headbands at Walmart, and though I am not a dress-wearing person, I liked the way it looked. She got out a fresh towel that was bigger than I was and soft and thick and smelled almost as good as the lilac scent of the water.

"Wash your hair, and when you get done, try this on," Sheila said. "I've got some white sandals I want you to try on too. And we're going to do your nails and trim your hair."

I sat back in the water, my arms behind my head, and relaxed. Surely this is what a queen feels like. People handing you things and putting out clothes and changing the sheets on your bed. I could get used to this in a minute.

I dried off and put the dress on, my hair shedding little drops of water.

Sheila walked in, put her hands on her hips, and shook her head. "If you don't look just like a picture, I don't know what does."

She stood me in front of the mirror and began brushing my hair, which is not an easy thing to do because my hair has always been the knottiest. It's like trying to straighten out an animal's nest. I usually give up on it and let it go wherever it wants. Sheila draped a dry towel around me and got out the scissors. What was supposed to be just a trim around the edges became a major cut because of all the tangles and knots, but I loved the way it looked and couldn't wait for Dad to see it.

"Let's do one more thing," Sheila said.

She sat me on the bed and put my feet on a folding chair and clipped my nails. Then she got out the prettiest pink nail polish I'd ever seen and went to work on my toenails. She put cotton balls in between my toes until the polish dried. She did my fingernails too, then put a little blush on my cheeks. To top it off, she'd bought a necklace that had a red flower in the middle just like the ones on the dress.

I was in front of the mirror looking at myself with her putting on the necklace when the engine of the RV cranked once or twice and then fired to life. Dad let out a whoop that we heard from the open window, and Sheila's face scrunched up like she'd just heard a car crash.

She fluffed out my new hairdo and smiled. "Let's go start dinner."

Dad changed clothes and looked as happy as I'd seen him in months. Men must feel like they accomplish something when they get a machine working. He took one look at me and his mouth dropped.

"Do you like it?" I said, twirling around and then holding out my fingernails and showing him my sandals.

"Where'd you get all that?" he said.

"Just a few things I picked out at work yesterday," Sheila said. "Every girl needs a new outfit and shoes."

He reached out to touch my hair. I think he'd become so used to seeing all the tangles that he couldn't believe it was so soft and silky. "You sure do clean up good, don't you?"

Sheila handed him a plate of ground beef, and he went to work. He'd bought onions and peppers and mushrooms and a couple kinds of cheese. He looked almost as happy making the burgers as he did fixing the RV but not quite.

An old truck rumbled up and Mr. Taylor climbed out. Walter ran over to him, wagging his tail and sniffing at his coveralls. Dad says a dog's nose is so sensitive it can smell things we can only dream about smelling, and it looked to me that Walter was in dog heaven. Mr. Taylor's clothes were like a full buffet at the Golden Corral. He walked behind the house where the smoke was coming from the grill and talked with Dad awhile. Mostly about what was wrong with the RV and how he fixed the burgers.

When Mr. Taylor saw me standing inside the screen door, he cocked his head like he was meeting a stranger and took off his John Deere hat. "Don't know that I've had the pleasure of making your acquaintance, ma'am."

I had to laugh at him as I opened the door. "Silly, it's just me."

He handed Sheila a jar full of something. "I've been waiting for a special occasion to open this. Some chowchow my wife made before she passed. Ought to be good with those burgers—don't you think?"

Sheila made a fuss about it, but I'd never heard of chowchow before, so I asked what it was. Sheila unscrewed the Ball jar and smelled the contents. "It's relish, sweet and good."

The pot on the stove was boiling, and it looked like there were enough ears of corn in there to feed a small village. Sheila had tossed a salad in a big green bowl and put croutons in, which I always called wood chips because that's what they look like to me. There were fresh cucumbers and tomatoes and just about everything you could think of in the salad, and I thought that staying with Sheila was a pretty good idea because I'd learn a lot about cooking. She'd also made potato and macaroni salad.

She asked me to pour the lemonade, and Mr. Taylor helped me get out the ice and put it in the big glasses. It was almost like having a real family with everybody pitching in and helping.

"So, is June Bug your real name?" Mr. Taylor said as we carried the food to the dining room table.

I shrugged, thinking about the picture I'd seen and wondering what it would feel like for people to call me Natalie. "It's what I've always answered to."

"Doesn't seem like a name fitting a pretty girl like you."

Dad brought a plate of burgers in and there was cheese running down the sides of some of them and juice still bubbling around the edges. "Her real name's June, but I added the *Bug*."

"You pick out the name or did your wife?" Mr. Taylor said.

Dad wiped his hands on a napkin and surveyed the table. "Guess it was a mutual decision." He looked at Sheila. "You didn't put out the caviar?"

Sheila laughed. "We're all out."

"Well, you have everything else. This looks fantastic."

We sat down and started passing food. There was something missing, and at first I couldn't figure out what it was. Then it came to me. I'd seen it in a lot of movies, especially ones around a big meal like at Thanksgiving or Christmas, which is what this felt like, even though it was summer and the flies were trying to get to the food before we did.

"We should pray," I said.

Mr. Taylor was cutting the corn off the cob onto his plate, and he stopped midway through the row he was on. Dad raised his eyebrows at me.

Sheila was the only one who nodded and bowed her head. "Why don't you do the honors?"

"I don't think I can."

"Sure you can," she said. "Just thank God for the food and anything else you want to thank him for."

All of a sudden my face felt hot. I couldn't tell if Dad was mad at me for bringing up the subject, or maybe he was worried that Mr. Taylor would be offended for some reason.

I scrunched my eyes closed and put my hands together so tight I couldn't tell which one was right and which one was left. I tried to remember the prayers I'd seen on those movies, but nothing really came to me and Mr. Taylor cleared his throat like he was some starving man in Africa who just wanted to eat.

"Dear God," I started. My voice didn't sound like myself—it sounded like some animal being strangled—but I kept on going. "Thank you for this food. Thank you for my new dress and the sandals. Thank you for our new friends. Oh, and the necklace too and my haircut. And help us to have a good time tonight. Amen."

"That was a very nice prayer," Sheila said.

"Straight from the heart, June Bug," my dad said.

Mr. Taylor kept cutting his corn, and I passed the butter to him and the salt for when he was done cutting it.

Walter whined at the back door and Sheila scolded him. Dad got up and took one of the burgers that was a little too done and gave it to him. The dog devoured it in one gulp and came right back to the door and whined louder. Other than that, all you could hear was the clinking of silverware on plates and Mr. Taylor groaning with pleasure over the taste of the meal. He spread his chowchow on the plate and mixed it with his corn, which looked disgusting to me. I wondered if his dead wife would have wanted him to open that jar at somebody else's table, but I wasn't about to ask that either.

Dad says you can learn a lot more from listening than you can from talking. I tried to just eat and not say anything until one of the grown-ups did, but the silence was about to kill me.

Finally Mr. Taylor wiped his mouth and sat back—at least as far back as he could with his shoulders being bent forward. "So what are your plans now that you've gotten the RV fixed?" he said to my dad.

Dad took a drink of lemonade. "Well, we need to take a trip back east. I have a couple errands I need to run."

I nearly dropped my burger on my new dress. "What errands?"

"Just a couple of things I need to do. We need some more funds for one. And who knows, I might trade the old junker in for something a little more updated."

"But I want to stay here," I said. "Why didn't you tell me we were leaving?"

I slammed my napkin down on the table and ran through the front door. I could hear Dad calling after me and opening the front door and running onto the porch, but I didn't stop until I got to Mr. Taylor's fence.

"June Bug, come back here!" Dad yelled as he crossed the basketball court.

I stood there with my hands tight on the fence, wishing I could crawl through and run until my legs gave out. Dad came up behind me and knelt down. He didn't say anything, so I started.

"Why didn't you tell me we were leaving?" I said again, trying to hold back the tears. But the thing is, the more you try to hold them back, the worse it gets and then you start to snort and I hate doing that when I'm by myself, let alone in front of somebody.

He put a hand on my shoulder and turned me toward him. "I didn't mean to hurt you. There're a few things I have to do to get us back in business. I don't expect you to understand that—"

"I *don't* understand it. This is the first time we've had somebody who cares about us and wants to do stuff for us." I pulled at my dress. "Like this. Why can't we just stay here? You could get a job and sell the RV, and Sheila likes having us around. She'd marry you if you'd ask her. And I could work for Mr. Taylor on his farm, and it could be like a regular family. I could go to school and have friends and go to sleepovers and stuff."

Dad glanced at me with that head down, knowing look. "You've been listening to our conversations, haven't you?"

"I might have heard a thing or two. But she's right. I don't want to live in that thing anymore." I pointed to the RV. "I like sleeping in a real bed and having a dog and being able to ride my bike in the driveway and down the path through the trees. Why can't we be like normal people? real people?"

"We are real people. It's just that . . ." His voice trailed off, and he ran a hand through his hair. "I thought you liked being on the road. I thought you liked the freedom and the chance to visit new places and see things. We've done a lot together. Been able to see a bunch of places other kids only dream of seeing."

It's hard to watch your dad act hurt over stuff, but sometimes you just have to spill out the truth. "Other kids don't dream of riding a bike in a Walmart parking lot. It's like being on vacation all the time. You know? You want to be free, but I don't know what we're being free from."

Dad rubbed his chin, staring off at the horse barn. "I've been thinking that maybe I'd make this trip by myself. If Sheila's okay with it and if you want to, you could stay here. I don't know how that would work with her needing to go off every day to—"

"I could babysit Walter," I said. "I'd be okay. But where are you going?"

"Back east. Tie up some loose ends, you know. Then maybe I'd be set to settle down. Stop all the driving around and sell that hunk of junk and buy us a place where you could make some friends and go to school."

My heart was soaring and breaking all at once. It was like listening to somebody give up on a dream, but at the same time, choose something better. You can't have the apple pie if you choose the cherry or the lemon meringue, but maybe apple is overrated.

"That would be nice," I said. "And I wouldn't be any trouble to her. I promise."

Dad stood, pulled me off the ground, and hugged me tightly.

Hanging there with my arms around his neck, knowing that I was going to sleep in a real bed for a while gave me the tingles all over. Then something felt wrong, like the whole thing was planned, though I knew he couldn't have planned to get stuck in the Walmart parking lot. "How long will you be gone?"

"As long as it takes," he said.

I pulled back and looked him in the eyes. "A week? A couple of weeks?"

"Something like that," he said, like he didn't want to pin it down. Like the winter we went to the Grand Canyon and he didn't want to say how long we'd stay there because he wanted to just sit for days on the south rim and watch the sun rise every day. That was back when he didn't want to sleep at night, and when he did he would wake up yelling and screaming and have to walk outside without a shirt on and kneel down and sometimes throw up.

"You're not leaving me, are you?" I said.

Dad put me on the ground. Then he leaned down and got in my face. "June Bug, how could I ever leave you? You've been in my heart since the first time I saw you."

He sounded so warm and tender and fuzzy, like a stuffed puppy. I couldn't help it. I couldn't hold it in anymore. "Are you my real daddy?"

He looked startled at first. "Why do you ask that?"

I shrugged. "'Cause I want to know."

"Why wouldn't I be?"

It was all I could do not to blurt out that I had seen myself on the board at Walmart. "Lots of reasons. I don't look like you. There's no pictures of you holding me as a baby. Stuff like that."

Dad smiled like Bruce Willis did in one of those movies we watched, kind of to the side and his eyes scrunched up. "Let's go back before the food gets cold. And tell Sheila the good news."

He took my hand, and we walked through the old pine needles and pinecones that lay rotting on the ground. It was right then, when he wouldn't answer my questions, that I knew something terrible was going to happen. Or maybe something terrible had already happened. Maybe that was why we were out on the road 24-7.

And as much as I wanted a mother and clean sheets and a nice bed and a dog and to have my nails done and to work with horses,

I knew I couldn't let my dad leave without me. I had to know what he was going to do. I had to know about my real mother.

❀ ❀ ❀

Stars were out as the three drove home from the movie. Sheila had watched June Bug stare at the big screen as if it were her first time in a theater. She laughed at all the funny parts and sat close to the edge of her seat during the love scenes. In the process, she'd eaten the lion's share of the large popcorn and then dived into the butter-slathered refill.

They stopped at Walmart to pick up some ice for John's cooler and a few more supplies. Sheila walked back into the parking lot with the girl while her dad paid.

"Must be kinda hard for you to shop at the same place you work," June Bug said.

"Sometimes you just know too much." Sheila leaned against her car. "Sometimes I go to the SuperTarget just to see what life is like on the other side."

The girl chuckled. She had a good sense of humor.

"How are you feeling about staying with me for a couple of weeks?" Sheila said. "You okay with it?"

June Bug sighed. "It'll be nice not to have to sleep in that lumpy old bed."

"Well, I think it'll be a lot of fun."

"I'm going to love playing with Walter while you're at work every day. And if you want me to do chores, I can. But I hope to read most of the time."

Sheila nodded. "I've arranged to take a few days off. Maybe we can take a day trip to Buena Vista or we could do an overnight in Glenwood Springs at the pool. They have a big slide, and the water's supposed to have special healing powers. Smells like eggs cooking to me, but . . ."

She noticed a cloud had come over June Bug's face. The girl looked up at her like she had just been told her birthday party had been canceled. Sheila wondered if she had ever had a birthday party. "What's wrong, honey?"

Her face brightened instantly. "Nothing. I just don't want you to take your vacation because of me. I'll be fine."

"I know you will, but I've been waiting for a special occasion to take some days off."

They stared at the sky for a while in silence. Finally June Bug spoke. "I miss the fireflies. Daddy calls them lightning bugs. When we travel down south we get out jars and put holes in the top, and I can watch them light up all night."

A cool breeze blew through the parking lot, and Sheila rubbed her arms. "Sounds nice."

"The roof of the RV has a skylight right over my bed. Sometimes I sleep at the other end because the moon's so bright. But a lot of times I'll finish reading and turn off my light and look up at the sky and try to count the stars. Sometimes I wonder if those same stars are the ones my mother sees. All bright and shiny."

"And what conclusion do you come to?"

"I'm not sure. I wonder if she's flown up to heaven and become an angel. Or maybe she's still down here waiting. Or she could have run off with the circus or something and doesn't care I exist."

Sheila started to correct June Bug's theology about angels but thought better of it. There'd be plenty of time to talk in the coming days. It was one thing she was looking forward to—late-night talks about God and guys and life. Some people look at children as beings you have to mold and shape. Sheila always looked at them as gifts God gave to help you learn.

"If you could do one thing with your mother, what would it be?" Sheila said.

June Bug traced her finger around some stars and cocked her head, one eye closed. "I think I'd want to just talk. Find out if she loved me. Ask her why she left. What she liked about Daddy when she met him. Her favorite places to eat. If she likes fried chicken as much as I do. If she ever thinks about me. Stuff like that."

"You wouldn't want to go to Six Flags or on a cruise? That would be fun, wouldn't it?"

June Bug sighed. "I think that's what I've learned from living in an RV. It doesn't matter *where* you are as long as you're with people you love."

Sheila stared at the same stars, trying to make sense of the seemingly endless expanse and the white dots that flickered against the deep blackness.

A smaller light moved slowly above them, and June Bug became excited. "Satellite!"

Sheila watched in fascination. It was the truth about everyone she had ever known. *We're all satellites sent out, circling the world until something stops us or we fall apart or wander from our orbit and burn.* Always drifting with the current, never resting or pausing.

Later in the evening after June Bug was tucked into bed, John came to Sheila in the kitchen. He'd dumped a couple bags of ice into the cooler.

"You get her all squared away?" Sheila said.

He nodded and crossed his arms, leaning against the stove. "It's not easy to leave, but I think this'll be good. Let her experience a real house." He got a faraway look. "She said she didn't want me waking her when I left. Do you think that's normal?"

Sheila placed a plate in the rack to dry. "My degree is not in child psychology, and I've never been a mother, but it makes sense to me."

John smiled. "You have a degree?"

"A master's. School of hard knocks."

"They gave me an honorary doctorate."

Sheila laughed and picked up another plate. "I think it's healthy. She's separating a little. Growing up."

Sheila wiped down the sink, squeezed the remaining dishwashing liquid out of the pink sponge, and placed it on the windowsill. "You never sent that article you promised."

His eyes were blank for a moment. "Oh, that. Sorry. I'll print it before I leave if I can use your computer."

She dried her hands and led him into what she called her office. She still used a dial-up Internet connection. "I'd love to read anything you've written. How did you get started?"

John seemed tentative. "I've been keeping a journal for a while. Some experiences I had in the military. Things that come back to me. I figured why not get paid for some of that pain instead of just letting it sit there? I'll print you something I wrote about her."

"She's going to ask when you'll be back. Is there a phone number I can use? somebody I can get in touch with?"

"I had a cell phone, but I let it go. She sees those pay-as-you-go phones and wants one so bad she can taste it. But who would she call? We don't know anybody."

"It might help her to hear from you while you're on the road."

"I'll use a pay phone. Let you know if I'm on schedule. It shouldn't take me long, unless I have more engine trouble."

"Take your time. We'll be fine."

Something creaked on the porch, and Sheila heard the familiar *bump, bump, bump* of Walter's tail against the floorboards as he scratched himself. She turned to walk out of the room and brushed John's arm.

"Sorry," he said.

Sheila stopped and stared at him, then tentatively reached out and held his arm. He was a strong man with a full day's growth of stubble. He looked like one of those pictures on the covers of romance books.

She softened her question with a smile, as if it were a joke. "You're not going to just leave, are you? You *are* coming back."

John put a hand on her shoulder. "I know it was a risk for you to do this. I appreciate it. And you don't have to worry about me just taking off."

"I know how much you love her." His hand on her shoulder felt warm, like she was being pulled into a mystery. She inched closer, still looking at his face and the scars.

And then it happened. Something strange and wonderful and scary. Something charged and electrical. A line of bumps rose on her arms and she shuddered, physically shook. How long had it been since she'd been spoken to so gently and with such respect? She wanted to ask him if there was a chance—just the slightest chance—that he could find anything more than a passing attraction to her. She wanted to tell him to come back to his daughter and her. They could make a life together.

But that felt too desperate. The emotions and past washed over her, and the possibility of rejection kept her silent and safe. Who was she to think that anyone would ever choose her? She was damaged goods, something for the Goodwill pile of life, and with the stains, rips, and tears of her life, there was a question whether she would even make it into that truck.

The negative voices sprang up in her mind, and instinctively she stepped away. "I should get to bed. What time you think you'll be leaving?"

"Hopefully before daylight. I'd like to be in Kansas before the sun comes up."

"I hate that drive," Sheila said. "Just flat and not a thing to look at but pig farms."

"You should drive through Texas," he said.

"I hear it's the same." She paused at the stairs and put a hand on the railing. "Have a good trip. Stay safe. Let her hear from you."

John nodded. "I'll print that article for you."

"Good night."

"And thank you again," he said. "You've been an answer to our prayers."

"I don't think anybody's ever told me that before." Sheila smiled but it didn't come easy. It felt weary, like cleaning the toilet. "Don't worry about her."

She went to her room, closed the door gently, and sat on the edge of the bed. Through the open window she heard the RV door close, then open again, and he walked across the porch. In a few minutes, the printer spit out some pages. It was all she could do not to run down and read it, but she told herself she needed to wait.

Sheila ran a tub full of water and added the lilac bubble bath until it foamed to the top. After she undressed, her clothes in a clump at her feet, she turned and looked in the mirror. The steam had clouded the view, and she rubbed at it and tried to assess her body objectively. Sags here and there, a bit overstuffed in sections, but overall, not bad for the wear and tear. If there were a Kelley Blue Book for people, she figured she'd be in the used category, private party value, in good condition, free of any major defects, clean title history, no major mechanical problems or rust, and all her tires matched. She turned and looked at her bumper. It had grown and flattened, but you don't pass up a car because of the bumper.

She sank into the tub, into the soothing, healing waters, and relaxed. For the first time in months she didn't think of her job. She thought of the girl. And him. And questions about the future and what might come from this spur-of-the-moment decision to take them in. And how if her manager hadn't been so hard-nosed, they never would have gotten together.

Life. How strange it is. How heartbreakingly random and odd how people find each other or miss each other in their chosen orbits. How surprising when they do find love or even the prospect of it.

Sheila fell asleep to the night sounds. Crickets and the wind in the pines and frogs *garumping* around the pond in Mr. Taylor's pasture. These were the best sounds in the world.

She woke up once, deep in the night, when the RV engine fired and drove off. Then she rolled over and said a prayer for John and went back to sleep.

8

When he couldn't sleep, John scrambled off the bed and walked barefoot into the RV's driver's seat. He'd worn a groove into the spot just under the accelerator that felt good to his heel, and he liked to drive this way, without shoes, the windows down, air filtering through the cab. The heat of the previous day had left the vehicle warm and stuffy. He'd tossed and turned, thinking what it would be like to sleep in Sheila's cool basement, until he finally gave up and drove away.

That was one advantage of this rolling house—he could pull over in a parking lot or a rest area and sleep as long as he wanted. That kind of freedom energized him, and the feel of the tires on the pavement and the rumble of the engine and the sensation of movement brought wholeness.

The stars were still out as he headed south on Route 83 into the Springs and then east on Route 24. Through the streetlights he noticed the faint outline of Pikes Peak, a red light warning low-flying planes. The air was cool, and like a child he stuck out a hand and let it wave in the wind. From the weather reports he was heading into an oven. Global warming, some said. He had his doubts. In his mind, summer was summer and tornadoes and hurricanes happened every year, and it wasn't because he drove his RV or didn't recycle his plastic water bottles.

He had carefully plotted his route on the worn Rand McNally map he kept in the holder by the front seat. His funds had dwindled to such a low point that just purchasing the gas to Arkansas was going to be tight. He'd dipped deep into his reserves for the RV part, and if he had to do it over again, he would have bought half as much meat for their barbecue. But it seemed like the least he could do for Sheila and Mr. Taylor for all they'd done for him.

Sheila was on his mind as he hit the eastern plains, a flat, barren landscape dotted with farms and a few head of longhorns. He'd worked hard at not getting entangled in a relationship, like the tumbleweeds that bounced along the pasture and over the road. He'd met plenty of eligible women—threats of relationships, storms brewing off the shore of his heart—but no one had gotten as close as Sheila. Her kindness and thoughtfulness at such a vulnerable time was hard to resist. She was right about June Bug. The girl needed more than the road, but settling down came with a cost.

John also knew the attraction was more than just finding June Bug a mother. Something tugged hard at his soul and other parts as well. Sheila was not his perfect match. She was shorter and a little frumpy. But he had felt the heat when she touched his arm. He had wanted to embrace her then and equally wanted to run. Everything was jumbled in his head. Complicated. And as he drove, he let his mind wander to a life in Colorado with a family. Something he'd never really experienced.

The sky lightened a bit as he rolled east, and when he neared the Kansas state line, clouds rippled and spread out above him like an unfurled, endless flag. The sun cast a golden glow on the underside of them, making ridges of yellow, white, and gold as if he were driving into a dream.

The first real stages of fatigue hit him between the state line and Hays. He pulled into an abandoned Dairy Queen parking lot and shut off the engine, stretching and walking around the building, taking a leak in the grass. He opened the cooler and rubbed some ice on his face, surveying the landscape. Everything was flat and hot and different from the world he had left.

Tires humming in the distance, the call of the road came again. John often wondered whether he and June Bug could make it as long-haul truckers. "It would be a smaller living space," she had said, "but you'd get to see more of the country and get paid for it."

Her eyes always sparked when she'd get an idea like that. She could see it all planned out, anticipate his next question and the negatives. But there were some negatives she couldn't anticipate. There were some things she didn't know, and he didn't know if he could ever have the heart to tell her. The stay in Colorado had brought it back again. She deserved to know what had happened and who he was. He knew that. But that raised new problems. Like whether she would love him if she knew the truth.

He took a long, cool drink and shook himself awake as he pulled onto the interstate. He traced the yellow marker on the map from Hays to Salina. He'd make the turn there and head south.

John was alone on the road for the first time in years, and he couldn't help thinking of the two of them getting up and having breakfast, talking and laughing and wondering where they might be.

The tires rolled. Trucks passed. Two people with New Mexico plates and the car packed so tight with clothes it looked like the windows would burst. Another couple, the woman in short shorts, her feet on the dash, her head turned toward the window, her mouth open and eyes closed.

He glanced out the window and saw a farmer on a tractor, dust billowing. A car on an access road racing for work. Or maybe a kid seeing how fast he could go. He went under an overpass and noticed a guy above, smoking, standing at the edge, and looking down at the oncoming traffic.

Seeing the old guy brought back that craving he'd given up years before. Cold turkey. It was a night in June when he'd last taken a puff of a Winston. That night he quit. If he'd have just done it for himself, he probably never would have quit. But he had heard all the stuff about secondhand smoke, and when the girl had come along, he decided it was time to quit. He'd fallen off the wagon a few times, but he'd been proud he never smoked in her presence again.

She'd changed a lot of things in his life. Including wanting to live again.

❀ ❀ ❀

Sheila stretched as the morning sun peeked over the horizon and lit the room with a yellow glow. Walter sat at attention, watching, wagging his tail, puffing his lips in anticipation, eyes darting. Funny how something as simple as being let outside could make him feel so excited, but that was the animal's life. She reached for her robe and stood.

"All right, but be quiet about it," Sheila whispered.

The dog scampered down the stairs, his nails skittering on the hardwood at the bottom and his paws sliding outward until he hit the door. He stood there whining as she opened it and let him out. He went to his favorite spot in the yard and lifted his leg.

She filled the coffeepot, fit the filter, scooped in some extra coffee, and turned it on, then made her own pilgrimage to the bathroom. She stared in the mirror as she washed her hands and studied her face at an angle. A few wrinkles showed around her lips, and she was startled at how much like her mother she looked. Her mother wasn't ugly by any means, but Sheila wasn't ready to look like a grandma.

Walter scratched at the back door, and she let him in. "Who's the hungry puppy? Who's the hungry puppy?"

The dog nearly wet the floor with excitement. He wagged his tail and twitched and snorted as she let the dry food clang in the metal bowl.

She topped off his water dish and wondered if the noise would wake June Bug. In fact, she was surprised she hadn't made it downstairs yet.

Sheila hurried through the kitchen to the office and checked the printer tray. Three pages waited, single spaced, and her heart jumped. She wanted to savor the article, so she placed it facedown on the table, poured a cup of coffee, and retrieved half a cantaloupe from the refrigerator.

Settling into her chair, she thought through breakfast and the amount of time it would take her to scramble the eggs, cook the bacon, and make pancakes. The pancake mix only needed water, and she promised herself that as soon as she heard June Bug's footsteps, she would stop reading and begin.

She turned the page over.

Little Illusions

Maybe it's the rumble and noise of the road. Maybe it's the freedom from anything permanent. Or it could be the uncertainty of each day, the take-it-as-it-comes, live-every-moment-to-the-fullest draw that attracts my daughter and me to the broken white lines. It could be any of these and a thousand others, but no matter what the reason, we have chosen to live as American nomads, vagabonds of the bypass, interstate drifters where life intersects the endless lines of asphalt and concrete through the land.

My daughter and I have been traversing the country from Alaska to Florida, Maine to California and everywhere in between since she was about two. There's a saying about life not being measured by the number of breaths you take, but by the things that take your breath away. It's cliché but true. Those sights are too numerous to mention here, but we have watched humpback whales breach in the waters off the Washington coast, combed beaches for treasure after hurricanes in Florida, seen the sunrise at the Alamo and sunset at Gettysburg. Together we've laid a wreath at Arlington, seen Old Faithful erupt in Yellowstone, and we've done it all on the price of a gallon of gas and parking privileges at Walmart.

Traveling has come easy to my daughter. She's learned the joys of adapting to new surroundings and living light, needing only a soft pillow and a good book. Learning to read and write came naturally, discovering the alphabet by watching passing license plates and sounding out words like exit *and* gas, food, and lodging. *She has taken to learning, all cylinders firing in her brain, and she'll soon become a better writer than her father.*

The other day she asked me why everyone doesn't have an RV. Why do people settle for living in a house built in one place that never moves unless a flood comes? Why would anyone live in one spot all their lives and hardly ever wander? It never occurred to her that people could be happy grounded, pulling their existence from the place they were born or the place they had chosen to call home. And perhaps this is the irony in her words. Her grounding has occurred in the midst of movement, in the subtle motion of traffic, searching for some impermanent destination.

I have spent the past few years listening to tires hum, air brakes crash, and the whoosh of a passing 18-wheeler in the rain. The twitter of hummingbirds searching for food at a rest stop. But the foreign sound most of us never hear is the beat of the human heart. Not the thump-thump of the organ but the sound of hope it brings. I hear it in every word, every decision, every road chosen or passed. It is a foreign concept to listen to the heart. We settle for consonants and vowels, responding to Xs and Os, ones and zeroes of speech, nuts and bolts of sentences that tell us nothing about what's inside.

In the process of listening for something beneath the surface, I've heard difficult things. Accusing voices of the past. Condemning words from people I trusted. And the voice of my daughter has risen above them all, questioning, showing that my search for a roadway to inner peace has few exits. By listening closely, I have seen that belonging arrives not with a space, not with movement and motion, but with miles and miles of heart.

I am not a painter, nor am I a wordsmith. I have not been a lover or a fighter for a long time. I don't sing, don't write songs, don't haul garbage, don't work nine to five. In fact, I can define my life more by what I am not than by what I am. And one thing I do not have is a home. This rolling bedroom is simply that, not a home but a rest area waiting to be set up or parked again in another place. A portable mattress awaiting exhaustion.

The road's romance began to fade the moment I realized my daughter was growing up and that she would not always be with me. It was a rude awakening. Her growth has helped me see that what I have is a relentlessly restless heart that knows only the peace of the passing sunset or the comfort of a billowy cloud over an ocean of wheat. I am working; I am plodding along these busy avenues of the soul, wondering and wandering through the past, one wheel stuck in the present, terrified of the future.

I am beginning to give up the little illusions that have come to define me and shape my migration. This life of an itinerant wanderer may seem idyllic to those looking in from outside, but the closer you look, the more you draw near to the cramped spaces we call home and the linoleum that long ago separated from the floor. Would you give up the comfortable flat-screen television and the convenience of a washer and dryer?

The smallest illusion that continues to hold is that there will come a time when I will arrive, when I will turn the key for the last time, pull it out, and be done. Be home. I am coming to believe that in this life that will not happen. There will always be a sense of movement, of striving, of contending for another mile.

In Florida, especially in the winter, it seems to the casual observer that the snowbirds from the North have completed their tasks and are simply waiting. But those watching have never tried to beat those people to the $4.99 buffet. Even in retirement there is movement and a plan for the future, no matter how short that future may seem to others.

Something deep inside, even deeper than the heart, tells me that my time with my daughter is coming to an end. The more questions she asks, the more she delves into the sinews and ligaments of our life together, the more I sense I can only live as a vagabond of the heart and not the road. A friend has told me such, that my daughter needs something different as she heads into the pubescent years. Change is on the horizon that will rock our worlds. I long to hold on to the innocence of this time, the discovery and wonder we've seen, the joy of fishing in a rippling stream in Montana or watching a Little League baseball game on a spring day in Iowa. We have not fought the crowds at Disneyland or Disney World because our joy doesn't have to be manufactured. But perhaps those joys are little illusions as well.

No matter how this turns out, no matter what choices are made and what results come from the decisions the days ahead will bring, one thing is clear. It is not the adult giving life to the child but the

*other way around. My daughter, June Bug, has given me more than
I will ever give her.
And that is no little illusion.*

Sheila stared at the page and finally breathed. There was
an earthy beauty to the language—mixed with an elegance and
thoughtfulness, as well as a rambling. Who knew someone so
tough-looking with rippling muscles and lean frame could produce
something like this.

Unless . . .

What if it didn't come from him at all?

She rose from the table and went to the computer, the screen
saver still working from the night before. She hadn't turned it off
because she wanted him to print the article. She pulled up a search
engine and typed in his name. A poet, a criminal, a recording art-
ist, a senator, and a guitar manufacturer popped up. There was a
MySpace listing for the same name as well as a Wikipedia article.
She searched through the listings but nothing matched, which
made her wonder which magazines or online sites he wrote for.
The article he had printed seemed new, or at least relatively recent,
and she wondered if she was the friend he mentioned.

She entered the title of the article and found a clothing company and several suppliers for magicians. She typed in the first
words of the article and a motorcycle dealer popped up, keying on
the words *rumble* and *noise*, but again, nothing about what she had
just read. Perhaps this was a work in progress, and he wanted her
to see it before it was published. But why couldn't she find anything
else he had written? Maybe it was the pseudonymn June Bug had
mentioned.

Walter scratched at the back door, wanting out. She picked up
her coffee mug, now cold, and opened the door. There was movement upstairs, or it could have been just the wind and sun making
the wood creak.

Sheila moved to the stairs and listened, staring up at the landing.
Suddenly a feeling of dread came over her, something she couldn't

explain. A scene from some old movie flashed through her mind. The camera looking down at her from the top of the stairs and then following each step she took. Was the man she had helped really who he said he was? Was he someone else? some*thing* else?

She took the steps two at a time, her heart racing, and scrambled to the bedroom door. She stopped to compose herself and catch her breath. It was the altitude and not her fear or the extra pounds she carried that made her gasp. Everything would be all right. The girl would be there in bed, asleep.

"June Bug?" she said softly.

Sheila turned the knob and pushed the door open. A lump under the covers. She let out a sigh of relief. No blood-splattered walls. No horror-filled room. The girl wasn't sitting on the edge of the bed, her head spinning around. Everything was normal.

Walter barked at something. Probably a squirrel. She eased the door closed and caught sight of herself in the hall mirror. She pushed her hair down in back, but it was as unruly as her thoughts. She was glad John had left and that she didn't have to work on it before he came in for breakfast.

She glanced at the clock as she let the dog in. The girl had to be up now, so she started breakfast and her morning ritual of watching the news. She'd missed the local station with their long weather report and the backdrop of Pikes Peak. The weather here was squirrelly, and it was said if meteorologists could predict the weather in the Springs, they could predict the weather anywhere. It was true; things changed quickly as clouds blew over the Sangre de Cristos and then the Front Range.

". . . with a high of ninety-five in the Springs and probably one hundred in Denver," a voice said over the weather map.

She cracked a few eggs into a bowl as the pretty people on the pretty set in New York laughed about something that had happened before they went to the weather. Watching people smile with all those white teeth always made her feel like she was on the outside of the joke.

She sprayed PAM in the old skillet and set the stove to high to warm it. At that point the laughter died, and the lead anchor on the set turned somber. Funny how she could make such an abrupt turn to the serious.

"A stunning development in a missing child case from seven years ago in a small West Virginia town. Four days ago a car was found, submerged in a reservoir near Dogwood, West Virginia, and the contents of that car have opened some old wounds for the residents."

The anchor looked to her left, and video ran of an old, rusted vehicle being pulled from the water.

The reporter's voice-over began as the screen showed a police officer looking inside. "Authorities feared they would discover a body in the back of this car that has spent the last seven years at the bottom of a lake. What they found has raised more questions."

A picture flashed on the screen. A toddler smiling. Something about it unnerved Sheila.

"Natalie Anne Edwards was reported missing by her mother, Dana Edwards, on a summer night seven years ago. The girl had been abducted. An unknown assailant had ambushed Dana and taken her car. The little girl was simply gone without a trace."

There was stock footage of grainy video taken in a police station with wood paneling. A young mother, who couldn't have been more than twenty, stared at the camera with red eyes.

"I just want my baby back," she said, her chin quivering. "Whoever has her, please let her go. She never hurt nobody."

"But the trail went cold," the reporter said over shots of police officers with bloodhounds searching fields and tree-lined gullies. "Natalie Anne simply vanished. However, this woman, Natalie's grandmother, would not give up hope."

An older woman with graying hair and a sagging face spoke from her kitchen table. A cuckoo clock ticked in the background, and an empty cake holder sat on a cluttered desk in the corner. The words *Mae Edwards, Grandmother* popped on the screen. "I know in my heart she's out there. And I'm not giving up."

"Mae Edwards went to several agencies that try to find missing children. One took Natalie Anne's picture and age progressed it to what she would look like today."

An egg dropped on the floor and splattered at Sheila's feet. She reached out a hand for the sink to steady herself. It felt like the room was spinning, like she couldn't focus on anything. Then a siren — had the police come already? Had they pieced it together that quickly?

No, it was the smoke alarm. The pan was billowing, and she pulled it off the stove and burned her hand. She stuck it under the water, the tears coming. Half from the pain of the burn, half from learning the truth.

But what was the truth?

She grabbed some ice from the freezer and stuck it in a Ziploc bag and turned off the stove.

The report was over, and they were back with the pretty anchor in New York with the pretty dress and the white teeth and perfect hair. A police officer, looking uncomfortable in the swath of white light, stood with the reservoir in the background. He swatted at a swarm of mosquitoes and tried to answer the questions of the pretty anchor.

Hand throbbing, Sheila studied the age-progressed photo when it appeared again. There was no mistake. There was no doubt in her mind. That was June Bug. Natalie Anne was sleeping in her bedroom upstairs, and her father, her abductor, or whoever he was, had left in the middle of the night.

She raced upstairs and opened the door without caution this time. Surely June Bug had heard the smoke alarm. She thought she might even find her cowering in the corner, scared at the sound. She'd probably never heard a smoke alarm in her life.

But when Sheila opened the door, June Bug was still there, a lump under the covers. She shook the girl's shoulder and whispered her name. But it wasn't a shoulder she touched under the covers. It was a pillow, folded to appear like a shoulder. And another pillow folded under that one. Sheila threw back the covers.

The girl — June Bug, Natalie Anne, whatever her name was — was gone.

PART TWO

9

Air brakes from a semi awakened him. Johnson yawned and stretched, sitting up on the bed, remembering where he'd parked. A sliver of sunlight shone through the broken shade and hit him full in the face. An older woman with a white dog walked through the parking lot of the truck stop, headed for a patch of grass beyond the asphalt. The dog walked stiffly, like its arthritis was just as bad as hers.

He had stayed dressed, except for his shoes, and now he put them on and clambered into the truck stop's café and found the restroom. It was eight thirty already, and he didn't want to waste time. He bought two Honey Buns and a plastic bottle filled with something orange and downed it as he headed toward the RV. He preferred the coffee at Dunkin' Donuts, so he hoofed it across the street rather than driving the RV.

When he returned, one of the Honey Buns was missing. He looked under the seat, thinking it might have slid to the floor, but it wasn't there. He looked around, wondering who would steal one Honey Bun. "Hope it was somebody really hungry," he muttered.

He returned to the road, flipping the radio past talk shows and morning farm reports. He and June Bug loved listening to local stations with low wattage and a small footprint. Teenage guys trying to sound older and more sophisticated. Older men caught in small backwater towns where careers stalled. Sunday morning preaching shows with singers camped around single microphones playing out-of-tune guitars. And the fiery preachers who followed.

He and June Bug had laughed at one preacher with a crackling whiskey voice, who almost sounded like a frog croaking well-memorized passages of Scripture. His wife would speak in the breaths and pauses of his rants, calling out encouragement. As the pastor's momentum built, so did his wife's, and they would speak together, roiling like a pot of boiling water, fomenting and running toward a climax of verses and positive thinking and you-can-do-anything-you-set-your-mind-to theology.

They'd been so captivated by the two that they found the church in a shabby part of a little town surrounded by boarded-up businesses. They parked across the street and waited hours, eating lunch together, watching, wondering if the approaching car would be them. When a shiny Lexus pulled up, two people got out. The "teacher" was a thin man and exited the passenger side in a nice suit, waving his arm and saying something to his wife. She shook her head and her finger at him and managed to pry herself out from behind the steering wheel, the car dipping with her weight, then rising after she stood.

"That's them?" June Bug had said. "That's not how I thought they'd look."

"It's always a little disappointing," he had said. "People on the radio never look like you think they do. You can bank on that."

Johnson thought about the couple as he continued down the interstate, the hot coffee energizing him. And then his thoughts turned to June Bug, what she was doing, if Sheila had planned out their day. They had to be up and getting started. Since the night everything had changed for both June Bug and him, they had spent every day together, almost every waking moment, and moments asleep were spent about ten feet apart. It was weird not hearing her voice, not listening to her soft falsetto as they crossed bridges.

It was nearing lunch when he crossed the Oklahoma state line. His stomach growling, legs cramping. It had been a few weeks since he'd done any hard driving, and he decided to push a little more. At each exit he'd survey the offering of gas stations and drive-throughs and decide to wait one more exit, push a little farther. He could use the bathroom in the back, but it wasn't flushing properly, so that was just for emergencies.

He got caught between exits, and he asked himself what he was trying to prove. When he noticed a particularly wide spot near an overpass, he pulled over, ran back to the tiny bathroom, and lifted the lid. The bowl was half-full, and that didn't make sense because he hadn't used this bathroom for weeks. He pondered this while he relieved himself, then wished he'd fixed the mechanism while sitting at Walmart.

Johnson was back on the road, checking the gas gauge, looking for a Long John Silver's, when he absentmindedly called out the name of the river they were crossing. He chuckled because he could almost hear June Bug's voice singing "I'll Fly Away" above. She would sing the song again and again, usually just a phrase or the first verse, until they passed over. When they'd approach a bridge, he'd try to distract her, talk to her about something else, but invariably she would see it. She saw everything.

One day after a long drive, they hit Memphis and the sight of the long bridge over the Mississippi sent her over the edge.

He pulled over and knelt in front of her. "Listen, honey, Jesus is going to take care of you, understand?"

Tears welled and her chin puckered.

He pushed a clump of hair from her face and cupped his hand around her chin. "I want you to sing a song with me, okay?"

June Bug sat there, staring. Finally she said, "What song?"

He shoved in the tape and let it play through the first verse, singing along in his guttural bass until she caught the tune. "Good, now let's try it again." He hit Rewind and she began to mouth the words as he climbed back in the driver's seat.

"Just close your eyes and sing, and pretty soon we'll be on the other side," he said.

She closed her eyes so tightly he thought she was going to burst a blood vessel. Her little chin tucked down, lips moving, arms shaking. He turned the volume up and it enveloped them.

When the song finished, she kept her eyes closed. "Can I open them now?"

"Take a look," he said.

Slowly June Bug looked out the window. Then she unbuckled and jumped on his bed and lifted the shades.

"We made it! It worked!" She ran back to the front. "It really worked."

"Works about every time," he said. "When you see a bridge coming up, just close your eyes and sing through the whole song and you'll be out the other side before you finish."

From then on, anytime they'd come to so much as a viaduct, she'd call from wherever she was in the RV, "Tape! Put on the tape!" It had its own special place above the visor. After each play, he rewound it to the right spot where he could use it next time.

One day when he pressed the Rewind button, the machine made a screeching noise and just sat there. He hit Eject, but nothing happened. Later that night, with a screwdriver and a flashlight, he pried the cassette from the player, the tape spilling onto the dash. He made a valiant try to repack the spool, but it was no use.

The next day he found a thrift store and frantically searched through the bins. Then he broke the news to her.

"I want the tape," June Bug said, her teeth clenched, face tight.

"Honey, I don't have it. It broke."

"I want the tape."

"We'll find another. Let's just sing together at the next bridge."

She shook her head. "I want the tape. Get the tape."

He explained it all again until her little face scrunched up in a red ball. She put her hands over her eyes, and the tears escaped and ran down her arms in dirty streams.

"June Bug, listen to me—"

"It won't work," she sobbed. "We have to have the song."

Johnson held her in his arms. "What is it, sweetie? What are you afraid of?"

He knew *why* she was scared. Knew it too well. Her fears were a mirror of his own—the past, the dreams, the flashbacks, the night terrors. He had spent his share of nights listening to her cries, staying awake so he wouldn't have to face his own memories.

"Every time we go over a bridge, I think we're going to fall," June Bug said. "I'm afraid we'll go down there, and I don't want to go under the water. We won't get out."

He held her close and felt the sobs racking her body. "That's not ever going to happen. These bridges are strong. They can hold up big trucks and all the cars you can put on them."

"It feels shaky when we go across."

Johnson nodded. "There's a little give to it, but that's normal. It doesn't mean it's going to collapse. People have been going across these bridges for years. You don't have to worry."

"But it still feels like we're going to fall," June Bug said, as if pleading for something he couldn't give. "I don't care if it's the strongest thing in the world, it still feels like it. I don't want to fall in. I don't want to get trapped."

The nightmares came and went. Cold sweats. Nights when she'd cry in her sleep, thrashing her legs until her covers were twisted in a tangle. That's when he bought the sleeping bag. Those first few months, probably a year after they came together, he'd hold her on his lap, with her all snuggled into the Sleeping Beauty sleeping bag until she fell asleep. He'd read stories, watching her eyes follow the words across the page until the eyelids became heavy. Then she'd surge again and he'd read some more. When she finally drifted off, he'd place her on the mattress above the cab and fit the safety bar so she couldn't roll out.

Her screams were like sirens. They tore at his heart. All the fear in the world was wrapped in those tiny lungs just waiting. He'd stay awake, trying to sense when she'd have a bad one. The worst nights came at the most unpredictable moments. He'd sit outside the door in a five-dollar lawn chair with a Coors Light in the holder on the armrest and a lit Marlboro, watching the stars come out or some dogs pick at the trash. Just when his body told him it was time to crawl into bed, when there was no way she'd awaken, he'd hear the telltale whimpers.

One night it was so loud that people in the camping area thought someone had been killed. A few of them ran over, banging on the door until he assured them it was only a nightmare.

"You sure you didn't hurt her?" a woman said, craning her neck to see the girl who was draped around his neck like a dime store Velcro monkey.

"I'd never lay a finger on this little thing," he said, and he must have convinced her because she and the others walked away. June Bug just held on tight.

The next day he had vowed not to park so close to other RVs and that they'd find lonely spots in campgrounds or avoid them altogether. When the generator finally went out, he decided to just use Walmart parking lots while they were on the road, moving from town to town.

The terrors continued for two years, subsiding at times but always remaining a possibility, like a golfer with a bad slice who never knew when a shot might wind up in the trees. Johnson found it difficult to sleep, waiting for the next round of wailing, and allowed her to curl up in her sleeping bag next to him. It was easier to calm her that way.

At times he could hear her singing in her sleep, the song that got her over the bridges, over the troubled waters and the falling. He thought about finding a child's sleeping pill, but then he thought better of it. No reason to mess her life up more than it already was.

In his mind now, he heard her soft, muffled voice singing into the pillow, like a familiar sound of the ocean lapping against the shore or shopping carts being collected by some teenager outside in the parking lot. This was part of the soundtrack of their lives, and try as he might he couldn't shake it.

The words to "I'll Fly Away" kept coming back, the ones he had first heard in his uncle's woodshop. It was a tin building with just enough room to fit the Ford F-150 on one side and all the tools and saws and a workbench on the other. His uncle had a nasally, tinny voice that rose and fell like the swell of a mountain stream that pushes against its banks.

There were times when he'd sit on a stump by the chinaberry tree and listen to the voices and laughter inside, the sound of an incorrectly tuned banjo mixing with his uncle's Martin D-28 he had won in a bet with a fellow who worked for a natural gas company who stumbled onto their weekly game of poker. His uncle kept it in a velvet-lined case right by his gun rack, and it came out only on special occasions.

> *Some glad morning when this life is o'er,*
> *I'll fly away;*
> *To a home on God's celestial shore,*
> *I'll fly away.*
> *I'll fly away, Oh Glory*
> *I'll fly away; (in the morning)*
> *When I die, Hallelujah, by and by,*
> *I'll fly away.*

To some, that was escapism, trying to slip the surly bonds and avoid the pain and reality of life. But there was so much more to it than that. More to it than you could ever read in a book or get from a newspaper interview. This was the national anthem of his life, the lament that ran through every fiber. The unknown soldiers and shadows of his youth, the indescribable loneliness of seeing the best and worst life had to offer, were all wrapped up in those words.

> *When the shadows of this life have gone,*
> *I'll fly away;*
> *Like a bird from prison bars has flown,*
> *I'll fly away.*

His uncle's garage smelled of stale beer and sawdust. There was laughter of genuine men. Fishing lures on the wall. A picture of soldiers in Korea. Metal stools dug into the earthen floor. And a cross. A warmth Johnson had never felt possible. He couldn't help feeling this was the pinnacle, to have friends and know them, for them to know him, to express in music what could not be expressed in mere words.

Just a few more weary days and then,
I'll fly away;
To a land where joys shall never end,
I'll fly away.

He shook his head at the memories and grabbed another cassette and shoved it into the player. His stash included bluegrass and country—tapes he'd found at garage sales and thrift stores, weathered by the sun and dusty from their travels. Everything from Willie Nelson to Trisha Yearwood to Glen Campbell. He turned up the volume and rolled down the window all the way until the wind rushed through so loud he could barely hear the warbling voices. He pushed the accelerator to the floor to make it up one of the last Oklahoma hills as he rolled toward Arkansas.

10

When Sheriff Hadley Preston wasn't herding the media cats, he was actually doing his job. Mae and Leason Edwards were all the help they could be in locating their daughter, but there are some things a parent can't do, and one of them is be responsible for their children's choices. Preston knew all about that.

His own daughter had run away at fifteen with a boy she thought was her life's love. Preston had spent three days tracking them down and, through a tip from one of the boy's friends, found them at a motel in Myrtle Beach. He and the family had called that their beach getaway, but after that, they rarely even spoke of the place. She became pregnant, and after a lot of tears and struggle, she decided to place the baby for adoption.

She settled down, finished school, then went off to WVU and landed a job with some PR outfit in Charleston. It paid well and she seemed to have some friends who cared about her.

So as Preston searched for the woman who had thrown their small slice of the world into a media circus seven years earlier and was now doing it again, the first thing he thought of was his own daughter and what might have happened if she hadn't gotten her life together. He and his wife had gone through it during her teenage years, and it hadn't helped that he was supposed to be an upstanding citizen and leader. Sneaking out late at night. Running with a bad crowd. He held his breath each time the phone rang, worried that she might have been arrested or found in some ravine in a mangled car. It was a constant fear until she graduated, and then his fears intensified as they dropped her off at college.

But something had happened there. She'd found friends who invited her to a Christian group. He still kept the letter she wrote him in the top drawer of his nightstand. The one that said she was grateful that he loved her unconditionally and how thankful she was to have her parents. She had found a good man and married and had given them two grandchildren. Just shows you have to play for the final quarter of the game and not halftime.

Though Mae was no help in locating her, Preston found Dana Edwards living with her current boyfriend in a two-bedroom house in Winfield, close to the interstate and within a crab-apple's throw of a fairly large liquor store. He was trying to get to her before the media.

Paint chips fluttered to the ground when he knocked on the door. He heard movement inside, a chair scraping across linoleum, and then cursing. A haggard face looked out the window, then let the shade fall. She was struggling to stay on her feet as she opened the door and had to lean against the jamb. Behind her was a kitchen table strewn with a couple of pizza boxes and empty bottles. The air in the house smelled of mildew, and her breath made him turn his head.

She was wearing a loose T-shirt and terry cloth shorts, but Preston could tell from her arms and legs that she was painfully thin. Her matted red hair stuck up in the back, but the general state of dishevelment did not seem to concern her. The face was unmistakable. She had Mae's droll mouth and eyes. A spitting image, as they say.

"Dana. It's been a long time."

She yawned and looked at his badge, then at his face. "What's this about?"

"I need you to come with me. It's your daughter."

She squinted, as if she hadn't heard correctly, or as if she couldn't remember even having a daughter. "Natalie? Did you find her?"

"I just need you to come with me. Get your clothes together. I'll wait in the car."

Dana disappeared into the darkness and reappeared a few minutes later wearing sandals that had been worn down to the thickness of cardboard. She put a long-sleeved sweater over the T-shirt and had run a brush through her hair a couple of times, but that only made matters worse. She crossed her arms in front of her and thanked him when he held the car door for her.

They set off on the winding two-lane road, passing a park and a lake and green hills that exploded with color. The sun was hot in the sky now, and he turned on the air conditioner.

"Tell me if you get too cold back there," he said.

"How'd you find me?"

Preston glanced in the rearview. "That's why they pay me so well. I'm part bloodhound, you know."

Dana looked out the window without smiling, wringing her hands like an old woman who'd lost her favorite cat. "I seen the news. All those reporters and cameras. How'd you find the car?"

"Scuba divers. Sounds like an oxymoron, doesn' it? West Virginia scuba divers."

She was turning something in her mind, and he let her do it as the squawk of the radio filled the blank spaces.

"You didn't find her in the car?"

"No, the car seat was back there, but there wasn't a body."

"After this long, couldn't it have just . . . dissolved? Or something could have eaten it?"

Preston took a moment at that one, contemplating her use of *it* rather than *she* or *her*. "Could have. But I think we'd have found bits of clothes or bones. The car was clean. We did find a blanket and a stuffed animal."

Dana grimaced and put the heels of her hands to her eyes, like she was trying to stop a migraine. Or maybe some memory that kept coming back. There had been a modest insurance policy that she collected after a couple years, but Preston assumed that had gone quickly. She wiped at her eyes and stared out the passenger window.

"That guy must have taken her with him. The guy who stole the car. Pervert. Who would do something like that to a little kid?"

He looked in the rearview again. Her face was taut and gaunt. Hollow eyes. Sunken cheeks so that her bones stuck out. Sallow skin in the sunlight. Painfully thin. "Your mother's always thought your daughter was still alive."

"My mother," Dana scoffed. "She kept Natalie's name on the prayer chain at her church for four years before they made her take it off. They said it upset people. I'll bet I'm still on there."

"Wouldn't disagree with that."

"A lot of good those people's prayers are going to do. Thinking God is going to cure their liver or shrink their hemorrhoids. I swear, those people would lay hands on just about anything."

Preston stifled a smile and watched a kid riding a bike without a helmet. He wanted to stop and chew the kid out, tell him he was going to wind up in a graveyard, but he wanted to get Dana to the station right now. He spotted the TV trucks before he even rounded the corner and told Dana to lie down in the backseat.

"What for?"

"Unless you want every reporter this side of the Mississippi chasing you down in those flip-flops, you'd better lie down."

She did and as they passed the trucks, Preston saw the camera guys standing together drinking their iced coffee or latte whatevers. He waved a big "howdy do" like you're supposed to when you're from some backwoods place and flashed his biggest aw-shucks smile and parked near the back door.

He herded Dana inside to the interrogation room, which doubled as their lunchroom. His deputy, Mike, was eating a sandwich and talking on his cell phone, his feet propped up on the table. When he saw Dana and Preston, he nearly fell over backward, quickly exiting the room.

Preston grabbed a cup of coffee for Dana and sat across from her as she sipped at the black water.

"So why couldn't you talk to me at the house?" she said. "Why'd I have to come down here?"

"I'm trying to piece a few things together. I thought you could help."

"I done told the police everything I know. About a million times."

Preston nodded. "Let's just go through it. Did Natalie know she was going for a drive that night?"

Dana lowered her eyes and cocked her head. "I couldn't get a babysitter. I went to a bar. I had a few drinks. She went to sleep in her car seat on the way over, and I checked on her every few minutes. And—"

"Who were you there to meet?"

"You know all of this. There was nobody in particular. I was thirsty. I needed to get out. It's not a crime to have a few drinks. Aren't you going to read me my rights or something?"

"I'm not trying to catch you, Dana. I'm looking for answers."

She cradled the Styrofoam cup in both hands and crossed her legs. A few stray hairs fell across her face and covered one eye. "I've been in the dark about it for seven years, Sheriff. I don't see what I could possibly tell you now that would help."

Preston leaned forward, his leather holster creaking. "I got a call yesterday about some old boy who used to live around here. They said he was at the bar that night. Said some things that led them to believe he might have known more than what he let on seven years ago."

Dana sat up. "Who?"

Preston took a mug shot from his chest pocket and held it up. The guy's face was almost as sunken and washed out as hers. "Remember him?"

She squinted. There wasn't a hint of recognition. She blew air out her lips and shook her head. "I like to think I never forget a face, but I'd say that's one worth forgetting. Who is the creep?"

"Graham Walker. They call him Gray."

"I can see why. He any relation to the Walkers over in Sissonville?"

Preston shrugged. "I couldn't say. He went to school around

here. Got in some trouble and moved to Ohio for a while and now he's back."

"What kind of trouble?"

Preston stared at Dana. "I didn't bring you here to question me."

"Maybe if you tell me something, it will jog my memory."

"We're getting a warrant, and then we're going over there to pick him up."

"Did you find something in the car that was his? DNA or something?"

"I can't comment on that." Preston leaned forward, and the table moved when he put his full weight on it. "But if you can think of anything that might help in our questioning, we'd appreciate it."

Dana picked up the picture and studied it. With her other hand she scratched at the back of her head; then she sniffed at her fingernails. Preston couldn't believe what he was seeing.

"Maybe I remember him. Off in the corner somewhere. I don't know. I didn't talk with him or anything. I guess it could have been him. How tall is he?"

"Listed at five nine, 165 pounds."

"Not much to him," she said, turning the photo over and sliding it across the table. "I can't think of anything that would help. I'd tell you if I remembered."

He nodded and stuffed the picture back in his pocket. "Something else is bothering me. It's about when you say the guy jumped you."

"He did. That's no lie."

Preston continued without the judging tone. "You said you had your keys out and he came up from behind."

"That's right."

"It was a pretty hot stretch that year. The records show it was in the eighties that night."

"Another reason I was thirsty. Back at the house it was like an oven, and the only room with an air conditioner was Mom's. They had that big window fan that made as much noise as a backhoe. Couldn't get any sleep with that thing."

"And you said he had on a leather jacket. Pretty hot for a jacket, wasn't it?"

"I didn't ask him about his wardrobe, Sheriff."

"Surely you didn't leave your daughter in a car with the windows rolled up."

"Of course not. I was parked under this persimmon tree, and there was a good breeze. I remember that. I had all four windows down so she could get the air she needed."

Preston pictured the baby, her hair matted with sweat. Flies from the trash bin buzzing around the car. Dirt in the folds of her skin at her elbows and on her neck.

"That man assaulted me at the car. I tried to scream for help, but he clamped his hand over my face and there was nothing I could do."

Preston held up a hand. "You don't have to go through it again."

"I struggled with him, my little girl laying asleep right there. Then he knocked me down and threw me in the car and drove farther out the hollow." The more she talked, the more animated she got.

Preston tried to calm her again. "I'm not asking you to relive that part of the story—"

She thrust a hand at her temple and pulled back the hair. "See this scar? I still got that from that night. And I still got the memory of seeing my scared little girl in that car seat behind me, crying and not knowing what was going on. And then never seeing her again."

"Dana—"

"I still got the knowledge that if I hadn't been in the wrong place at the wrong time, my little baby would be walking to the elementary school with her lunch box, having a birthday party, and playing in a tree house or something. Me going to talk with her teachers about what a smart girl I have. Me watching her sing down at the church."

Dana was tearing up now and Preston had to look at his boots. He couldn't imagine this woman at a PTA meeting, but who was to say her life wouldn't be different? Losing the child wasn't the reason for her downward spiral. From everything Preston could tell, Dana Edwards was not an upstanding citizen before that night, and she certainly hadn't done much to enhance the résumé after it. But that didn't make her a criminal.

"Every night I lay awake and wonder what happened," she continued, digging her finger into the table. "Every night I go to sleep and wake up with the thought that I could have done more or done something different. But I didn't. And I have to live with it. But if you can catch the pervert who took her and get him to tell us what he did with her, you do that, Sheriff. And I want to be here the minute you bring him in."

Someone knocked on the door and he waved them in. It was his secretary, Mindy. "That warrant's ready, Sheriff. Good to go."

"Could you ask Mike to come back here? I want him to give Dana a ride home."

The two stared at each other, Dana gritting her teeth. Preston finally picked at his ear, something he did when he was nervous or wasn't sure what else to do. Fiddling with some new hair growing like a weed.

"We're going to find her," he said. "I don't know how, and I don't know what condition she'll be in, but if it's the last thing I do, we're going to find her."

11

Johnson rolled into Bentonville, Arkansas, in the afternoon and ordered the biggest platter of fish and shrimp he could at Long John Silver's. His back was so stiff he couldn't think about sitting down to eat, so he pulled into a regional park and walked through it, thinking of June Bug and Sheila as he crunched the clam strips and fried cod. At some restaurants it didn't make sense that they put all those napkins in the sack, but this was so greasy he used one for every piece of fish.

At the top of a knoll was a pair of tennis courts, and he leaned against a flagpole near a veterans' memorial and watched a teenage boy trying to teach a teenage girl how to play. The girl wore a cheerleader's dress and shoes that made white marks on the court. It was clear why the boy was teaching her, though probably not to the girl. He'd hit to her backhand repeatedly and she'd swing and miss, and then the boy would watch her walk to the fence, staring as she bent over to retrieve the ball.

Over the hill was a Little League field and two teams were at it, though from the sounds of the parents yelling and clapping this was more like the seventh game of the World Series. He dumped the box of spent tartar and cocktail sauce holders as wasps swarmed over the empty cans of Coke and Sprite piled high.

He stretched out on the side of a hill by an oak tree that looked like it had been there since before the Civil War and watched the game. The right fielder for the home team seemed more interested in the dandelions. The kid at bat, #14, swung at three consecutive pitches, not even coming close, and Johnson's childhood fears flooded back. Playground picks and squabbles over captains and who would pitch. He'd never played organized ball until his uncle signed him up for a team when he was ten. He wore his uniform to school the day after he received it and the other kids laughed.

"I think it's a wonderful uniform," his teacher said, taking him aside after class had begun. Miss Bailey spoke softly, and he could smell the sweet mints she kept in her desk's top drawer. Seeing her red lipstick so close nearly took his breath away.

The truth was, he had worn the uniform to impress her. She was soft and sweet and curvy like the women on TV shows, and she smelled like a bouquet of flowers. But the draw was her eyes and that smile, and he couldn't help wondering what it would be like to have a mother like her. Someone to read him a story at night and tuck him in bed and sing — her voice was like an angel's — and she could play the piano and knew more about math and science and writing and social studies than all his other teachers combined.

"I'll bet you're going to be a big leaguer someday," she said softly in his ear, and a tingle spread through his body.

Those words had made the mocking bearable, and that day he decided he would become a teacher. If a sentence or two from Miss Bailey could do this to his heart, he was in. He walked home proudly, shunning the bus and the teasing of the high schoolers that was sure to come. That was a good memory from his elementary school years.

However, Miss Bailey's comment about his baseball career had not been prophetic. During his first game, he stepped to the plate against a mean kid from the next town who recognized him and called his catcher out for a meeting. They spoke quietly through gloves held to their faces. A round canister showed clearly through the seat of the pitcher's back pocket, and there was a bump on the kid's lower lip. The laws of children and nature sometimes take a backseat in the West Virginia hills.

The umpire scraped some dirt off home plate as the catcher returned. The kid held his mask at his side and got close enough for John to hear. "Tom says your mama's a whore lady. He says she works out at the truck stop."

The catcher smiled and showed the gap between his top front teeth, two of which seemed to be growing in opposite directions. He fit the mask on and gave the pitcher a thumbs-up. The umpire took his position and waved at John to step into the batter's box, then pointed at the pitcher.

The first pitch was high and tight, and John tried ducking but lost his balance and sat in the dirt.

The pitcher laughed and so did a few parents from the opposing team. A couple players from his team clapped and told him to "hang in there."

He heard the deep voice of his uncle encouraging him. "Stay in there, John. Knock it out."

The ball hit the metal fence behind him and rolled to within a couple feet of home plate. The catcher had chased it and ambled toward him.

John picked up the ball and placed it in the kid's mitt. "Tell Tom to watch himself."

The catcher tried to act tough and shake off the threat, but there's something in the eyes of prey that gives away fear and John sensed it.

"Put another one in there, Tom!" a man with stringy hair shouted. John guessed from the resemblance that it was Tom's father. He was at the edge of the dugout sipping something jammed into a holder that said *Drink Coke*. "Let's see what you got!"

Tom overthrew the next pitch outside and in the dirt, and it skipped to the backstop again. John swung a few times, staring at the pitcher with the hint of a smile. The kid walked off the mound and spit, then took the throw from his catcher. He stared in at the sign, his right arm dangling. His form was first-rate, not herky-jerky. Fluid and smooth. He grooved the 2-0 fastball down the middle, and John saw the stitches and swung, connecting with the resounding ping of the metal bat. He put his head down and ran to first, stealing a glance at the left fielder, who stood at the fence with his back to the field.

There was a smattering of applause behind him, and when he hit first base, he took an immediate left and ran toward the pitcher's mound. Tom was staring at the still-rolling ball and some kids chasing it past the concessions stand. John put his helmet into the back of the pitcher and drove him hard into the infield dirt. The air came out of the kid's lungs, and John drove him face-first into the hard ground. There was yelling after that and a catcher's mask on John's back, then a couple of coaches pulling him off and his uncle dragging him away.

John didn't get to touch home plate and didn't play another inning. He was kicked out of the league.

His uncle didn't speak until they got into his truck. "You want to tell me what that was about? I paid a lot of money for you to play baseball, not big-time wrestling."

John sat silent.

"That was a great hit. Actually two great hits. One on the ball and one on the pitcher. Unfortunately you're not playing line-backer." He started the truck and put it in gear, then held his foot on the brake. "Did that catcher say something to you?"

John nodded.

His uncle sat for another moment, rolling something in his mind. He opened his mouth to speak; then he must have thought better of it because he just drove off.

People said the rage was understandable. The next Monday he heard the titters and whispers of kids and the more hurtful words of teachers who cast a wary eye at him on the playground. When Miss Bailey saw his eye and the scrapes on his cheek and the deep gash on his arm, she asked what had happened.

"Baseball game," he said.

"This needs to be looked at right away. Come with me."

She took him to the school nurse, who wasn't there yet. Miss Bailey swabbed hydrogen peroxide on the cuts that were turning a dark yellow. The liquid bubbled and stung, but he didn't let on that it hurt.

"There're still some little pebbles or something under the skin, John. Didn't anybody look at this at the game?"

"They didn't really have a chance to," he said. "I got in a fight with another kid."

She was kneeling in front of him. "What happened?"

At that moment he knew he had a choice: to open up and tell her what was going on or to keep it inside. Maybe it was the perfume. Maybe it was how warm he felt being touched by someone so beautiful who seemed to care. Maybe it was the dam in his heart that had backed up a wall of emotion that had cracked. Whatever the reason, he spilled the whole thing in a choking, gasping effort that both scared and humiliated him.

Except she was crying too.

She listened to the whole thing. The feelings the boys brought up, what they said about his mother. The fact was, he hadn't seen his mother in more than a week, and then she was drunk. And his father had worked midnights over the weekend, which meant he slept most of the day. John had eaten alone, except for the hot dog and ice cream he ate at Dairy Queen with his uncle, and he'd waded through the dirty clothes to find something to wear to school. He had thrown his bloody uniform in the trash after the game.

The more he talked, the more she cried, and it felt good to have someone listen—really listen—as he told her about the way the ball flew off the bat and how good it felt to drive that kid into the ground and watch him get dirt and rocks in his mouth to mix with the pinch between his cheek and gum.

When John was done spewing the disconnected stories, he saw something else in her eyes. Something akin to a loving revulsion. Pity mixed with horror. He had said too much. He had let her inside to see what was really there. Though Miss Bailey had compassion, it seemed to him like she was treating a wounded snake. No matter how much she helped, he was still going to have to slither off into his hole.

At that point he stopped talking, stopped looking at Miss Bailey as someone who would listen, and began the damming process again. He learned he needed to hold on to the feelings. Though others—his uncle and a few teachers and coaches—tried to break through, John kept himself in check. He steeled himself against the pain of having an absent father and a mother who floated in and out of his life.

When high school rolled around, John became known as one of the most fierce linebackers in the state. It felt good to drag his opponents to the ground. It felt good to feel anything. But when the game was over, he went back to his template, keeping things pushed down and controlled.

Several girls had been interested. And he was certainly interested. But something kept him from commitment. Something kept him from opening up, and sooner or later, they would get tired of the strong, silent routine and move on.

After high school, when a few colleges offered scholarships, John went to his uncle. He didn't have the grades for college, mainly because he hadn't applied himself. His uncle encouraged him to give it a try, but John felt it a waste of time. His uncle suggested the military, which made perfect sense. It was there, in preparation for battle, that John finally found himself, his calling. Things clicked and he put his mind and body to work. His physical talents shone, and his superiors recognized his abilities. Again, he stepped into the challenge of the SEALs, going through the rigorous training, the mind-bending assaults on his body to bring it into subjection, to take him places he'd never been before and prepare him for places he hoped he would never have to go again.

Now, under the oak tree, he looked out over the mass of uniformed young boys and saw himself in right field. Saw himself rounding first and slamming the pitcher to the ground. Saw the parents in the stands and in folding lawn chairs cheering and remembered the loss of never having his mother or father watch him. Whether it was the closeness he saw there or the empty feeling of loss or the growing feeling that something drastic was about to change his life, John began to tear up. A wave of emotion hit him, and he lay back in the grass and let it come, tears flowing, eyes stinging. There was plenty in his life to weep for. Plenty in his life that would have felled a lesser man.

He lay there a few minutes, listening to the game's end—the

high fives, the squeals of younger brothers and sisters at the play-ground, the plastic wrappers coming off fruit snacks, and empty Gatorade bottles tossed in trash cans.

Johnson glanced at the concessions stand beyond the left field fence and saw a young girl in an outfit just like June Bug's. He'd bought it for her at Walmart in late spring. In fact, the way the girl moved away from the stand toward the parking lot reminded him of her, her hair bouncing when she ran. She skipped when she was in a hurry, putting her left arm out and hopping along. The girl disappeared behind a playground wall. He was really losing it if he thought he was seeing June Bug.

He checked his watch and stood, walking to the parking lot with parents and siblings of sweaty players. A kid with #14 passed him and John couldn't hold back. "Nice swings out there, 14," he said.

The kid looked at him, thick glasses, red lips from the Gatorade, and he flashed a smile. "I didn't hit anything."

"Yeah, but when you do, it'll go for a mile. Keep swinging."

The kid's father put a hand on his son's shoulder, and the two walked away.

John watched them climb into their Prius and drive off. Then he fired up the RV and found the intersection from memory. It was a rural farming region without the nice backyards and wooden fences of the suburbs. The road dipped, and there were willow trees growing on either side of the little red house with the short drive-way and the porch swing.

He parked in the gravel next to the mailbox and stared at the For Rent sign in front. It was nearing dinnertime with the sun still high in the sky. He swatted at a few mosquitoes as he walked to the front door. It was muggy, and there was a creek nearby that had eaten away at the bank and standing water in a little cow pond beside the house. He knocked on the door and waited.

After a louder knock, he looked in the window by the swing, cupping his hand so he could see inside. The uneven, hardwood floors ran throughout the empty house. No furniture. No phone. Not even a kitchen table.

He walked to the side, hands on his hips, and saw movement at a farmhouse. He cut through the edge of a cornfield and up the long driveway. A man was working on the wheel of his tractor, his Razorbacks hat stained with sweat and axle grease.

"Excuse me," John said. "I was wondering if you knew anything about the lady who lived in that house."

The man turned, propping his arm against the huge tire, but it took him a few seconds to look John over and speak. "Mrs. Linderman?"

"That's her. She didn't pass, did she?"

The man stuck his tongue in his cheek and dipped his head to look over his glasses. "She passed from that place down yonder; that's for sure. But not from this world. Who wants to know?"

"Sorry. I'm a friend of her son's."

"You knew Calvin?"

"We were in the service together. Fought in Afghanistan side by side."

He wiped his hands on his coveralls and with great effort stood, sticking out a rough and rugged hand. Callouses from hard work. Lines on his face from years of life and dark veins that showed through sunburned skin. "Thank you for what you did for your country, son. You're not John, are you?"

John let go. Surprised. "How'd you know?"

"Margaret mentioned you anytime she talked about Calvin. She hoped you'd come back around here." He glanced at the house and a woman working in the kitchen. "You and your daughter want to come inside and have supper with us?"

"My daughter?" John said, confused. How would he know about June Bug?

The man nodded toward the road. "She looks like she's with you. Isn't that your daughter?"

John turned to the road. June Bug was bounding up the driveway toward him, a big smile on her face.

12

I hugged my dad, and I swear he looked like his teeth were going to fall out of his head. He just stood there, his mouth open, about a million questions in his eyes. I'd stayed as quiet as I could, singing into my pillow as we crossed bridges. The hardest part was finding something to eat. I'd brought some bread from Sheila's kitchen and a couple of pieces of cheese, but after I ate those, my stomach started gnawing at itself.

One of the big draws of me coming with him was to find out what in the world he was doing and what was so all-fired important about the trip, and I figured I was missing something with this man. Maybe it was his daddy. Maybe the uncle he talked about from time to time who had taught Dad to fish. I wondered if this might be the man who made all the memories.

Instead of letting my dad ask me anything, I took his hand and swung it back and forth, smiling at the older man. "Are you friends with my dad?"

"I am now," he said. "Just asked if he wanted to come have supper with us. Are you hungry?"

"I'm starving," I said. "Can we eat supper with them, Daddy? Please? I know it's going to be good because I can smell it."

"I'll go in and tell the missus to set two more places at the table." The man walked off, leaning to one side with one of his arms held tight against him.

When he made it to the steps which were cinder blocks, Dad

turned to me. "What are you doing? You were supposed to stay with Sheila. Have you been in the RV all this time?"

I nodded.

He ran a hand through his hair. "She must be going out of her gourd. She might have contacted the police, thinking you ran away."

"She wouldn't do that. She'll figure it out."

"I got to get to a phone."

"The people in there will let you use theirs. Do you know them?"

A bunch of worry lines came on his face, and for once he didn't seem fully with me. Most of the time when I had my dad's attention, I had all of him. But I could tell there were things going on in his head now that took him away, took his thoughts to some other place, like he was on some deserted island but thinking about Alabama or Tennessee.

"I knew the lady who lived in the house next door. That's who I came to see."

"What for?"

He looked at me and gave me a stare that said, *I can't believe you are asking me questions when there are so many questions I have for you.* But he also did it with a smile. "I have never spanked you in all these years, young lady, but I'm as close as I've ever been. What were you thinking hiding like that?"

I tried to pout and put my head down. He put his hand under my chin and lifted it up so he could see my face. I guess there were tears in my eyes because things were sort of blurry.

"I just want to know," I said.

"You want to know what?"

"About you. About me. I knew if I asked you wouldn't let me come. And if you found out I was in the RV anywhere close to Colorado you'd have turned around. So I stayed up there as long as I could."

"I should put you on a bus in the morning. I should send you straight back there."

"But I want to go with you and find out."

"Find out what? What are you talking about?"

The screen door creaked, and the old man stuck his head out. "You two come on inside and get washed up."

"We'll be right there," my dad said. He got down on one knee and put his arms on my shoulders. "What's this about? I thought you'd be happy to stay with Sheila."

And then the tears started to roll, and once they start there's no way you can stop them; I don't care how old you are. I didn't like to cry in front of him, and most of the time when I do, I make sure it's in my bed at night when he's asleep or out getting food. But I couldn't help it. "I want to go back with you to Dogwood."

He squinted at me like I had three heads. "What do you know about Dogwood?"

"My mama is back there. I just know it. And I thought if I came with you, you'd explain things. Explain why we're not living there and what happened. I want to know what happened to her."

My nose was running now, and I wiped it on my shirt. Then I wiped my eyes and wasn't able to see much, but I could see the look on his face. And that was enough to send me into more crying and snorting. I fell into his arms, and he gathered me onto his chest and held me there as I sobbed. Getting it out felt good in a hard kind of way. It was sort of like eating way too much candy, like one time I had a whole bag of Twizzlers. I made it to the parking lot before it all came spilling out, and Daddy said he was afraid I had burst something inside because it was red. I told him it was just the Twizzlers, and then he laughed and shook his head and gave me a wet paper towel.

He kept patting me on the back and whispering in my ear. "Shh. It's going to be okay. It's all right," he said about a hundred times.

Then he pushed me away so I stood on my own, and he took out a handkerchief from his back pocket. I blew my nose hard, and we both laughed because I can really make it sound like an air horn.

"How did you find out about Dogwood?" he said.

And then it all came spilling out. I told him about the poster

I saw in Walmart that had my picture on it and recited exactly what it said, like I'd done about a million times in my head.

Daddy kept wringing his hands, folding them over and over like he was trying to wash something away. Again I asked about Dogwood and if we could go back, and he shook his head and muttered something about never being able to.

"Why not?"

"It's complicated." He looked toward the road, and there were lines on his face I'd never seen before. Finally he said, "Which do you like better, June Bug or Natalie Anne?"

"I don't think I could ever get used to anything other than June Bug."

His chin trembled and he pulled me close.

The screen door squeaked behind us. "Food's on the table," the old man said.

"We were just coming," Dad said.

He picked me up and walked into the house and took me to the bathroom down a long hallway with hardwood floors that creaked underneath our weight. I had a feeling that they'd creak under the weight of a mouse. The house smelled musty and old, and there was dust in the corners that old people must not see. The bathroom fixtures were rusted and dripped even when I turned the handle off really hard, and there were brown spots on the towels.

I tried to make it look like I hadn't been crying by rubbing cold water on my face, but my eyes were still red.

Daddy's hands were brown and strong, and he cupped my face in them from behind and kissed the top of my head. "You look great. Come on."

The old woman wiped her hands on her apron and smiled like I was her grandbaby. She shook my dad's hand and told him she was proud to meet him. Then she hugged me so tight I thought I wasn't going to be able to breathe for a day.

She showed me my place at the table while she turned down the TV volume. I couldn't believe all the food she'd prepared for only two people, and I wondered if she'd pulled out more stuff just for us. A big plate held a mound of meat that she called her special recipe meat loaf. There were green beans in a bowl, still steaming, and a dish of red things that I found out were beets. She had baked four of the biggest potatoes I had ever seen—they were almost bigger than me—and she cut mine open and put a slice of butter on there and it melted.

"That's cow butter," she said. "And there's homemade apple butter for your biscuit. Try some."

Her face was kindly, with more lines than the map we kept in the RV, and she had a way of talking that her husband didn't. She'd talk and talk and ask questions, and the old man would just sit there like he was watching a ball game. Then, on the off chance that he got a word in, she'd correct him and he'd go back to eating.

"Warren tells me you knew Margaret and her boy. Served with him over in Afghanistan."

"That's right," Dad said. "I was through here a few years ago to see her after Calvin died."

She shook her head. "Her life's changed a bit since then. We'll call her after supper."

Dad looked at me. "And if it's okay, I need to make another call. Long distance."

She flung a withered hand in the air. "Call as much as you like. And park your RV by the barn tonight. You two are staying here."

"We couldn't do that," Dad said.

"Nonsense. This little thing needs some meat on her bones. Least we can do is fatten you up a little and give you a good breakfast."

"Can we stay?" I said, mashing the potato down with my fork and getting the butter mixed in until it turned yellow.

"We'll talk about it," he said.

I'd never tasted anything better in my life. The meat loaf had a red sauce like ketchup on top of it, but it was sweeter. Part of it was that I was starving after all that time eating next to nothing in the RV, and part of it was the freedom I felt now that I had my secret out. It felt like the pack off the back of that guy in the *Pilgrim's*

Progress story. Daddy started reading it to me but it got a little hard to understand and we moved on to something else.

"And what's your name, young lady?" the woman said to me.

"It's Natalie, but everybody calls me June Bug."

She covered her mouth with the paper towel in her lap and put her head back to laugh. "If that don't beat all. I don't think I've ever heard a name that fit a person any better. We had a boy who lived down in the hollow, went to high school with him . . ."

Her husband smiled and nodded as if the man were sitting right in front of him.

"Cow Pie Reynolds," she said, tapping her husband on the shoulder. "You remember Cow Pie?"

"I do."

"I don't know where he got it, but everybody called him that all through school, at least until he dropped out and started working at the plant. His mama had the pleurisy and his daddy died years before that and he basically took care of her the rest of her life. He was one to tip back the bottle, if you know what I mean, and that did him in." She shook her head, and the gray hair waved like a lion's mane.

"He sat in a cow pie once," her husband said.

"That's how it got started?"

He nodded. "Sat in a cow pie."

She took a bite of a biscuit with apple butter on the edge and wiped at some sweat on her forehead. "I think he was sweet on me, to tell you the truth. Spent his days just filled with regret that I wouldn't marry him." She stole a glance at her husband, and he gave a sheepish grin. "Warren here stole my heart."

"I married her for her meat loaf."

Daddy pushed back from the table. "Then I'd say you made a good decision. That was the best meal I've had in years."

I wanted to ask if that was a criticism of Sheila's cooking because of the good food she'd made, but I didn't get the chance because Dad went for the phone. The black one hanging on the kitchen wall looked like it had survived a war. I pointed it out, but the woman seemed to know he needed privacy and showed him the one in the living room, around the corner and into the dust.

"Where are you two headed?" the woman said when he'd gone. "Do you go to school anywhere? You must be in about the third grade, right?"

"I don't really go to a regular school. My dad teaches me in the RV."

"Homeschooled. That's what they call it."

"RV schooled," I said.

"What's that?" She leaned closer.

I repeated it, and she covered her mouth with the paper towel again. And then she started in on another story.

Pretty soon Daddy came back in and sat down at the table.

"Did you make your call?" the woman said.

"There was nobody home. I'll call again later, if that's okay."

The woman was up like a flash. "You call as many times as it takes. You want some coffee?"

"Love some."

"Get me a cup too," the old man said.

She picked up a small towel and uncovered a pie on the desk in the corner. "And I baked this cherry pie this afternoon. Let me heat it a little in the oven so it'll be nice and toasty when I put the ice cream on it."

Dad drank his coffee black, which I could never understand because I tried it once and it tasted like drinking week-old rainwater out of a shoe. The four of us sat around the table listening to the old woman talk about her pains and ailments and how doctors didn't care about people anymore.

I focused on the TV and the news stories that were flying by. There was something on about the economy and the words *Economic Crisis* flashed up there with a jagged arrow pointing down. I finished all but the skin on my potato and the green beans, which I am not as thrilled about as old people seem to be.

She got the cherry pie out of the oven and pulled a plastic tub of vanilla ice cream from the freezer, all the while talking about her diverticulitis and how she couldn't go to the bathroom—if you can believe that. I glanced at the TV again and saw a reporter holding a microphone in front of a police station. He was older, with gray hair and a face like a mole. The words in the corner of the screen said *Dogwood, WV.*

I tapped Daddy on the shoulder and pointed. He asked the man if he would turn the sound up but the woman beat him to it and she turned it up about as loud as it would go.

". . . being described by local police as a person of interest in this baffling case that has scarred this West Virginia community like a strip mine," the reporter said.

While the reporter talked, a skinny fellow in a white T-shirt was being led inside the building. When he saw the camera he put his hands over his face and looked the other way.

"Though national attention has been drawn to this small West Virginia hollow, the residents here still speculate about what happened to a young girl who went missing seven years ago."

The camera showed a tree with some flowers surrounding a picture. Underneath it said *Natalie Anne Edwards,* and it just about made me sick to my stomach.

The old man shook his head. "It's a shame what this world is coming to."

Daddy got up and turned down the volume just as the reporter showed an older woman with white hair talking and waving her hands. Daddy stood in front of the TV and leaned back against the table. "That's the town I'm from. Didn't ever think it would make the national news."

"Well, I hope they caught the fellow who kidnapped that poor little girl," the woman said as she put a bowl of pie and ice cream in front of me.

"Why can't we watch the rest?" I whined, trying to move and see.

"There are some things little girls shouldn't have to worry about," Dad said.

"You got that right," the old man said.

The woman put her hand on my back and patted it. "Your daddy's going to take care of you. He's not going to let anything happen. Is that what you're afraid of?"

"No," I said quickly, and from the reaction in the room I guessed I said it a little too loud and angry. "I mean, I'm interested in what's happening there."

Daddy spooned in a few bites of pie and ice cream. "Maybe I ought to call Mrs. Linderman and find out if she'll see me. Then we'll get out of your hair."

"Now you're no problem; you know that," the woman said, rustling through some papers and finding a yellow address book. She wrote a number down on the edge of an old newspaper and tore it off.

He walked into the living room, and I moved my ice cream around until it made a little ice cream pond on the pie. Cherry is one of my favorites, though I like the turtle pie at Denny's the best. But I just couldn't eat anything after what I'd seen on TV, and it made the whole thing jumble in my head.

Dad laughed in the other room as he talked on the phone, and the old woman asked if I wanted to take a piece of pie with me. I shook my head because I wasn't really hungry anymore.

"She said to come right over," Daddy said. "I suppose we ought to head out."

The woman said something about keeping rooms open for us, but I think she knew we weren't coming back. I walked over and hugged her and she hugged me back. I did the same to the old man who was standing like a statue by the door. He hugged me and said, "You take good care of your dad."

The two were standing on the porch waving as we drove away. Dad turned around in their driveway and headed up the road.

13

Sheriff Hadley Preston was not pleased at the media's knowledge of the arrest of Graham Walker. He asked Mike why he had ignored his pleas not to discuss the case. The young man's face had turned redder than the Ohio State practice shirt he wore under his uniform. There was a cute young thing from Channel 13 who had camped out by the cruiser, a young lady with a short skirt and long eyelashes, and Preston figured she had pried the information from him.

"You beat all; you know that?" he said.

"I didn't tell her much, Sheriff."

"You told her all she needed and now look at it out there."

Walker was in the same interview room where Dana had been, fiddling with a Styrofoam cup of coffee. He wasn't much to look at, just skin and bones and hair that reached his shoulders and covered one eye. The man had a severely pockmarked face, scars from unattended acne, Preston guessed. From the looks of him, the 165 pounds was being generous. Preston could see the man's ribs through his tight T-shirt. His arms were small and spindly like broomsticks. Either a drug addiction or a metabolism that was higher than he deserved.

"You want a lawyer?" Preston said as he pulled a chair back and sat, plopping his hat on the table.

"What do I need a lawyer for?"

"You don't. They just make me ask that."

"I haven't done anything wrong."

"For how long?"

"What do you mean?"

"It's not true that you haven't done anything wrong. I took a look at your record."

"That was a long time ago, Sheriff. You can't hold that against me. I've changed."

Preston nodded. "That's good to hear. You still working at the Tire Works?"

"I quit a couple months ago. Still looking around for something."

"You quit or you were fired?"

Walker paused. "I'd say the parting was mutual. I wanted different hours, and my boss wouldn't give it to me."

Preston poured himself a cup of coffee. "From what he said, you didn't want to show up on time. Ever."

Walker didn't answer.

Preston stood by the door, leaning against it with one arm. "There're a few things in that report and a few things I've heard that made me bring you down here. You remember working at the mini golf?"

Walker shifted in his chair. "Yeah." He looked away and then back at the sheriff. "What about it?"

"You got fired from that job too."

"It was a dead end. Just something I did to make some spending money."

"I hear you made advances on a young girl and the manager got wind of it. Is that fair to say?"

Walker opened his mouth, ready to speak. But nothing came out.

"She was thirteen," Preston said.

"Sheriff, that girl did not look thirteen. I can guarantee you that. And all we did was talk."

"In your car?"

"Look, I don't know what that has to do with me now. Is that girl accusing?"

"Just trying to put the pieces together." Preston stared at the man. "It was about that time you moved away to Ohio. Akron, wasn't it?"

"I have a brother who lived up there. Worked for Goodyear. He let me stay with him and his wife."

"And you were in Hartville about a month when the neighbors started complaining."

"How did you . . . ? Is this what the fuss is about? Something that happened in Ohio?" Walker's face was a sunken mixture of neglect and incomprehension.

"Not really." Preston moved back to the chair and sat, leaning forward with his elbows on his knees. "I just like to get things in order. It helps to know the whole story. Where a person has come from. Know where they sit before you find out where they stand."

Walker scrunched up his face, as if the sheriff were speaking a foreign language.

"I'd encourage you to level with me on what you say. Shoot straight."

"I am being straight." His eyes shifted away from Preston, like a dog ashamed of something he did on the carpet.

"From what I hear, you agreed to leave that area because they caught you looking in windows, scaring people. Young women."

Walker shrugged. "I liked to take walks at night. I wasn't a Peeping Tom, if that's what you mean."

"The search warrant we have for your home covers anything electronic, like computers. We found a laptop there."

Walker locked eyes with Preston, his arms tensing. He finally leaned back with a nervous smile.

"We going to find anything we don't want to see on that hard drive?"

"Nothing that's probably not on every one of your computers here," Walker said.

"We'll see about that," Preston said, picking up his hat and rolling it. "You like looking at pictures?"

Walker stared at the sheriff's hand. "You been married how long, Sheriff?"

"Almost thirty years to the same woman."

Walker shook his head. "Thirty years. It's been thirty years since you dated a woman. Let me tell you something. Things are different now."

"I suspect they are."

"No. There's no way you could understand. Women today . . . it's like they're waiting for you to make some mistake. Say one thing wrong. Do something that hacks them off. Then they get up and walk away. That's pressure, especially if you have to pay for both dinners."

"You tried those online dating things?"

Walker scoffed and pointed at his own face. "No matter which side I take of this, it always looks like a mug shot. They take one look and keep clicking the mouse. I saw this one guy the other day in a pool next to a dolphin. Said he was a nature lover and liked to read books and take long walks. And he had this baby face that made him look like some retired Backstreet Boy."

Preston laughed. The guy was weird, but at least he had a sense of humor.

Walker leaned forward and jabbed a finger at the tabletop. "Women today don't even give you a chance to make an impression. They're looking for guys with looks and the six-figure income. Last thing they're looking for is a guy like me. I got a good heart, Sheriff."

Preston nodded and stared at him. "Is that why you favor the young ones?"

"What are you talking about?"

"Some of the pictures we found on the computer. We haven't gone through it all, but Mike found some stuff that's not good for your public image. And some conversations you had in chat rooms. You want to explain that?"

"First of all, there's nothing illegal about talking with people on the computer. How am I supposed to know how old they are?"

"When they say they're twelve, that's a pretty good indication —don't you think?"

"Maybe so, but people lie. You know that."

Preston nodded. "True, but pictures don't lie."

Walker put up his hands. "I didn't have anything to do with that. Honest. I had a friend staying with me a couple of weeks, and when I found out he was downloading stuff, I told him to delete it and he said he did."

"You might not want to blame other people, Gray. Be straight with me."

Walker sat back and pulled his hair into a ponytail. "I admit I'm a little stuck. Back in high school or whatever. I don't get along with older women. I've tried. The younger ones don't have all that resentment and pain. You know?" He cursed. "I didn't know this was going to be a counseling session."

Preston tried hard to make it seem like he was just a good old boy sheriff who was uncovering rocks to see what he'd find, but there was a method to his approach. When he was talking with some slick lawyer from Charleston or a media hound from New York, he could say the things they wanted to hear. But he felt most at home with his own people. Those whose faces had been slapped time and again by life. People like Walker.

"You had that mini golf job back in 2001. Is that right?"

Walker looked away in thought. "Yeah, that was the summer before 9/11."

"And the next year toward the end of June, you were at a bar, the Dew Drop."

"Sheriff, I'm not going to lie to you. I've been in a lot of bars over the years, so it might be a little hard to pinpoint."

"You were in that bar the night that baby girl disappeared. You remember that?"

Walker cocked his head slightly. "The lady whose kid went missing?"

"That's the one."

He laughed. "I can't believe this."

"Have you seen the news?"

"I saw they found the car in the reservoir."

Preston nodded and looked at him.

Walker crossed his arms, his elbows sticking out like the ends of matchsticks. "Well, I don't know what I can do for you."

Preston studied his hands. "Somebody came to us and told us about a conversation you had."

"Who?"

"Not important. They said you were talking not long after the child went missing." He unbuttoned his shirt pocket and fished for a piece of paper. Unfolding it, he held it a little farther away, almost a full arm's length. "'I think somebody stole that little girl and dropped her in some lake. They'll never find that girl.' That's what you said."

Walker's arms tensed and his face creased like a dried apple. "I never said anything of the sort. How would I know where that little girl went? Whoever told you that is lying through their teeth."

"She seemed pretty sure of herself."

"She? It was a woman?" He shot up from his chair and put his hands on the table. "Then you might want to check her story out. Maybe she's the one who nabbed that kid." He walked to the rear of the room, near the refrigerator, turning his back and running a hand through his hair. "I swear, Sheriff, I've done a lot of stupid things in my life, but I did not have anything to do with that girl's death."

Preston stared at the back of Walker's head.

Then Walker turned, a look of surprise and horror on his crimson face. He looked like a trapped animal in a cage. "I didn't mean that. I don't know if she's dead or not. But I didn't have anything to do with it."

"So you know more than you're telling me. Is that what you're saying?"

Walker paced, his shoelaces flopping as he walked. The ends of his jeans were nothing but loose strands. "Look, when I get drunk, I can say a lot of things. I've been in fights I don't even remember. Maybe a long time ago I was trying to figure it out like everybody else and I said something like that. I don't know."

"Why would you choose to mention the part about the bottom of the lake?"

"Sheriff, that wasn't me. That was the Jack Daniel's talking. I was just guessing, probably, if that's what I said. People have opinions about stuff all the time, and they don't get arrested for it."

Preston looked at the paper again and waited. Just sat there. Like a pause in a musical score meant to bring out the longing for completion. Clouds had gathered outside and the room darkened.

Preston finally spoke. "She also said you knew that lady's car was at the bottom of a lake. Not that you *thought* it was there, but you *knew it*."

"That's not true. How would I know where that car was? I was sitting in the back of that bar having a couple brews."

"So you admit you were at the Dew Drop that night."

"No, I don't admit that. I'm just saying whoever told you this could have been some woman I was trying to impress in a bar."

"You didn't say this at a bar, Gray. You were stone sober." He folded the paper and stuffed it back in his pocket. "A relative of yours reached out to us. Told us about the conversation. She thought it—"

"Relative?"

"—might help us. At first she said—"

"Who?"

"—she didn't think anything about it, but when the car came up so did the memory of the—"

"Who told you that?" Walker shouted.

"—conversation."

"What lying skank told you that?"

"Just calm down."

"Don't tell me to calm down. Some lowlife is trying to pin this on me, and I want to know who it is."

The door opened slightly and Preston waved Mike away. He leaned forward and looked up at Walker. The man's face was tight, the pockmarks drawn and quartered.

"I swear, Sheriff, you need to tell me who told you that because they're lying to you."

"It was your mother, Gray."

Walker's eyes became dead pools. His shoulders slumped, and he fell into the chair as if a bullet had just crashed through his brain.

Preston had seen men felled by gunfire before. An old boy who had abused his wife and daughter holed up in a hog pen with a shotgun. It was clear he didn't want to come out alive. And he didn't. He'd fallen among the hogs, just dropped like a stone after a well-placed shot. Walker acted the same.

"My mother?" he said, whining.

For a moment, Preston thought he could see into his life, the neglect and fear. She was a big woman with a face every bit as hard as Gray's. The woman had to be brutal, both in her words and actions. He could tell that by the way she talked about him during the interview. Preston actually felt a bit of pity for the guy, knowing what he'd come from.

"Did she just call you up and tell you that?" he said.

"She did. She asked to come down and we sat right here and she told us everything. I don't see any reason for a mother to lie to me, do you?"

His face betrayed him, a searching, lifeless stare into the void.

"There's something else. Another piece of the puzzle."

Walker shook his head, as if the dam of his life couldn't take another word.

There was a commotion outside in the hall, some yelling. Preston excused himself and opened the door to find Mike standing in the middle of the hall, blocking Mae Edwards. Her husband, Leason, was behind her, nervously following.

"Is he back there, Sheriff?" Mae shouted.

"For the love of pete," Preston said, striding toward her.

"I tried to keep her out, Sheriff," Mike said.

Preston edged in front of him and came face-to-face with Mae. She had the look of a determined bulldog.

"I saw it on the news. Has he confessed?"

Preston looked at Leason. "Get your wife out of here." Then to Mae, "Turn around and go home."

Leason turned and reached for his car keys, but Mae grabbed his arm. "Has he told you where she is? Has he told you what he did with her?"

Preston caught sight of a video camera coming through the front door, and he pushed Mike forward. A light came on and bathed them in white. "Take care of that, would you?"

Mike held up a hand in front of the camera. It was a scene played over and over the next few news cycles. A man in a uniform pushing the cameraman backward, the sheriff trying to calm a grieving and inconsolable grandmother. It was human interest squared, all happening in a small town setting that could be Anywhere, America.

"Mae, the best thing you can do for your granddaughter is go home. Leason, bring the car around back."

This time Mae let Leason go and the camera lights flashed again.

"Did he do it?" Mae said, her lips trembling. "Is he the one who took her?"

"Mae, I don't know. Now let me do my job. You know I'll be the first to call if I find anything. Why don't you trust me?"

"It's not that and you know it." She talked as the sheriff led her toward the back door, past the interrogation room. "I'm the only one in this town, the only one in my family that's ever held out any speck of hope. And if he knows where she is . . ."

Preston showed her through the door as the car pulled up. He tried to shield her from the cameras and questions of trailing reporters. She got in and Leason tried to back up, but Preston pecked on the window and pointed to the alley. The cameras turned toward him when the car left.

Preston smiled and turned to go inside, but the door was locked. He banged on it and cupped his hand around the window, but Mike was still in front.

He walked around the building, the gaggle of mics and cameras following him like babies behind a mother duck. Inside, he frowned at Mike, who Preston knew had to be feeling at fault. He hurried back to the interrogation room, and as soon as he opened the door, he knew the commotion was just beginning. The room was empty and the window was open.

14

They drove in silence in the RV, with June Bug in the passenger side and John staring straight ahead. He pulled into the parking lot where there was a laundry and a pizza restaurant and just sat there taking up two spaces.

"I can't believe you did that," John said. "I can't believe you disobeyed me and stowed away."

"I got the idea from you," she said.

"What are you talking about?"

"Remember the story you told? the one about your mother leaving and you went out in the backseat and covered up so you could go with her?"

John looked out the windshield at the pay phone by the convenience store. He rifled through the change in the cup holder, grabbing as many quarters and dimes as he could.

"Aren't we going to the old lady's house?"

"It's not a house," John said, slamming the door and walking across the lot to a grassy area between the buildings.

June Bug followed, trying her best to keep up. "If she doesn't live in a house, where does she live? An RV?"

"No. Go back to the RV. I need to talk to Sheila alone."

"I need to go to the bathroom."

He reached the phone and glanced at the convenience store across the lot. "Try in there. And watch for traffic."

She ran across the lot and inside. She disappeared into the

store, then came back to the front to talk with the woman at the cash register who was chewing gum like a cow chews its cud. The woman handed her a key, then said something to June Bug. She pointed toward the window, and the woman looked outside. John waved at her, and June Bug did her potty dance. That's what he had called it when she was younger. She'd dance down the aisle in the RV and he knew it was time, like a dog walking in circles or clawing at the back door.

"Hello?" Sheila said.

He hesitated. "It's John. She's with me."

A huge sigh on the other end. "Why did you do that?"

"I didn't. I had no idea she was here until a couple of hours ago. I've been trying to call you. She hid in her bed and stayed there."

"Don't lie to me."

"I'm not ly—"

"I mean it, John. I can take the truth. But I won't take another man lying to me, especially about something as important as this." Her voice trembled with pent-up emotion.

"I wouldn't lie to you."

"Are you her father? Answer that. Are you really her father?"

John paused. "No."

"Then you've been lying to me all along. Don't you see?"

"I never told you I was her father."

"*She* thinks you are. You're lying to her every day. That's even worse. And you posed as her father. I can't believe you'd do this. I don't know what's happened or what brought you to this, but I can't be part of it."

"I understand. And I wouldn't ask you to be part of it. Just listen to me for a minute."

Sobs on the other end. The worst sound in the world, a woman crying. All because of him. He wanted to hang up the phone. He wanted to get June Bug and leave. This woman had invited them into her life; he hadn't pushed his way in.

But she was right. He had misled her. He had misled everyone they had met the past seven years. This was why he didn't get entangled with other people. He just stood there, leaning against the phone, listening to the woman's cries.

Sheila finally spoke through her tears. "What does it say about a little girl when she chooses to hide away in an RV instead of staying with someone who loves her company? I'd have treated her like a princess."

"I don't know why she came with me—"

"John, she's just like the rest of us. She wants to know the truth."

He smiled. "That's exactly what she said to me."

"Then why don't you tell her? Why do you keep up with the lies? You're not a freelance writer, are you?"

"No."

"You've never sold an article in your life, have you?"

"It's not that I haven't tried . . ."

"Your writing about her is beautiful. It took my breath away. But that's not who you are."

Silence. Then he spoke again. "It's complicated, Sheila. About June Bug. I didn't want to hurt her. I thought I had a few more years, but I guess if she's asking questions, it's probably time. And with what's going on back there . . ."

"Go to the authorities right now."

He watched a semi pass. June Bug bounced to the front of the store and gave the key to the lady. The woman took it and hung it on a peg behind her. "I just wanted you to know she's safe. I thought you two would be having fun together. When I saw her, you could have knocked me over with a feather. I knew you'd be worried."

"*Worried* is not the word. I've been going crazy wondering who you are and what you're doing with her."

"I can promise you, I've never hurt her. I've always tried to be the best . . ." His voice trailed off.

"You're not just lying to her. You're lying to yourself. Where are you?"

"Arkansas. I'm meeting with an old friend."

Sheila sobbed as if anything he said would make her cry. "Have you seen the news?"

"I saw a clip. Not a whole lot. Have you called the police?"

There it was. The only question he really had for her. Other than letting her know June Bug's whereabouts, this was what he wanted to know.

"Is that why you really called?"

I swear, John thought, *this woman picks up on everything.* "No, scratch that. I don't care whether you called them or not. I just wanted you to know she was all right. And I wouldn't blame you for calling them if you have."

She sighed. "I've picked up the phone about a hundred times. Every time I get this picture in my mind. I think of that little girl . . ."

June Bug ran up to him. "Is it her?"

He nodded.

"Can I talk to her?" Her face lit like a Christmas tree.

He put up a hand and mouthed, "Just wait." Then to Sheila, "What picture do you get?"

It sounded like she was wiping her nose. "I see that little face as she rode her bike. And I see you watching her all the way."

"You saw that?"

"On the video camera in the pharmacy. John, I've never seen a little girl so in love with her daddy, but that's not what you are. And if you can't bear to tell her the truth, then something needs to be done."

"I think you're right. Here, she wants to say something to you."

John handed June Bug the phone, and she hopped with excitement. "Sheila."

He couldn't hear the other end of the conversation but he could imagine. June Bug said she had played a trick on them and not to worry, that she'd be back.

"I'm sorry I wasn't able to stay. I had to go with Daddy."

There was a long pause and several *yeah*s, and June Bug finally said, "Okay. I will. Bye." She handed him the phone and ran for the RV.

He held the phone and heard the soft sounds of Sheila crying. "I guess we'd better get going."

"John?" It was a question that just hung there. A question that carried a thousand words rolled into one. Finally she said, "Are you going to keep running?"

"I'm not sure."

"They're holding a man. They think he had something to do with the disappearance."

"Yeah, I gathered. Don't worry. I'll do what's right. I promise."

"All right," Sheila said.

"Whatever happens," he said, his voice strong and steady, "we both appreciated what you did. She'll never forget it. And neither will I."

He waited a moment. When he didn't hear anything, he said, "Good-bye, Sheila."

He placed the phone on the cradle and held it there for a moment before returning to the RV.

❀ ❀ ❀

The building looked more like a castle on a hill than a nursing home. A Graceland for the aged. The security guard at the gate took their information and gave Johnson a pass. "There's larger vehicle parking just to your right, sir," the attendant said.

They parked and walked hand in hand toward the visitors' entrance. June Bug was entranced by the bees hovering about the flowers, and she gasped at the building. "It looks like the house where the president lives."

The doors opened and they were greeted by falling water against rocks. Fish swam in a decorative pool.

"Can I help you, sir?" a nicely dressed woman said.

"We're here to see Mrs. Linderman."

"You must be John. She's expecting you in the garden. Right this way."

They followed the woman through the glistening hallway. He'd expected that antiseptic, alcohol smell of the aged, but there was none of that. It was a natural flower-and-earth-and-water smell that squelched other odors.

They walked past the dining area being readied for breakfast the next morning. Crystal and napkins arranged to perfection. There was another sitting area by a fireplace, tucked away with a filled bookshelf.

Mrs. Linderman sat in a wheelchair in a garden area surrounded by roses and concrete benches. A huge American flag flapped lazily above her as she watched the orange and yellow sunset. She looked like some old general to John, tired of the fight and ready for one last ride.

She shifted in her chair and smiled through the wrinkles, reaching out her left hand. "I knew you'd come back. I just wondered if I'd be around when it happened."

He bent to kiss her, and she cupped her gnarled hand around his cheek and held him there, as if drinking in the past. She looked at June Bug, who stood mouth agape. "And who do we have here?"

"Mrs. Linderman, I want you to meet June Bug." He glanced at the girl. "Mrs. Linderman is the mother of a friend of mine. A real special person."

June Bug held out her hand as the withered one enveloped it. The old woman's eyes twinkled. "You're just as pretty as a picture, aren't you? John, where in the world did you find such a beauty?"

"Just lucky, I guess," he said.

"It's nice to meet you," June Bug said. "I wish I could say I've heard all about you, but I haven't."

Mrs. Linderman threw back her head and laughed. "I suppose this fellow here is a little quiet about his past."

As June Bug nodded, John put a hand on the girl's head. "We're working on talking more. Telling each other the truth."

June Bug looked up at him. "We are?"

"Yeah."

"Well, I think that's a great idea," Mrs. Linderman said. "Those who don't remember the past are condemned to repeat it. That's what I've always heard." The woman sighed, took John's hand, and gazed at new leaves swaying in the breeze. "I like to come out here each evening and watch the sunset. God puts on a show for me." Though the heat was still oppressive, she rubbed her arms like it was the middle of winter. "Would you mind pushing me to my room, sweetheart?"

June Bug got behind her, and the woman bent down and released the brake on one wheel. "Through the doors and straight on till morning," she cackled.

John walked beside her, holding her hand, slowing June Bug. "This is a bit different than your other house down in the valley."

"I suppose. Of course, it's nothing compared to the townhome I was living in. But I had a fall and needed somebody to watch me." She waved at one of the workers and smiled like they were best friends.

"Break anything?" John said.

"Chipped a hip," she said. "It was downhill from there. So I sold that for a nice profit before the real estate market fell and moved up here to my Versailles, as I call it. They spend as much time on the flowers as they do the medical treatment." She craned her neck to look at him. "You don't think it's too highfalutin, do you?"

"I'd say you deserve everything here and more. But how can you afford it?"

She cocked her head at him with a knowing glance, almost surprised at the question. "You don't know?"

"What? You hit the lottery? They find oil under that town-home?"

"No, and I didn't go to Vegas."

June Bug stayed quiet, listening and pushing slowly, taking it all in. There was tile in a fancy array that led to carpet in even fancier arrays, and it seemed she was having a hard time concentrating.

"Up here on the right, June Bug," the old woman said. "This is my home away from home. My final resting place."

The room was large, with a sitting area and kitchenette and

an open bedroom next to a window that stretched the entire wall. Mrs. Linderman had the shades open, and there was a pond nearby with ducks and geese swimming and waddling on a path near some cattails. The valley below was green and inviting and seemed to fall away in the distance.

"Nice view," John said.

"I'm a very fortunate old lady. June Bug, wheel me over to the chair if you would."

June Bug did and the old lady positioned herself next to it, hit a button that raised the chair, and then she managed to perfectly seat herself and let it down. She took a deep breath and motioned for them to sit on the couch. There were two pictures on the end table facing her—an older man, smiling, and a younger man in a uniform. The men looked identical except for the years between them.

"So, what brings you to my humble abode?" she said.

"The question isn't what brings us here; it's what brought you here. Tell me. How can you afford this?"

She shook her head. "You have the same fortune in that box I gave you."

John sat forward uneasily. "What do you mean?"

"Yeah, what do you mean?" June Bug said.

Mrs. Linderman looked at the girl. "A long time ago your father did something kind and considerate for my son. Now, your daddy didn't think it was kind at the time, and he came to see me after my son died. He was filled with lots of bad thoughts. He blamed himself for what happened."

"I still do," John said.

"What happened?" June Bug said.

"We can talk about that later," John said.

Mrs. Linderman paused. "I gave him a box. It had some money and other things in it."

"I took it from you and the cop brought me back."

"I gave it to you. I explained all that to him."

"Wait," June Bug said. "The police brought you back where?"

John stood and walked to the window, ignoring the question.

"I used the money to buy the RV. That's the money we've been living on the past few years, June Bug."

"But there was more in the box," Mrs. Linderman said. "Those certificates I endorsed."

John turned. "The stuff in the envelope?"

Mrs. Linderman nodded. "You didn't open it?"

"I want to hear about the police," June Bug said.

Mrs. Linderman held up a hand. "It was a misunderstanding at the worst. A friend of my son who was looking out for me."

"You didn't have to do that," John said.

"Now we finally agree about something. I didn't *have* to, but I did for a simple reason. I knew you were a good man, John. I knew you were going to do something terrible. So I had to do something drastic. And that's why I put the box out there. In a sense, it was payment to bring you back to your senses."

"Wait, wait, wait," June Bug said, shaking her head as she tried to take all the information in. "What happened with you and the box and . . . the police?"

John knelt before the girl. "I'll explain later."

"No," June Bug said. "I want to hear it now. I want to hear her tell it."

"She's got spunk," Mrs. Linderman said. "Just like you."

John took a breath. "She's not my daughter."

"What?" June Bug said, almost jumping out of the chair.

"Settle down. I'll tell you."

"She's not yours?" Mrs. Linderman said.

"No. I mean, I've been her father since she was little. And I've been the best one I know how to be, which isn't saying much."

"You find her hiding under a cabbage leaf?"

John moved to the floor in front of both of them and crossed his legs. "Why don't we take one story at a time?"

"How could you not be my father?" June Bug said.

"I'd rather take the box first," John said.

June Bug crossed her arms. "Fine, as long as you get to both of them."

John looked at the floor and began. "I was in a bad place. I hadn't been out of the service for—"

"What's *service*?" June Bug said.

"The military. Her son and I were in Afghanistan together."

"What did you do there?"

He rubbed the back of his neck. "I guess you could say we killed people and broke things. Bad people. Men who wanted to kill us. People who hate freedom."

"And something happened to your son?" June Bug said to Mrs. Linderman.

The old woman nodded to John, as if to say, *Let him tell it.*

"We were in a firefight—a bad battle with lots of guns going off and mortar shells. We'd been sent to take care of some enemies, and we thought there were only a few. But there turned out to be a lot more. So we were caught. Pinned down. And a couple of our guys were hurt. Her son was a medic, took care of people's wounds, so he started off for them. I tried to talk him out of it. I tried to tell him they were gone, but he wouldn't listen. He had a job to do." John kept rubbing his hands and the more he told, the harder he rubbed.

June Bug sat rapt, studying his face.

"I tried to cover him, but there were too many. And I was getting low on ammo. Then the air strike came, but Calvin made it to the injured. There was smoke and fire everywhere, lots of explosions, but there he was, putting bandages on them and trying to stop their bleeding."

A tear trickled down Mrs. Linderman's face. She put her chin in her hand and leaned forward. "You were there for him."

Overcome with emotion, John shook his head. "No, I wasn't. I didn't help."

"That's not what the report said."

"I don't care what the report said. I know what happened. I didn't do everything I could."

"You were a hero."

"I was a coward. I let him crawl out there alone. If I had listened to him earlier . . ." John put his hands to his head, trying to put a finger in the dike of memories. He looked at June Bug. "You asked me once why I sweat at night. Why I sometimes wake up yelling. This is why. Her son. And the other guys who were with me. It was my fault."

"You didn't pick the mission, John. You followed orders. You were being a good soldier."

"A good leader anticipates. A good leader doesn't get in a situation like that. In a place where they had no chance."

"You survived," June Bug said.

John nodded and pressed his lips together. "That's part of my problem."

"A good leader lays down his life for his friends," the old woman said. "That's what you did."

"No. Your son did that. And his sacrifice haunts me. I should have listened to him."

Silence in the room. Just an old clock ticking on the mantel. The sun was gone now with just a silhouette of the hills in the gloaming. The three sat like statues waiting for someone to bring them to life.

Finally June Bug slipped from the couch onto the floor beside him. "I don't think it was your fault. I think you're being too hard on yourself."

"She's got that right," Mrs. Linderman said. "You did everything you could. There's not one ounce of you that wanted to see your friends hurt. And if they could be here right now, not one of them would ever hold it against you."

John looked up at her, his eyes stinging.

She continued. "Now you have to do one more thing. Maybe the hardest thing. Let it go so it can let go of you. You know Calvin wouldn't want you to feel this way. He'd want you to go on living. He'd want you to use your life for good."

"I've tried. The only thing that's kept me going this whole time . . ." He glanced at June Bug. "She's the best this world has to offer."

"Well, I don't doubt that," Mrs. Linderman said. She looked at the girl, who sat with a blank expression. "How did you two meet?"

John held up a hand. "Not yet."

"I thought he was my dad," June Bug said. "I always have."

"Well, if he took good care of you, he was. Has he been a good father to you?"

June Bug nodded slowly. "We've been lots of places together. He's taught me a lot about history and what side of a tree moss grows on and stuff like that."

John stood and ran a hand through his hair, unable to cross into uncharted waters before leaving these. "How did you know it would work?" he said to the old woman. "How did you know giving me the money would keep me from . . . hurting myself?"

Mrs. Linderman sat back. "To be honest, I didn't. I knew you didn't want to live. That what happened weighed on you. But I prayed God would love you through it. That he would break through the darkness. And that you'd come to your senses." She paused, the wrinkles of her face lessening as she looked at him. "Actually, if you want to know the truth, my prayer wasn't about you at all."

"What do you mean?"

"We need men like you. As much as our country doesn't want to admit it, we need men who aren't afraid to stand up to evil. We need men who will answer their country's call without flinching. Every time something comes up in the world that everybody else is afraid to handle or simply can't, American men do. We need good men, and that's what you are. So when I thought about what the pain was doing to you, I just flipped things around. I asked God to bring someone into your life who would need you. Someone who would teach you what real love is all about. I figured it would be some old stray dog or cat or maybe a woman. But he did something more wonderful, didn't he?" She looked at June Bug. "Where's your mama, honey?"

June Bug hesitated. "I'm not sure."

The old woman looked back at John.

"It's complicated," John said.

She nodded. "Life generally is. I don't want to overstep my bounds, but I think my prayer was answered. And the important thing is, you came back. Just you sitting here in my room is an answer to my prayers and shows God is still on his throne. And every day since then, I've been asking God to give you a peace and a rest. You deserve that, son."

"Wait," June Bug said. "What about the police and the box? I don't understand."

John sat with his back against the stone fireplace. "I had a little money left after I was discharged. I used it to come out here and keep a promise. My plan was to bring her the things Calvin had given me. Then I was just going to go off and . . . not be here anymore."

"And she gave you a box?"

"No, she told me I needed to stay with her. She lived in that little house by the farm. She gave me Calvin's room and sometime between dinner and bedtime she got out this gray box and while I was watching, she put money and an envelope in there. Later that night I took it."

"You stole it?" June Bug said, wide-eyed.

He nodded. "I took off after she went to sleep. I was in a bar, with that box on the table, taking money out and buying drinks, when an officer noticed me. He came over, asked if he could look inside. He takes some paper out and says, 'I know Mrs. Linderman.' That's when he gets out his gun and puts the cuffs on me."

"What happened then?" June Bug said.

"The officer drove me over there and knocked on the door. It took her a while to get there."

"I was just playacting," Mrs. Linderman said. "I knew as soon as I saw the cruiser in the driveway what was up."

"She opened the door, saw me in the cuffs, and just about chewed that officer down to a sapling."

Mrs. Linderman laughed. "I threw into him like nobody's business."

"The officer thought she was going to thank him for catching a crook, and she nearly slapped him. 'Get those cuffs off him. Do you realize this is a war hero? You don't even deserve to be standing beside this man.' That kind of stuff."

June Bug laughed at John's imitation of Mrs. Linderman.

"Then she says, 'John, I'm glad you came back. I forgot to endorse those certificates. There's no way you can liquidate them without my signature.' You could have knocked me down just by breathing on me. I thought for sure she was . . ." The emotion overcame him and he put his head down.

Mrs. Linderman picked up the story. "The officer couldn't believe it either. You should have seem him fumbling with the keys to those cuffs. Just as if I'd planned the whole thing, I took the box and got that envelope with the papers out and started signing. And when I looked up and saw the officer, I yelled at him to get out of there unless he wanted a lawsuit for unlawful arrest."

June Bug laughed again.

John shook his head. "I'll never forget what you did next."

"Wasn't anything special."

"It saved my life."

"What happened?" June Bug said. "What did you do?"

John stood and walked to the window, waiting for her answer. When it didn't come, he turned and crossed his arms. "After the officer was gone, she closed the box and gave it to me. I said I couldn't take it and she said, 'You're not taking this. It's a gift.' She said there was enough to make a new start."

The old woman chuckled. "I had no idea how right I was."

"She said she was buying something valuable with that box. My soul."

June Bug scrunched her face. "How do you buy somebody's soul?"

"What I meant was," Mrs. Linderman said, "that he was a valuable creation of God. And that he shouldn't throw away that gift. I told him he needed to take that gift and go make a difference."

"What did you say?" June Bug said.

"I didn't say anything, as I remember it. I just took it and left. Wandered back up the road and sat in a field and thought about my life.

"The next morning I went into town. I'd counted the money in there and figured I could buy a nice car, but then I saw an RV and it made sense. I could live there and head back home."

"She gave you enough money to buy our RV?"

"And more," John said. "But that still doesn't explain how you can afford to live here."

"You didn't cash those stock certificates, did you?"

"What's a stock certificate?" June Bug said.

"It's something a company gives you that makes you part of that company. If you own a share, you have a say in what that company does and a part of their profits or loss."

John searched his memory. "Walmart," he said. "You worked at Walmart, didn't you?"

Mrs. Linderman smiled. "Worked at Sam's first store. And over the years I received stock in the company."

"Who's Sam?"

"Sam Walton, the man who started Walmart. I still remember him driving around in that old truck. I moved around a few times to different stores, but I worked there for nearly thirty years. At about the time I was to retire, my husband passed and I got worried whether his life insurance and my Social Security would be enough.

"I had some family members over for a barbecue—and one of my nephews is a financial whiz. I cornered him and asked him what I should do. He asked if I had any investments. I told him about the stocks I'd kept and he went through them. I'll never forget the look on his face when he came outside. He said, 'You don't have a money worry in the world.' Turned out those stocks were worth a few million dollars. I nearly dropped my dentures. I don't care what anybody says; old Sam knew how to take care of his workers."

John's mouth hung open. "But you gave them to me."

"No, I kept all the memories and insurance papers. I just put in some cash and signed over a few certificates. What did you do with them?"

"I left them in the envelope in that box. I'd never seen a stock certificate before and figured it might be worth a few hundred dollars at most. But with my state of mind, I wasn't about to go to some stockbroker."

"Where are they now?"

"Dogwood."

"And you didn't cash them?"

John shook his head.

Mrs. Linderman's gaze wandered from his face to June Bug's. "There's a story all over the news. A little girl in West Virginia that went missing years ago. Along about that time . . ."

"I've seen a little about it," he said.

"John? Is this her?"

He looked at the floor. "Can we turn on your TV and see what they're saying?"

She picked up the clicker with a gnarled hand and gave it to him. He clicked the Power button and found a news channel.

15

It felt good being in Mrs. Linderman's house, kind of like what I'd pictured having a grandmother would be like except without all the fancy furniture and the round-the-clock help. I imagined having cookies and lemonade and laughing and hearing stories about riding in a covered wagon. I also thought a grandmother would give you stuff, like earrings or a doll or maybe a new outfit she saw at Target and just couldn't pass up.

But with all the good feelings, I still felt nervous. I now knew my dad wasn't my real dad, and that brought up a bunch of questions. I always thought the biggest one in my life was who my mama was and what was she like and what did I get from her like a nose or my eyes or some disease. But it only takes something like a visit to an old woman's house to let you know there are other questions floating around out there like butterflies and that it's hard to catch the answers. There's not a net big enough for all my questions.

When my dad clicked around to the news station, he landed on one with a lady wearing a pretty scarf tied around her neck, and I thought it might be the wrong time of year for that but what do I know. She looked like she had on all the makeup in the world and it made her face look like some doll in a store window, smooth as porcelain and shiny, and I doubted that was the way she looked when she got up in the morning. She said something about the "top story" being about a missing child case in West Virginia. We'd seen the story at the farmhouse, but it was hard for me to concentrate there. I moved up real close to hear the reporter's voice. Seemed to me like the last place on earth he wanted to be was Dogwood, West Virginia. He had perfect hair and a nice face except for these beady eyes that seemed suspicious of everybody.

They showed a picture of me as a kid and then the age-progression one and said my mother was a lady named Dana Edwards. That was a new piece of information. Then they showed an older lady who was walking from her car into a house and shielding her eyes from the lights. The reporter said she was the grandmother.

"I've told them all along she was alive," the woman yelled. She looked a little bit angry. "And now they've let the man who took her go!"

I think the news people like it when people scream or cry or throw something. I don't get to watch much, but every time I've seen the news, somebody is pitching a fit about something. Gas prices or an election or some issue that has their veins sticking out on their necks. My dad, even though he's not my real dad, always says that what gets people riled up is what makes the news. I wonder if they ever covered the fight he had in the war and his friend who died. That seemed to get him riled up.

The reporter's voice came in over a picture of a crumpled-looking man with a scary face and hair to match. I got the creepers all over when I saw him.

"This is Graham William Walker, a suspect in the disappearance of the girl. He was being questioned at this police station when he escaped authorities."

Then they switched to an older guy in a uniform standing outside the station, and there seemed like there were about a million microphones shoved in his face. He had his hat pulled down so you could just barely see his eyes. The man looked a little uncomfortable to me.

"The suspect is now at large," he said, and the way he talked made me feel warm all over, like I was listening to somebody from home, which I guess I was. "He exited through a side window while the interrogation was in process."

"Was he under arrest?" the reporter said, and there were about a hundred other voices asking the same thing.

"No, we were just questioning him when we had a situation in the office and he was left unattended. . . ."

He said some other stuff, but that's when it all became real to me. It's one thing to see your picture on the wall and wonder where in the world you came from, and it's an entirely different matter to watch TV and see yourself.

"Did he give you any information, Sheriff?" the reporter yelled. "Do you believe he was involved in the girl's disappearance?"

The sheriff stared at the reporter and said, "I can't comment on the ongoing investigation."

The reporter with the beady eyes wrapped things up, though I wanted him to talk with the grandmother or the woman he said was my mother, but there's probably a time limit. The woman with the makeup came on and shook her head, like she couldn't believe what she was hearing, and then she said something about the economy and there was an arrow behind her that went down and I knew my story was over.

When I turned around, I realized how quiet it was behind me, and I found my dad kneeling beside Mrs. Linderman. The woman had her hand over her mouth, and he was whispering to her. When I jumped up, she jerked back like I was a ghost, and there were tears in her eyes. She looked at me with the saddest face I've ever seen on a human being, and she reached out a hand that looked more wrinkly than a raisin. "You come here, dear."

She took my hand and had me sit with her in the chair, which wasn't hard because she didn't take up much room. She hugged me tight and kissed my cheek. "The Lord used you, June Bug. Just as sure as we're sitting here he did."

I looked at her, but I didn't really know what to say.

"Do you understand what's happening? what's going on back in that place?"

"I think so."

Dad just knelt there with his head turned and his thumb to his mouth, like he was chewing on it.

"Tell me what you know," she said.

"That he's not my real dad. That I come from a place in West Virginia and that my mom and maybe my dad are back there."

Her eyes lit up, like she didn't expect what she was hearing. "Anything else?"

"They think that guy with the weird face took me."

She nodded and hugged me tighter. Dad sat with his back to the chair, staring out the window. It was quiet then, except for the chatter of the news and then a commercial about hair loss and how some men are using a new process to restore themselves to their natural condition.

"We have to go back," he said. "I have to take you back there."

"Really?" I said, sitting up.

Mrs. Linderman winced like I had broken her hip bone and I realized I had my elbow in her side and I said I was sorry.

"We'll head back there first thing in the morning."

I guess my face showed something because Mrs. Linderman smiled and hugged me again. "Is that what you want to do? Go back and find your family?"

I nodded. "More than anything." And then I saw the look on Dad's face. "Except I can still stay with you, right? Your family is there, right?"

He just stared at me like he was looking for some answers, and the cold shivers came over me and I tried to push them down.

"We better go," he said.

The woman grabbed her purse from her wheelchair and dug inside. She pulled out some wadded-up bills and shoved them into his hand. He tried to give them back, but she scolded him like a little boy. "You take that. This is to help you both."

"I can't take any more of your money," he said.

"I've got a lot more where that came from. Now get on out of here." She grabbed his hand and looked at him like he was her own son. "You're a good man, John. I'm proud to know you." Then she turned to me. "You take good care of him, you hear?"

I nodded and hugged her as tight as I dared. Then I took my dad's hand and we walked out.

We got in the RV and drove to the interstate. When we passed a Wendy's, he stopped and got me a Frosty with some of that lady's money. He drove with me sitting in the passenger seat and the sound of the road rushing up to meet us. I was glad I didn't have to stay hidden anymore and that we could be together, even though he wasn't saying anything. I had a million questions, but I figured now wasn't the time to ask them.

"You getting tired?" he said when I yawned real big.

"No, I'm fine."

"Why don't you go on up and crawl into bed?"

"How far are we going?" I said.

"Till I get sleepy. We won't need gas for a while."

"You're not tired?"

"Nope. Driving helps me think."

"Think about what?" I said.

"What to do next."

"And what're you going to do?"

"That's why I need to keep driving and not talk, chatterbug."

I giggled. He called me that when I asked too many questions. I unbuckled and crawled behind him.

Dad patted me on the back as I passed him. "You have some sweet dreams. I'll see you when you wake up."

We have this thing about reaching out and touching fingers. He'll do it at night when I'm going to sleep, and if I get scared and he's in his bed, he'll just reach out a hand. It's kind of dumb, I know, but it's kind of comforting too. Just reaching out to someone you love.

I turned and hugged him, then kissed him on the cheek, and there was something sad to his face that I wished I could change.

"You don't think it was your fault about her son, do you?" I said. "It wasn't your fault that he got killed. It was the bad people who shot him."

He nodded. "I know that in my head. It's just that some things stick in there and you can't get them out."

"Do you wish you could get me out of your head?"

Dad looked up from the road and locked eyes with me and he didn't need to say a thing. But I'm glad he did. "I have a lot of regrets but you are not one of them. You're the best thing in my life, June Bug. And if I had it to do over a thousand times, I'd take you with me every one of them."

I hugged his neck again and then jumped in my bed and tried to sweep away some of the crumbs that I'd left up there. Then I kicked off my shoes and snuggled into my sleeping bag. I didn't know much, but I did know somebody who loved me was down below. If you believe that, even if you have questions, you're in a pretty good place.

It wasn't long until my eyes were closed and I fell into a deep sleep.

We were standing on a hill overlooking a valley, with craggy rocks all around. It was out west somewhere because there was nothing but tumbleweeds and rocks and a clump of trees in the distance. He was standing there with his hat pulled low, the way he always looks when he's outside.

Go on; take it.

I don't want to.

You have to figure it out sooner or later.

I don't want to.

I had a whine in my voice, which he says he doesn't like. Don't whine, he always says, and I try not to but sometimes it gets the best of me and I have to. And then I heard the sound, the little yip yap of a dog. I've probably asked him about a billion times if I could have a dog of my own because I know better than to ask him for a cat. There are dog types of people and cat types of people and he is not a cat type.

The pup, all furry and black, ran up to me with his tail wagging and his ears back and his eyes soft and warm. I just wanted to hug him to death. He sniffed around my legs and licked my hand and then was off down the hill. I followed him with my eyes blurry, just giggling at how funny he looked and how happy I was.

You'll have to learn how to shoot one of these someday, he said. Might as well be now.

Guns are for killing and I hate them. I'll never shoot a gun.

He got that far-off look in his eyes he gets when he talks about leaving for the winter. I've wondered why he does this, but I guess deep down I don't care because it's so much fun to go places with him.

He's staring off and looking at nothing, and then he says, Guns are not just for killing. They're for protecting too.

I could see his point, but I said I still wasn't ever going to shoot one.

He whistled into the wind, and the dog just kept running a trail back and forth toward a sandy patch of grass. The clump of trees was to the right along with some taller grass that grew straight up and only bent for the wind. The pup was having a hard time deciding which trail to sniff, and it looked so funny I thought it should be a movie.

Life is a series of choices, June Bug. Sometimes you have to choose what's good and then what's best. What's good may be saying you'll never shoot a gun. But what's best is knowing how to shoot one in case you have to.

I don't know a thing about what you're saying. I don't want to shoot it.

He looked off again, and I'd never seen the steely look. Take the gun, June Bug. He said it almost in a whisper, and it made me shiver. Now.

I rolled my eyes and took it. It was heavy and I didn't see how I was ever going to even hold the thing up, let alone shoot it. Then the gun came up and I was looking at the little nub at the end of the barrel, wondering what to do.

He put his hands under mine to help me. You line up the back and the front sight square with what you're aiming at. Now you should never point at anything you're not ready to shoot.

I let go because when my eyes were focused in the distance, I saw he was pointing right at the dog in the clearing. Take the gun back.

No. Hold it up now.

I grabbed it, but my arms were shaking and the tears were starting to come. Don't make me shoot him, please.

Stop whining and listen.

Please.

Stop it.

He pushed the gun to the right a little, pointing to the tall grass by the trees. I caught sight of something furry, something crouching in the grass, inching forward. Then two eyes and a long snout and pointed ears.

You see that?

What is it?

Doesn't matter. It's hungry and it sees a hot meal.

Take it back. You shoot it.

No, aim and pull the trigger.

Please, I don't want to.

You want to see that little pup in the jaws of that coyote?

No, but you shoot.

He let go of the gun and the barrel dipped.

My heart raced as I looked at the pup waddling toward the grass, hopping like it was playing at a park. He's headed right for it!

Then aim and shoot.

What if I hit the pup?

Aim and shoot, June Bug.

I pulled the gun up and couldn't see the coyote in the grass anymore. Then his strong hands were underneath mine and he was behind me, his breath on my shoulder, his face down near mine. I saw a flash of fur as the animal sprang from the grass. His finger squeezed mine on the trigger, and then again, and there were two cracking sounds.

Dirt kicked up in front of the coyote, and he stopped dead in his tracks and glanced at us. And then he fell, twitching for a moment before lying still. Just a piece of fur in the grass. The little pup barked at it as he ran toward us, looking back, stopping, and barking some more.

You killed him, I said. I just wanted to scare him away.

Some things you have to kill. Some things you don't mess with or they'll kill you.

The pup ran back to us, his tongue hanging out, scrambling over the big rocks. He crawled into my lap and I hugged him close. Daddy got up and walked back to the RV and I followed him with the pup in my arms, the little thing squirming and licking and kicking.

Just as I was about to put him down, I looked back at the valley and saw the coyote. His head was up and he was grinning, if you can believe that, and saying something. The whispers drifted over the barren land, carried by the wind, and I strained to hear them but I couldn't. And then he laid his head back down in the grass and never moved again as far as I know.

16

Sheriff Hadley Preston had just arrived home to fried chicken, biscuits, and coleslaw when his cell phone buzzed. He hated carrying the thing and most of the time wanted to roll down the window and toss it out. As far as he was concerned, cell phones had been invented by wives to keep track of their men.

"Just let it go," his wife, Macel, said. Her eyes were pinpoints in the kitchen's bright light. The skin around her eyes was wrinkled and cracked with age. "You've been working too hard. Let it go and eat something."

Macel Preston was a good woman. Stocky and short with a few streaks of black hair still showing through the gray, a strong and jutting chin. She looked built for some athletic pursuit, and their life together had seemed to him a marathon of trouble. Trouble with their daughter, trouble with the job, trouble with the family as their parents grew older. She had suggested they move his parents in with them when their health had failed. Shortly after they were gone, her mother had been diagnosed with Alzheimer's and she moved in for the last six years of her life.

When asked how they were able to stay together so long, Preston gave his wife the credit. "She's a patient and forgiving woman," he would say, and that was the truth. Forgiving to a fault. He had heard secondhand how she had stood in the midst of the little church on Wednesday nights and asked the congregation to pray for his salvation.

But she was not the goody-two-shoes type to go around with her nose in the air thinking she was better than everybody else and you had to believe like her or you'd burn forever. It was more of a quiet and gentleness that spoke so loud he could hardly stand it at times. It's one thing to preach, and it's another to know every jot and tittle of the Word and be able to argue a Jehovah's Witness under the table and still love people you don't agree with.

Preston had watched her care for a son of one of her church friends who'd gotten mixed up in an alternative lifestyle. The mother had him on the prayer chain and detailed his wayward life, the gay bars and multiple lovers, until he moved home, his body ravaged by disease. He needed round-the-clock care toward the end, and though the people at her church abhorred that lifestyle, Macel had gone to the house every day for months and cared for him like he was her own. She talked to him about God's love and forgiveness and the open arms of Jesus until the boy's death. At the funeral it was hard to tell which one was the mother because Macel's tears flowed freely. It was hard to argue with a faith like that. Hard, but not impossible because Preston did every chance he got.

He opened his shirt pocket and pulled the silver vibrating thing out and checked the screen. He expected it to be Mike, but a different number popped up. "Preston."

Nothing on the other end. Just noise of a TV in the background.

"Hello?"

A crackling voice began, wheezing and rattling with emphysema. His deputy had talked with Walker's mother, who had no more information. He couldn't imagine who this was.

"I know where that boy is. The one you're looking for."

"How'd you get this number?"

"Your deputy. What's that got to do with it?"

Preston shook his head. "All right. Where is he?"

"I heard a car rumble past here last night."

"Where is 'here'?"

He listened a few moments, first reaching for a pen, then closing his eyes and following the directions in his head. He knew exactly where the place was. He'd been there in his childhood.

"You know where I'm talking about?" the rattling voice said.

"Yeah, I got it."

"I can't give you an address because there ain't one."

"Thank you."

"You giving any kind of reward if you find him?" The caller pronounced the word *reeward* like Preston had heard it all his life.

"Yeah, your *ree*ward is knowing you did the right thing telling me where that scumbag is."

He flipped the phone shut and pushed back from the table, looking at the chicken. Macel had made it flakier than the Colonel and the slaw was homemade, with just the right amount of mayonnaise so that it didn't run all over the plate and soak into the biscuits.

"You don't have to go," she said. "You can at least stay and eat a piece of chicken. Or have Mike look into it."

"If I start in, I won't be able to stop. Your chicken does things to a man he can't explain."

Macel smiled as he stood and walked around the table. She sat there staring at her plate.

He put a hand on her shoulder. "Can you keep it warm for me?"

"I'll put the slaw in the oven."

He chuckled and rubbed her back. When she got peeved at him, her humor turned sarcastic—the one chink in her spiritual armor. "I'll be back in a bit. You wait up."

She didn't move for a moment, but when he lingered behind her, she turned, her eyes saggy and pained. "I've been thinking about that little girl," she said. "You think this guy did something to her?"

"I'm not sure what I think anymore. And I'm not sure it matters. The dead float to the surface eventually, and it's the same with the truth. That's all I'm looking to know."

"If he did have something to do with it, he'll be like a cornered rat. You won't be able to bring him out alive."

"Which is maybe why he ran. But he might have just been scared by the whole thing. Don't worry—"

"I am worried. You're not as young as you used to be."

"It usually happens that way when you have more than fifty birthdays."

"Hadley, I'm serious. You ought to call in backup to bring this fellow in. Then you can figure out what he did with her." She turned back to the table and fidgeted, looking like that old man in the picture on the wall with the loaf of bread and his hands outstretched and praying. "I don't want to lose you," she said in a little girl voice.

"You're not going to lose me. Now stop worrying. We've been through this a thousand times and it's never bothered you."

"I had a dream last night."

"I have to go."

"I was at your funeral. And everybody was saying what a good man you were."

"Well, there's good news." He bent down and kissed her forehead. "It's going to be all right. We'll bring him in and figure out what happened. Something's not fitting and I want to find out what it is."

"If you don't think he's guilty, why can't it wait?"

"I didn't say he's not guilty. I said things aren't adding up. He knows more than he's telling us. And he ran. You can't abide that."

"What if he has a gun? He may be guilty of something else you don't even know about."

"If he is, I'll find it out and deal with it. Now I have to—"

"I don't want to lose you to some no-account."

Preston reached for the door and opened it. "I thought you believed everybody has worth in God's eyes."

"They do, but that doesn't mean they have a right to kill my husband. They can have their worth behind bars."

He put his hat on and stepped onto the front porch. "Just keep the slaw warm, and I'll be back before the pie's done."

In the cruiser Preston watched her through the window as she spread her hand across the tablecloth, ridding it of wrinkles. When he backed out of the driveway, he could still see her raking the slaw from his plate and putting the chicken in the oven.

❀ ❀ ❀

Sheriff Preston met Mike at the parking lot of the Dairy Queen on Route 60. Mike climbed into the cruiser with a hundred questions, asking who it was who called and what they said and where they were going.

Preston scanned the parking lot and streets, ignoring the questions. "Any of those reporters follow you?"

"No, sir, I made sure."

"You talk to anybody?"

"No, sir, not even the wife."

He drove into the night without speaking, running the scenario through his head, windows open. Preston hated using the air conditioner. He made a few turns to make sure no one was following them, then headed east on Route 60 until they hit Dogwood, passing the old elementary school.

His family had lived here in his childhood, before moving west of Huntington. His father had brought him to the redbrick building on the left when he was little. His dad called it the Feed Store, though it said *Dogwood Farm Implement Company* on the front. It was a place with a thousand smells of freshly ground corn and molasses and sweet hay and new machinery. His father always let him get a bottle of pop from the refrigerator and a candy bar, and as they passed where the building used to stand, now replaced by a tiny strip mall with a place to have your nails done and a dry cleaners, he could almost taste the Zagnut bar and Mountain Dew, a sweet communion of the past.

The memories came back, flooding like a dam bursting above an unsuspecting town. The kindergartner who was killed at the elementary school crosswalk. The young girl who was with him when he broke away from her grasp. Another scene of flames and people standing around a house engulfed and the screams of a mother whose children were inside. And watching an old dog run down the side of a hill to chase a car, only to see the car slow and then go on. His own dog lying there in the road, lifeless, tongue lolling.

"You think he might be armed?" Mike said.

"I think he might be drunk, and if he has a gun, he'll probably shoot at anything. We're going to talk to him, not try and rush him. You got it?"

"Yes, sir."

They drove into the gathering darkness, their faces illumined by the dashboard light. When they passed a Country Kitchen, Mike shifted in his seat. "You ever eaten at that place? I had some of the best fried chicken in my life, and you can get as much fish or meat loaf or shrimp or whatever you want."

"Is that how you keep that youthful physique?" Preston said. The kid was nothing but skin and bones and probably had to dance around in the shower to get wet.

"I'll be honest, Sheriff. I've always been able to eat anything I wanted and as much as I wanted. My daddy said I had the metabolism of a tree squirrel."

"I suspect he was right."

"My wife, she can't eat a thing without having to think about it. Walks around looking at herself in the mirror, turning this way and that, wondering where that banana split's gonna show up."

"She's a pretty little thing," Preston said. "I hope you tell her that."

Mike furrowed his brow and sat back. "She knows I love her."

"How?" Preston slowed and turned onto a smaller road that led into the hills.

"I tell her she's pretty and all. She knows."

"Just a little advice. You think she knows what's going on in your head. But unless you tell her, she's always wondering."

"How'd you come by that?" Mike said.

"Just go home and ask her after this is over."

"Ask her what?"

Preston slowed and swerved left when he saw two deer heading for the road. Mike put up his hand, pointing his index finger at one as if pulling the trigger.

"Ask your wife if you could do anything to let her know you love her more. See what she says."

"You think I don't love her enough?"

"Didn't say that. That's not the question. Question is, does she know it? If a woman doesn't know she's loved, she's always asking the question."

Mike mulled it over a moment as they hit a dirt road and slowed. "So how do you do it? How do you tell your wife you love her?"

Preston turned off the headlights and pulled the car to the side of the road, turning the key. The moon was high overhead and peeking through the clouds, casting a white glow on the trees that seemed to hover over the road. "Didn't say I did. Just said I know she needs it."

Mike laughed and they sat there, the engine clicking as it cooled. Crickets and a million night sounds filled the air, and Preston heard the trickle of a creek nearby.

"If I'm right, the shack is on the right about a hundred yards. If you cross the creek and go up the ridge right here behind that big oak, you should be able to angle over and come out behind it."

"What are you going to do?"

"I'm going to head up the road and walk to the front door and raise a ruckus, like there are about five hundred of us. When he bolts out the back door, you'll be right there." Preston looked at him. "And that's what I want you to do, wait until he runs. You got it?"

"What if he starts shooting?"

"Then we got us another problem, don't we?"

"I suppose so. You want to maintain radio silence?"

Preston nodded. The kid always wanted to make it sound like they were on some military mission, but he could tell it was just nerves. "Yeah, turn your radio off. I'll watch for you. When you're in position, give a couple of blips on your flashlight."

I woke up to the sound of air brakes and a fluorescent shining through the skylight and knew we were at a gas station. There are some things you just know after living on the road, like when you're going over a bridge or when you'll be driving through the night. Plus, I smelled oil and gas.

The first thing I thought when I realized we were at a gas station was that I needed to tell my dad (even though I knew he wasn't my real dad) about the dream. I couldn't shake it out of my head, kind of like the time I got lice and we had to shave my hair off way down to the skin and wash everything in the RV and even toss out my old mattress. At the time we were living near a family that had set up next to us, and I'd go over there and play with the little girl whose name I can't remember. She had this pretty kitchen set with all these pots and pans, and we'd pretend we were cooking meals for our husbands. I took a nap over there with the girl shortly before I had to get my head shaved, and maybe that's why we moved on so fast.

There was a siren in the distance getting louder and louder, and then I could even see some red and blue flashing in the skylight before it turned onto the interstate and sped away and then I lost it in the night sounds and the talking and laughing of the truckers.

A gas station late at night has to be one of the loneliest places on the planet. You can get any kind of soda pop you want and all the cherry turnovers or slushies or hot dogs, but the people who work there have the saddest eyes and it always smells like smoke to me. I usually don't like going inside at that time of day because it feels creepy, but sometimes you just have to go to the bathroom and that's when my dad goes with me.

When I go to sleep, Dad likes to turn on the radio and drive into the night. One time this doctor lady who gives out advice to anybody who calls said that your parents aren't necessarily the people who gave birth to you. She said something like, "Anybody can be a sperm donor or give birth to a child, but it takes love to make you a mommy or daddy." I don't know what a sperm donor is, but I think she was saying it's the people who love and care for you who count the most. So maybe that's why I still want to call him my dad instead of something else.

I slid to the side of my bed and started to open the curtain, but just when I did, there was a noise—the door opening. I thought it had to be my dad, but instead there was a man and woman whispering.

"This is perfect," the guy said. "Got a big bed in the back."

"It's a dump," the woman said.

"It'll get us out of here."

I stayed real quiet, trying not to breathe or move. My dad made the curtain so I could have some privacy. It's only a piece of cloth, but every time I pull it I feel like I'm in my own little world. I had pulled the curtain before I went to sleep, but I could just barely see through the middle and look at the two as they stood there. The light from outside lit up the back of the RV so I saw their faces in the shadows. The guy was big with cutoff sleeves and he had tattoos on his arms, though I couldn't see what they were. He had a short haircut and tattered jeans. The backpack he had strung over his shoulder looked pretty heavy, and he put it down by the bathroom door with a thud and got something out.

The girl was scrawny-looking, like she had been the runt of the litter. I could see her cheekbones sticking out, and her arms were thin and tiny. She had hair that was as wild as a tangle of chickweed, and I wondered if she had ever heard of a hairbrush. Made me feel kind of sad for her because I thought she could be really pretty if she took a bath and maybe got a haircut.

She had this suitcase she was carrying, and it looked like it weighed as much as she did. They both were nervous about something. In fact, he pulled the blinds in the back and tried to cover all the windows.

"I think that's him," the girl whispered, pointing to the front of the RV.

"Get in the back," the guy said, and from the drawl and gruff sound of his voice and the way she scampered away, it seemed he was a mean guy used to having people do what he said.

The door opened and the RV dipped as my dad got in. The little buzzer sounded as he put the key in and he started it. There's a sound to a big engine like this that's the best thing in the world, I guess because I've heard it not be able to start.

The guy below hunkered down trying not to be seen. I wanted to shout out to Dad, but I was afraid that might not be the best thing for us. In the end it didn't matter because Dad noticed the fellow back there and the guy held up what was in his hand.

"Put it in drive and pull out of here and you won't get hurt," the fellow said.

We just sat there and I figured Dad was thinking about me. The girl walked up behind the big guy, and I guess I moved because she glanced up and pulled the curtain back.

"Lookee what we have here," she cooed.

"June Bug?" Dad said.

"I'm okay," I yelled.

The big fellow stood and I saw he had a gun. Then I heard another siren and it was closing fast.

"You don't get this thing on the road, it'll be the end of your daughter. Drive."

Dad shifted the RV into gear and moved forward, going around some of the big rigs parked at the truck stop.

"Just head toward the interstate and go west," the man said.

"June Bug, you come down here," my dad said.

"Nope," the guy said. He grabbed my arm and pulled me down so fast that I thought I was on some ride at Six Flags, and the next thing I knew we were all on the floor because Dad jerked the RV to one side.

The guy pointed the gun at me. "You try that again and this June Bug gets squashed, you understand?" He said it like he meant it, and there was a dull sound to his voice like he wouldn't care if he had to pull the trigger any more than somebody asked him if he wanted ketchup or mustard on his hamburger. His eyes were the meanest things I'd ever seen, and I've seen a lot of mean things. His tattoos ran from the back of his hand all the way up his arm to his neck. It was some snakelike thing, and right at the top it said *Angel of Death*.

"Ow, you're hurting me!" I looked at the scrawny girl, but she wasn't doing anything to help.

"I got no problem offing this girl," the guy said.

"Let her come up here beside me, and we'll take you wherever you want to go."

The guy spoke through clenched teeth. "You don't get it, do you?" He pointed the gun at Dad this time. "You either drive now or she's in the ditch."

I was able to sit up enough to see my dad's eyes in the rearview. He always said there was really no reason to have the mirror because you can't see out the back except for a sliver if the shades aren't pulled down. But at the moment I was glad it was there.

"You okay?" Dad said to me.

I nodded and tried to get up, but the guy pushed me back on the bench and this time the scrawny girl sat down beside me and put her arm around my shoulder.

"Drive," the mean guy said.

"But that's not the way we're headed," I said. "We just came from there."

The police car racing toward us turned onto the interstate. The woman leaned back, and it felt like she was trembling as it passed.

"It's all right," Dad said to me. He had a tone of voice when he was talking to me and another when he was talking to other people. "We'll take these two wherever they want to go, and then we'll be on our way."

The mean guy snickered, which I didn't think was very nice, but I guess you can't expect much from such people. Dad put the RV in gear and pulled out. We had to cross a bridge to get over the interstate, and I closed my eyes and started singing.

"Shut up," the guy said.

I stopped singing and started humming.

The woman pulled me closer. "What is it?"

"We're going over a bridge. I get scared, so I sing a song and it helps."

"That's the dumbest thing I ever heard," the guy mumbled.

"Why are you scared of bridges?" the woman said.

"I don't know. I'm afraid of falling in the water."

"There's no water down there," the guy said.

"Doesn't matter. I still have to sing." I felt my breath getting shorter and I started to pant, this big knot starting in my chest that made me feel like I couldn't breathe.

"You go ahead and sing then," the woman said.

And I did.

Another police car passed on the interstate below us and Dad turned left, finally getting off the bridge. We headed west, the way we had come, and I wondered if we'd ever make it to Dogwood.

That's when I noticed the funny smell. It wasn't just the cigarette smoke; it was like they hadn't had a bath in years. I thought maybe they were carrying something dead in that backpack. I wasn't about to ask. You might think that her putting an arm around me was a good thing, but when you can't breathe because of the panic and the smells, well, you can see I was in a bad position.

I pulled away and said, "I need to go back to bed."

"Stay right where you are," the mean guy said. He flicked the gun toward me like he was ordering a dog to stay in its kennel.

The guy opened the refrigerator, but there was nothing inside except some water bottles and cans of pork and beans and fruit cocktail. I told him the generator hadn't worked for a long time and he just grunted. He grabbed a bag of potato chips from inside one of the cupboards and munched on those.

"Where you two headed?" I said. I figured talking with them might be a good idea as long as I didn't ask the wrong question, but from the look on the man's face, that was what I had done.

"Shut your piehole."

I looked at the woman, and she looked down at me with eyes that had big red lines through the whites. "What's in the bag?" I whispered.

She frowned. "Nothing you need to know about." She put a finger to her lips. "Just be quiet."

They say there's a peace that passes all understanding, and that it's available to anybody who wants it. I believe in Jesus and I know he lives in my heart, but right then I didn't have any peace because I thought the guy would rather shoot us than look at us. Sometimes having Jesus in your heart makes you feel good all over, like you know there's somebody who loves you no matter what, but it was hard to focus on that.

"Watch your speed, Jimmie Johnson," the mean guy said to my dad. He smirked like he had said the funniest thing ever. "We don't want them pulling you over and me having to shoot the lot of you."

I was trying hard to think of something good, and I remembered when I'd first become a Christian. We were down in Florida at this RV park that wasn't far from a big church and the signs said Vacation Bible School. Some people came by handing out invitations. One man had this hat with mesh netting that hung down, like you see on an African safari. One of the older women oohed and aahed over the Little Mermaid dress I was wearing and said I should ask my mama if I could come. She didn't know I didn't have one, but I didn't let that bother me.

I showed my dad the invite and he wadded it up and was going to toss it, but then I started to bawling and he said, "We don't even know what kind of church this is."

I said, "I don't care what kind it is. I want to go. It starts tomorrow, and they said it doesn't cost anything."

The next morning he walked me there, and it seemed this wasn't something easy for him. We'd been in little country churches out in the boonies before, but this was a big church with big windows and a new parking lot. The lady at the front desk was dressed in a safari outfit too. That was the theme of the week, and they even brought in a real elephant one day which I couldn't hardly believe. Dad gave the lady my information and said we were staying at the campground.

Instead of being escorted out because we weren't as well off as everybody else, the lady made me this real nice name tag that said *June* on it, and she gave me a brand-new shirt with a giraffe on the front. I put it on over my other shirt because the air-conditioning was turned up so high it felt like they could have invited penguins for supper. She pinned the name tag on and told my dad where I needed to go, and then I was off in a river of kids to the south wing of the church.

My dad stopped at the big doors, and a lady took my hand and led me down the hallway. I looked back and waved, and when the class started I saw him through the window walking back to the campground, staring at the ground. I couldn't help but feel sorry for him because he had to spend the next three hours alone, and I couldn't imagine what he was going to do with himself.

But I didn't let that keep me from having fun because they taught us some songs and had us do motions with hands and feet. It was funny watching the grown-ups because you don't expect it. I still remember a couple of the songs, and if anybody asked I could sing them, but nobody does.

It was the end of the second day, after they'd gone through the stuff about God making all the animals and that Jesus was the one who created everything and actually came to earth and lived a perfect life so he could be punished for our sins. I didn't understand it at first because it didn't make sense that somebody who was perfect should have to die for somebody else who wasn't.

But the more I listened, the more something inside felt like it was being stirred up—like that natural peanut butter that has all the oily stuff on top and doesn't taste good until you mix it. My dad and I had read Bible stories at bedtime before, but this made it all real. Everybody had done bad things, and instead of turning his back on us and just blowing the whole planet up, God sent his Son to make a way back.

When I heard that, I was the first one standing with my hand raised, wanting to pray with one of the adults. It wasn't one of those crying things like on TV, where people come up and they're carrying their handkerchiefs and wiping tears. It was more like I knew this was what I needed to do and I wanted to.

That afternoon I told Dad what had happened as we were walking back home. I didn't know what he would say, but I was glad when he smiled and squeezed my hand. "That's great, June Bug. I'm proud of you."

Even if he isn't my real dad, it sure felt good to have him say that, and I don't think I'll ever forget either feeling—the one when I asked Jesus to come in and change me and the one when my dad smiled and told me I'd done a wonderful thing.

He came the last day when we performed and every dad there had a video camera except mine. He sat in the back row and watched. Some of the older kids had speaking parts and the leaders tried to corral us as best they could, like we were some wild animals—which, in truth, there were a few of the boys who should have been taken to a zoo and put in a cage, if you ask me. They were just as wild as any jungle animal, but I guess that proves what the teacher was saying, that we're all sinners and need somebody to forgive us.

That was the extent of my church education, except for the occasional visit and late-night stories Dad told me about guys in the Old Testament who knew how to use knives and swords. I don't know where he came by that information. Maybe they talked about "Ehud, the left-handed Benjamite" in the military or something, but his eyes lit up when he talked about it.

That's what I was thinking about when the man with the gun got the woman alone and whispered to her at the back of the RV. I caught Dad's eyes in the rearview, and he seemed to be telling me something, motioning with his arm, but I couldn't figure it out. The mean guy saw and he grabbed me and flung me onto the bed. I cried because he hurt my arm, and when I hit the mattress, all the air came out of me.

The mean guy looked out the window at a blue sign. "There's a rest area in ten miles," he yelled. He pointed the gun at Dad. "Pull in there and I'll tell you what to do."

18

Sheriff Hadley Preston measured his steps on the dirt road, taking in the sounds of crickets and watching fireflies ascend. His eyes adjusted to the moonlight and shadows of tree branches.

There was movement along the ditch as an animal crept along. An opossum lumbered across the road, fat and sated on some carrion, its long tail dragging. He always had a mixture of revulsion and respect for the bottom-feeder. Like an above-pond turtle, eating anything dead it could sink its sharp teeth into. Preston nearly picked up a stick and threw it, if only to see it roll on its back and snarl its mouth into a death pose. It protected itself by making predators think it was already dead, kind of like most of Congress, he thought. But he thought better of making noise.

With all of its ugliness and impurity, there was something noble and likable about an animal that would do whatever it needed to protect its young and provide for them. The possum was just trying to get by, and there was honor in that.

Preston listened to Mike move from the cruiser and across the creek. The kid had made a loud splash and cursed, and Preston rolled his eyes and couldn't help but smile. Mike made his way back into the hillside with relative ease and little noise, made easier by the presence of life springing forth in the early summer heat. The ground was wet and pliable now, not stiff and crackly like in the fall when things died and fell and became noisy underfoot.

A mosquito sucked blood from Preston's neck and he swatted

at it as a few deerflies tried to get in on the action. A swarm of gnats surrounded him like a cloud. He waved his hat like a horse swishes its tail. He figured there was some stagnant water nearby, and he caught a whiff of something rotting. He picked up the pace, waving his hat and spitting out a gnat that had flown in his mouth. The swarm finally lessened, though a deerfly did find the vulnerable spot on his neck. Life is harsh and unforgiving in the woods, and when something dies, something else lives, and the rest pay the price.

Preston spotted the cabin, if you could call it that, on a little rise away from the road. Just four walls and a small window in front and a pipe sticking out of the roof. Two doors, one in front and one in back. There were bigger gaps in the rotting wood around the cabin than he remembered, and the window had only a few shards of glass left. Ancient shingles on one side of the roof looked like they were moving in the moonlight.

Preston had been here with his father and mother, searching for her brother, an Army veteran from the Korean conflict. The man had gotten lost in the bottle so many times his body had wasted to next to nothing. There was a pattern to his life—he'd straighten out, spend some time at the VA hospital in Huntington, and then resume his concrete work. He was one of the best concrete flatwork finishers in the county. He'd even show up at church a few times, thanking people for their prayers and saying he hoped he would never find himself in that position again. But he'd eventually get mixed up with the wrong people, and one day he'd just be gone, disappearing into the shell. Preston's mother would start looking, asking where he might be, and it led her here one winter, on a tip from one of his drinking buddies.

Preston's father had gotten out of the car and stood there, his breath floating in the chill wind, staring at the countryside and the little building. "Wait here," he had said, and Preston had never seen the lines of worry on the man's face like that.

His mother and father walked up the hill together over the frozen ground, peeking in the window and cupping their hands to see inside. His mother scraped at the frost. Then they opened the door and went into the darkened shack, and Preston wondered what they had found inside. Just his imagination kicking in to the horror. Half of the fear of life is not knowing something that you wished you knew, and the other half is knowing it.

Preston took a breath and let it out, standing there as a grown-up, watching the two in his memory, carrying the sack of bones that was his uncle down to the car, his mother crying and struggling over uneven ground, his uncle trying to put a foot out every now and then, and his father carrying most of the weight with one arm, like a sack of grain that had a hole in the bottom and was spilling out. Preston had held the car door, but his uncle stopped short and tilted his head and retched until he finally tossed the contents of his stomach on the ground. A mixture of brown and red splattered Preston's shoes. The man's face was like a ghost's when he stood.

"Sorry about that, Hadley," his uncle said as if just noticing him. "How you doin', boy?"

"I'm okay."

And then they all got in and drove out of the hollow, his uncle rolling down the window and trying to get his mouth positioned outside. His clothes stained, his beard and stubble growing around chapped lips, his skin sallow and shrunken, drawn so that there was nothing but skin on bone. His eyes had scared Preston the most. It almost looked like he was another person now, and in truth, he was.

His father had Preston get out at the end of their road—it was about a mile walk to the house from there—and he told him to head home and stay there until they got back. That was okay with Preston. The last place he wanted to be was the VA hospital with all the sick people and the crying and the smells. To this day Preston had a hard time with any hospital, and he was pretty sure it had started with one of those trips.

Over the years, the cabin had been vandalized by young people until the property owner boarded up the entrances and put Posted signs around it. The occasional hunter now occupied it, but few would ever stay overnight. There was a sickly, moldy smell about the place, as if water had soaked the wood so much that it was beyond repair. As Preston stood there in the moonlight, he could feel the familiar ache of the spot, like a pinpoint on a map of the heart that brought back hurt just by looking at it.

Something moved to the right up the hill. Preston spotted Mike snaking along the ridge behind the cabin. The kid was moving quickly with his revolver out and his hands spread to catch himself if he fell. A wall of dirt stood behind the cabin, and Preston was surprised with all the slippage of the land over the years that it hadn't already caved in.

A little farther was a small car pulled off to the side. Someone had made a feeble attempt to hide it with stray branches and an uprooted bush or two. From the back it looked like a Toyota. He clicked on his flashlight and saw the reflection of West Virginia plates.

As soon as Mike was behind the cabin and out of sight, Preston saw two quick bursts from the flashlight in the trees overhead. He signaled the same and moved up the hill. There was no light inside the cabin and no movement that he could tell, other than the ghostly moonglow on the shingles.

As he stepped onto the front porch, a raccoon darted out and streaked past him. Preston nearly fell backward, but he caught a sapling and regained his balance. He listened for a moment and heard no movement inside. Maybe this whole thing was a ruse. Maybe it wasn't Gray's car up the road. But when he set foot on the porch and the first board squeaked like some haunted house's front door, Preston heard a click inside that sounded like a shotgun.

"Gray, it's Sheriff Preston. I want to talk to you." His voice sounded strained, even to himself, as his words echoed through the hills.

No response.

He released the snap over his holster and pulled out the gun, then took a step to his left, away from the door. He didn't think the boy had the nerve to actually open fire on anyone but himself. But if he had enough liquor in him and was scared of going to jail, who knew what could happen.

"Nobody has to get hurt here, Gray. Come out and let's talk."

Preston hadn't trained at hostage negotiation or talking someone down from a ledge, but he knew enough that calm and reassuring words could go a long way. He had to be careful not to use Walker's name like a used car salesman. He'd done that one too many times with a young fellow in Hurricane he'd found holed up in his high school chemistry room. It was one of those images stuck in his mind he couldn't shake. The kid holding a handgun to his chin, scared as a trapped mouse.

"I'm done talking, Sheriff," Gray said, his voice muffled and groggy, as if he'd just come out of hibernation. "You done made up your mind about me."

"That's not true. I haven't made up my mind about anything. I don't know what went on that night. I'm trying to get answers. Now come out and we'll just talk."

"Right. The lawman always *just wants to talk*." He said it in a mocking tone, like something he'd seen on a sitcom that deserved a laugh track. "And pretty soon I'm strung up in some tree. I'm convicted already, and you know it."

"Nobody's going to string you—"

Gray cursed loudly, interrupting him. It sounded like he was pacing. "You judged me from the minute you saw me. And what did you find on the computer?"

"Just some pictures, and you already explained that your friend was the one who downloaded them. Now come out and let me hear your side of that night."

"Fine. Here's what I got to say: I didn't do nothing to that little girl."

"And I believe you," Preston said.

Gray muttered something Preston couldn't hear, and the boards kept creaking inside.

"That might surprise you, but I've had a sense about this whole thing that you're not the one we're after."

"Then you know you're barking up the wrong tree."

"But how do I know? You ran off, which makes people think you're guilty. So come on back with us and we'll get this settled."

"I come back with you and I'll wind up in jail the rest of my life."

"How can that happen if you didn't do anything?"

"Jails are full of innocent people; you know that. They've killed a few who they found out didn't commit the crime."

Preston knew the more he could drag words out of Gray, the better chance they had of bringing him in. "You got me there, and that's why I want to talk. I don't want to hunt the wrong person. I believe you didn't have anything to do with this, but I also think you know more. So come on out and we'll discuss it man-to-man."

"There's not going to be any man-to-man stuff. Do you know what they'll do to a guy like me in prison?"

Preston's mind was flying with thoughts about what he meant by "a guy like me."

"Graham, don't get ahead of yourself. Nobody gets sent to prison for just talking about some old case. Now I'm getting eat up by gnats out here, and the deerflies are starting to form a frontal assault. Come out and I promise you'll get a fair shake."

"You're just ticked off because I got away. Made you look bad."

Preston laughed. "I'll admit I'm not too happy about it. You got those newshounds laughing their butts off and calling me Barney Fife. But I'll take all that if we get to the bottom of this."

There was silence, then a clink of glass inside. It sounded like Gray was taking one more drink. He hadn't planned a long conversation—didn't think the boy was capable. Preston hoped Mike would stay put and not do anything stupid.

"That should show you how guilty I think you are," Preston said. "If I thought you were the one, I'd have put an armed guard on you. But I was just asking questions."

Something banged inside, a bottle on a table, a gun on the floor—he couldn't tell. This was the point where Preston could set the hook if he played it right. It was also the point where the whole thing could fall apart.

"Here's how I figure it," Preston began again. "You come with me, and you can sleep it off. Then in the morning I'll head over to the Village Inn and get some sausage and biscuits and you can tell me what you know. Simple as that. How's that sound?"

"I'm not hungry," Gray said, his voice a little softer now.

Preston inched closer to the door, trying not to make the boards creak. "If we don't see any connection with you and the girl, you're free. Now I'm shooting straight."

Gray's voice came as a whine. "You don't know. You just don't know."

"There's nothing you've done that can't be worked out."

"It don't matter what I have or haven't done; you've already decided I'm guilty."

"I have not! Gray, I haven't decided anything." Preston was right next to the door, his nose almost against the wood. "And believe it or not, I'm here to help. Your thinking is off. Your head is clouded and that's understandable. So just come on out and—"

Something cracked loudly, like wood splintering, and then there was an explosion. Someone yelled—it sounded like Mike— and something banged against the floor. Preston kicked at the door, but the thing was sturdier than it looked and he fell backward. He got up and kicked again, and the door crackled and fell in. He crouched there in the doorway waiting for another blast, but all he heard were footsteps out the back. Then the heavy panting of Mike on the floor.

"He ran out, Sheriff," Mike said, gasping.

It was dark in the room, and Preston could only make out the silhouette of his deputy. The back door teetered, held on by one hinge.

"I'm sorry. I tried to surprise him."

Preston clicked on the flashlight expecting to see a crimson stream somewhere on the boy's body. Instead, he smelled a sickly aroma of a man who had lost control. Mike sat against a wall, covering his face. "You okay?"

Mike nodded.

"Stay there. I'll call for an ambulance."

"I don't need an ambulance. Go after him."

The Toyota fired up in the woods, that familiar *clickety-clickety varoom* of those tight engines.

By the time Preston got outside, the car had sped off. There were several ways Gray could make it to the main road, and it would take Preston a while to get back to the cruiser.

He looked again at Mike and the boy was shaking. He was lucky not to have a hole in his head.

"Just wait here," Preston said.

19

The skinny woman sat with me on the bed and told me it was going to be okay, rubbing my arms and saying, "Shh," and stuff like that.

There was something wrong with her, but I couldn't tell what. My dad told me once that there's something deep down inside that God gives everybody, and he didn't know what to call it, but it was like a metal detector that beeps when you pass over an old tin can or a buried spoon. And that something deep inside tells you when there's something wrong with a person or a situation, and whenever you hear that beep go off inside, you should run from it.

I'd pretended I knew what he was talking about when he told me that, but I didn't. It made sense to me that you could feel something deep inside, because it happened to me a lot. The deep ache of thinking about my mama. Wondering why we never stayed in one place. Making a friend and then having to leave. Wanting a dog so bad I could taste it but knowing we couldn't have one. But I'd never been able to fit together what he had said about knowing something was wrong in the pit of your stomach and being able to understand it until sitting with that woman.

I don't think I'd ever been so scared, and it wasn't the gun that made my stomach queasy. It was the look in the woman's eyes. It was almost like some rabid animal my dad had talked about. He told me the story of a friend of his in his hometown who had been bitten by some animal out in the woods, and the boy didn't tell anybody for a long time. And when he did, he told my dad. As soon he did, my dad said there was something that made him think he needed to tell somebody quick. An animal in the woods running up and biting a person is unnatural, and my dad knew it. But by the time he told someone and they checked the kid out, his disease was so far along that they couldn't do anything. The whole thing gave me the creeps. If a squirrel ever jumped out of a tree and landed on my shoulder and sank his teeth in, you can bet I would tell somebody right away.

Well, that feeling my dad had when his friend told him was the same feeling I got when I looked into that woman's eyes. There was something wrong, something not there that should have been or was there in place of something else that was supposed to be. I don't know how to explain it, but the thing hit me like a wasp. My dad says people start running with people who aren't any good for them when they run out of love or hope or both. Maybe that was why she was in with this guy who seemed like Satan himself. That's another thing my dad told me, that if you get that feeling you shouldn't try to figure out what's wrong, just get out.

We turned into the parking lot of the rest area, with its brick building and trucks and cars parked around with sleeping people. And then I thought about the motion my dad made and I knew. He wasn't telling me to come up front but that when he stopped I should try to get away.

"Everything's going to be all right, you'll see," the woman said as my dad pulled around some of the big rigs and headed into a spot.

That thing in my stomach gurgled up and I wanted to believe her, but the feeling wouldn't let me. "I think I'm going to be sick," I said.

Dad put on the brake kind of hard and the guy stepped forward.

I shot toward the door and ran out.

"Go after her!" I heard the guy yell.

I ran into the dark like I was on a mission from God, which I guess I was. The woman came out and ran around like an old woman, her legs turned in and her arms flailing. I was in a dark spot beside the bathrooms in some big shrubs.

I wanted to yell, "Cold!" because that was a game my dad and I would play sometimes when we'd do Easter egg hunts in the RV. He'd hide a piece of candy from me and I'd go hunting all over looking for it and he'd just say *hot* or *cold* and it nearly drove me crazy until I found the candy bar or Peppermint Pattie or whatever.

I could see my dad in the front seat and the Satan guy yelling at him and I thought it was going to all be over, but then they both settled down.

The door opened on the RV and the guy yelled, "Donna, get back here."

Dad was still behind the wheel, looking out at the night, not knowing where I was, but wanting to tell me something. He put up one thumb in the air and then with both hands out pointed down. "Stay there," he mouthed. "Stay there."

I'm sure he couldn't see me because he was staring ahead like a blind man, not looking at anything in particular, just in a general direction. So I hunkered down and watched Donna, the rabies woman, huff and puff back to the RV like the big bad wolf. She climbed in and the light came on and I watched my dad buckle his seat belt tight and start the engine.

The other part of my stomach started getting rickety and queasy because it dawned on me that I was watching them pull out and I didn't want to be left alone, so I ran out. But by the time I made it to the light, the taillight of the RV (only the left one worked) blinked on and then off again and they turned onto the interstate. It was the loneliest feeling in all of the world, and I started to cry because I was sure those two would hurt my dad. It's one thing to feel bad because somebody you love is about to get hurt, and then it's another to be lonely in a deserted place at night, alone with that feeling.

A car came barreling into the rest area, its high intensity lights about blinding me—even through the tears—so I turned around and went back into the shadows and watched. It was a mom who got out and a little girl about my age. They were African American.

I remember the first time I met an African American I was down south in Florida playing on a beach, and there was this family playing beside us. I went back to where my dad was sitting and asked him if I could play with "the brown girl." He laughed real hard and then he took my hand and went out with me to meet the family and they were real nice and even let me borrow one of their buckets. Dad sat right there with me, and we made one of the prettiest sand castles. Even people passing talked about how good it was.

That family left and the two of us kept working until the sun set and then we got a couple of hot dogs and stood up at the railing and watched the tide. I cried when the water first touched the sand castle, and my dad hugged me tight.

"The tide comes in every evening and every morning, June Bug," he said. "Just a fact of life. And everything that's built gets flattened."

"I don't want it to get flattened."

"Well, there's something good about it. Every day you get a fresh start. The ocean cleans up the beach, and then in the morning you get to begin all over again. Kind of like a fresh canvas to paint on."

I hadn't thought of it that way, and I suppose it's comforting in its own way that the earth takes care of itself. Water smoothing out the rough places and making things new. It's funny how you remember stuff like that when you think your dad isn't going to come back alive.

I watched the mom take the daughter into the building, and the dad sat there in the car with a couple of kids asleep. Their license plate said Pennsylvania, and I wondered where they were heading.

That's when the game we played came back to me. Dad would say the state where the car was from and make up a story about the people, using something from that state in the story. Like this one time he said the driver of the car used to be Brutus, the mascot for the Ohio State Buckeyes football team, but he did a flip one day and landed on a cheerleader, and that's who the woman was in the passenger side, his wife the cheerleader who never recovered. I laughed till I cried because he made up all kinds of stuff about their kids who were back at home with Brutus costumes on for trick or treat and how they were driving west to see the San Diego Chicken for advice. You wouldn't know it just by looking at him, but my dad has a really good sense of humor.

So in my head I started thinking about this family from Pennsylvania, just to pass the time and, to be honest, to make me feel a little less scared because I find that thinking about something else is a good way to keep yourself from being scared.

So I imagined this mom and dad and their three children were going to Chicago to see relatives and they were in a hurry, traveling overnight, because their grandma was sick and if they didn't get there fast she would die and they would never get to say good-bye. That was such a sad thought that it made me think of my own dad out there with those two people.

The toilet flushed inside and the water made this big gushing sound and pretty soon the woman and the little girl came out. It was hot and sticky and there was no breeze whatsoever, but the woman hugged the girl so close that you'd have thought it was January in Minnesota. The mom put the girl in the backseat, and she snuggled down into a pillow that looked so soft it could have been a marshmallow. The dad waited until the seat belts were on before driving away.

Then I thought I had it wrong. They weren't going to visit Grandma. With all the stuff in the back of their car, they were moving. Maybe this man was a pastor and he was heading to a small church in Iowa and everything they had in the world was stuffed in that car. He was preaching on Sunday about this world not being our home and we're just passing through. They were probably sad to leave their friends in Pennsylvania.

About that time, I heard the door of a semi truck shut, and there came a mountain of a man heading for the building behind me. He had on jean coveralls and a T-shirt and a hat that looked like it was older than he was. He was squinting into the light, and I thought it was strange he was walking this way because the men's room was on the other side.

As he got closer I noticed a gray thing around his neck and that it was a beard that was growing every which way. It almost looked like his beard was leading him toward me, and when he got to the edge of where the light was shining he dipped his head.

"What are you doing in there, girl?" the trucker said. I expected him to have a voice like God's, deep and scary, but it was pitched up high like a woman's. "Are you singing in there?"

That's when I realized I was singing "I'll Fly Away" and didn't even know it. I didn't say anything. I scooted back a little bit and hoped he would go away.

"I see you in there. Now come out and tell me what happened. Did somebody leave you?" He was looking into the dark, and then he went down on one knee in the grass. "I saw that woman in the RV looking for you and then they took off. I saw the whole thing."

When he turned this time I could see the light reflecting in his eyes, and they weren't anything like the other lady's eyes that were all hollow. It seemed to me like they were full of something, but I didn't know what. I was trying to figure out what feeling was in my stomach and if I should trust him or turn and run.

"You're not hungry, are you?" the man said. "Because I've got a sandwich in my fridge, and I'll bet I could rustle up a Coke or a Dr Pepper."

He glanced at his truck, and something moved in the windshield. Then a dog barked and the guy said something under his breath. "You stay right there. I'll be back in a minute."

He ran to his truck, if you could call it running. It was more like waddling or a person's fat just rolling in a wave. My dad has told me not to make fun of fat people and I'm not doing that; it's just an observation. Dad says it's not kind for people who have my kind of metabolism to make fun of anybody. Still, it's hard not to stare because it's like watching a tornado. You don't get to see one that often, and when you do, it's hard not to gawk.

So he rolled over to his truck and opened the door and out jumped the cutest little beagle you've ever seen with brown, floppy ears and his nose to the ground running across the parking lot, heading straight for me.

He jumped onto the sidewalk, ran to the first tree, and hiked up his leg. I just about busted out laughing because I thought it was me he was so excited about. And, boy, did he have to go. He stood there a long time with the stream going and I thought if my dad could see this he'd let me get a beagle because this one could hold it longer than I could and my dad called me a camel.

Then, when he was done, the dog came to me, sniffing my shoes and my leg, and when he looked up I was actually glad I had been left at this rest stop. I sat down right there, and he crawled into my lap and let me pet his head and scratch his ears.

"He likes you," the trucker said. "He doesn't do that to everybody. You must be special."

"What's his name?" I said.

"Fred."

I laughed. "Why'd you call him that?"

"I don't know; it just seemed to fit."

The night sounds of the cars and the crickets and the occasional engine starting gave me a peaceful feeling, but I wasn't sure if I was supposed to feel afraid in my gut. My dad had told me there are mean people in the world who want to hurt little kids, but this guy didn't seem like one of those types, though I didn't know what those types look like.

"What's your name?" he said.

"June Bug."

He chuckled. "I like that. Almost as good as Fred."

That made me laugh too.

"You want to tell me what happened?" he said. "Was that your mama out here looking for you?"

I shook my head. "No, that was just a lady with the man who had the gun. Donna was her name, but that's all I know. They came into our RV while my dad was getting some gas, and this mean guy held the gun up and said he'd kill him if he didn't drive off. We were headed toward West Virginia, but they made us turn around."

He listened closely, I guess trying to figure out what was really going on. Sometimes you tell people a story, and they can't hear it because they're trying to figure out some other question than what your story is about. "So your mama wasn't with you?"

"I don't have a mama."

He groaned a little. "But that was your daddy driving?"

I nodded because I knew I couldn't explain all about him not being my daddy.

"And you don't know where they went?"

I shook my head.

He thought a minute, then looked at me with an angry or mean look and it kind of scared me. "Then let's get to the truck. I need to call the police."

That made sense to me, and I followed him back there with Fred going ahead of us, his tail wagging. The man opened the door, and Fred jumped in the passenger seat. It was a long climb for me, and as I was going up the man said, "No, get down, Fred. We got company."

I know dogs can't scowl or smile or anything like that because every time I say that I saw a puppy smile my dad tells me it's not true, but I could swear Fred gave me a mean look before he jumped onto the floor. I got in and sat on his cushion.

The man took his phone down from the visor and dialed. "You know your license plate number?"

I told him I didn't, and then he talked with the police and told them where we were on the interstate and that two people had abducted my dad. He answered all their questions, though there was a lot he didn't know, and when he pushed the End button, he just sat there for a while chewing on his lower lip and the straggly hair below it.

"What did they say?"

"They're sending somebody." He put the phone back and looked straight at me, wagging a finger. "Your dad's gonna be okay, you hear? I don't want you to worry. I'll bet he can take care of himself."

"He was in the military," I said, my voice shaking.

"Then he'll be more than all right. I don't imagine that RV will be too hard to find this time of night."

Fred nuzzled my hand and licked at it, and I petted him on the head. It wasn't exactly my dream to be sitting in a big old truck and petting a dog without my dad, but it did feel good.

"What's *your* name?" I said.

"My real name is Ronald, but my friends on the radio call me Big Mac. You know, like Ronald McDonald and the sandwich?"

"What radio?"

"The CB." He pointed to a little radio with a microphone attached to the side. "I use it to talk to my friends out here on the road. This is my office. I've run up and down these roads longer than you've been alive."

"Do you like it?"

"I get tired of it every now and again, but it's a steady job. What's your daddy do?"

"Oh, he writes things on his computer and sends it off." It was right then that I wondered if he really did any of that. Was the writing and sending off stuff a lie? Or maybe he did it but didn't get paid for it. I went back to petting Fred.

Big Mac rummaged around behind him and brought out a bag of Lay's potato chips. I was getting pretty hungry and the chips tasted good. I dropped one and Fred was on it fast, crunching the thing in his mouth. Big Mac and I laughed.

"You gotta be quick with that boy. He'll eat your whole lunch if you don't watch out."

Big Mac looked out the window beside me and craned his neck.

"What is it? The police?"

"No, I thought I saw somebody. Probably just the shadows."

He had the windows down to get some air in the cab. He handed me a Dr Pepper in a can that was so cold you could feel the sweat dripping down the side. I can never get my finger under that tab, and I asked if he would do it for me. When the top popped, I also heard a voice outside whispering my name. At first I wondered if it was the voice of God. I've heard people on the radio talk about following God's voice in their life and telling people if they don't listen when God calls they'll be in big trouble. So when I heard that loud whisper, I thought that God was calling me and that he was going to make me some kind of prophet or maybe he was calling me to be a long-haul trucker.

But as it turns out, it wasn't God—it was my dad. I saw him over by the bushes in the shadow of the lights, and I wondered how I had missed the rumble of the RV engine. I opened the door faster than a jackrabbit, and Fred must have heard the voice too because he barked and followed, with Big Mac trying to get him to be quiet. The dog ran straight for my dad in the bushes and barked, but I caught up and held on to his collar.

Dad hugged me and picked me up in his arms and just about squeezed the life out of me because I guess he was scared that something awful had happened. "I was so worried," he said.

"Well, I was worried that guy was going to shoot you."

Just then the trucker came over to us and Dad put me down.

"This is Mr. Big Mac," I said. "His real name is Ronald, but people call him Big Mac because of Ronald McDonald. He called the police and let me pet Fred. That's his dog. Isn't he nice?"

A guy in a truck in the parking lot yelled something about shutting that dog up, but Big Mac and my dad ignored him.

My dad shook Big Mac's hand. "Thanks for taking care of June Bug while I was away."

"She said you got abducted," Big Mac said. He was squinting and looking sideways, like he wanted to hear more of the story before he believed it.

Dad nodded. "That was pretty much the size of it. What did the police say?"

Big Mac looked toward the interstate. "They should be on their way."

Dad took my hand. "We have to scoot."

"Hold on there," Big Mac said. "What happened with the ones who abducted you?"

"I took care of them," my dad said.

He held tight to my hand, and I noticed the blood on his fore-head running down the side. I pointed it out and he just wiped it away.

"I've got a first-aid kit back in the truck," Big Mac said behind us.

"We have to go," Dad said over his shoulder. "I appreciate your help."

We kept going at a fast clip, but Big Mac called to us. "Wait up." I thought he was going to have a heart attack the way he was gasping. He put a hand on my dad's shoulder and caught his breath. "I'm a vet too. Da Nang. '68 to '70. First Infantry."

My dad nodded, like he knew that score, but I'd never heard of a team called Da Nang.

Big Mac took a deep breath. "If you're in some kind of trouble, I can help."

There were sirens in the distance, and Dad's gaze darted from the man to the interstate. Finally he said, "The RV's totaled. I swerved off the road up a piece and ran it into a few trees."

"And those two probably went flying," Big Mac said.

"Pretty much. I got the gun from the guy and tossed it into the woods a ways in case he came after me. Cops'll find them and that stash of whatever they have in there."

"Why don't you wait for the police?" Big Mac said. "They prob-ably have a reward."

"Yeah, can we stay?" I said, kneeling and petting Fred. "We could use the money to get back to West Virginia."

"I don't think we're going to make it back there, June Bug."

"Why not?" I said, and the look on his face was what they call stern, I guess. I could see the lights of the police car coming down the interstate now.

"We have to go," Dad said, pulling me up.

Big Mac grabbed Dad by the arm. "Wait a minute. Tell me what's going on."

Dad looked at the man a long time, like when he was going

fishing and trying to figure out how deep to put the hook under the bobber. Then he said to me, "Stay here and pet Fred, okay?"

"Okay." I sat down on the asphalt, and Fred leaned against me while I scratched his ears. I was trying hard to listen to what my dad was saying, but I could only pick up a few phrases.

". . . headed back to West Virginia . . . when she was little . . . traveling around in that RV . . . the guy they have in custody . . ."

I wasn't following it but Big Mac seemed to understand every word. My dad can tell a story better than just about anybody because he knows how to pull you in with details. Like what kind of trout he caught with the fly he tied that morning. I swear he could make the phone book interesting just reading it, and maybe that's because he doesn't talk much except when he has something to say.

When my dad finished, Big Mac stood there and watched the police car make a U-turn in the middle of the interstate. I wasn't sure why we didn't want to talk to the police because my dad has always been one to obey the law. He always drives the speed limit because the RV can't do much over it.

"You two crawl on up in my sleeper and stay out of sight," Big Mac said.

"All right, but we're trusting you," Dad said.

We crawled in the man's sleeping compartment, which was so small I didn't think he could ever fit in, and both of us hunkered down. There was a big man smell back there, but the bed was soft. Dad found a bag of barbecued corn chips, the Fritos kind, and he dug out a handful. I wished Fred were with us, but he was outside. I gave Dad the rest of my Dr Pepper, and he guzzled it in one swig.

"So, we can't go back to the RV?" I said.

"Nope."

"What about all our stuff?"

"Like what?"

"My clothes. My journals."

He sighed. "I suppose we can get it from the police after they haul it away."

"When?"

"Keep your voice down."

"But when can we get it?"

"I don't know. Now stay quiet."

"What are you scared of? You didn't do anything wrong. Those people came onto our RV and pointed a gun at you."

"Yeah, but there's more to it than that."

"More to it? What do you mean?"

"It's hard to explain. Just lie down."

I whispered, "What did you tell Big Mac? Why did he agree to help us?"

Dad looked at me with that stern look, and then he softened. "There's stuff I can't tell you. Stuff you deserve to know and that I want to tell you, but I don't know how yet."

"Just tell me."

"It's not as simple as that."

"That's not what you always say. You always say if there's something on my mind I ought to say it."

"You ought to be a lawyer is what you ought to be."

"So tell me."

His face was still half-worried or mad and half just melting because of something. "You'll know the truth pretty soon. But right now here's what's on my mind. We need to make it back to West Virginia. We need to get that box of stuff from Mrs. Linderman. I need to clear up a couple of things, and then . . ."

"Then what?"

"I don't know. We can move on."

"What does that mean?"

"Keep your voice down."

"What do you mean we can move on?"

"Get on with life," he said. "Put the past behind us. Now we can replace all that stuff in the RV—"

"Not my journals!"

He clamped his hand over my mouth, not hard and meanlike, but just to keep me from squalling. I could see his eyes and there was something serious there. Something hurtful and kind at the same time. It's funny how a person's eyes can tell you so much, but I believe it's true.

"June Bug, you have to listen. We can't have those police finding us. As soon as we get to West Virginia, we can buy a whole truckload of journals and a new RV. And I'll do my best to get those back. But I can't promise you something I can't be sure of. Understand?"

I nodded and he took his hand away, but I couldn't keep the tears from rolling and I felt my chin puckering, which is a terrible feeling because there is nothing that will make it stop once you try to unpucker it. I've tried.

"Don't cry. Everything's going to be all right. I promise."

I only half believed him. There was something bad waiting to happen. It felt right then like there were a million bridges between where we were and where we were going. It felt like I was losing something, and not just the RV and all the stuff in it. But I couldn't put my finger on just what it was, and it made me more nervous than having somebody hold a gun on my dad.

20

Mae rocked herself as she prayed in the pitch black of night. Even with the fan going in the back room and all the windows open, it was stifling hot. She had soaked through her nightgown. And with Leason's snoring and his hot body next to her, she had come to the screened-in porch and sat and rocked, trying to exhaust her mind.

She said the same prayer over and over, the same one she had prayed the first night Natalie disappeared. *Bring her back, Lord. Bring her back and keep her safe. And bring Dana to you. Don't let her go so far that she can't come back.*

As she moved, the rocker creaking on the porch, she ran over the same verse that came every time she thought of her grand-daughter—Romans 8:28. "And we know that all things work together for good to them that love God, to them who are the called according to his purpose."

Mae didn't care much for the new translations. If King James was good enough for Jesus, it was good enough for her. But no matter how many versions she read, she couldn't make sense of those words in relation to Natalie.

Lord, you know I love you. I want to do your will. I have since I can remember. But I can't for the life of me figure out how in the world this could do anybody any good. And I can't see any purpose at all. You don't have to explain anything to me. I know you're God and your ways are not my ways, but I don't see what's all-loving about keeping us in the dark about her. It's just stealing the life from me, and you said you came to give us life. This is not what I see as abundance, and I don't mean to be ungrateful because you've done a lot, but I'm being honest that I can't see it. I truly can't.

Something moved in the front yard and she glanced out. There were no animals she could see, so she sat back and kept the *squeak-squawk* of the floorboards going.

Mae looked at her praying as a running one-sided conversation, much like the ones she'd had with Leason. She'd talk and he'd listen and sometimes grunt or scowl or roll his eyes or shake his head, but he pretty much listened. What he'd said the other day to her was as much as she'd gotten out of him in years, and to tell the truth she kind of liked it better when he was quiet. She'd wondered what she'd ever do if God would actually speak to her while she was praying. Some of her friends, particularly one over in Point Pleasant, had encouraged her to get slain in the Spirit as if that would change things between her and God. She'd already been slain as much as she needed as far as she was concerned.

As a young girl she'd attended a church with a friend who lived in some hollow where men had carried burlap sacks from a back room into the service and everybody stood and clapped. She pushed forward to get a look and wound up standing on one of the pews when a bag filled with snakes emptied. People danced and stomped, hopping around and whooping, and then somebody actually picked one up and danced around with it. A copperhead held so close to a guy's face that Mae had to look away. And she had thought right then and there that if being a Christian meant making friends with snakes, she didn't want anything to do with it.

She preferred a silent God who just listened and helped her make sense of life by going along with whatever she said. Until times like these, when the weight of the world hovered over her like some tornado and she wanted answers. She wanted God to tell her exactly where that little girl was. Even if it meant finding a body.

Bring her back, Lord. Bring her back and keep her safe.

Mae knew one reason she hadn't slept was her dreams. The recurring one of men combing the woods, dogs barking and sniffing the earth. It was fall and the men wore coats and the trees were bare. They moved in a line across the hillside, trying not to trip over downed trees and stumps. Then someone would yell, and the men and dogs would run to a shallow grave and a tiny, decomposed hand sticking out of the leaves. That was the one she had most often.

But there was another dream. She'd be in the field, bent over and weeding the garden, when she pulled up what looked like the top of a turnip. Instead, a baby came out and it was Natalie. It sent her reeling each time.

Maybe that's what kept her awake, the risk of dreams. Maybe that was God speaking to her, getting her ready for the truth, softening her heart for the discovery of the shallow grave. That was another reason she liked the God of silence, the God who slumbered and listened, if he listened at all. She liked to think she was in control and not him, because if he really was in control and would allow some of the things to go on that she'd read about every day, then she wasn't too sure how far her faith was going to take her.

A train whistled in the distance. Two longs, a short, and another long, which meant the train was approaching the crossing in Dogwood. Her dad had been a trainman, and she knew all the whistle codes. When her mind was active and her body fatigued, she could slip into that netherworld of the past and see him at the swimming hole, down from the ramshackle home of their youth. They'd grown up dirt-poor but made great fun out of the little they had.

Mae remembered the bucktoothed grin of her brother and the sight of him jumping from the creek onto the bank naked. None of them could swim, but the creek wasn't deep enough for anyone to drown.

At times like this, deep in the night and with nothing to hold on to but her faith and the worn edges of the rocking chair handles, she found it easier to chase the days of the past rather than the pain of the present. She had always wondered what her mother went through, watching them grow up to find their way—or not find it. She wondered what her mother would say about Dana and what should be done, as if anything could be. She was sure what her father would say: that she needed a good switching until she changed her ways.

She craned her neck to see the kitchen clock, but it didn't matter what time it was—she wasn't going to sleep much, if at all. Her eyes were heavy, her legs and back ached, and her face felt so hot she thought it would melt.

Mae picked up an old newspaper on the table and began to fan, which brought back another memory. That's all she had now. Dana had come down with an earache—she always had the most piercing illnesses, that child. Mae would try to rock her to sleep and sing her songs to calm her. One night she was rocking Dana, singing "The Old Rugged Cross." She was on the final verse, the one that said:

> *To the old rugged cross I will ever be true,*
> *Its shame and reproach gladly bear;*
> *Then He'll call me some day to my home far away,*
> *Where His glory forever I'll share.*

Dana looked at her with those big eyes, and she could see the pain on the little girl's face. "Mama, why do you always sing about the cross?"

She'd thought about giving her a theological answer, something about the substitutionary atonement for little minds, but then thought better of it. "I suppose it's like singing about somebody you love," Mae had said.

"Like 'Tom Dooley'?"

"Not exactly. 'Tom Dooley' is a tragic song about losing love. 'The Old Rugged Cross' is a victory song because love didn't lose; it won."

"Don't sing it anymore. I want to hear 'Tom Dooley.'"

That was the first time Mae had felt Dana reject her faith, and it was a small thing that had grown bigger. There had been distance between them off and on, especially at the end of grade school and into junior high. Mae had taken a job at the bank about that time, and she always wondered if not being home when Dana returned from school had been the start of the trouble or if it was something inevitable, that she was just going to go her own way no matter what.

Of course, Mae had blamed herself when Dana had run off with boys in high school, a different one every weekend it seemed, and she'd be gone from Friday until late on Sunday. Mae considered calling the police, but the girl would eventually drift home, half-drunk. Leason had scowled and huffed about the house, talking about "raising a hussy," but he didn't do anything more.

For Mae, it ate at her every day, and as Dana's ways became more erratic—dropping out of school and moving in with a guy on Barker's Ridge—Mae became more spiritual, more in tune with God. She always felt the folks at church judged her and didn't understand. How could they? The worst thing their kids did was toss toilet paper at some trees in people's front yards. Other than that Hatfield boy who ran those kids down on the road early one morning, most of the people in town were upstanding citizens. But instead of giving in to the pressure and cutting off the relationship, Mae tried to love her daughter through the hard times. She wasn't sure that was the right thing, but when she looked back at it, she believed keeping that door unlocked was a good idea.

It wasn't until Dana showed up on their doorstep with a muskmelon-shaped belly that things changed. She had moved on to several other guys and was living in Huntington with a "room-mate." She was thinking about going back to school, but whoever was paying the bills at her place had thrown her out when she wouldn't have an abortion. She'd come home asking for help. Begging, actually. Mae saw the whole thing as a second chance and an answer to prayer.

There was a rhythm to the hills, a certain cadence to life that she had grown up with. Living and dying and living again, with life springing from the most unlikely places. Sometimes trees grew at odd angles right out of the sides of rocks or plants grew between the cracks in the concrete. There were some things you simply couldn't pave over, and life was one of them, and that girl having a baby was a sign to Mae that there was a God and that he was faithful to his promise, just like "The Old Rugged Cross." Sin would not only find you out, it would hunt you down and stick a foot on your neck. But the fruit of this sin had come home in a car seat and was so cute Mae could hardly breathe.

Mae had set Dana up in the side bedroom that used to be the laundry room and put fresh linens and soft pillows on the bed. She loved her with kind words that would have turned around the most hardened criminal, but instead of being thankful, Dana had almost punished Mae. She laughed at Mae. Leason asked Mae why she endured it, and she shook her head. "The Lord put up with a lot from me. I reckon I can put up with some from her."

There was talk of adoption and even selling the baby to some rich couple over the state line, but once that red-haired beauty had come into the world, Mae knew it wouldn't happen. Surely Dana would see the error of her ways and would become a responsible mother.

Mae began caring for the child full-time, being more than a mother to her, and letting Dana go about her life. Mae couldn't remember Dana ever changing one of Natalie's diapers. She'd just let the child sit in her own mess. Mae knew she had raised a monster—or as near as you could get to one—but every time she looked into that angel's eyes, her little Natalie, she forgot about the bad choices and knew God had brought something good out of something bad. Natalie was living, breathing proof of Romans 8:28. Mae even called the girl Roma after that verse, but now the taste of it on her mouth felt bitter and useless. All the work of loving and what good did it do?

The moon was bright and almost full as a car came around the bend in the road. One headlight was out, and it slowed at the downward slope and stopped altogether by the line of rosebushes on their side of the blacktop. The road had been just a rut-marked patch of dirt until a few years ago when the county paved it. Now cars flew in and Mae knew it was going to get somebody killed.

The car inched forward, then turned into their driveway. Gravel crunched under the tires and the engine bogged down as the car came over the incline. She wished she'd kept the light on at the end of the walk so she could see who it was. The driver parked and just sat there.

It wasn't the sheriff's car; she knew that by the sound of the engine. She equally hoped and feared the sheriff had caught Graham Walker and that he'd confessed and told them where he put Natalie. As she peered into the darkness, she wondered if this could be Walker himself, needing to make amends for what he'd done.

She stood, her nightgown stuck to her back. Half-wanting to run in and get the loaded .22 Leason left by the trash can at the back door (for the groundhog he was constantly warring) and half-wanting to just stay and watch, she edged toward the screen door and opened it, standing there in the moonlight. If it was the wiry man she saw on the news, she swore she would scream, doubting that would wake Leason with the fan on, but still it might scare Walker away.

The car door opened and out stepped a female with straight hair and an angular nose.

Mae squinted. "Dana?"

The girl sauntered up the walk like she'd never missed a day of calling and checking on her. Straight up to the porch she came, arms dangling, staring at Mae.

Mae tried to hug her, but it was clear from the stiffness Dana wasn't going to return the affection.

"I been driving by here at night looking for a light on," Dana said.

"*You* been driving by? What for?"

Dana looked at the floor. "Just to see if anybody's here. If anybody cares."

Mae edged back. "I'm not sleeping too well these days. Came out here because it was hot. It must be two o'clock in the morning."

"Three thirty," Dana said. She looked stick thin and almost haunted.

"Do you want me to fix you a sandwich? You look like you're starving."

"I always look like I'm starving to you, Mama." Dana laughed with derision. Then she sat in the rocking chair, her feet propped on the railing.

"Whose car is that?" Mae said.

"It's mine. Delbert gave it to me."

"Who's Delbert?"

Dana rolled her eyes. "I'm not going to tell you. You'd just judge him."

Mae collected her thoughts in the quiet and sat on the front step, where there was just enough room. She could think either the best or the worst. Maybe this was God's way of giving her another chance with her daughter.

"I was sitting out here thinking about you as a little girl. Remember when you used to get those terrible earaches?"

"They weren't that bad."

"That bad?" Mae leaned against the front door. The same one Dana had slammed and broken years ago. The hinges had never been the same. "You'd squall and holler about the knife in your ear and that you needed somebody to take it out. It was awful."

"You're making that up."

"I wish I was. Every time those infections would come, it cut me to the quick, you in all that pain. I'd have taken that from you in a second if I could have."

Dana chewed on a thumbnail, and it looked to Mae like she'd gone as far as she could go with it, just staring with those hollow eyes. There was something more to this visit than old infections.

"I need some money, Mama."

"I suppose we could all use some."

"No, I mean it. I'm leaving. I'm probably not coming back. There's just too much of the past here."

"What about Delbert?"

She shrugged. "He's not what I'm looking for."

"What's the hurry? Why now?"

"I can't take all the news and cameras. I can't relive that." She put her hands in her hair and pushed it up. It looked like dry spaghetti.

"Where you headed? The news is the same all over the country."

"I don't know. Some place where I can make a fresh start. Where people don't judge you."

"Well, if you find it, tell me where it is because I've never been there before."

"I'm serious. I can't live here."

It was too dark to see the walnut tree on the other side of the driveway. But in her mind Mae could see its gnarled branches and the way the tree had struggled. *Trees are like people,* she thought. *It's all about the roots.* "How much do you need?"

Dana shook her head, a bit of light coming into her eyes. "I'll take whatever you can spare."

"What I can spare and what I have are different amounts. But I have to know you're going to use this for a fresh start and not a fresh high."

"I swear to you. Just once more and I'll be out of your life. I'll be gone. I'm going to do something with my life."

Mae looked off in the distance to the headlights passing on the interstate. She thought of the hope she used to have for her daughter and all of those dark nights and times she wished her daughter had never been born. And then of Natalie. Always of Natalie. "Let me talk with your father."

"You know what he's going to say."

"I have a good idea."

"And I need it now. I want to leave right now. So don't wake him up. Just give me whatever cash you have and I'll make do."

Mae looked at her hands and then back at her daughter. "What's wrong? What's got you so worked up?"

"I told you, it's the news." She choked up like she was actually going to cry. "I can't take it. I need help."

Mae turned away from the tears and stood. "All right, Dana. I'll help you. But I have a condition."

"Condition?"

"I need something before I give you any money," Mae explained.

"I don't have anything but that old car and a few clothes I took from Delbert's house."

Mae shook her head. "I don't want that. I want the truth."

"The truth about what?"

"About that night. About what really happened."

Dana rolled her head back on her shoulders as if doing some sort of stretching exercise. "I've told you and the police and anybody who cared to listen what happened."

"I don't think so," Mae said evenly. She had spent her life trying to keep the young woman from yelling and pitching a fit. Somehow it didn't seem right anymore. "Tell me what happened to Natalie."

Dana clenched her teeth and stuck her hands in her hair again, grabbing it and pulling. "See? This is what it always comes back to. That little girl. You care more about her than anybody. Especially me."

"How can you say that?"

"It's true," she shouted. "Natalie got a lot more attention in one day than you ever gave me my whole life."

"Dana," Mae said, "how can you think that?"

"Because it's true. She was a mistake and you treated her like royalty."

Mae was horrified. "What have you done?"

"I haven't done a thing. I'm just asking you to think about me for once."

"What happened to her? You've known all along, haven't you?"

"I don't know what happened," Dana said quickly, crossing her arms.

"Did that Walker boy have anything to do with it? Did you . . . ?"

"Did I what?"

"Did you sell her to him? or trade her away for some dope? Tell me that's not what you did."

Dana looked at Mae with a contempt the woman had never seen. "How could you think that?"

Mae put out a hand to steady herself. "I'm trying to imagine what could have happened. If what you've said all along isn't true. If you've been lying. Just *tell* me."

"Oh, Mama, you can't imagine the worst. 'Cause if you could, you wouldn't be able to look at me or live with yourself."

"What do you mean? Why couldn't I live with myself?"

Dana cocked her head. "I been thinking. Especially since they brought that car up. And you know what I came up with?"

Mae shook her head, the feeling of a little girl creeping back into her heart. The emptiness and soul-drenching fear bubbling.

"You're the problem," Dana said. "If it wasn't for you, Natalie would still be alive. Having a birthday party soon."

"You *know* she's not alive?"

Dana stepped forward and pointed a crooked finger at Mae. "I didn't say that. But it was you. All that doting and all the bows in the hair and the presents. You made it worse."

Mae slapped her hard across the face. "How dare you speak to me like that. Now tell me where that girl is." Her voice was shaking now, uncontrollable, and the adrenaline caused her to grab Dana's arm, the skin turning white under her fingers. "Tell me the truth or you'll never get another dime."

A sick smile came over Dana and she jerked away. "Look in the mirror, Mama. You want the reason she's gone, go to the mirror."

"Where is she!" Mae screamed, grabbing at her again, but she was gone through the screen door and it fell hard, hitting Mae in the face.

"Have that money ready when I come back," Dana shouted over her shoulder.

Mae sat down hard in the rocking chair as the car headed down the driveway. The taillights were dim and seemed like two eyes staring at her.

The door opened behind her. "What was all that yelling about?"

"Nothing," Mae said. "Go on back to bed."

21

Sheriff Hadley Preston awoke to the sound of sizzling bacon and cursed when he saw the sun through the window. He'd meant to sleep only a couple of hours, but he glanced at the clock and rose, still dressed. He'd fallen into bed with everything but his shoes and his gun belt on. There was a greasy pain in his stomach, no doubt the chicken he'd eaten in the wee hours.

He undressed quickly and stepped into the shower, figuring this was his one shot for the day. If last night was any indication, it was going to be a long one.

Macel had biscuits and eggs ready when he sat, the water beading and dripping from his hair onto his starched collar.

"Late night?" she said.

"Thanks for keeping the chicken warm."

"What time did you make it back?"

He told her.

"Did you catch him?"

"No, ran into a little trouble."

"What kind?"

"Walker had a gun. He got away."

She nearly dropped the pan with the gravy. "What in the world happened?"

Preston laid it out as best he could without frightening her. The last thing he wanted was to upset her before he even finished his breakfast. "Nobody got hurt; that's the good news. Bad news is he got away."

"That could have been you," Macel said.

He separated a biscuit and the steam rose. He poured honey over both halves and gravy over the biscuit next to it. "I suppose, if I'd have been dumb enough to charge into that shack. I think he would have come out on his own if Mike had waited like I told him."

His wife stared at the tablecloth. She was deep water. There was no doubt about it. She could laugh with the best of them, but when she got something in her mind, it was best just to leave her be until she came back. He put some hot sauce on his eggs and moved the melted cheddar cheese. This was how she'd made them the past few years.

Finally Macel spoke. "You don't know what you've got until you almost lose it."

"What's that supposed to mean?"

"Just means that I'd miss you if you didn't come home. I prayed all night."

"Not all night." He smiled.

"As long as I could hold my eyes open. And then some."

"Well, I could feel it."

She cocked her head. "You could?"

"Don't get your hopes up about my soul. But, yeah, there're times when I feel like there's something bigger out there watching over me. Some call it white light or good feelings, and some call it God or Jesus or the Spirit. I don't know what it is, but I think it's more than just hoodoo."

"Well, that's a start, I guess," she said.

His cell phone rang in the bedroom, and before he could get up, she'd retrieved it for him, holding it out so he could see the tiny screen. He had to move his head back like some insect in order to see.

He answered it, went to the front room, and looked out on the yard. He needed to mow it today or tomorrow or she was going to get that Reynolds boy to do it. The kid charged them twenty dollars, and Preston thought that was a crime.

"Who was it?" she said when he returned.

"Mike's wife. Says he's not coming in today."

"I can't blame him. He might need counseling after that close of a call. Post-traumatic stress."

Preston wanted to say if anybody needed counseling for PTSD it was him, but he didn't. She would have agreed. She sipped at her coffee, and he grabbed his gun belt from the mantel.

"You didn't finish your breakfast." The biscuit with gravy was still sitting on his plate.

"Got enough to make it to lunch. It might be a long day, judging from last night." His cell phone rang again, and he looked at the number. He just let it go.

"If you're going to be gone, I might eat over at Brud's house," she said. "Leslie invited me anytime you're working late. Unless you think you'll make it for dinner."

"No, that sounds good. Go on over there. If things calm down, I'll call on you."

"Call on me?"

"Yeah, like it used to be. Your brother never liked me much, as I recall."

"He knew you were just after my beautiful body." She said it like Jonathan Winters used to say it on some comedy show long gone, and they both laughed. Things were like that now. They'd been together so long all it took was a look every now and again or a word from a joke somebody told years ago and they were right with each other. Time can do that, at least partly.

He bent and kissed the top of her head and she patted his hand.

She called to him as he went through the front door. "I'll be praying for you."

He nodded and let the door slam. They'd been good for each other. Not the perfect marriage, but who has that?

On the road he dialed the office, and his secretary picked up. "We got a few calls from people who said they might have seen Walker's car. I can give them to you if you want to follow up."

"Did they see him before or after midnight?"

"Before," Mindy said.

"Just hang on to those until I get there. Anything else?"

She went through a litany of names of law enforcement personnel willing to help with the investigation. The elephant on the phone line was what had happened the night before. He knew Mindy and Mike were close, probably closer than they should have been, but giving her information would make her dangerous with the media. He sensed she was writing down what he said.

"I'll fill you in on what happened when I get there," he said.

"Yes, sir. Oh, Sheriff, there's one other call here. Some lady from Colorado said she needed to talk to whoever's in charge."

"In charge of what?"

"That missing little girl. She said she has information that could help."

Preston shook his head. Probably another psychic. He'd talked with them from all over. People who had seen the news story and said they'd had a vision of where the girl was buried. Everything from the trunk of an old Buick in a trash dump to body parts being scattered along the Appalachian Highway. Every one of them as sincere as they could be but all dead ends. "She reading tarot cards when she called you or just tea leaves?"

"Not that I could tell. But she sounded upset. I think she's legit."

Mindy had a good sense about people. "Give me her number."

Mindy gave it to him, and he wrote it on the side of a McDonald's coffee cup. He dialed as he headed for the drive-through. A machine picked up, and the lady said her name and to leave a message. He was halfway through leaving his number when she answered.

"Sheriff Preston?" she said.

"You got him."

"I saw you on the news. Thank you for calling back. I was just walking out the door to work."

"If you want me to call you back —"

"No, no, this is fine."

He took the new cup from the drive-through girl, and when he went to hand her the two dollars, the older lady behind her waved him on with a smile.

"Can I ask what this is about?" he said.

She took a breath, and it sounded like she was trying hard not to cry. "It's about that little girl. Natalie. The one who's missing."

"What about her?"

Preston half expected her to say she'd had a dream and wondered if he knew a place where two trees crossed because the girl was buried by a bush underneath that looked like Elvis's mother or something like that.

"I think she's been living at my house."

He was taking a swig of coffee and nearly choked. He coughed and held the phone away from him as he pulled into the last parking spot. "And why would you say that?"

"She was traveling with her father. At least, that's who I thought he was. He'd parked his RV in our lot while he waited for a part."

"He'd broken down?"

"Right. I work at a Walmart. And this cute little thing . . ." Her voice cracked.

He took a sip of coffee. Another news truck had exited the interstate heading for Dogwood. "How old would you say she is?"

"Nine, I think. If the information is right, she'll be ten on the twentieth."

"How would you know that?"

"That's what it said on the missing child poster we have on our wall. She's the spitting image of little Natalie."

She seemed genuine enough, but Preston was skeptical. He'd tried to discourage Mae from going to those missing children people for this very reason. People see someone who looked somewhat like the missing person and then all the calls and false leads and a couple of years later some bones turn up and you realize it was all just blind hope.

"Did you get a good look at the guy in the RV?"

"Not just a good look, he stayed here."

She briefly explained how that happened; then Preston asked

for his name and she gave it and he wrote it down. Something about the name rang a bell, but he couldn't place it.

"What about the license on the RV?"

She'd written it down in her room and she went to the other extension.

"Is there any other reason you think this might be the Edwards girl?" Preston said.

"Yes. From the things he said on the phone, from Arkansas. He said she's not his daughter."

"Johnson told you that? Why did he call?"

"The girl was supposed to stay with me, but she left with him. He had to make a trip to Arkansas. I'm not sure why. And when he called, he said she had stowed away and he didn't know she was there."

"You don't believe him."

"I don't know what to believe. But in the middle of that conversation I put everything together."

Preston was jotting more notes.

"Honestly, Sheriff, he's a good man. He's a good father to that girl, even if he isn't really her daddy."

"As far as you can tell."

"That's right."

He thought a minute. "What took you so long to call?"

She paused and he could hear the tears. "I think something inside me just wanted to think the best. Wanted to think it could work out for all of us. I would adopt that little girl as fast as anything. She's as smart as a whip and she can read better than most adults, so she hasn't lacked for an education. But I couldn't get that family out of my head. There's somebody out there with an empty bed where that little girl deserves to be."

Preston thought of Mae and everything she'd gone through. This could be some crackpot or some publicity hound, but he didn't think so. Maybe Mae had been right all along. Maybe there wasn't a body in a shallow grave. Maybe there was a living, breathing little girl riding around with a fellow in an RV. A fellow who had abducted her, like Dana Edwards had said. And what did that mean for Walker?

He let the thoughts sift through his mind. He wasn't going to figure this out with a phone call, and if there was one thing he knew, it was that people were very seldom what they appeared to be. A lonely woman who took in strangers from a Walmart parking lot probably did not know the whole story. If this guy was using the girl in some unseemly way, he was a monster. And monsters ought to be hunted down and locked up or killed.

"Please let me know if you find him," the woman said. "I think they're headed back your way."

"Why would you think that?"

"Because he's from there. The hills. I think there's something there he has to do."

"I'll keep an eye out for him."

"Don't hurt him, Sheriff. Something really bad happened to that little girl a long time ago. But hurting him won't erase any of that."

PART THREE

2.2

I liked curling up with Fred on the bed as Big Mac drove. We went back by the RV and there were lights flashing all around and Big Mac saw a couple being loaded into the police cars. I hoped they'd get what they deserved. There was news of some drug-related shooting on the radio, and Big Mac said he bet those two were responsible.

As we passed the RV it felt like what some people must feel like when their house gets hit by a tornado or a flood. Losing the RV was all in my head until I saw the mangled thing on its side.

I grabbed Dad's arm. "When this is over, can we go back to Sheila's place?"

He was staring out and watching the white lines go by. "I don't know, June Bug."

"But my bike is back there!"

"We'll see."

"Why do you call her June Bug?" Big Mac said. I don't think he liked it when I raised my voice. "That can't be her real name."

"It's all he's ever called me," I said.

"Take a look at her," Dad said. "If you can think of a better name, go ahead."

"I don't know," Big Mac said. "Maybe something like Julie or Carrie or Guinevere. Anything but June Bug."

I laughed when he said Guinevere, and Dad put an arm around me. "Minute I first laid eyes on her I thought, 'June Bug.'"

"And when was that?" Big Mac said.

"Long time ago. It was in June, which is another reason the name fits. You can call her whatever you want, but she'll always be my June Bug."

Fred gave a big sigh and put his head on my leg. It was a good feeling to hear my dad say that, but it was sort of empty too, knowing what my real name was. Sometimes the best feelings come with other feelings you can't escape.

We were heading west, away from our destination, but Big Mac told us not to worry. He knew another driver that would be coming from the other direction who owed him a favor. He called the guy's cell phone and left a long message. I must have been asleep when he called back because the next thing I knew Dad was waking me up and Fred was going crazy about something and I had drool running down my arm.

Big Mac was standing in an empty Best Buy parking lot talking to another fellow whose truck was parked alongside. There was fog all over the place, and the sun hadn't come up to burn it off yet.

I only got to pet Fred one more time before Dad lifted me into the truck and set me down on the sleeper again. This man's name was Bill, and he went by Coyote on the CB. I guess because he howled sometimes. He didn't seem happy about us riding with him, but like Big Mac said, he owed him.

"I could get in big trouble doing this, you know," Bill said to Dad as we pulled away.

"We're not telling anybody," Dad said.

Bill didn't have a dog, but his bed smelled like he'd had one a long time ago and there were enough crumbs and stuff back there to feed a couple of pups for a week. I was so tired I closed my eyes. The next thing I knew we were stopped at a Bob Evans and the sun was up and it was getting hot even with the little fan Bill had stuck on the curtain between the bed and the front seats.

Dad helped me down, and we walked across the parking lot because you can't park one of those big trucks in a regular spot.

"Where are we?" I said.

"Bob Evans," Bill said, and he snorted like he thought that was funny.

"Kentucky," Dad said kind of soft. "Not too far from West Virginia."

I asked Dad about my journals again, and he got down on my level. "June Bug, I want you to listen. We're in a bind. A big one. I have to get to this place I haven't been in a lot of years and find something. And then . . ."

"And then what?" I said.

He stared over his shoulder, keeping his eyes from me. I thought for a minute he was looking at the Bob Evans, but when he turned back his eyes were watery and red. "And then we figure out what to do next. Let's get something to eat, and we'll get back on the road. One step at a time."

After that I decided not to ask too many more questions because I don't know about you, but I hate to see anybody cry, especially my dad. We sat down and the waitress came. She was an older lady with funny colored hair. She smiled at us but it was one you know doesn't come from the heart and is there only because you're supposed to smile and you know you're not going to get much of a tip if you're not pleasant.

I got some orange juice and happy face pancakes with warm syrup.

Bill watched me as he ate, cutting up his sausage and biscuits, and he snickered. "She can really put it away for a little thing. How long you two been on the road?"

Dad looked at me, and from that I figured he didn't want me saying anything.

"Didn't know it was top secret," Bill said when we didn't answer. He stuck another whole sausage in his mouth, and the grease rolled over his lips. "So Mac told me you wanted to get to West Virginia, but he never said whereabouts."

"About an hour across the state line," Dad said.

"Dogwood," I said. "You heard of it?"

Bill wiped his mouth with a napkin. "Seems like I have heard about it on the news lately."

Dad crumpled up his napkin and put it on his food. Then he stood, reached inside his wallet, and pulled out a couple of twenties. I could see Bill's eyes going wide as he looked at the wad of cash from Mrs. Linderman.

"We'd better head out," Dad said.

"Hold on," Bill said. "I'm nowhere near finished."

"I'll make it up to you at lunch," Dad said. He put the money on the table without even getting the bill.

"I need to use the toilet," I said.

"It'll have to wait," he said.

"Daddy, I have to go!"

He picked me up and held me close to his whiskery face like he used to when I was little. Now that I've grown up, he doesn't do that, so it surprised me. But then I noticed the police car parked outside.

Bill caught up with us at the door and Dad turned. "Get in the truck and meet us across the way at the gas station."

Bill answered him with not very nice language saying something about him not being the boss and he should just pull out and leave us behind. He had a soggy biscuit in his hand and was still complaining about not being able to finish breakfast.

"We'll make it worth your while," Dad said, and then he didn't say anything more. He marched out the door, put me on the ground, and took my hand. I didn't let go once as we crossed the street and went inside the little store to the bathroom. Boy was I glad I didn't have to wait until some rest stop. I think orange juice has a way of making you glad there's a bathroom nearby.

When I came outside, Bill was there and Dad handed him a brown coffee cup through the window. I guess to make up for what he was missing at the restaurant. We climbed in and Dad craned his neck to see the police car.

Bill flipped on the radio, and as it turned out, he liked listening to Rascal Flatts really loud which was okay with me. One time I heard this preacher say that the only musical instrument God ever created on earth was the human voice, and I like that. Angels are supposed to have harps and stuff and they sing too, but listening to Rascal Flatts made me glad God made people who could carry a tune.

We got back on the interstate, and the first thing we did was go over a bridge which made me plug up my ears and sing. Bill heard me because he turned around and said a few more of those bad words. Dad tried to explain about my being afraid of bridges, but the guy just didn't understand. I curled up again with the taste of those pancakes in my mouth and the loud music going and the wind rushing through the windows. But all I could think about was the tears in my daddy's eyes.

I was pretty tired because the next thing I knew Dad was shaking me and pointing to a sign that said, "Welcome to Wild, Wonderful West Virginia." I looked out the window and saw we had gone over a big old bridge, and that just shows how much my dad loves me, that he would wait to wake me up.

By this time Bill had turned off his music and was listening to the CB. I didn't understand half the words he used. I did find out he was going to Charleston with the load he was pulling, but my dad said we'd be getting out before then.

As soon as we hit the state line, the roads started going up and down, and there were so many trees and bushes at the side of the road that it looked like a garden. The whole place just screamed life at me, and I wondered what it would be like to live in one of the houses I saw up in the hills with the big columns in the front and the yards that looked like they went on forever. Then I got to thinking about our RV and all my stuff and that it would feel lonely in a big old house without any of my journals.

"I have a brother who went to school over there," Bill said, pointing to a town I could just barely see off to the left. "Played football for the Herd."

I didn't know what the Herd was, but I figured it was important to him to mention it.

"What's he doing now?"

"Sells insurance over in Columbus. He messed up his knee his first year. Still can't walk right. Hobbles around worse than our old man. I never played ball, but at least I can walk, you know?"

Dad looked out the window like he was reliving something. Any time I go to places I've been before, I think about the last time I was there and all the stuff that happened to me, so I figured he might have been doing the same thing.

"You grow up around here?" Bill said.

Dad nodded. "I was a kid when the plane went down. I'll never forget that."

"Yeah, that cut the heart out of this place; that's for sure. But the team came back. National championships and all that."

"Never brought back those people," Dad said.

"You got a point there," Bill said.

We passed under a big bridge and Dad pointed to the right. "When I was a kid, there used to be a drive-in theater there."

"What's a drive-in theater?" I said.

Dad explained that it was a place you watch a movie in your car. It sounded like a fun way to watch a movie.

"I never got to go, but I remember driving by and looking back at the screen," Dad said. "These big images flickering out over the parking lot."

"Why didn't you ever go?" I said.

He shrugged. "I guess there was nobody to go with."

We drove on with the sun up high. There's no exit for Dogwood, so we got off at the one before the town, and Dad told Bill to find a place where he wanted to eat. Bill chose a Wendy's and parked in a vacant lot. Dad and I walked over and came back with burgers and fries and a big Frosty. Dad handed Bill several twenties and thanked him for his kindness. I didn't think *kindness* was the right word necessarily, because it seemed he was just doing this to get Big Mac off his back.

He stuffed the money in his shirt pocket and frowned. "I think you can afford a little more than that."

"I gave you about all I had."

Bill nodded toward the radio. "All I got to do is hop on this radio and have somebody give the local constable a call. You want them looking for a weird guy with a little girl?"

I knew if Dad had a do-over, he wouldn't have shown his money, but I guess he was just scared of the police for some reason. I wanted to tell him not to give him more, that the guy could still call the "local constable," whatever that meant.

Dad reached into his wallet and pulled out more money and handed it over. Bill took a look, then glanced at Dad's wallet where I could see only one more twenty, and the man tipped his dirty hat toward us.

"Hope everything turns out all right for you two," he said. Then he fired up the truck and took off.

I guess if you had passed us right then on that vacant lot with the weeds grown up and the sun beating down with not much money and just the clothes on our backs, you would have felt sorry for us. You would have seen two drifters making their way where there wasn't one.

But part of me was so excited because I felt we were both closer to home than we'd ever been. And the music that washed around in my head could have filled the hills around us. I held my dad's calloused hand and couldn't help skipping in the dirt. For some reason I felt like there was real hope for both of us to find what we were looking for.

"Come on. Let's get out of the sun," Dad said.

Instead of walking to Wendy's, we hiked to Dairy Queen. It was cool inside, and I sat down at a booth while he got us a couple of Mr. Misties. He got me a lime-flavored one, and it was so cold I wanted to go back outside to get warm.

"What are we going to do now?" I said.

He took a long swig of his drink and when he talked I could see his tongue was green and that started me to laughing. He shook his head at me and smiled, and I knew then that we were going to be okay, even if we didn't have money or the RV. My dad once said that if you have somebody who loves you in the world, you don't need a whole lot more.

"We need to find us some wheels and head out to the reservoir," he said.

"How are we going to do that? We don't have any money."

"I've got an idea, but it might mean taking a hike. You up for that?"

"Mountain climbing? Sure!"

"Not mountain climbing. Just a long walk." He checked his wallet again.

"We got enough money?" I said.

"We'll be all right," he said. "Let's go."

23

Sheriff Hadley Preston filled a Styrofoam cup from the coffeepot and glanced at the news trucks. The vultures were still there, but he knew they only circled so long before they pounced. They had reported about the missing suspect but hadn't heard about the incident the night before, and he hoped they wouldn't for a while. He was trying to work out the sequence of events from long ago, but the more he thought about it, and the more he looked at the pictures of the car they'd pulled from the reservoir, the less sense he made of the situation. The whole thing reminded him of a spent candle that just leaves a smoke trail that circles up and up and then disappears into the air. Maybe there was something to this lady in Colorado. Maybe Dana had been telling the truth.

Mindy put a report on his desk. "This is about that license plate you had me run. And that reporter fellow from the *Herald-Dispatch* is on the phone."

"You know I don't want to talk to—"

"I wouldn't have bothered you if he hadn't said he had some information. I think you ought to talk with him."

"Information about what?"

"He said he knows about Gray Walker."

Preston cursed.

"I swear, I didn't tell him a thing," Mindy said.

"No, he probably got to Mike and promised him a box of chocolate-covered cherries or a six-pack of Coors."

Mindy smiled. "He'd sell his soul for a Budweiser."

"All right. Close the door for me." Preston picked up the phone and put on his reading glasses.

"Sheriff, it's Todd Bentley from the *Herald-Dispatch*. I'm in your neck of the woods. Okay if I come by?"

"I don't think that's a good idea, Mr. Bentley. You know how territorial reporters get. Stick one microphone in front of me and they start having babies right in front of your eyes."

Bentley chuckled. "Well, I think you'll be interested in what I have to tell you. It's about Graham Walker."

"You know, not everything you drag out of one of my deputies is the gospel."

"I didn't get this from Mike. Though I do know about the shooting."

Sheriff Preston sighed and rolled his eyes. This guy was good. A real go-getter. He probably saw this story as a way to move up to some other paper. Maybe Cincinnati or Lexington. Anything to get him out of the hills.

Preston pulled the report Mindy had given him closer. It always helped keep his emotions in check when he was focused on more than one thing. The West Virginia license plate the lady from Colorado had given him had been inactive for years.

"What makes you think there was a shooting?"

"Because he told me," Bentley said.

"My deputy told you?"

"No, Graham Walker told me your man broke through the back door of the shack where he was staying."

Sheriff Preston nearly dropped the phone. "Is that so?"

"Fired his birdshot over the deputy's head, which made the deputy—how should I say this? Lose control? Do I have that correct?"

Preston remained silent.

Bentley continued. "Walker said he didn't know who it was, and he reacted on impulse. You evidently had him engaged in conversation out front, and that's why he was startled. He said he believed you when you told him you were alone."

Preston had never said he was alone. Bentley was trying to corner him for information, but the reporter also had clearly spoken with Walker. "Mr. Bentley, you know you could be accused of interfering with an ongoing investigation."

"I'm not here to interfere. Walker called me. What was I supposed to do, refuse?"

"You should have told him to turn himself in."

"I did. And that's what he wants to do."

"He told you that?"

"Yes. He wants to come in, but he wants assurance that he won't be held responsible for your mistake."

Preston flipped to the second page. It listed an incident report in Kentucky where state police had recovered several pounds of cocaine from an RV with West Virginia plates. Two suspects were apprehended at the scene. They were implicated in a shooting that had left three men dead at a warehouse several miles away. They also found several hundred thousand dollars in the RV. The vehicle had been wrecked and the two suspects were unconscious when police arrived. The vehicle had been impounded in Kentucky.

"My mistake?" Preston said. "And I suppose you want to be there when Walker gives himself up, with somebody taking pictures. Not to get the story, of course, just to make sure your fellow human being is treated fairly. Is that right?"

The occupants of the RV claimed the drugs and money weren't theirs. They claimed a man had used a young girl to gain their trust and then held them at gunpoint. The man fled on foot when the RV went off the road and wrecked. There was no word about the whereabouts of the girl.

"I just want to get to the bottom of what happened," Bentley said. "There are a lot of people who have a huge hole in their hearts regarding this Edwards child, and if this man can help tie up those loose ends, I want to be there." There was an edge of sincerity in his voice.

"That's a pretty convincing speech, Mr. Bentley. How long you been working on it?"

"Ever since I got off the phone with Walker," Bentley said. "But seriously, the one I keep coming back to is the grandmother, Mae. You can see the pain every time she talks about her granddaughter."

"Mm-hmm."

"I've also talked with the mother, though she didn't know I was a reporter."

"Dana? What did she tell you?"

"She was high at the time and made a pass at me."

"Are you saying she wouldn't have if she'd been sober?"

Bentley went on. "Most of what she said didn't make sense. She told me all about the loves she's had and lost, and it sounded like it was quite a list. How does a sweet old woman like Mae Edwards have an offspring like that?"

"You think Mae is sweet?"

Bentley laughed. "Well, she's a little territorial, but I'm sure she's good at heart. She just wants to see her granddaughter again."

"Did Dana talk about her own daughter?"

"Not on her own. I threw a couple of lines out there to see if she'd take them, but it was buried deep. I don't know if she's just shut it out or if there's guilt. I finally said something like, 'Have you ever lost something that you wish you could get back?' And she made a joke about her virginity. Then I steered her toward kids, and she said she once had a daughter but that she was gone."

"When was this?" Preston asked.

"After they pulled the car out of the reservoir," Bentley said. "Took me a while to find her."

"How come you didn't do a story on her?"

"You'd be surprised how much you have to know before you write something true, Sheriff. Probably a lot like your job. You know more than you let on when you're talking to someone. Like this Walker character. You must have some pretty good suspicions about him to go after him that late."

"Yeah, with me and Mike. A whole posse."

"Do you think he knows something?"

"I think he knows a lot."

"I mean about the Edwards case."

"You're the one who talked with him. Did he say anything to you?"

"Unfortunately he wasn't in the talking mood, other than to ask my help coming in."

Sheriff Preston pushed the report away on his desk and leaned back in his chair. The air conditioner made a rattle anytime it was turned on high, so he kept it on medium, where the hum dulled the senses and cut the heat to about eighty-five. Sweat trickled down his neck, and he could feel the stains spreading under his arms.

"Mr. Bentley, I can tell I was wrong about you. There is a caring bone in your body. You're not in this just for the story."

"What are you getting at?"

"Help me bring this boy in. Tell me where he called you from and I'll find him."

"That's what he's afraid of, Sheriff. He thinks you're going to come in with guns blazing because he shot at an officer."

"I gotta tell you, it doesn't make me too happy that he pulled a gun on my deputy, but I can assure you I'm not going after him with guns blazing."

"Well, that's why he called me. I'm just telling you what he said. And if you want my help, I need to be part of him coming in."

Mindy stuck her head into the office. "I've got one of the troopers from the Kentucky State Police on the line if you want to talk to him."

Sheriff Preston nodded. "All right, Bentley. How did you leave it with him?"

"He said he'd call me and set up a meeting place and I'll call you."

"Let me give you my cell number. But don't be surprised if you don't hear from him."

"What's that supposed to mean?"

"He might change his mind. That's been my experience. He'll either turn tail and run or do the job himself."

"Meaning suicide?"

"If he doesn't see a way out and the liquor talks to him, yeah."

"I'll let you know what I hear," Bentley said.

24

We headed out toward a little town. The streets were torn up with potholes, but it seemed like a nice place. There was a funeral home, a post office, and a shoe store, but a lot of the places looked like they had gone out of business.

With my hand in his I got this tingle in my belly that something good was about to happen, and I thought maybe he was taking me to see my mama. Maybe she was sitting in a house waiting for me, praying I would come back.

We turned down an alley and walked and walked until we passed a big brick church. I haven't been in many of them, but from the open windows I could smell that old wood and those pews and something inside sparked a memory.

"Is this Dogwood?" I said.

"No, Dogwood's down the road ten miles or so. Why?"

"Because I think I remember this place. That church smell."

We walked over the freshly mowed grass with a few dandelions trying to come up and some crabgrass growing near the building. It was shady in that area, the big cross above us blocking the sun. He stopped and lifted me to one of the stained glass windows that was open, and that's when it came back to me like a flood. An older woman smiling at me and holding me up. I closed my eyes and saw a blurry vision.

"What is it, June Bug?"

"The strangest thing. I remember this woman holding me up. It smelled just like this. And she called me a name."

"Natalie?" Dad said.

He held me up so I could keep smelling and looking, though I had my eyes closed trying to see that old woman's face. When I couldn't bring it back, I looked in and there were all these pews sitting empty in the sunlight. "No, it was something else. She held me up and laughed."

I glanced at the big organ over on the other side of the church and the piano on this side and wondered what it sounded like in there with all that music going and people singing. People in choir robes swaying, that's how I pictured it.

"What are you thinking?" Dad said.

I rested my chin against the cool concrete windowsill. "I know living out of an RV is fun and you get to see lots of places, but wouldn't it be nice to live in a house and go to a church like this? have our own yard? maybe a playground with a little swing set? and a dog? a little puppy I could train to sit and chase a ball and fetch your paper in the morning?"

Dad's face lit up a little bit, but at the same time he looked sad. Like he knew what I was saying wasn't ever going to happen. "I suppose it would," he said.

"Can I help you?" someone said behind us. Sometimes people can say that to you in a store and what they mean is "Get away from there." But this voice sounded like the man actually meant it. He had on nice clothes and looked a little older than my dad.

Dad put me on the ground, and I tugged my shirt down in the back.

"Just looking inside," Dad said. "You have a nice church here."

The man came over and said he was the pastor. I wanted to ask him all kinds of questions, but Dad told him we were taking a walk.

"I hope you'll visit us this Sunday," the man said.

"We're just passing through," Dad said.

The man stared at us like he knew there was something wrong.

He looked Dad square in the eyes and said, "Are you two okay?" He said it like somebody told him to ask it. I don't know how God works with people and if he does that anymore. There's all sorts of stories in the Bible about him talking to people from bushes and such. I suppose if you want to hear God talking to you he'll do it in a way that you can hear eventually.

"Yeah, we're fine," Dad said.

My heart went pitter-patter when the man turned around. I thought that was the worst answer Dad could've given, so I couldn't help saying, "Except that our RV got wrecked and this truck driver took all our money."

Dad poked me on the shoulder, but the man turned and looked us up and down. "You poor things."

"I've got relations that live here in town, Pastor," Dad said, putting his arm out and pushing me behind him. "That's where we were headed. We just made a little detour to look at your church."

"What's the name?" the pastor said. "Your relations."

Dad hesitated. "Johnson. First name is Franklin. If I remember correctly, he lives on Third Street." He tilted his head to one side, pointing down the street.

The pastor bit his lip and looked down. I thought that was a bad sign. "Son, Franklin passed. It must have been four, maybe five years ago. Had a heart attack over at the Big Bear. Sweetest man I ever met." He snapped his fingers. "Went just like that."

"Is that so," Dad said. He said it kind of soft, almost like a prayer.

"I think that house was sold. Mrs. Johnson moved back to Cleveland to be close to family. A sister, I believe."

Dad nodded and I stared at him and he just looked at the church like there was something interesting he could see in the bricks. I wondered if that was his daddy.

"Franklin had a brother who lived over in Dogwood, didn't he?" the pastor said.

Dad nodded. "Henry."

"Why don't you hop in and I'll give you a ride over there."

"No, thank you. We'll be all right."

"Are you sure?" the pastor said. "It's air-conditioned. Sure would feel good to get out of this heat."

"It sure would," I said. I wanted to get in that car worse than anything. Almost worse than getting a dog but not quite. Dad stood there looking away, and I came out from behind him. "How many people go to your church?"

"Depends on whether it's Christmas, Easter, or some other Sunday," he said, smiling. "At the peak we probably have a couple hundred. On Wednesday nights it's a handful."

"Is it fun being a pastor?"

"June Bug," Dad said, telling me to stop.

"No, she's all right," the pastor said. "I enjoy it. It makes me feel good to know that I'm helping people. And at other times it makes me sad when people get stuck and won't accept God's forgiveness."

"I'm a Christian," I said.

"I could tell just by looking at you."

"Really? Is that something every pastor can do?"

He chuckled. "Well, I don't know if everyone can, but there's something about the way a person looks sometimes, the way they smile or talk, that helps you tell they know the Lord."

"Where were you going when you stopped to talk to us?"

"June Bug," Dad said.

The pastor ignored Dad this time and glanced at his watch. "I was headed for some lunch over at the diner and then on to the hospital to see one of my church members." He looked at Dad. "But I've got plenty of time to take you wherever you need to go. Seriously, I'd count it a privilege."

I turned to Dad. "Please, can we ride in the air-conditioned car?"

Through the buildings came a siren and Dad looked more like some animal that was cornered than anything else. "I suppose if you have the time, it would be a help."

The man smiled from ear to ear like we'd just made his whole day. Some people smile when they take your money and others smile when they help you. Right then I thought about Sheila in Colorado and the way she smiled whenever I'd find some new thing in her house. It's like uncovering a buried treasure when you find people like that. Of course my dad and I have seen a few of the other kind too.

I hopped in the backseat and Dad got in the front. As soon as the pastor started that car the air felt so good I never wanted to get out. The seats were leather, and though they were hot when I got in, they turned cool fast. The pastor reached around and showed me how I could change the direction of the air. There was also this music that came on soft and low and soothing, and I could tell it was church music. Not the kind with the organ blasting and a choir but just one person singing about "the Lamb" or "the Father" and stuff like that. I figured he kept the sound low so we could talk because that's what he did most of the trip.

We pulled out and Dad said for him not to skip lunch, but the pastor said he could afford to and he patted his belly. He said he went to the diner because his wife had him on what he called the John the Baptist Diet.

Dad didn't ask, so I did because that sounded like the strangest thing in the world.

"A locust for breakfast, a locust for lunch, and a sensible dinner," the pastor said. And then he cut into laughing, saying he'd used that joke the previous Sunday and the people in the church got a kick out of it.

I laughed but I guess I don't know enough about John the Baptist.

We drove through the little streets with the pastor pointing out the houses of different people who attended the church. It seemed to me that a lot of people who went there had either died or were sick because just about every one of them had ailments. The pastor said one woman had surgery for a gallbladder and another man had prostate cancer and in another house the son was killed in Iraq. I was glad to get out of the neighborhood to tell the truth because it was getting depressing, but pastors must think about those kinds of things a lot.

As we drove this windy back road, I could tell Dad was looking at things and noticing stuff, though he wasn't saying much. "Do they still have the Halfway Market along Route 60?" he finally said.

"You bet they do," the pastor said. "Expanded it not long ago. They'll have some of the best sweet corn this side of heaven in a few weeks."

When we passed it, the pastor slowed down and let Dad look. I wondered why he would ask about it.

"I used to have a job in high school, and I never took anything to eat for lunch. Every day I'd get hungry just before work, so I'd stop in there and buy some chips or a Little Debbie cake."

We drove on and the pastor showed us the new post office and the elementary school. Dad had gone there when he was a kid, and I couldn't for the life of me imagine that he was ever as little as me.

The pastor snapped his fingers. "Now I remember. You were in the military, weren't you? Special forces."

"Yes, sir."

"I remember seeing the write-up in the *Cabell Record*."

"Then you've got a good memory," Dad said.

The man laughed. "I'm a stickler for details. I can tell you the starting lineup for just about every team in the majors from '68 to '75. National League, of course. That kind of attention to detail helped me out when I started memorizing verses and studying Greek. And then remembering names and faces each Sunday."

We passed a police car with its lights on, sitting behind a beat-up old car with two guys in it. The pastor slowed down to have a look at them and then pursed his lips. "That was one of the Meadows boys driving. He's been on the prayer chain for one thing or another since he was about twelve. His mother's going to be beside herself."

We kept driving, and I tried to pick out the house most likely to have my mother in it. The ones with the white picket fences were my first choice, but there were others that were made out of brick that looked nice. And then there were a few trailers that seemed like a mansion to me because of living in an RV.

"Now if I remember correctly, Henry's house is up Virginia Avenue and then left toward the interstate."

Dad nodded and looked to the right and left. "If you wouldn't mind, why don't you just pull in here and let us out."

"I can drive you all the way back there. It's no problem."

"I know." Dad looked out the window again, like he was expecting to see someone he didn't want to see. "I think it would be best if we walked back."

The pastor turned left and didn't slow down, and the veins in Dad's neck bulged. "I want you to stop now!"

The pastor had his foot on the brake as fast as a squirrel can run up a tree. "You don't have to shout."

"I'm sorry," Dad said. He got out of the car and opened my door while I unbuckled.

"He didn't mean anything by it," I said to the pastor. "I think he's nervous."

The man nodded and reached down in the middle of the seat for something, then turned around to pat me on the shoulder. He slipped a little white piece of paper into my hand that had his name and phone number on it as well as the address of the church. "You take care, June Bug. And if you ever need anything, you call me. You hear?"

I nodded and got out. Before he closed the door, my dad leaned down and said, "I thank you for the ride. Didn't mean to scare you."

I don't know what they said after that because I was taking in all the sights and sounds and smells. There was a horse barn across the street and small houses in a row. Some of them looked nice; others looked old and dingy. The electric wires ran by the road above us and almost seemed like they were sizzling in the sunshine.

As the pastor pulled away, my dad took my hand and we started walking. Just then, the prettiest black dog came out of a house across the street and stood on the top step and barked. You wouldn't think that a dog barking could make you feel welcomed, but right then it felt like I had set foot in a place that should have been home a long time ago.

Dad can walk really fast when he's on a mission, but this was about the slowest walk I'd ever been on with him. It was almost like walking through a cemetery only there weren't any tombstones.

First we walked to the right of the street, and he paused at this little white house. He stared at the mailbox. "My best friend used to live here. Used to ride bikes with him."

"What was his name?"

"Dale."

"What happened to him?"

"Your guess is as good as mine. He got married; I know that. I was his best man."

A little farther along he stopped at another house, and I asked him who had lived there.

"A girl. Connie was her name. She was the smartest in our class by far. While the rest of us were reading *Dick and Jane*, she was reading *Jane Eyre*."

"Who's Jane Eyre?"

"Just a famous book. I still haven't read it."

"Did you like her—the girl who lived here?"

He nodded. "It was impossible not to. She was real quiet, though. I always wondered what happened to her. She could draw pictures so good the substitute accused her of copying her artwork out of a book. She cried because of that."

I'd never had a teacher accuse me of anything because the only teacher I'd ever had was my dad. My curiosity was getting the best of me, so I headed to the sidewalk. "Why don't we go see if she's still here?"

He squeezed my hand and we kept walking toward the end of the road. A sign said *Dead End*, but it looked to me like it went on forever. To our left was a field that sloped and rolled along a creek.

"I used to work for a farmer who owned this field, baling hay and putting it up in his barn. He didn't pay much, but it sure was fun riding on that wagon. He had a big house, and every time we'd bring a load in, his wife would come out with a pitcher of the sweetest lemonade."

I closed my eyes and could almost imagine Dad younger and working in a field with that hay. Maybe with his shirt off and his muscles growing. Him and his friend Dale sweating in the summer sun, drinking lemonade, and working hard. "How much did he pay you?"

"Five dollars for a day's work. Seemed like a lot back then."

I thought maybe I could catch him off guard while he was thinking about the past, so I said, "Does my mom live around here?"

He kept walking and looking out at that field with the bark of the dog fading. "We seined for minnows down in that creek and then rode our bikes to the reservoir. Caught crawdads and even a few snakes."

I didn't say anything and he finally looked at me. "I don't know about your mom, June Bug. I told you I can't answer that."

It was hot again, and the sidewalk had ended and we were walking along the dirt. The flies had found us, I guess because we were sweating and they could smell it, and then the gnats joined them and swarmed. I tried to swat at them, but they were just as persistent around my head as I was about my mother.

Toward the end of the field on the left there were a bunch of trailers packed in like haulers at a NASCAR race. Some kids were out running and giggling. One little kid with long hair just had a diaper on, no shoes or shirt. At the end of the road there was a fence that kept you from going up to the interstate, and on the right, across from the trailers, was this old brown house that looked like somebody had tried to paint it a long time ago and the paint was peeling off and the roof was sliding down on itself. There was a cracked window in the front, and it looked to me like a kid with a black eye.

Dad let go of my hand and knelt in the dirt by the road just staring at it.

"Is that where you grew up?" I said.

He nodded. "I lived there until I went into the military."

"Did it always look this run-down?"

"Not like that. There used to be a little birdbath in the front. Rocks around it and some flowers."

The front yard was nothing but weeds and thistles and dandelions. Either someone's lawn mower didn't work or somebody didn't care. The driveway led out back to a shed that was leaning to one side. A stiff wind could have blown it down.

"Who lives here now?"

Dad pointed to the mailbox, and the word *Johnson* could almost be seen through the rust. "I'm thinking it's my dad."

I stood there looking and swatting while he knelt in the dirt. A truck pulled out of the trailer park and the driver lifted an index finger toward us and my dad waved. Seemed like the least the guy could have done was raise his whole hand, but maybe that's the way they say hello here.

I put my hands on my hips and stared at him. "We going to go over there or just stay here and collect dust?"

He stuck his tongue in his cheek like he was trying not to smile and squinted at me. "Why don't you go over there and knock on the door? See what happens."

"What do I say?"

"I don't know. Act like you're selling Girl Scout Cookies."

I looked at the house and I couldn't help but feel it was haunted. "Why can't you go with me?"

"I'll be along directly."

He didn't say that too much, but when he did, it had a bunch of different meanings. *Directly* could mean two minutes or a whole hour, depending on the situation. But I was so hot and the bugs were so bad that I walked across the road and climbed on the rickety porch. There was one lawn chair outside the door that looked like if somebody sat in it they would fall clear through. Beside it was a Maxwell House coffee can that was full of cigarette butts.

I glanced back at my dad and he was still on the ground watching me, his hands together in front of him as he knelt. I pushed the doorbell, but there wasn't any sound inside. So I knocked on the screen door, which didn't have a screen in it, and the thing rattled like some angry snake.

The front door was wooden, and when nobody came, I reached through where the screen should have been and knocked. It made a dull thud like it had gotten wet and wasn't really supposed to be used as an outside door in the first place.

I didn't hear anything inside, so I started to leave, but then the doorknob turned and the meanest-looking man I had ever seen was standing there. He had whiskers all over his face, white ones, and there was some brown stuff coming down the corner of one side of his mouth. His hair was all swirled on top of his head like he'd been sleeping, and the white T-shirt he was wearing had big stains under the armpits. He stared at me with the kind of sneer that you would use when looking at worms in your salad bowl.

"Can't you read?" he said. He almost growled. He pointed at the sign on the side of the house that said *No Solicitation.*

"I don't know what that means," I said.

"Means whatever you're selling I'm not buying."

It was a really terrible feeling talking to somebody who did not even want you to exist, but at the same time, I could tell there was something in that voice and in the eyes that reminded me of my dad. Sometimes when you see something awful, you can't help but stare at it. I almost wanted to sing a verse of "I'll Fly Away," but I didn't.

"You get on out of here and leave me alone."

He was about to close the door when I said, "But, sir, do you know a John Johnson? Used to be in the military? Fought in Afghanistan?"

He pulled the door open again, and it creaked at the bottom where it was coming apart. "What do you want with Johnny? He don't live here anymore."

"I know he doesn't. But he used to, right?"

His eyes narrowed.

"You're his daddy, right?"

He muttered something under his breath about stupid kids in

the neighborhood bothering him and started to close the door. Then he looked up over my head, and I felt a shadow engulfing me and a hand on my shoulder.

The old man stared at my dad in a mix of anger and surprise. Then he opened his mouth, and I could see his teeth were either yellow or black. "I thought you was dead."

"You thought wrong," Dad said.

"I thought you killed yourself. Everybody did. Thought you'd wash up on some beach."

"I washed up here. Can we come in?"

"We?" the old man said. Then he looked at me. "This your daughter?"

"This is June Bug. June Bug, this is my dad."

He muttered something about my red hair before turning around and looking inside. I guess he wondered what he should pick up.

My dad opened the screen door and we walked in. It was dark, even in the middle of the day, because all the blinds were pulled and there wasn't any light except the one coming from the TV. The sound was off but there was some fishing show on. Newspapers were strewn all over and a couple of bowls that needed cleaning long ago. I wished he had a dog, but then again, I wasn't sure what would happen to a dog if he couldn't take care of himself.

The old man wobbled when he walked and just inside the kitchen door there were lots of medicine bottles, the brown kind, with the name Henry Johnson on them. The kitchen wasn't much better than the front room as far as being clean, and the floor was coming up in different places. There was a funny smell about the whole house, like when you get your socks wet and hang them up, but they don't dry, and I wondered if it had always smelled like that.

"Where was your room?" I said to my dad.

He pointed down a hall. "Last one on the right."

"Can I go see it?"

Dad stared at the old man. "Yeah, go ahead. Just watch out for wild animals."

The floor creaked with every footstep, and that's saying something because I really don't weigh that much. I kept waiting for the two of them to start yelling at each other, but it was quiet behind me. There was carpet as thin as sandpaper in the hall. The bathroom to my left had a brown ring around the bathtub as dark as the old man's teeth.

I got to the door at the end of the hall and pushed it open. There was an old bed in there and a dresser with a couple of the drawers falling off and dust everywhere. I stepped inside and saw a bookshelf, which was just a couple of cinder blocks with a piece of wood between them. On there were a few Hardy Boys books, the blue hardcovers, and several paperbacks. *Where the Red Fern Grows* was one of them, and I knew that was one of Dad's favorites. A story called *The Old Man and the Sea. To Kill a Mockingbird.*

And a little red book that turned out to be a Bible. I picked it up and opened to the first page. "To Johnny, from Uncle Franklin. Walk with the Lord. December 1982."

I looked in the closet and there was a uniform in a plastic bag. Black boots stood on the floor with dust all over. I kept looking for any of my dad's toys or games or maybe an old baseball glove, but there was nothing like that in the whole room.

I heard their voices from the end of the hall, but I wanted to look under the bed. I lifted the cover and found a shoe box. I pulled it out and blew off the dust. When I opened it, I couldn't believe what I saw, because there was this skinny little boy with the same grin my dad has and I knew it had to be him. There were a whole bunch of pictures thrown in there, and one was of a lady with lots of lipstick holding him and giving him a big kiss. There was only one that had the boy and the old man. They were standing a yard apart and staring into the camera. There was something sad about it, but I couldn't figure out why.

There were also a few pictures of him in a football uniform and one with a graduation outfit. And then several in a military uniform where his face looked hard as a rock. I shoved a couple pictures in my pocket and took the rest with me into the hall.

"And where's her mother?" the old man said.

"I don't have an answer to that," Dad said. I thought it was interesting that he didn't call him Daddy or Dad or Pop or even any name.

"Is she dead? Did she run off? Something must have happened to her."

"You're right. I'm sure something did, but I don't know what."

I just stood there, afraid if I walked they'd hear the floor creaking.

"What did you come back here for?" the old man said. "If you're looking for money, you're going to be sorely disappointed. I've been on disability since after you lit out, and I can barely get by as it is."

"I don't need money," Dad said. "I need to borrow a car."

The old man cackled. "If I had a car, I wouldn't be sitting around here. Truck's all I got but the transmission went out last month. Don't have the money to fix it. What happened to yours?"

"Wrecked it. We lost everything."

"Insurance ought to cover that."

"Didn't have insurance."

The old man groaned. "I raised a infidel." There was silence for a few moments. "When you came back from the war, where'd you go?"

"I had to say good-bye to a friend of mine. Pay my respects to his mother."

"And then what? You just went out and got a woman pregnant?"

"It wasn't like that."

"How'd you get the girl, then? Buy her at Goodwill? If so, I'd say you got cheated. Red hair like that? Ugly as sin."

"Shut up," Dad said. "You've got no right to talk that way."

They just sat there not saying anything, and I wondered if this was how it was back when Dad was little.

"Don't say another word about her," Dad finally said. "She's the best thing in my life and about the only thing that kept me going."

I wanted to cry and smile at the same time. I'd never heard anything so mean in my life. I always felt ugly compared with the kids I saw at the stores, but this was the first time I heard my dad stick up for me like that.

The old man must have raised his hands and let them fall on his lap because that's the noise it made. Just kind of a slap sound. "Well, from my perspective it don't sound like you have reason to come in here all high and mighty. You should just take her and get out."

I walked down the hall and handed Dad the shoe box. He took it and leafed through the pictures. The old man muttered something about thinking he'd thrown them away.

"How do you get to the store?" Dad said.

The old man leaned back. "I call the widow Perkins. She'll come get me every week or so and take me down to the Big Bear. Or I walk to the Foodland. Prices are higher, but if I get in a pinch I can go there."

"Where does she live?"

The old man shook his head. "No, you're not gonna bother her and mess up my chance of getting a ride next week."

Dad pulled me close to him and kept looking through the pictures.

I pointed out the one with the woman and him. "Is that your mama?"

He nodded.

"His mama would have liked you, little girl."

"Shut up," Dad said to him.

The old man gave a wheezy cough. "She liked to throw away the good things and hang on to the worthless."

"I told you to be quiet," Dad said.

"It's my house, if you didn't remember. It's not much, but I get to speak my mind. If you don't like it, get out and take that ugly thing with you."

Dad jumped up as fast as lightning and stood toe-to-toe with him. Dad was about a foot taller, but that was because the old man had shrunk. I guessed they had probably been about the same height at one time, judging from the pictures.

"You don't scare me," the old man growled. "I'll call the police quick as look at you."

Dad looked around. "You don't have a phone."

"Neighbors do."

Dad just stared at him, turning his head while he was looking, and finally in a squeaky voice, he said, "Why? Why didn't you take care of your own? What did I ever do to you that made you care so little?"

With all the emotion in my dad's voice, I thought maybe the old man would say he was sorry or something or try to explain it away, or even give his son a hug.

But he gave a sick grin and all those black teeth showed through. "Is that what you came back for? Some kind of apology? To boohoo about what a bad parent I was? Get over it. Grow up. Life's not a bed of roses, if you hadn't noticed."

Dad reached around and took my hand. "Come on."

I grabbed the pictures in my other hand and followed him.

"You leave those be," the old man shouted. He reached out and tried to take them from me but I avoided him.

"Those are my pictures," he yelled. "I been looking for them. That's all I got left of the memories."

Dad took the box from me and dropped it on the table behind us. He opened the front door and it scraped against the metal frame something awful, taking a couple strips of wood with it. Instead of walking toward the road, he went to the shed out back.

The old man followed, cussing and ranting and telling us to get off his property.

Dad got an old rusty shovel from the side of the shed and tested it out, and I guess he was satisfied because he walked toward the road past the old man. I was scared that he was going to hit his dad with it, but when the man yelled, "Leave that shovel alone," Dad kept walking.

The old man stumbled off the porch and came down the side of the yard. I was surprised at how fast he could go. Inside he could barely move, but now he was churning his legs, and his hands were balled into fists. He jumped right in front of my dad and grabbed the shovel. He was breathing heavy out of his mouth, and his face was white. "You want to know why I couldn't take care of you? You want to know why it was so hard? why I left you alone?"

Dad stared at him like he was from some other planet while both of them held on to that shovel.

"Because every time I looked at you, I saw her," he said, and there was a whine in his voice, like a tied-up dog that wants to run free. "Every time I looked into your eyes, I saw her eyes. Every time I saw you, it reminded me she was never coming back."

"I was a kid," Dad said. "I needed a father. All you could think about was yourself."

The old man pulled back, and his voice got meaner. "I'm not excusing what I did. I'm saying that's what went through my head. I don't need your forgiveness, if that's what you're thinking."

They were both still holding on to the shovel, which would have looked funny if it hadn't been so sad.

"You'd be real proud of the man your son's become," I said, and both of them turned like they'd heard a ghost. The look on my dad's face was priceless. I could tell what I'd said had hit home.

But the look on the old man's face wasn't as nice. "What would you know about men? You probably don't even know who your father is."

Dad pushed the shovel against him, and the old man let loose and fell on the little hill beside the driveway. He grunted and groaned, but I don't think he really got hurt.

"Come on, June Bug." Dad took my hand in his, and off we went down the road with that rusty shovel being the only thing he took away from the house.

The old man shouted something behind us, but I couldn't tell what he said.

When I asked my dad, he hugged me close and said, "Don't look back."

I did look up at him once, and there were these big tears running down his face that he wiped away real quick.

25

So this was Dogwood. It didn't look like a place newspeople would come, but I guess they don't get to decide when and where the news is going to happen. Dad and I walked down the road and had to move to the side a bunch of times because there were these big trucks that passed us, blowing the weeds by the road, and it felt like we were going to roll down the hill. He was walking fast, as if he didn't want to spend any more time here than he had to.

Off to the left there was this nice brick house, but right beside it was a trailer park with weeds coming up in between. I saw a couple of people outside, one guy with long, stringy hair and no shirt. He was smoking, and when he glanced up I wondered what could make him look like such a shell.

"Where are we going?" I said.

"I used to know a few people in town. Maybe we'll find a ride."

We walked behind a grocery store, and there were a bunch of blue bins in the back and some rats gnawing on stuff, crawling around underneath. It gave me the creeps. Then we went by this tiny gas station and crossed onto the other side. There wasn't any sidewalk here, just road and yards.

He took a road that looked sort of like an alley, but there were no houses on either side and I wished I had my bike because I could have ridden it up and down all day. The end of that road stopped at the volunteer fire department, which Dad said had burned down when he was a kid. That made me laugh—not that a fire is funny, but that the very place that's supposed to protect you from a fire would burn down is just a little humorous. There's a word for that, I think, but I don't know what it is.

On another street were more houses and next to them gardens growing with big stakes holding up vines with green tomatoes. Dad said there were corn, cucumbers, and probably potatoes in those rows, and when they were ready, the people inside the houses could come out and pick off the vine for their lunch or dinner. I thought that was like a drive-through without the driving.

It was sweltering hot, and every chance I had to get into the shade I took. In fact I ran ahead of Dad and jumped into the shade and waited there for him as he looked along the road.

"Sure has changed," he said. "This used to be a dirt path we'd take to my grandparents'."

"You didn't tell me you had grandparents," I said.

"Everybody has grandparents. It's just that some of them are alive and some of them aren't."

"Do I have grandparents?"

The shovel clanged on the blacktop. "Yeah. I'm sure you do."

"Then where are they?"

Dad kept walking into the shade of a big tree. "I don't know the answer to that."

"I don't understand," I said. "Do you know my mama or not?"

He stopped by a little green house with a porch swing and an apple tree in the front. "Wait right here."

I followed him up the sidewalk anyway because I wasn't about to be left out of another conversation.

An older woman came to the door, and my dad asked if a Mrs. Burris lived there.

"Law, she hasn't lived here for years," the woman said. Her cheeks hung on the side of her face, and I couldn't help but watch them bounce up and down when she talked. At the bottom of her arms was the same kind of skin, just big globs of it swinging back and forth when she lifted one up to scratch her head or point. "Last I heard they was headed down to Florida. Had a son or daughter that lived down there. Boca Raton, I think. Or maybe it was Tampa. I can't remember which. I bet I could find out from a friend of mine over in town a ways; she keeps up with them."

"No, that's all right," my dad said.

The woman looked past him at me and smiled and lifted her glasses. "Who you got here?"

"That's June Bug," he said, putting his arm around me and patting my shoulder.

"She's a cute one. I love that red hair of yours, darling. You all want some lemonade? It's hot out. My lands, you must be about ready to melt out here."

I was so hot I could feel my face turning red and inside was the low hum of an air conditioner and it looked cool and inviting. I could just about taste that lemonade and feel the water running down the side of the glass on my hands, and I pictured myself putting that cool glass to my forehead.

But there was a noise behind us and Dad said, "We have to be moving along. Thank you."

"It won't be no trouble," the woman called after us, but Dad was already off the step and headed toward the road. "I can bring it out to you."

There was an old truck that rumbled past and then stopped at an intersection. When the driver saw Dad come out to the edge of the road he turned around, smoke coming out the back of the truck and gears grinding.

"Why can't we have a glass of lemonade?" I said, and I could tell by the way Dad didn't look at me that I was whining.

The truck was blue with a bunch of white places all around, as if somebody had changed their mind what color they wanted it to be. Where the truck bed was there were rusted-out holes and you could see the tailpipe. My dad has taught me to look at tires carefully because a blowout when you're riding in an RV can be a life-changer or a life-ender. So other than the rust and the holes, I noticed that the tires were about as smooth as the floors at Walmart. The truck stopped with both windows down. I stood on my tiptoes and was surprised to find it was the old man, Dad's father who had been so mean.

"Put that shovel in the back and get in." He said it more as a command than a request.

Dad looked at me, then at the old man. Then he opened the door and climbed in to sit in the middle, which I thought was nice that he wouldn't make me sit next to the old codger. I didn't want anything to do with him, and I just stood on the road.

"Come on," Dad said. "We need to go."

"He's mean. And he told us his truck doesn't work."

Dad glanced over at him. "She's got a point."

"I told you the truth. My truck doesn't run. This is a neighbor's. Said I could use it in an emergency if I needed it."

"Why didn't you tell us that before?" I said.

"Get her in here. There's somebody coming behind us," the man said.

"You said I was ugly."

"I was upset. You're not that ugly."

Dad held out a hand, but I crossed my arms and stood there thinking about the lemonade I was missing and the fact that this was the meanest man on the face of the earth that was offering us a ride.

"June Bug, this is the best we're going to do. Now come on."

The car behind slowed, then went around the truck. If this was the best we were going to do, we were in a bigger pickle than I thought. But I got in anyway, slowly, and closed the door. I didn't do it hard enough, so Dad had to reach over and open and close it again.

"Now where do you need to go?" the man said.

"Reservoir," Dad said.

The old man stepped on the gas, and the truck chugged a couple of times, hesitated, then took off. The lady was still on the front porch watching us, and I waved at her because anybody who says I'm cute is nice in my book. I wondered if I'd ever see her again.

If I were my dad at that point, I would have done all kinds of yelling and asking questions and giving his dad what for, but he didn't. The two of them sat right there next to each other and didn't say two hoots, and it liked to drive me crazy because I knew what had to be going through my dad's head. Why did the old man go to the trouble to find a truck and then come looking for us? Was that supposed to erase all the hurt and the pain? Or maybe he was going to get back at Dad for pushing him down. It was just the most perplexing thing and I half wanted to scream about it but I didn't.

"Things have changed a lot around here," the old man finally said. "Everything's built up."

"I've noticed," Dad said.

"They put in a Sam's Club just up Route 60. You don't have to drive all the way to Cross Lanes anymore."

Dad glanced out the back window, and I asked him what was wrong. "Used to be a Brazier Burger right there." He looked at his dad. "You took me there once for a hot dog, and I can still taste those toasted buns."

"I took you there?" the old man said.

"Maybe it was Uncle Frank," Dad said. He stared straight ahead and rubbed the sweat from his hands onto his jeans. After a few more minutes he reached out to the radio and turned it on. It was tuned to a Christian station because I recognized the song that was playing.

"Turn that Jesus stuff off," the old man growled.

I leaned forward and looked straight at him. "You think Jesus is ugly too?"

He closed his mouth and didn't say another word until we came to this big sign that listed the reservoir and a wave pool. I thought that sounded like the best place to be in the whole state. Dad said he didn't remember that road being there.

"I told you, they've changed a lot of things. You won't recognize the place."

There were lots of cars parked along the side of the road, and from the looks of things everybody had the same idea about being at the pool. I asked if we could go, and Dad shook his head. "Not today, June Bug."

CHRIS FABRY

I wasn't sure that old truck could get all the way up the hill, but it did, and then he veered right, away from the promised land of the pool toward another road that led into the woods. Right then the news came on and I heard the words *suspect* and *Dogwood*, and Dad turned the thing up real quick.

"Sheriff Hadley Preston said in a news conference this afternoon that there's a person of interest being sought in the disappearance of Natalie Edwards seven years ago. The suspect's name is Graham Walker, and if you have any information, you're urged to call the sheriff's office. The suspect is believed to be armed and dangerous."

"I hope they catch that fellow," the old man said. "Anybody who would hurt a child like that deserves to be strung up, if you ask me. We used to take care of that kind ourselves."

Dad stiffened like he had a stomachache or something.

"Go to the right," Dad said when we came to a fork in the road.

"That don't lead to nothing but a big parking lot," the old man said.

"Go there anyway."

We turned and when we did I saw the most amazing sight. Below us, through the trees, there was this big lake that stretched as far as you could see. Little boats dotted the inlets and choice fishing spots, and men in their hats fiddled with fishing lures. The reservoir spread out among the hills and snaked around to another area I couldn't see.

"They've changed it," Dad said. "Down there was the dock and it's . . ." His voice trailed off, and I could tell he was trying to orient himself.

The old man stopped the truck and turned off the radio. We were just sitting in the middle of the road. "Where to now?"

"Right down there," Dad said, pointing. "Does the road go that far?"

"I told you there's a parking lot there."

We rumbled through a turn and then down into the trees. The lake kind of disappeared, and then we came out a little above it. All around were picnic tables under trees, and it looked to me like the people who couldn't afford to get into the wave pool had come here because there were kids splashing at the edge of the reservoir in an area where there was sand and rocks.

We stopped and Dad got out. He walked a few steps and looked back at the reservoir, then retrieved the shovel and headed down toward the bank. The old man came over to me, and I didn't know what to do but inch away from him.

"What's he looking for?" the old man said.

I wanted to say, *He's your son — why don't you ask him,* but I didn't. I just said, "I think he buried something here."

We followed Dad past the parking lot to a grove of trees. He acted like he was looking for something in particular, rooting around in some bushes and plants, which I later learned were rhododendron. His shovel clanked on something, and when I walked over there I could see it was a big rock that seemed to roll right along with the hillside.

"There was an oak tree about . . ." He walked toward the water, stepping off really wide like he was counting them. He stopped at a picnic table and trash can that were set in the ground with concrete. "It must have been here. The big oak tree."

Then he turned around and looked at the parking lot and his face fell. He stepped off about fifteen or twenty paces and glanced back at the stone, then where the tree used to be. He was on the parking lot, right at the edge of a yellow line. He put the shovel head down on it and looked up. "It's right here."

"What is?" the old man said.

"Something valuable."

"Cash?"

"Not exactly."

The old man surveyed the lot. "Son, the people who put this in probably found whatever it is you buried when they leveled the lot. Or they could have pushed it over the hill yonder."

Dad shook his head. "I buried it deep. Didn't want anybody finding it."

The old man stared at the blacktop. "Well, you're not digging through there with that shovel. And you'll do nothing but gather attention if you try to do it in daylight. The place closes at sundown, so I can bring you back. I got a mattock in the garage you can use."

We walked to the truck and drove away. I sat in the corner with my face pressed against the window, and Dad must have noticed I was moping because he asked what was up.

"I just want to go in that wave pool."

Dad thought for a minute. "Where's the nearest Walmart?"

"Next exit off the interstate."

"How much cash you got on you?"

"Not anything," the old man said. "Check comes next week."

"Take us to Walmart."

The old man looked over at me and smirked. "It's not cheap to get in that pool."

"In this heat, a little girl deserves a swim—don't you think, June Bug?"

❀ ❀ ❀

The bathing suit was $7.96 plus tax. That left us with about $7 from what my dad had left from the Dairy Queen. I asked what we were going to do for dinner, and Dad said I could drink pool water, which made me laugh. He was dead set on getting me into that pool.

We pulled up and the two of them followed me to the window where you pay. There was splashing going on and screaming kids and lifeguards blowing their whistles and telling them not to run and that kind of thing. And there was this wonderful pool smell—I guess it's the chlorine—and that made me just ache to get in the water.

"Day pass is fourteen dollars," the girl at the counter said.

Dad said, "Are there any discounts for this late in the day?"

"It goes half price at four," she said. "We close at eight."

Dad checked his watch. "It's almost three. I got seven dollars left. You think she could get in now?"

"I'm sorry; I can't do that."

"Don't make a lick of sense," the old man muttered. "Highway robbery is what it is."

There were a few people behind us now, and Dad moved closer to the window. "Is there anybody I can talk to? a manager or somebody?"

"He's not here right now. I'm sorry. I'd do it if I could, but it'd get me in trouble."

"I understand," Dad said.

Dad shoved his hands in his pockets, and I saw the old man do the same thing. It was sort of eerie to watch because it looked like an older and a younger version of the same thing.

Dad stood by the fence and looked at the top. "You think we could just throw her over?"

The old man chuckled. "Oughta go back and get the shovel and I'll dig her a tunnel."

There was a line of people now and we sat there watching. It was like being hungry and wanting just a crumb from Old Country Buffet but not being able to get even one piece of chicken. I studied the different pools and the slides, and I pictured exactly what I'd do once I got in there and got changed into my bathing suit. I'd never seen such a big bunch of water and people.

At three thirty when the line was gone, the girl who was chewing her gum called me over. "Just give me the seven dollars and you can go on in."

I ran inside so fast I almost slipped on the watery floor. I looked back and Dad was grinning and waving.

I changed and wadded my clothes up in a little ball and then went through the sprinklers overhead and then outside. I ran over to the side where Dad and his dad were standing, and I put the clothes on the ground.

"Where you gonna go first?" Dad said.

I pointed to the big slide where there was a long line. And then up the stairs I went. I waited and inched ahead, glancing down at Dad every now and then. He was smiling at me, and when I got to the top I watched all the kids in front of me get handed these tubes. When it was my turn I grabbed my tube and looked down, which turned out to be a mistake.

"You can go now," the girl said. She had on a tight bathing suit and shorts and wore sunglasses and looked like she'd been out in the sun all her life.

My heart fluttered and I handed the tube back. I thought it was going to be so much fun, but my knees were shaking and I couldn't breathe and it didn't seem as fun anymore.

"Come on," somebody said behind me. "Move it."

The girl with the tube looked upset with me. "You need to go."

Then I looked down at my dad and he was waving at me and putting a thumb in the air, and even his dad was standing up and had his arms hanging over the fence watching me. I half wondered if this is the way God is. Some think you have to go down the slide in order to please him. But maybe he's just standing at the fence, smiling and reaching out for you.

I grabbed the tube from the girl, slapped it onto the top of the slide, jumped on, and that became just about the scariest, most wonderful thing I have ever done. When I hit the water, the tube flew out from under me and went sailing and I went under. The water was warm and cool at the same time and was the best feeling. I knew I couldn't stay by the slide because I'd get smacked by somebody, so I dived to the bottom like Dad had taught me, blowing bubbles out of my nose. I looked up when I got down there and saw the sun shining through all those bodies above me, legs flailing and arms going. It was like being in my own watery cocoon.

I rose to the surface and fought my way through all of them playing games and got out of the pool. I got turned around and tried to remember the fence where my dad was, and then I saw him. He was still smiling and giving me a thumbs-up as I walked over. I was almost shivering now because I was actually cold in all that heat if you can believe it, and I think I was shivering because that slide was so much fun.

"How'd it feel?" he said.

I nodded again and again and laughed.

"You were going lickety-split down that thing, weren't you?" the old man said, a big smile on his face.

Dad reached through the fence and wiped some water off my face because it was dripping down from my hair. "Was it scary?"

"Scary *and* fun."

I didn't have a towel and we were in the shade under the tree and there was this breeze that was blowing just enough to get the goose bumps going on my arms.

"You going to do it again?" he said.

I nodded and ran off for the stairs. There was this little girl in front of me, even shorter than me, and she had the shiniest blonde hair I've ever seen, almost like a Barbie doll. She held both rails as she climbed and she kept her head turned around, which meant she ran into the people in front of her.

"Have you ever been down this?" I said.

She looked at me like she was scared my head was going to pop off and a big monster was going to jump out. "Not by myself."

She said it with the cutest Southern drawl and a little lisp, and I found out that she was from Georgia and was visiting her grandparents who lived nearby. She told me her name was Melinda, and I thought that fit her pretty good.

We talked and she laughed when I told her my name was June Bug. When she got to the top, she took one look at the slide and lit out of there like a scared cat, her face scrunched up and her eyes starting to turn red. I've had that feeling before, besides the ten minutes earlier when I did the same thing, so I felt sorry for her. The girl with the tight bathing suit tried to get her to go ahead. Melinda pushed by everybody to get to the ladder, but that was not as easy as it sounded because there wasn't much room for even one person going up.

I took Melinda by the hand and went ahead of her, announcing to everybody that we were coming down and a few of them heard and moved.

Her mama was at the bottom waiting, and she gathered Melinda in her arms. "Did you get scared? Aww, that's okay. Looks like you made a friend."

Melinda unburied her face from her mother's shoulder and said, "That's June Bug." She got down and looked me straight in the eye. "You want to be my friend?"

I looked at her mama and she said, "It's okay. Who are you here with?"

"My dad's over there," I said, pointing.

She turned and looked but I don't think she saw him. "Well, you two have fun. Now come back in a few minutes because we're going to eat dinner at the picnic table."

"Okay," Melinda shouted as she ran away.

She had this raft that her big brother wasn't using, and the two of us went out on it and floated and splashed and giggled. And then a big wave would come and knock us off and we'd laugh some more and swim around until we could get back on. I was having so much fun I almost forgot about Dad, but when I looked, he was still there watching. There was a sad smile on his face and I wondered if that was because he wanted to come in but we didn't have enough money. That made me a little sad, but I knew he'd want me to have fun.

After about half an hour Melinda's mama called her over to eat. She asked if I wanted to have something, and I was about to starve to death because when I swim, I have to eat something or I feel like I'm going to die. So I said I needed to go ask my dad.

"They want me to eat with them. Is that all right?" I said.

He was hot and sweating and his dad moved down to the shade. "That's fine with me. You having fun?"

"It's the most fun I think I've ever had. I wish you could come in."

"Yeah, me too. Maybe next time."

I ran back and found the family eating. The mama had made cheese spread sandwiches and ham and cheese, and they had potato chips and pudding. I was so hungry I just ate and ate. The mama laughed at me, not a mean laugh, but one that said she was glad I had an appetite because Melinda picked all the crust off her sandwich and maybe ate two bites of pudding. Her older brother was a squirrelly looking kid with lots of freckles and big ears. I don't think he liked having me around because he just took a few bites and ran.

"Why isn't your daddy coming in with you?" the mama said.

"We didn't have enough money for both of us. The lady at the gate let us in almost a half hour early so we didn't have to pay the full price or I probably wouldn't be in here. Plus he doesn't have any swimming trunks."

She looked toward Dad and then back at me. "Do you all live around here?"

I told her it was a long story, but no, we're from out of town. "My dad came back to find something he'd lost, and our RV got wrecked down in Kentucky."

She pushed the plate of sandwiches toward me and said, "You poor thing. Where are you staying?"

"I'm not sure yet, but my dad's dad drove us here."

"So you're with your grandpa."

I didn't know how to answer that one. "He's my dad's dad, but he's not my grandpa."

That seemed to puzzle her as much as it did me, but she didn't ask me any more questions.

When I was full to the point where my stomach felt like it was about to pop, the mama told Melinda and me to lie down and rest awhile, so we got these big chairs that had been out in the sun and lay back in them and it was so warm to my skin I almost went to sleep. The mama covered me up with a fresh towel and smiled, and I wondered if this was what it was like to have a mother.

Pretty soon after that Melinda got fidgety and wanted to go back into the pool and she pestered the Cheez Whiz out of her mother until she said, "Okay, you can go."

I thought that would never work with my dad because he would just tell me to stop it, and if I whined some more, he'd say I couldn't swim the rest of the night and we'd leave. But I guess not every parent is like my dad.

I saw Melinda's mom talking with her husband who was nice-looking with a lot of hair on his chest. When he called Melinda to get out, he was wearing jeans, and she started bawling and rowed out into the middle of the pool and wouldn't come, so I helped tow her in and said if she didn't behave she might not get to come back.

"Are you going to be here tomorrow?" Melinda said.

"I don't think so. But maybe." I told her it was nice to have met her and that she was a real good friend, and the little thing hugged me before she left. The mama gave me one of their towels, which made me feel like a queen.

I watched them walk through the gate and head down the side-walk and something inside hurt and I can't explain why. The sun was going down and people were picking up their stuff and leaving. My hands and feet were getting pruny from being in the water so long and I took a look outside to see if my dad was there, but he wasn't by the fence. A few minutes went by and I got out of the pool and looked down the hill and saw the old man still in the shade, eating something, but my dad wasn't with him.

That's when I heard his voice behind me, and just as I turned I saw him in the air about to crash into the water and the biggest splash in the history of that pool came over me and my dry towel. And he laughed as loud as you can imagine because of the look on my face.

"Come on. Jump in!" he said, and I recognized the swim trunks from Melinda's dad and I thought that was about the sweetest thing I'd ever heard of and I still do.

We had only half an hour before the pool closed, but I can tell you we made the most of it. We went down the slide together, we rode the waves as long as they'd allow us, and we had a diving competition.

Dad is a really good swimmer—I guess he learned in the mili-tary—and when he swims, he kind of glides in the water instead of flailing like most people do. I could see a couple of the moms who were still hanging around looking at him and talking to each other and I wondered what they were saying, but then I didn't want to know.

We were the last out of the pool when the lifeguards blew their whistles. I could have stayed in there all night if they would have let us. There was a sign that said their Saturday night movies started in July where you could come and watch a movie on a screen and swim while the pool stayed open late, and I thought that was a great idea. They called it a "Dive-In" movie and I thought that was funny.

I grabbed my wad of clothes and got changed and then we went back to the truck and there were all of the sandwiches we hadn't finished from Melinda's family. I put two and two together and figured those people must have been Christians. They even put some more cash in the swim trunks my dad had on and never left their number or anything.

I think that's probably what it was like for Jesus people way back—they'd just give you the shirt off their back if you needed it, even though I don't think they had wave pools.

26

Sheriff Hadley Preston fiddled with his cell phone and listened to the squawk of the radio. He had parked at the back of the waste-treatment facility, which he thought was ironic given the people and circumstances he was working with. His job brought him into contact with people wasting their lives in some vain pursuit of satisfaction or happiness or what they thought could bring a moment of joy. Empty pleasures for a second or two that left a lifetime of pain for them and others. More often than not they got caught up in some pursuit that doomed their chances. A failed love affair that ripped a marriage apart and led to murder. A late-night joyride that left some teenager injured or dead. Stupid choices people made that they probably wouldn't if they'd thought about it for a split second longer.

Preston knew the little silver Honda that Bentley drove. He'd seen it at several accident and homicide scenes, so he watched the parking lot of the Kwik-Mart that sat about five hundred yards below him. A couple of straggling cars pulled up to the gas pumps, but most people went across the street to save five cents a gallon.

Something about this didn't add up. There was no question that Walker was guilty of firing on his deputy and that he'd serve time, but as far as the Edwards girl, Preston wasn't sure. He'd talked with the Kentucky State Police about the impounded RV. They'd told him that other than the cocaine and the money, the vehicle was a dead end. It looked like somebody had been living out of there for a while, but it didn't appear it was the perpetrators. If the people who'd been arrested were to be believed, it was a man and a girl—which was borne out by some of the contents of the RV. The woman in Colorado believed the missing girl was traveling with a man in it, but that still felt like a long shot, even though she seemed credible.

The silver car zoomed into the lot and parked in the space by the air pump. Preston kept a pair of binoculars in his glove compartment, usually to watch the deer on some distant hill, a grouse feeding in a field, some diversion amid the monotony. At times the field glasses were useful in police business. There were two people in the car, and Bentley, in the driver's seat, craned his neck to see inside the store and the rest of the lot.

The edge of the sun had dipped behind one of the hills, so there was still light. Everything around was sprouting with life and green as it would get all year. He'd heard from a buddy that the fish were biting down at East Lynn Lake, and he would have given anything to be down there in someone's bass boat, drinking a cold one and putting a line in the water. Didn't matter if he caught anything, of course, it was just being there. That's what most people didn't understand about fishing. It was just being in the moment, being fully in the water or on it, with the sights and sounds and smells and memories. Catching something was gravy, and he couldn't remember the last time he'd actually kept a fish he'd caught. He always released it back into the water and watched it swim away, glad to have been part of the story.

He waited as the passenger in the car got out. The man had something slung over his neck, and as Preston figured, it was a camera. This would be front-page news tomorrow if everything worked out like they planned. The photographer walked into the Kwik-Mart, out of sight, and Bentley climbed out and stood by the car, folding his arms, glancing one way, then the other at the road. Probably wondering if there'd be a line of police cars showing up to scare away his big story.

It was a waiting game no matter how you sliced it. Most of his

work was. Most of life was. A few years earlier Preston would probably have stayed up all night exhausting his energy and resources
looking for Walker, turning over every rock and dragging people
out of bed. But time had taught him that waiting was sometimes
best. Just like fishing. Sitting and watching, keeping a line out,
fresh bait.

He also knew that the easiest time to lose the fish was right
when you were pulling him into the boat. The hook could slip and
the fish would flop back in the water, leaving you with nothing
but the memory of that silver beauty flailing and squirming until
it found freedom. It had happened more times than he wanted to
count, and he didn't want it to happen here.

He heard it before he saw it, the old beater of a car rumbling
below him, heading west down Route 60. Muffler sounded like
the tailpipe had separated and was dragging. When it came into
view, sparks lit up underneath as the car slowed and wove its way
across the double yellow lines until it made the agonizing turn into
the Kwik-Mart, scraping the curb. It was mud-splattered and the
hubcaps were a distant memory. The car finally came to rest near
the store, then chugged a few times before it quit and black smoke
plumed.

Preston tossed the binoculars aside and rolled down the hill. By
the time he made it to the Kwik-Mart, Bentley was standing with
Walker and the photographer was busy as a hillbilly paparazzo.
When they noticed the cruiser, Walker put his hands above his head
and Bentley stepped in front of him, his recorder to his lips.

Preston parked behind the old beater and reluctantly put his
lights on. He didn't want to draw any more attention than he had
to, but this was needed. He checked for the cuffs on his belt and
struggled out of the car.

As soon as he was out, Walker yelled, "I swear to God I never
meant to hurt anybody up there, Sheriff. I didn't know who was
coming in that door. I swear."

"We'll work this out at the station," Preston said, holding up a
hand to calm him down. He tried to read him his rights, telling him

anything he said could be used against him in a court of law, but it took several times to get through.

"Do you understand what I just said?" Preston said.

"Yeah, I understand."

He turned him around and cuffed his wrists, then led him to the cruiser.

A crowd had gathered inside the Kwik-Mart, their faces pressed to the windows. A few people who were driving stopped or slowed down to gawk. Bentley had his notebook out, asking what he'd be charged with and for a statement from the sheriff.

"He shot at my deputy," Preston said. "I'm going to charge him with that first."

"What about the Edwards girl?" Bentley said. "Do you have reason to believe he was involved?"

"Watch your head," Preston said as he guided Walker into the backseat. He was about to close the door when Walker looked at him, talking through the Jack Daniel's or the Two Buck Chuck or whatever it was that he'd gotten his hands on. Preston had almost closed the door on him before he said the words that changed everything.

"I didn't kill her," Walker said. There was something about being arrested that always brought out the emotion. Maybe the finality of it or the relief or the fear. "I didn't even know she was in the car. You can't convict somebody for something they didn't know, can you, Sheriff?"

Preston glanced at Bentley, who had his recorder held out and a look on his face like he'd just found buried treasure. Preston grabbed the recorder and tried to find the Stop button but it was too small and complicated, and he probably could have stayed there all night and not figured it out.

"You didn't hear that," Preston said.

"I heard what I heard," Bentley said.

Preston handed the recorder back. "If you want to get the whole story, you didn't hear that. Not in tomorrow's paper. You understand me?"

Bentley took the device and nodded.

Preston slammed the door and reached in the front and rolled up all the windows and put the air conditioner on high. Then he walked to the other side and got in next to Walker. "What are you talking about?"

Walker looked like some scared little kid. "I want immunity or whatever it's called. And that thing about your deputy, I don't want to be charged with that."

"Gray, that's not going to happen. You could have killed an officer of the law."

"But I didn't know that's who it was. He busted in."

"Tell me what you know about Natalie, and I'll make sure you get the best deal possible."

Walker stared at him. "You promise?"

"I give you my word, and that's about as good as you're going to get around here."

Walker nodded. "I believe you're a fair man."

Preston let his words hang there. It was the hardest thing not to say something, to just sit and wait, but that's what he did.

Then Walker began. "That night, it was her that put me up to it. Said it was for insurance or something. I don't know."

"Her?"

"That woman. The mother."

"Dana?"

"Yeah. Skinny with big lips and lots of curves. She said if I'd take her car to the reservoir and drive it in that she'd . . ."

"That she'd what?"

Walker looked up with guilty eyes. Like a teenager who'd been caught parking over on Gobbler's Knob. "She promised me and her would get together. I told her I wasn't going to do something that she'd accuse me of later and have me thrown in jail."

"Back up," Preston said. "How'd you meet her?"

"Friend of a friend. I'd seen her around, but she'd never talked to me before until she called. Told me to meet her at the Dew Drop and she'd buy me a drink. And maybe more. That's what she said. Just like that. 'Maybe more if you're good to me.'"

"So you met her there."

"Yeah. It was mid-June. She was flirting around with a bunch of guys when I got there, and I watched from outside. They were hooting and hollering, and she had them all going. Then she saw me and came outside and told me to wait, so I did. She finally came out and said she had something for me to do. I asked what it was." He looked up again. "I swear to you, I didn't know she was back there."

"What happened?"

"She said she wanted me to drive her car into the reservoir. And I said why would she want me to do that. She said insurance or something. That there'd be a big payoff. I don't know what was going on in her head. I swear that girl was half-loony. She had a hot body, but she was off in the head, you know?"

"So you drove the car."

"Not right off. I said I needed payment before I did the job and after. And she smiled and we went to my car." He stared out the window at the gathering crowd, like a kid caught tipping cows or soaping windows. It was almost like he was stuck back there, like he'd been a prisoner of what had happened.

"Sheriff, you gotta believe me. This thing has eaten me up inside. All these years I never told anybody. I never let on what happened except a couple of times it slipped. And I guess that came back to bite me."

"Why didn't you tell? If you weren't guilty of anything, why didn't you come to us?"

Walker cursed. "Guy like me. You going to believe a guy like me over some mother crying her eyes out?" He shook his head. "I lit out of here as fast as I could. Next day I was gone. Drove up to Cleveland. I saw it on the news, her standing there crying, saying what she said. I couldn't take the lies and I figured the truth would come out, but I turned it off. I couldn't think about it after that. Something just shut down."

Bentley was right at the window leaning down and Preston wanted to drive away, but this was like hooking two fish at the same time and dragging them into the boat. He knew he had to see it through.

"So you two go back to your car. What happened after that?"

"She was a big tease. She made it look like she was all hot to trot. Kissing me and doing stuff and whispering things. I was excited; I'll admit it. There's not a man on earth who's still breathing that wouldn't be. But all of a sudden she just stopped. She said it was time to get to her car. And she told me right where it was deepest and how to do it. It was like she'd thought the whole thing through and planned it out right down to telling me to make sure there was at least one window rolled down."

"And that's what you did? You drove up there?"

"Sheriff, I was half out of my mind before I even got to the Dew Drop. I don't know how I remember any of this. But, yeah, I took her keys and she showed me her car. I got in and drove with her driving my car behind me. We snaked up that road—you remember how narrow that thing used to be. It's a wonder I didn't drive over the side, the shape I was in."

"You didn't see the girl in the car seat? How could you miss that?"

"I swear, I never even looked back there. It was pitch-dark and the car's dome light didn't work. You couldn't hardly see the dashboard to tell how fast you were going. It never occurred to me there'd be somebody, especially a little kid, in the back."

"So you drove up there . . ."

Walker took a breath. "I drove up to the incline. It was just dirt. There was this drop-off at the edge where the water was pretty deep, and I knew why she'd picked that place. Nobody'd find the car there unless the whole lake dried up. She had planned that out right, I can tell you. I was maybe twenty yards from the water at that point. And I got out and saw her parked above, waving and giggling. I left the front door open and put it in neutral—then I shifted it into drive and pulled the brake off and let it roll. As soon as it picked up speed, the front door closed and I remembered about the window. I'd forgotten to put it down. So when it ran over the embankment, it hit the water nose-first, then flattened out and floated there for what seemed like an hour, but it was probably only a few minutes. Then it pitched forward and sank." Walker closed his eyes, like something was stinging them.

"What?" Preston said.

"I remember in the back window, this stuffed animal sitting there. I think about what that little girl must have gone through every day of my life."

Preston let the story sink in. He couldn't afford to get caught up in the emotion of the moment, so he pushed forward. "Then what?"

"I ran up the hill to her while the car was about under, and she screamed something about her daughter. Why hadn't I gotten her daughter out of the back? And I said I didn't know there was anybody there, and by that time there wasn't nothing I could do. She was bawling her eyes out and hitting me and screaming about murder and if they caught me I'd go to jail for life or maybe get the death penalty. Looking back I see how she had the whole thing planned out like some dance at halftime. I bought it hook, line, and sinker, Sheriff."

"So you got out of there."

"I hightailed it to my car and turned around. I had to go down to the switchback, and when I came barreling back, she was in the middle of the road with her hands out, yelling at me that I was going to jail and that I better get out and stay out. I just drove away. I can see now the whole thing was an act, and when I saw later on the news that she had accused some stranger of carjacking, it came together. She wanted that little girl dead. I don't know why, but that's the truth."

Preston took off his hat and rolled it in his hands, staring at the cage from the backseat.

"I wish I'd have had the guts to tell somebody, Sheriff. I truly do. Maybe none of this would have happened. Your deputy. All those people looking for her. But I figured me coming forward wasn't going to do that little girl any good. Wouldn't bring her back."

"It would have helped the grandparents if they knew where she was."

Walker nodded. "I'm not saying I'm proud of keeping quiet, but I swear to you, I never meant to hurt anybody."

Preston was still processing the information. What he couldn't figure out was where the body had gone. Water will do strange things, but there should have been something in there, even after seven years.

"What's going to happen to me?" Walker said. "What are you going to do?"

"It's over," Preston said. "You don't have to worry about it. You did the right thing turning yourself in, and I'll make a note of it."

Walker nodded and put his head back on the seat. "You don't know what it's like to carry something like that. You don't know what it's like feeling guilty every day. Living with what you did and knowing there was this innocent thing who's never coming back."

Walker's shoulders shook and he leaned forward, his forehead on the back of the cage, mouth open, saliva dripping from the corners of his mouth.

When the camera flashed, Preston got out and climbed into the driver's seat. Walker's car needed to be impounded, but that could wait. He backed up and headed to the office.

Mae had managed to stay awake all day thinking about her conversation with Dana. The words and looks tripped around her mind at the strangest times. She'd regretted slapping her, but she wasn't sure it was the wrong thing. She'd read about tough love, and though that probably wasn't the best way to show it, what was done was done. You had to move on at some point.

Leason had left her alone most of the day. She guessed he thought she was just in one of her moods. He'd taken the tractor out on the ridge by the old logging road behind the house, and she could see him every few minutes through the trees, cutting the hay and doing whatever it was he did by the water tower all day. Work always seemed to give him comfort. On the day after Natalie disappeared, he had exhausted himself driving around looking for her, then came home and worked on an old car. It had seemed the strangest thing to her, that he could do anything like that when there was so much at stake, but now she understood it better. He was only trying to cope.

When he came in late in the afternoon, he took a Ball jar and held it under the tap until it was cold and then downed it in one gulp and got another. He stared out the back window as the few cattle he had left lumbered down from the upper field for a drink. He asked what was for dinner without even looking at her.

"Sub sandwiches."

They ate in silence with the night both behind and ahead of

them. She didn't want to bring up anything about Dana, and of course he didn't. She couldn't help thinking they were growing apart in their old age instead of growing together and that something needed to happen or they were going to drift off like sticks in the creek, one getting caught in the weeds while the other one rolled on with the rising tide.

After supper, he turned on a game and sat in front of the TV with a bowl of buttered microwave popcorn. Normally she would sit with him and read or doze until he got tired. Tonight she just couldn't sit there and watch another nine innings of life slip away. She went to the porch and gazed at the clouds and the slipping light, thinking about what her daughter had said, trying to decipher the meaning. Maybe there wasn't anything to decipher. Maybe those were just the spiteful words of the crack or meth or whatever it was Dana had taken to numb her pain. Or maybe there was more.

"She coming back tonight?"

The voice startled her. Leason stood behind her, the echoes of the sparse crowd at the game still whistling and clapping in the other room.

"I know she was here for money," he said. "I heard you talking."

Mae waved at a fly and wiped her head with the paper towel she'd been holding since she'd dried her hands doing the dishes. Still staring at the clouds, she said, "I think it's the right thing to do. I think it might be our last chance."

"Last chance to mess up her life for good, you mean. You give that girl any more money and you know exactly where it's going."

Mae straightened her apron. She'd forgotten to take it off after the dishes. Actually she'd worn it all day. "I'm not arguing with you. I know what she'll do with it. But maybe this is the bottom. Maybe it'll take this to turn her around."

Leason stood there at the door, his face clouded gray by the screen. He picked at a popcorn husk in his teeth and then looked at it on his finger, finally flicking it away. "It's throwing our money down the toilet. You know I love her, but I can't stand to see the life just sucked right out of us because of this. We've paid enough — don't you think?"

She looked at him. "How much is enough for a life? You stop praying for her?"

Leason's face showed pain, as if the question were a knife. He shook his head. "If that's what you want to do, go ahead."

"I don't want to do anything of the kind," Mae said. "I'm trying to do the honorable thing. This may be our last chance with her."

"You've said that about a hundred times. And every dime she gets she spends on the drugs and the booze."

She folded her arms. "Well, this time it's true. This might be our last chance at a breakthrough."

He looked like he was going to say something else, but instead he went back to the game.

Mae stood up and went for a walk down the driveway. Gravel under her house shoes bit into her feet. She walked in the grass, then switched back to the gravel, not caring about the pain anymore. When she got to the end, she sat on the brick casing Leason had built for the mailbox so nobody could hit it with a baseball bat. It had only given the vandals a reason to become more creative. They'd stuck an explosive in there, a blasting cap, and then Leason had given up. It made a good place to sit down but a lousy place to get your mail.

She turned and faced the house, set up against the hill like it had grown there naturally. The way the land ebbed and flowed in and around it was like some picture, especially with the soft light above the trees showing the fading pinks and oranges. She saw movement above the house at the treeline and watched a deer edge out into the open. Soon another and then three more joined it, and they all looked up at the same time when a car came around the bend. It passed her, and out of the corner of her eye she saw someone wave and threw a hand up.

She watched the animals move farther down the hill as darkness descended. They were beautiful creatures, and she remembered as a girl wanting more than anything to be one of them. Just become a deer and run through the woods without a care.

Her legs and back ached, and as she stood, she heard the rattle of the old car. When it reached her, she turned and watched it pull into the gravel and stop. Mae stared at the deer again when her daughter got out and left the door open, a buzzer sounding.

"I was just thinking about the times we used to drive to Myrtle Beach when you were young," Mae said. "You sure loved splashing in the water."

"Did you get the money?"

Mae looked at Dana and a deep well of emotion stirred. She could see her daughter as a child, skipping and laughing in the surf, looking for seashells and digging in the sand. How had she come this far? And where had Mae gone wrong?

"Or did he tell you not to waste any more of it?" Dana said.

"I'm sorry I slapped you. I shouldn't have done that and I apologize."

"Assault and battery is what it was." Dana smiled and there it was, that familiar gap-toothed grin, though it was only a hint of what the young girl had been. The sun had gone down on her life and it looked like the darkness had just taken over and there didn't seem to be a chance at a sunrise.

"I was so hurt by what you told me," Mae said.

"Now you're going back on it —"

"No, I'm not."

"Either you're sorry you slapped me or you're not. You can't say you had a good reason."

Mae bit her cheek. "You said Natalie disappearing was my fault."

"Forget it. Do you have the money or don't you?"

"Dana, please. Tell me what happened. What did I do that was so bad?"

"I'm not arguing with you anymore. Just give it here and I'll go."

"Was it that man? the one who came by looking for you? Surely you wouldn't hurt your daughter over a man."

Dana lifted her head and sighed. "Mama, forget it. It's over. Done."

"You mean with Natalie? You *know* she's not alive?" Mae's voice sounded more like a whimper now. Even to herself.

"I don't know what happened. All I know is, she's gone. You have to accept it and live with it. Stop looking for her. Stop putting flyers up and talking with the missing children people. It won't do any good."

The moon edged up over the treetops and cast a ghostly glow on the cornfield behind them. Mae felt her legs giving way, and she sat back on the bricks and put out her hand to steady herself. She wanted to ask more, probe deeper, but she couldn't. She'd believed all her life in the words of Jesus, that the truth would set you free. But she was beginning to believe that there was some truth that didn't. It just wrapped itself around you like a wisteria vine and choked the life out of you. Took your breath away until there wasn't any left.

She reached into the apron pocket and pulled out a thick envelope. She'd spent the morning thinking of what she wanted to say and wrote it in a note she'd tried three times to write before she came up with a good line or two. As she handed it over, she wondered if Dana would even read it or if she'd toss it out the window.

Her daughter took it, but Mae held on, locking eyes with her. "This is the last. There won't be any more."

Dana pulled, but Mae still held on.

"Okay, I get it," she snapped, and Mae let go.

When Dana got in the car, Mae followed. "I love you, honey. I hope you know that."

The woman in the car was not her daughter. She was someone else, looking slack-jawed and spent. "Yeah, I know you loved me the only way you knew how, which wasn't much."

"Call me?" Mae said. "Let me know where you're going. Where you wind up. You think you'll—?"

Before she could finish, the door slammed and the engine fired, and without buckling, Dana backed onto the road and was gone.

Mae watched the taillights wink at the corner, and then she set her face toward the house, willing herself forward, across the sharp gravel like it was the Via Dolorosa. She thought she was all out of tears until she made it to the front porch and the sobs began.

28

I pleaded with my dad to let me go back to the house with the old man, and he finally let me. He told me to watch myself, which I guess meant stay out of the man's way if he got mean again, and I told him I'd be fine.

We drove back to get the mattock, which I found out was this rusty old thing with a point on it that looked like it could do some damage. I always thought my dad was strong enough to do just about anything, but all those layers of blacktop are pretty hard to get through without the right tool.

The old man didn't talk much on the way to his house, and when we got there, it was almost dark. He went straight out to the shed and rooted around until he found what he was looking for. I hung around the front porch watching the lightning bugs rise and catching a few. He returned and threw the mattock in the back of the truck, and I thought the thing would have punched a hole in the bed.

He looked at me. "You want you a jar?"

"Excuse me?"

"When Johnny was little, he'd get him a jar and poke holes in the top and fill it full of them bugs. Put it on the windowsill in his room and let them light up all night."

I thought it was interesting that he'd be telling me something about his son because from what I could tell he didn't take much thought to him when he was a kid. "Sure," I said.

He went inside and brought back a mason jar that looked like it had had some beans or something in it before, and I wondered how those lightning bugs would like it in there. Then he pulled a pocketknife out and poked holes in the cap.

"Do you know where the Edwards live?" I said.

He kept working on the jar, his head down. "Just up the road a piece."

"What road?"

He pointed behind him. "Next street over and past the interstate, then left. They got this big house by the water tower. Why do you want to know?"

"Just wondering."

"Leave those people alone. They've had enough trouble the past few years."

"I don't want to cause them trouble," I said.

"Here," he said, handing me the jar. "You hang on to this and we'll see how many you can catch when we come back from the reservoir."

I'd been wondering how I was going to say what I was about to say, and this seemed like the perfect opportunity. "I don't want to go back there. That place is spooky at night. Let me stay here and I'll have this jar filled by the time you get home with my dad."

"You think *that* place is spooky and you want to stay here?" he said, his forehead wrinkling. "That house behind you has more ghosts in it than all the others combined."

"I don't believe in ghosts," I said. "My dad would let me stay. He really wouldn't mind, as long as he knew I wanted to stay."

"Is that so?"

I started collecting the bugs and giggling and putting on a good show.

He took off his hat and scratched his head with the bill. "I guess if you want to stay, it's okay with me. Just don't bother the neighbors and don't wander off."

When he drove away, I was still catching the bugs but when he went around the corner I stopped. I went inside the house and rummaged around in the drawers in the kitchen and the pantry, but it wasn't until I looked in the hall closet that I found a flashlight. Lightning bugs are okay, but you just can't see with that little bitty light.

The flashlight weighed a ton. When I turned it on nothing happened, so I opened it up, which wasn't very easy, and these big batteries fell onto the floor with all this gunky stuff on them. It took a long time to realize he didn't have a stash of batteries like we did in the RV and that I was basically out of luck, though I don't think luck has anything to do with life. I think the things that happen are for a purpose, though at the moment I didn't know what the purpose of not being able to find a flashlight was.

I grabbed the jar and walked out the back and went through a couple yards with that jar held out. The moon was up and peeking around the few clouds in the sky, so it didn't take long for my eyes to adjust. The houses looked old, and there were a few junk cars sitting around like forgotten children.

I found a spot between two houses that were close together and saw the road down the hill on the other side. There were people talking and laughing in one house, like they were having a party, and in the other house it was just a man and a woman yelling at each other, something about how much she was spending and how he couldn't keep up with her.

When I got to the front I heard a noise that made my skin crawl. It was something growling, and if you have ever been walking in the dark and heard that sound you would know why I stopped and nearly peed my pants. A dog was on the porch, but he came at me, lunging at the screen and barking his head off. The people inside were the ones who were fighting and I guess didn't pay much attention. I took off down that driveway and didn't judge the incline too well because I tripped on a rock and went flying headfirst and the jar crashed into a million pieces and that just got the dog going crazy. I didn't have time to check myself because a light came on, so I got up and ran to the street and headed toward the interstate, the way the old man had said.

There was something pulling and tugging at my heart. I suppose other people have this same feeling and never do anything with it and just stay where they are. But I'd thought about this a long time. I believe you have to let things be the way they are and accept them sometimes. Like the whole thing with me and a dog. I still have the dream of having a puppy and training it and going to sleep with it at night, but there are some things that aren't going to be, at least anywhere in the near future.

But there are things I can change. And I'd decided that now was the time. And the biggest thing hanging in the back of the closet of my life, though I have never had a closet living in the RV but you know what I mean, is the question about my mama.

So on that moonlit road, without a flashlight and with my jar broken on some driveway behind me, I started walking toward the interstate underpass. I felt something sticky on my arm, and when I reached around, there was a bunch of blood coming from a gash. I hadn't even felt it, probably because that dog was barking so loud.

I imagined some big magnet pulling at me and drawing me down that road, and that was the only thing that could do it because it was so spooky walking under that bridge holding up the interstate. There was a bunch of stuff spray-painted all over it, and some of it was about a guy named Will. Most of it I couldn't see because it was too dark, but I could imagine the types of words there.

When I got to a little ridge, there was a street going left, and I figured this was the way because the old man said there was a water tower near the Edwards house. I didn't know what a water tower was, but as soon as I saw it I knew what it was because it rose over everything like a metal monster with big legs. On the side of it was the word *Dogwood* all lit up by the moonlight. Down below were trees and a hillside and a house that sat back from all the other houses.

A car was coming, so I got off the road as far as I could, but even with all of that, I thought whoever was driving was going to run me down. They didn't even slow when they saw me, if they ever saw me, and then the car just kept going around the bend without stopping. I got back on the road and kept walking until I came to a driveway with a mailbox that said *Edwards* and a little pile of bricks that looked like a monument to something but I don't know what.

My heart was going about a hundred miles an hour, and I looked up the long driveway to the house that sat there in the dark. There was a flicker of a TV in one of the windows but not much else, and I wondered if the people inside were my family. It's scary to think you know where you come from and then find out you don't really know the truth. But sometimes the truth can be scarier than not knowing.

Since I saw my face on the wall at Walmart, I've had this thought that someday I'd find a whole passel of people related to me. Instead of just me and my dad, there would be sisters and brothers and uncles and aunts and cousins. We'd have picnics and reunions and parties, and everybody there would have a dog. I know some people will say that's just a little girl dream, but it's what I thought about as I walked up that driveway with the gravel crunching and the lightning bugs rising. I swear, I thought I could run right out there in that field with the creek snaking through it and lie down in the grass and watch the stars come out and put on a show. And I got this warm feeling deep down inside, but at the same time I got this terrible feeling that things were about to change.

When I got to the concrete walk that led to the house, I stopped and looked around. There was a tractor parked beside the house, and it had this long thing attached to it. There didn't seem to be any playgrounds or bikes, so I figured kids didn't live here.

There was a noise, like some animal had been wounded, and it seemed to be coming from the house. And then it stopped and the light came on, not a light in my head telling me something, but an actual light at the end of the walk. Somebody said, "Hello?"

I thought about running away. I thought about heading for the field. But in a voice that didn't seem like it was mine, I said, "Hi?"

Someone moved off the porch and came down the step and stood there looking at me. "Can I help you?"

"I don't know," I said. "Is this the Edwards house?"

She walked a couple steps closer, staring at my face, but I was standing in front of the light and when that happens you just see the light as some kind of halo. It was an older woman who was coming toward me slow, like she was walking on a patch of ice. And then I recognized her from the TV news. It was the grandmother. She didn't answer my question.

"What are you doing out at this time of night all alone?"

I took a step back into the light, and when I did she put a hand over her mouth. I thought she was going to faint or that she was having a spell.

"Leason!" she shouted. "Leason, get out here!"

I felt like running now because her face was all twisted in pain. I watched her as she came toward me and grabbed me by the shoulders and turned me around full in the light.

The screen door creaked and an older man came out. "What's wrong? What is it?"

The old woman whispered, "Natalie?"

I stared at her face. "Are you my grandmother?"

That's when she pulled me into her arms and started crying like I have never ever heard anyone cry before. It was just the deepest soul-wrenching sob you can imagine, as if something terrible has happened and there's no way to describe the pain except for letting your body do it.

Dad told me once that you can only be as happy as you've been sad, and I didn't understand it until that moment. It seemed to me like the sobs reached down inside that woman and scooped out a part of her, like people inside an ice-cream parlor getting a double scoop out of the big container. But when her sobs were done—or at least when they were halfway over—there was something else there to replace them. It was laughter, a deep belly laugh that shook the woman, and it was something to hear.

The old man came down the walk and into the light, and when he saw my face, it was like he'd seen Elvis himself at Graceland. Dad took me there once and told me all about Elvis and how some people thought he was still alive and that his death was a hoax. I almost wanted it to be true just so all those people who were still crying about him wouldn't have to anymore.

"It's her," the woman said in a half sob, half laugh. "Just look at the birthmark on her cheek, Leason. It's her."

She finally let go of me and noticed some blood on her hands. "Leason, she's hurt. Get her inside. And you call Sheriff Preston right now. This second."

29

Sheriff Preston was headed home. Walker would have a lawyer in the morning who was assuredly going to try to undo the damage his client had inflicted upon himself. After writing up the report and having what must have been his tenth cup of coffee, he headed for home and then remembered Macel wasn't there. He turned around, passing a couple of news vans coming the other way. Bentley had been interviewed on the Channel 3 News about his experience, as much or more a part of the story than Walker was. The whole thing would be written out in the *Herald-Dispatch* the next day.

He was only a few minutes into his drive when the radio squawked. A concerned citizen had reported someone vandalizing the reservoir parking lot. He was near the road but didn't have the energy to pick up the microphone, let alone deal with some hoodlums overturning trash cans or smashing beer bottles. Still, that old feeling in his gut leaped and made him grab the mic.

"This is Sheriff Preston. I'm coming up on the reservoir. Which parking lot are we talking about?"

The dispatcher gave him the location, and he turned onto the road that snaked back toward the water. How or why a person would vandalize a parking lot was beyond him, but kids these days would carve up their arms and legs like pumpkins at Halloween, so how could you tell anything?

It took him a few minutes to get to the right lot, and when he did, his lights shone on a single figure with some kind of tool striking at the surface of the blacktop. The man looked up when his headlights hit him and went back to his work, as if he were in a factory and the boss had just walked in.

Preston shook his head and drove over near him and parked. He stepped out of the cruiser as the man took another swing and sank the tool deep into the asphalt and let it stay there. A lean guy with shaggy hair. A tight build, and from first glance, he appeared he could be former military. He had the look of someone you would want on your side in a fight. Square jaw. Arms as strong as steel. Straight back. Preston checked his holster to make sure he was ready if the guy tried anything.

"Nice evening," Preston called.

"Sure is, Sheriff."

"You know, there're probably better places to dig for night crawlers."

He smiled. "I wish I was digging for night crawlers. I truly do."

Preston walked closer. There were three types of men in the world. Those you approached cautiously. Those you approached with your gun drawn. And those you didn't approach. This one looked like the first type, though he'd been wrong about people before. "Mind telling me what you *are* digging for? And why you're out here after closing?"

The man looked down and took a step away from the mattock. "I didn't know it was a federal offense."

It was Preston's turn to smile. "It's not, but we don't have a lot to do around here these days."

"Not what I heard."

"So what's under there?" Preston said.

The man glanced at Preston's eyes, as if he were gauging whether or not he could share the story. He scratched at his cheek and looked at the crumble of asphalt. "I was here a few years ago, before all of this was put in. I buried something and I was hoping I'd find it."

"Buried what? A body?"

The man laughed. "No. A metal strongbox. To keep valuables in."

"And why would you do that?"

"Seemed like a good idea at the time."

"How do you know it's still here?"

"I buried it deep. I don't think it would have been dug up."

"Must be important to make you dig through six inches of asphalt."

The man nodded.

Preston stepped forward and reached out a hand. "Hadley Preston. I'm sheriff here in Dogwood County."

"Johnson," the man said. "John Johnson."

The name sounded familiar. Where had he heard it?

"I'll pay for the repair of the parking lot after I'm done."

Preston kept thinking. He'd taken a dozen calls, but the one from the lady in Colorado stuck out. "Any relation to the Johnsons in Dogwood?"

"My dad still lives there. Henry."

Then it clicked with Preston. "You won all those medals. Purple Heart in Afghanistan."

"That's part of what's in the box."

"Is that right," Preston said. And like fireworks going off in his head, the pieces fit. He hadn't connected Johnson's military service to the call from the woman. "About how long ago did you bury this here metal box?"

"Seven years."

Preston looked at the lake. Seven years earlier there were trees here and a little clearing where people camped. Back then it was deserted and you could still see the stars and the dogs ran free without leash laws and if you caught a fish and wanted to eat it, you scaled it and put it over a campfire. "I got a call about you today, believe it or not."

Johnson didn't respond.

"Lady from Colorado saw the news story about that missing girl. Said she knew you. And that you and a little girl were traveling together. Stayed at her house. That ring a bell?"

Johnson nodded.

"Where's the RV?"

"We ran into some trouble."

"What kind of trouble?"

"Some no-goods tried to hijack us. They showed up at a gas station with a gun."

"What happened to them?"

"Let's just say they didn't understand the importance of buckling their seat belts."

Preston smiled. He liked this man. The questions were partly to test his ability to tell the truth and partly because he was curious. "What about the girl?"

Johnson sighed and crossed his arms. He looked off, like there was something painful going on, and Preston had a bad feeling. Had he done something with her? done something *to* her?

"Honestly, Sheriff, if I could just dig this up and get out of here, I think it would be better for you and me both."

"No. I don't think you're in a position to tell me what's best, to be honest, John. Now I've got this old boy in jail tonight who says he—"

"He didn't do it," Johnson interrupted.

"Didn't do what?"

"Take the girl. If you're holding him because of her, you've got the wrong man. That's part of why I wanted to come back."

"And how would you know he's not my man?"

"Because I was here that night. I saw everything."

Preston stared at him. There wasn't an ounce of flinch or hesitation to him. He looked away and noticed a picnic table, then pointed toward it and they both walked over. Preston let out a big sigh as he settled. "What you say to me can be used against you. You understand that."

Johnson nodded. "What I say to you or what I say to anybody is the truth. So I guess it doesn't matter if it can be used against me."

"Fair enough. What were you doing here that night?"

"Planning my funeral."

"What do you mean?"

Johnson put his hands out in front of him. Strong hands. Battle scarred and nails bit to the quick. "I'd come to a place where I didn't want to live. I'd let my best friend down. He was dead. I didn't have a family to speak of. And the stuff I remembered of the war kept coming back every time I closed my eyes. Maybe it was post-traumatic stress; I don't know. But I was pretty sure I didn't want to go on, and I didn't want anybody related to me getting what was in that box."

"What's in there?"

"My medals. An old letter my uncle wrote me. A Bible my buddy gave me. And an envelope of stuff from my friend's mother. Supposed to be worth something now."

"So if you were going to kill yourself, why didn't you just burn it?"

"I can't answer that one. I guess my mental state at the time wasn't too clear, but digging the deep hole kept me busy and helped me clear my head."

"Thought about how you were going to do it?"

"Just drive to the ocean and jump in. Start swimming and not stop until I was tired. I can swim a long way, Sheriff."

"SEAL?"

Johnson nodded.

"How did you and the girl get acquainted?"

Johnson looked at him squarely again, piercing eyes. No flicker or twitch. "I didn't find her, sir. She found me. God brought her to me as sure as we're sitting here."

Preston let the information sink in, urging Johnson forward with his silence.

"For a long time I thought I was the one giving to her," Johnson said. "That I was the one who'd brought her back. Saved her. But it wasn't that way. It wasn't that way at all."

Preston hated asking the question, but it was the obvious one. "You ever hurt her?"

"Yeah. Every time I said no to getting a dog. Every time she got sick and I tried to treat her myself without taking her to a doctor, afraid that somebody might ask questions. Every time she'd make a little friend at some campground and people would get too close. I'd get scared and we'd leave."

Preston just watched him.

"Not in the way you mean," Johnson said. "I could never hurt that girl. That would be like killing your guardian angel."

The words came out true, but Preston still didn't understand. "If what my prisoner said is true, that girl should be dead. Is he lying about what happened with the car? the woman involved?"

Johnson shook his head. "I brought her out of the water unconscious. It was probably about three minutes before she came around. Longest three minutes of my life."

"Wait. Back up."

Johnson tensed. "I've never told anybody this. Especially her." His shoulders slumped and he took a breath like a pitcher ready to deliver his best fastball. "I'd dug this deep hole, put the box in, and covered it up. I cursed at God for not being with my friend and me in Afghanistan. I was mad at him for not showing up. But my friend's mother had been kind to me, and I didn't feel worthy of the gift she'd given me.

"I was about to head out when I heard a car on the road. I walked out of the trees into the moonlight and saw it sitting by the water's edge. There was a second car above it on the switchback, had its lights on. This little guy gets out, and as soon as I saw him, I knew something was wrong. He leaves the door open, then puts the thing in gear and it rolls toward the water. The door closes and it tumbles over the embankment and floats there, like it's being held up. Then it tips and goes under. Just sinks to the bottom.

"And then I hear this woman yelling from the other car. She'd stepped out to watch, I guess, and she was saying something about her baby. That there was a baby in the car. She's yelling other stuff, but as soon as I hear that, I lit out, kicking my shoes off and taking off my shirt. Those two were arguing and yelling and then the car pulled out. I was still sore from the surgery I'd had, and I didn't get there as fast as I would have. When I did, I dived in where that car was bubbling up and pulled myself down.

"I have this thing about penlights. I always keep one in my pants pocket, and I took it out and turned it on and held it in my mouth as I swam. When I made it down to the bottom, I could see all the windows were still up. And then . . ." Johnson's voice broke.

Preston was surprised to see water in the man's eyes. "What?"

"I saw her. The water had seeped in through the undercarriage and was filling it from the bottom. It was about up to her feet when I got there, but it was rising fast. I grabbed hold of the door but it wouldn't budge. Front door too. There was just no way it was going to open, and I was losing the air in my lungs. I tapped on the window to let her know I'd be back, but the look on her face. I can still see it." Johnson wrung his hands together like some old woman sick to death about a wayward child.

Preston took a breath. He had to remind himself to breathe.

"I rose back to the surface and got some air," Johnson continued. "At a time like that you just want your training to kick in, but I'd never been in a situation like that. I've seen the fear of men who are about to die, but I swear, I've never seen such a look on a child's face and it just about did me in. And the hardest thing was, I knew I was going to have to let her go. I had to let that water rise before I could break through the glass."

He took a moment to compose himself, and Preston looked off at the moon shining on the surface of the water. He tried to imagine the child in the water, the fear, and there being only one chance for her survival.

"By the time I got back, she was struggling, trying to raise her head enough to get a breath. I knew the pressure inside would be about right, so I kicked on the window with my bare heel, but again I couldn't get it to break. So I got out my knife, the one I'd carried with me in Afghanistan, the one my uncle gave me before I left. I pushed the point right into the center of that window until it cracked, and then I was in. She was buckled into her car seat, and her arms were floating beside her. Her little mouth open."

He jammed his palms against his eyes and muttered something Preston couldn't hear. "I couldn't get the thing unbuckled. I tried and tried. So I took the knife and sliced the straps over her shoulders, and then I was back to the surface as fast as I could kick. As soon as I came out, I was yelling for anybody to help. That other car was gone. There was nobody around.

"I got her to the edge and laid her out there and tried CPR. I knew how to help a grown man, but someone that small . . ." Johnson's chest heaved as he talked.

Preston shook his head. The radio was squawking again, but he couldn't make out what they were saying and at the moment he didn't care. He took off his hat and ran a hand through his thinning hair.

"I don't think I've ever prayed so hard in my life. I just kept saying, 'Please, God, please, God, help me, help me,' and not ten minutes earlier I was cursing at him for not being there in the war. I kept asking him to bring her back, and I'd push on her little chest and blow into her lips, and after a while I thought I'd lost her." He looked at Preston. "I almost gave up. I think that's what haunts me the most. I almost sat back and let her go."

"But you didn't," Preston said.

"No, sir. She came around. That first cough was the best sound I've ever heard. Just water gurgling up, and then I turned her on her side and all that water gushed out. I picked her up and held her. She was so cold and wet. And she started crying and calling out for her mama. I'd never held a child in my life, and giving comfort to someone so innocent did something inside."

Preston just took in the information. His mind ran to the legal implications of what happened next. "So you pulled her out, brought her back to life, and then what?"

For the first time, Johnson looked a little scared. "I didn't know what to do. I took her back to the RV and wrapped her in a blanket and sat there thinking it through. If her mama had been part of this, with that friend, I didn't want her going back there. And if I took her to the authorities, that's exactly where she'd go. My sense was that whoever had done this thought they did their job, that she was gone. So I figured I could take her and find a place for her. Out of reach of the people who wanted to hurt her."

"So you took off."

"I drove out right then and didn't stop until we got into Pennsylvania. She slept the whole night and woke up wet in the morning, and I knew I had to find her diapers. I swear, if I didn't have Walmart, I don't know what I would have done."

"Why didn't you give her to someone in some other state?"

Johnson laughed. "You've never met June Bug. You have to, Sheriff. I guarantee you, one conversation with her and there's no way . . ." He looked away for a moment. "No way you could let anybody else take her. She puts a spell on you."

"So if you're attached, why come back here? It has to be more than just what's buried here."

Johnson nodded. "Part of it was the fellow who's accused. I couldn't stand the thought of somebody going to jail for killing someone who wasn't dead. From what I saw, I have a feeling he didn't even know she was there."

"He's going away but not because of the girl."

"Fair enough. The other reason was the news reports. When I saw you'd found the car, I knew it was only a matter of time until somebody discovered the truth. And then I saw that grandmother and all the pain she'd been through and how much she believed her little grandbaby was alive. It tore at me the whole way here. The final straw was June Bug herself. She needs more than I can give her now. I know that in my head, but in my heart . . . I guess I know it's time to do the right thing."

Preston thought through his next words carefully. "You know I can't just look the other way on this. But if what you say is corroborated by the girl and the family doesn't have a problem . . ." He shook his head. "But then there's the mother."

"I can't have her going to someone who's going to hurt her," Johnson said.

"I understand. You gave her life back to her."

"Yeah, and she gave it right back to me."

CHRIS FABRY

"It'd be a shame to go through all you've gone through and then have something happen to her. And then there's the media to deal with."

"You couldn't pay me enough to do your job, Sheriff."

The radio squawked again and Preston stood. "I need to answer that."

"I'll keep digging, if that's okay."

Preston hurried back to the car. "Sheriff Preston, go ahead."

The dispatcher sounded agitated. "I've been trying to get ahold of you, Sheriff. Leason Edwards called. They've found the girl. She's alive. Can you believe it? She's alive!"

Preston glanced at the man working on the parking lot. "Yeah, I believe it."

The grandmother liked to hug the stuffing out of me. It felt good to know I had grandparents. He wasn't as touchy as the grandmother was, though he did stand there grinning a lot and looking at me like I was some kind of china doll from outer space.

The grandmother bandaged up my arm and sprayed some stuff on my legs that were scraped, and I thought it was going to hurt but it didn't. Then she went off and phoned somebody while the grandfather asked if I wanted anything to eat, which I did, and he started a pan to heating on this old stove and was going to make me a grilled cheese sandwich. But when the grandmother saw what he was doing, she shooed him out like he was an old fly and took over and made the most toasty and cheesiest sandwich I have ever had. It was like she had been waiting all her life to make me a sandwich and she wasn't going to have anybody else do it. The grandfather just smiled through it all like this had happened a hundred times.

"How's the sandwich?" she said.

"Great," I said, but my mouth was full and they laughed their heads off.

That's when the grandmother started crying again. She would cry one minute and laugh the next. It was the weirdest thing. And then the grandfather came over and put his hand on her, and I didn't know what to do except keep eating. Dad says some people cry because of what's happened and others cry because of what's not happened, but I figured it was a little bit of both for her.

"How did you find us?" she said after she wiped her face with a paper towel and blew her nose.

I told her about seeing my face on the wall at Walmart. "And when my dad was taking a trip, I thought maybe he'd be coming here, so I hid in the RV, and he didn't find me until we got to Kansas or Arkansas. I can't remember which."

They stared at me and finally the grandmother said, "You have a father?"

"Yeah, we've traveled around so many places, the beach and out west and to Civil War battlefields and all kinds of places."

The grandfather rubbed the back of his neck and turned around.

The grandmother leaned down with a serious look. "Did your dad ever . . . hurt you?"

"You mean spank me? He doesn't do that because he says all I need is a strong look and I just melt. He's yelled at me before when I wasn't looking where I was going in the parking lot."

The grandfather turned around. "So where's your daddy now?"

"Over at the reservoir. He had to dig up something and his daddy brought me home." I jumped up from the table. "I need to tell him where I am."

"No, no, you sit right there," the grandmother said. "The sheriff will be here any minute."

"Sheriff? You called the police?"

"Natalie, it's important we find out what happened. And who's responsible for this."

It was a special thing to hear your real name called and strange at the same time.

"Responsible for what?" I said.

"We'll talk it through with you later. The important thing now is to get you settled and checked out."

I didn't know what that meant, but I felt safe, so I didn't ask more questions.

She got out a glass and poured cold milk in it and cut a slice of cake that looked like it was bigger than me, and we just talked and the grandmother smiled and kept staring at me. It was a perfect meal until there was a commotion outside and the porch was all lit up and the grandfather said a bad word. He looked out and mentioned something about the media.

The grandmother took me into a bedroom down the hall and took my shoes off and told me to snuggle under the covers and stay there. Then she brought me the prettiest doll I have ever seen with a fancy hat and hair that just swirled down the doll's back. It was a sight; I'll tell you that.

I listened to the commotion, and a little later a car pulled up with a siren on and there were these lights, blue and white, dancing on the wall across from me. The front door opened and closed, and there were voices low and whispered. I sat up to listen but I couldn't understand what they were saying, except I did hear the grandmother start into crying again.

Then the floor creaked outside in the hall and the grandmother came in, smiling and trying to hide her red eyes. Behind her was this giant of a man in a uniform. He had his hat in his hand and was looking at me like he had never seen red hair in his life. He just stood there looking.

I glanced from one to the other and said, "What?"

That set them to laughing.

"It's just so good to see you; that's all," the man said. "I'm Sheriff Preston."

I recognized him from the TV and when he held out a hand I shook it and he seemed surprised at how strong I was. My dad always told me not to hand anybody a dead fish.

"Pleased to meet you," I said.

"How do you like your new place?" he said.

"What new place?"

"This house. This is where you're going to be living."

I sat up in the bed. "What do you mean? What about my dad?"

"He'll be all right," the sheriff said. "He's fine."

"Do you know where he is?" I said.

"Sure I do. I met him over at the reservoir. Nice fellow. We're just trying to work this whole thing out."

CHRIS FABRY

I had a queasy feeling in my stomach and I jumped out of the bed and headed for the door, but the sheriff caught me and said I shouldn't go outside until the media was done with whatever they were going to do.

"I want my dad!"

"Let's settle down now," the grandmother said.

"I want my dad!"

"Natalie," the grandmother said in a stern voice that let me know she meant business.

The sheriff got down on one knee, and I could tell by the way he winced and the thing cracked that it wasn't the best position for him. He looked me straight in the eyes, and I could see that he was sorry for me.

"I want my dad," I said, this time the room getting cloudy with tears.

"I know, honey. And he knows too. We're going to work everything out, okay?"

"Can he stay here?"

The sheriff turned his head and rubbed his chin with a big hand. Then, as if he knew I wanted somebody to look me in the eye, he did. "It's June Bug, right?"

I nodded.

"June Bug, I'm known as a straight shooter. Do you know what that means?"

"That you don't beat around the bush with your words?"

"Exactly. And for any other little kid, I would probably pat their head and tell them to get back in bed and stay there. But you're not just any little kid. You've been through a lot. So I'm going to tell you the truth."

"Okay."

"Your dad is a good man. It appears he did something when you were little that saved your life, and he's been taking care of you ever since. Do you know about that?"

I felt my chin puckering and shook my head.

"Well, if what he's saying is true, you two have had a life together on the road. And it's been fun. But he knows it's time for you to be with your real family." He pointed a thumb at the grandmother. "This lady here has been watching and praying for you for seven years. She never gave up hope."

The grandmother's eyes were red again, and she took off her glasses and wiped at them with the paper towel. The grandfather took her in his arms and patted her back, and the old lady just went to bawling.

I couldn't stop looking the sheriff in the eyes. It seemed to me he was one of those people who knows a lot more than he lets on. "Will I get to see him again?" I said, and one of those lonely tears rolled down my cheek and hung there, like a balloon that's had most of the helium taken out.

Sheriff Preston reached over with a big hand, all wrinkled and gnarly, and took the tear from me with just a finger. I think that's about the kindest thing a person can do for another one and it surprised me.

"If your grandmother thinks it's okay, I think we can work that out. But we have to be quiet about all this. Those media people out there get hold of your dad, and he'll be gone."

"When can I see him?"

"June Bug, look at me. I promise you'll see him again. I can't tell you right now when that will be. But I promise it will happen, okay?"

I nodded, still looking into his eyes. And then another tear came and my whole face felt like it was going to shrivel up. "But he needs me. And I need him."

That big old sheriff pulled me close and hugged me, and I got his shirt wet. I could picture my dad out there at the reservoir all alone, digging up that box he was looking for and then wondering where I was. Just walking around calling my name, reaching out a hand. I kept thinking about Colorado and Sheila and all the places we'd been. And then Dad letting me go swimming.

"You promise?" I said into the sheriff's uniform.

The sheriff patted my head, and I could hear his voice kind of shaking. "I promise, June Bug."

❀ ❀ ❀

I was beginning to think that old sheriff wasn't a man of his word because a few days went by, and there was no talk of my dad. On the news they kept showing our house and the sheriff talking to reporters. The grandmother didn't let me watch any of it, but I found a newspaper in the trash basket and read the story.

There was something about a man named Graham Walker who had been charged with shooting at a sheriff's deputy and that he was somehow involved in my disappearance. I didn't understand much of it, but the important thing was that they didn't write a word about my dad. It was like it was our secret and nobody could know and I think it was because if they did, my dad would have to be dragged in front of the cameras or something, and I know he wouldn't like that. And you couldn't drag that stuff out of me if you tied a hundred horses to me and tried.

I had to go to a doctor and get checked out, and he asked me all kinds of personal questions. It wasn't that big of a deal. Then after a couple days they let me go into the backyard and play because most of the news cameras had left. A few days later the grandfather took me on the hill on his tractor, and he even let me drive it. It was about the most fun thing I'd ever done.

We came up to the big water tower that had *Dogwood* written on it and we stopped and the grandfather let me down. There was a man standing at the bottom of the tower, and I recognized him right away and started running toward him.

My daddy. I know he wasn't my real daddy. But he was my daddy. And I was giggling just to see him. He moved toward me and then got down on one knee and took something from behind him and put it on the ground. I just about died because it was the prettiest little white puppy I had ever seen.

I fell on the ground and that little puppy came over and licked me on the face and then we rolled around on the ground and the fresh-cut grass got in my hair and it was just about the closest thing to heaven this side of the pearly gates.

I jumped up and grabbed Dad around the neck and hung on. "Thank you! Thank you! Thank you!" Sometimes that's the only thing you can say to your daddy.

"I told you when the time was right, you could have a dog," he said. "Time's right."

"I love him," I said. "What's his name?"

"It's a her. She doesn't have one. They say the person who loves a thing the most is the one who should name it. So go ahead."

The puppy had waddled over to the grandfather and was gnawing on his shoe and both of us laughed at that. I threw out a bunch of dog names like Shep and Whitey, but none of them seemed to fit.

"Take your time," Dad said. "You don't have to decide right now. Noodle on it."

I turned back to him. He was kneeling on the ground, and though he had always looked a little sad to me, he looked really sad and happy at the same time. "You're leaving, aren't you?"

He nodded.

"Why can't you stay? They've got a lot of room."

He took me in his arms and hugged me so tight I thought I was going to bust. Then he pushed me back so I could see into his eyes. "Remember when I told you about when I was a kid and we'd tie a string on the leg of a june bug?"

I nodded and the tears started.

"I knew someday I'd need to let the string go. I did the best I could, and we had a lot of fun out on the road. But it's time for you to fly, little girl. These people here love you a lot and they'll take care of you. You can go to school. Have sleepovers with your friends—"

"I don't want sleepovers. I want you!" I buried my face in his chest.

He patted me on the back again and again. "I know you do and I want to stay. You don't know how hard it is. But I won't be gone, really. You have me in your heart. And I have you. I'll always have you in my heart, June Bug. Don't you forget that."

I tried to stop my crying, but it was too hard. It wasn't until that puppy came over to me and started licking at my bare leg that I laughed through the tears.

We played a little more, and the grandfather asked him a few questions about the sheriff and what they'd worked out with the law. And then I knew it was time. Dad stood up and shook the hand of the grandfather.

"I want to thank you for what you did," the grandfather said.

"Thank you for loaning me your granddaughter," Dad said. "She did more for me than I ever did for her."

"Where will you go?" I said.

He looked off into the distance at the interstate that snaked through the valley. "I don't know. I was thinking of heading west."

He got this big grin on his face, and I knew who he was thinking about. "Why don't you take me with you? It's not fair."

"June Bug, there's a lot of things I don't understand about life. Why one person dies and the other lives. Why people do hurtful things to innocent people. If I could keep you with me the rest of my life, I would do it. But in my heart I know this is the best, and you're just going to have to trust me."

I nodded because in my heart I knew he was right, but sometimes your heart and the rest of you don't go in the same direction.

He picked me up in his arms one last time and swung me around so that my hair flew out and the puppy started barking and the world started spinning and it felt like home. It just felt like home.

The grandfather put me on the tractor and we drove away with that puppy in my arms and the best dad anyone ever had standing on the hill. We moved into the trees and I lost sight of him, and when we got down to the clearing, I looked back and he was gone. Just like that.

❀ ❀ ❀

About a week later, I went to the mailbox with Papaw. There was a box sitting on the ground with my name on it and we carried it back to the house and opened it. Inside were all my journals and stuff from the RV and about everything I ever had of any value. Along with it was a picture of the two of us standing in the sand by the ocean, smiling. And packed up inside the box were a bunch of medals. I didn't know what they were for, but I thought they were pretty.

There was also a letter inside addressed to Leason and Mae Edwards. When Mamaw opened it, she grabbed her mouth and said, "Have mercy."

"What is it?" I said.

"John sent a letter and a check. He says it's for you to go to college."

"That's enough to *buy* a college," Papaw said, and he laughed and shook his head.

I took the letter and looked at his handwriting. It was my dad's, no doubt. I wondered how he had gotten all that money and if it came from the box under the parking lot at the reservoir.

❀ ❀ ❀

I had my first sleepover with Jennifer at the end of July. It took me a long time to work on Mamaw because she liked to have me close to her almost all the time. Jennifer's mama made us s'mores and let us sleep in a tent just out the back door and watch a movie on a TV we plugged into an extension cord at the side of the house. After Jennifer went to sleep and it was quiet, I crawled out and looked up at the stars and picked out the Big Dipper. Dad had taught me to do that.

They lived next to the interstate, and I heard the rush of semis going past and the whir of tires. I closed my eyes and it took me back to those days on the road. There's something about living in a house that's cozy and warm that you don't get in living out of an RV. But I guess if you're with people you love, it doesn't matter where you live.

I've seen some pictures of my mama, but I've never met her. Mamaw says she doesn't think she'll ever come back, but I wish she would. I'd like to see her and get to talk with her and ask her dumb questions.

I don't see his dad, Mr. Johnson, much. He doesn't have to drive somebody else's truck because he has a new one. And Papaw said his mortgage is paid off, and I think that would make my dad happy to know.

Mamaw and Papaw take me to the big brick church, and I have this Sunday school teacher who asks me to read the verses each week because the other kids stumble over the words. The pastor is a good friend now, and he said he would baptize me when I'm ready.

❀ ❀ ❀

Not a day goes by that I don't think about him. I'll see an old truck pass with an arm out the window and my heart will quicken. Or in some Walmart parking lot I'll see an RV with worn tires and curtains drawn and think of our life. Sometimes when I'm playing with Roma—that's what I named my dog—I'll look up at the water tower and think about what it would be like to see him sitting there looking down on me, laughing as I play or when I tie a string to a june bug and follow it around like he did.

He comes to me in my dreams and my dreams are never enough. I wonder if he'll be in the audience when I'm in school and singing at a Christmas concert. I wonder if he'll watch me graduate or get married. I don't think that will ever happen, but if it does, I'd want him to be there and maybe walk me down the aisle.

At night sometimes, when I'm in bed and under the clean covers in the back bedroom, I'll close my eyes and reach out a hand toward him. And I'll wonder if he ever does the same for me.

I wonder what made him such a good father if he never had children. I wonder if he's started a new life with Sheila. And I wonder if he'll ever forget me. I don't think he will because he said he wouldn't. And he always kept his promises.

Some people know every little thing about themselves. Not me. And I don't need to anymore.

Acknowledgments

This past year has been a long journey for my family, and I want to thank the Fabrys and Kessels and Marts for standing with us, as well as our Tyndale and Moody families, many listeners who became involved, and several people who have walked the hard road closely, including the Rings, the Parmelees, the Doyles, our church family at Tri-Lakes Chapel, the HPOA, and many others who have enriched our lives through their love, prayers, and friendship. It was fitting that as I edited *June Bug*, I was in Jim Ring's camper in our front driveway. But that's another story. I'd also like to thank Laura Gomez, whose courage and humor amaze me. Our prayers are with you. Thanks to Karen Watson for being so excited about this book from the moment I explained it. And to Lorie Popp for making it much better as always.

And thanks to Andrea, my wife, who has been through the desert with the kids and me. Your love and encouragement are like a cool drink of reverse osmosis water to a tired soul.

About the Author

Chris Fabry is a 1982 graduate of the W. Page Pitt School of Journalism at Marshall University and a native of West Virginia. He is heard on Moody Radio's *Chris Fabry Live!*, Love Worth Finding, and Building Relationships with Dr. Gary Chapman. He and his wife, Andrea, are the parents of nine children. You can visit his Web site at www.chrisfabry.com.